BY IMMORTAL

HONOR

BOUND

OF ALCHEMY AND ANGELS
BOOK ONE

DANIELLE ANCONA

This book is dedicated to the pioneers in philosophy, mathematics, medicine, and alchemy—which has segued into chemistry and scientific methodology. Pioneers who forged on in their passion to seek knowledge and truth under the most arduous of circumstances. To name a few bright points of light of this sky full of shining stars: Socrates, Galileo, Mary the Jewess, Paracelsus, Laura Bassi, Marie Curie, Joseph Lister, George Washington Carver, Lise Meitner, Albert Einstein, Katherine Johnson.

*And to my mom, Patti, and the nun who taught her grammar.
Grammar which Mom recalls with razor sharpness.
Those corrected paper copies shall always be treasured.*

Acknowledgements

This book would not have happened without the contributions of many people I deeply respect, and beloved family and friends.

A special thanks to my supportive husband, Dan, who offers non-stop encouragement and hours of proofreading. My mom, sisters Nancy Jo and Sharon, my children—who often dealt with take-out and distracted answers given twenty minutes after the question was asked, my niece—Morgan. And my friends—Becky, Brenda, Judi, Anna, Deb, and Gary—who truly kept me going.

Thank you as well to several talented writers who have lent me invaluable insight, candor, friendship and encouragement: Rowena Tisdale, C. Beth Anderson, Ryen Lesli, Daniella Shephard, D.K. Marie, Eric Lahti, Erinne Lansing, T.J. Torrington, Willie Handler, Hanson Oak, Michael D. Nadeau, J. M. Grenier, C.D. Storiz, and Brad Collins.

Last, but most certainly not least, B.K. Bass, Sam Hendricks, and Crystal L. Kirkham of the Kyanite Publishing family. You truly are family, in so many ways. Thank you for your belief in Malachi and me, and all of your magic and hard work on this book.

BY IMMORTAL

HONOR

BOUND

PART I

IMMORTAL GUARDIAN

495 BCE THROUGH 281 CE
EGYPT AND GREECE

There is only one good, knowledge,
and one evil, ignorance.
— *Socrates*

CHAPTER ONE

495 BCE ~ Meadow Oasis, Egypt

CONJURED magma collided with the ground the warrior angel, Malachi, had just vacated. Sweat beaded, ran down his sooty face. The heavy odor of scorched soil surrounded him. Thunder reverberated about the meadow and echoed off the surrounding hills. The shock wave blew his sable hair across his face, blocking the light of the sun from his vision for a moment, a few strands stuck in the perspiration on his forehead. He shook his head to chase away the itch.

Silence swept in and held the valley captive, the air hot and still. Then, just as quickly, it convulsed and released. Dirt and pulverized rock rained about Malachi and his opponent. The sharp sting of debris dug into his flesh while Mother Earth's silent wail of pain cut through his soul. An undeniable urge to offer comfort stole into his concentration. Malachi shoved this aside to remain focused on the battle at hand. A battle between himself, a Celestial warrior angel, and Gideon, a fallen archangel and leader of the Seraph Insurrection. A battle which could be to the death for either of them—immortal otherwise, yet equally matched.

Realization dawned: he now had the strategic advantage of time. It was time Gideon would need to again gather energy for a weapon after conjuring the magma ball. Resolve and determination abounded within Malachi while he gathered Elemental forces. With a flash of cobalt blue, he forged his sword of carp's tongue blade. An ethereal light radiated from within the length of the fierce weapon, seemingly to have a life of its own.

He lunged toward Gideon, swiping at the dark one's neck, his muscles rippling with the effort.

Still weaponless, Gideon jumped back as his swarthy cheeks flushed with anger. He slid a scornful glance over the cobalt sword and unscathed warrior angel.

"Celestial," Gideon graveled as he spat to the side and moved with ease, ducking another slash from the warrior's humming blade. His silver hair ruffling as it passed close by. "You would allow our Mother Earth to be ravaged for the sake of lowly humans and self-important Celestials?"

"She is not 'your' Mother Earth," Malachi countered with vehemence as he stalked closer, his sword held at the ready before him. "You betray her with every step you trod upon her." His obsidian eyes flared with a sudden cobalt blaze as he challenged Gideon's assertion. "You claim you avenge the innocents of Sodom and Gomorrah, yet you herd humans like cattle for your expendable use." Malachi's voice dripped with disgust and the ethereal elements in his blade pulsed with his ferocity. "Humans are to have free will," he ground out as he swung at Gideon's neck.

Angling back, Gideon avoided the swift arc of Malachi's blade. He turned and stood with his profile narrowed, taking advantage of the moment Malachi needed to recover from his spin. Shifting to the demeanor of a savvy diplomat, his palms lifted in feigned supplication, he explained, "These humans live a peace-filled life with me, Angel." A smile crept across Gideon's firm lips and into his silver eyes. His tone was beguiling. "I gather the humans to me to protect them from the fire and brimstone judgment of your Celestials."

Malachi's countenance darkened upon Gideon's audacity. "Is that what you tell humans while you rob them of choice and action?" Incredulity flashed in his eyes and imbued his question. Intrepid, he advanced further on the former archangel. His sword swung like a pendulum, as though counting Gideon's remaining moments on Earth. The lethal blade glinted in the sun.

Gideon stole a quick glance down to Malachi's weapon, then a shrewd light shifted across his eyes. He motioned toward the warrior with a welcoming, open hand. "Angel, you pray to Mother Earth and Sister Moon more than you do the Celestials." He again threw his gaze to Malachi's sword, then slid back to his opponent's face with temptation imbuing his silver eyes and his crafty smile. "You command elemental powers with skill and ease. Celestials are discomforted by you. Come, join me, Malachi, where you can relish your reign over the Elements."

Malachi drew himself to his full height, his eyes hardened. "To help you wipe out Celestia, the balance to the Dark Forces?" he asked, grimacing with distaste.

"You fool!" bellowed Gideon as silver flames burgeoned in his eyes. "Celestia is the Dark Force!" He spat on the ground in disgust. "Your Celestials decimated Sodom and Gomorrah without thought to the Innocents lost: the children, the beasts of burden."

"Celestia gave the citizens many chances to redeem themselves," argued Malachi as he advanced another step on Gideon.

"Redeem themselves? For being weak humans?" Gideon questioned, bitterness ringing in his harsh laugh.

"Indeed, Gideon. Redeem themselves."

"Angel, you flirt with Immortal death," slithered Gideon, the words cold and predatory.

With a ruffle of his muscular wings kept close to his body, Malachi advanced on his silver-haired opponent and tightened his grip about the handle of his weapon. He created an ethereal barrier behind the cast-out archangel, while simultaneously lifting his sword and lunging toward Gideon.

Backing away from the wrathful warrior, Gideon jumped and bent to dodge the rapid, lethal swipes of Malachi's thrumming blade. His back came against the impassable barrier and panic flitted across his face. Then, as determined optimism replaced fear, his jaw and eyes hardened.

Malachi's advantage had passed, Gideon's stalling tactics successful.

A dark, low, and insidious incantation in the ancient tongue of Babel slithered from Gideon. His eyes lit from within with an unnatural, silver-like flame. The air about the two preternatural beings pulsed. Gideon siphoned the blackened energy of corruption from the ethereal realm while he conjured his sword. The deadly sterling and black blade grew from the hilt before Malachi's disgusted gaze, seething with souls of the condemned.

With a depraved grin, Gideon brandished his weapon and lunged.

Malachi jumped back, turning sideways to narrow his profile. He parried the blow and charged at Gideon. His blade vibrated, the elemental hum of power growing the closer they drew to one another. Malachi adjusted his breathing as his black linothorax armor increased in density to better protect him. He tensed and flexed his wings. While dodging Gideon's thrusts, he surged forward and swiped his sword toward Gideon, knowing the venom of the souls embedded in Gideon's blade would surely poison him were the weapon to hit its mark.

Over and again their blades clashed. Metal on metal rang through the meadow, pulsing cobalt blue meeting hellish black. Gideon heaved Malachi's sword aside with an upward thrust. Sweat streamed down his face and neck. Massive gray wings appeared at Gideon's shoulders with a leathery ruffle, remaining folded close to his body. He snarled, spun, lifted his sword, and cut across Malachi. Malachi turned and leaned away as the seething blade arced past his torso, whistling through the air.

Searing pain blossomed through Malachi as the sharp edge bit into the flesh of his upper left arm. Cobalt-blue flashed in his eyes as he willed the venom of Gideon's blade from his bicep into his linen armor. He firmed his grip about the hilt of his sword. Disgust and ire crested as he caught sight of the trapped souls in Gideon's silver blade licking and imbibing his shed blood as it ran along its edge.

Crimson poured from the slash across Malachi's upper arm and ran in rivulets down his dirt and sweat-streaked wrist before dripping onto the ground. He whirled with a great battle cry, his teeth bared. Perspiration, spittle, and blood flew from him in a spray of droplets as he swiped his blade toward Gideon's neck.

Gideon countered the mighty stroke. A low, preternatural growl came from between his teeth, gritted in a grotesque parody of a grin. His shoulder and neck muscles bulged as he shoved aside Malachi's sword.

Malachi grunted and reeled with Gideon's torque. A strategy quickly formed in his mind around the venom he had pushed out of his body into his heavy armor. Dancing backward and to the side, he drew Gideon in to engage. He parried blow after blow and studied his opponent's patterns.

Malachi watched, timed, then set his trap with his rib cage near his right elbow now made open and vulnerable.

Gideon's silver gaze landed on the flash of the opening at the warrior's ribs. A triumphant, sinister light entered his eyes.

A momentary sense of conquest wound through Malachi when he noted Gideon taking the bait, but he strove to keep his expression one of being in the battle.

Gideon thrust his blade into Malachi's ribs. Surely, a death blow for the Immortal.

Malachi transmuted the venom from Gideon's sword, now imbued in his armor, into silver and cobalt teeth lining a yawning mouth. He turned quick as lightning and the blade slid between the waiting rows of teeth. The ethereal mouth grasped the sword and the envenomated teeth severed Gideon's weapon, then dropped the blade to the ground.

Malachi drove his black leather heel onto the detached blade. Mother Earth snapped blue granite about the seething metal, encasing it. The teeth and mouth faded from Malachi's armor. He stepped back, his chest heaving as he worked to draw breath.

Gideon stared at the blade stuck in blue stone while he grasped the now useless hilt. He threw his head back and howled with hellish rage wrathful enough to strike fear in demons. He pinned Malachi with his quicksilver gaze.

"Angel," he said as his fury bowed back the trees about the meadow and blew back Malachi's sweat-laden hair from his head, "you will regret not coming with me to join the Seraph!" He paused, eyed Malachi through his churning gray gaze. "The weak-willed humans and insolent Celestials will not be worth the cost I shall exact from you!"

With a flash of silver motes, Gideon disappeared, leaving only silence and the odor of sulfur to fill the void.

CHAPTER TWO

463 BCE ~ Temple of the Goddess Artemis
Foot of Mount Olympus, Greece

MALACHI'S SECOND IN COMMAND, Josiah, rode up to the command post in the Temple of Artemis at the forested foot of Mount Olympus. From the left, he dismounted his dappled chestnut Arabian, Talia, with one smooth motion. Josiah rushed up the steps of the verdant temple, the linen pteruges of his armor smacking against his thighs. The trees and lush vines obscuring portions of the limestone pillars did not register in his periphery. He made a beeline to the teak table where Malachi and the tall Katherine the Adamantine—immortal lioness warrior of the Sekhment bloodline—were conferring with a member of Celestia. Josiah waited to be addressed. He deliberately looked past the Celestial whose white robes reflected as a blinding light in the Grecian sun, her face obscured by the glow which effused about her.

Malachi turned toward him. "Speak freely, Josiah. You obviously bring word to us." The weight of somber concern in Malachi's stern countenance lifted somewhat as his gaze landed upon his trusted second-in-command.

"Malachi, Sir." Josiah saluted his commander and then gave a respectful nod to the warrioress.

Taciturn, Katherine returned his nod and her cinnamon braids sifted over her bronzed, burnished shoulders as she did.

He then looked to the Celestial and bowed his head.

The Celestial's brightness did nothing to disguise the haughty lift of her head and lack of return greeting, her silence thunderous in its disdain.

Malachi's lips tightened at the imperious stance of the Celestial.

Josiah turned his attention to both Malachi and Katherine. "Sirs, three new pieces of information: our spies have indeed spotted the goddess Artemis held behind Seraph lines in the Temple of Bia, and the Seraph have successfully recruited Bia, goddess of Force. They also report Bia is working to actively recruit her brother, Kratos, god of Strength."

Malachi's jaw hardened at the second piece of news. "Gather your officers and intelligence personnel. Devise two plans to recover Artemis. We will convene here in two notches of the sundial to confer. I know you are aware there is no time to waste. Artemis could woo many women over the eons into the fold of the Seraph, were she recruited."

Josiah saluted. "Yes, Sir."

Malachi looked at each operative gathered around the maps and charts strewn about the table, urgency darkening his eyes. "It is imperative we recover Artemis before the Seraph recruit her. Knowing Artemis, she would prove impossible to turn back or dispatch once recruited."

Turning to his second-in-command, Malachi added, "You are dismissed, Josiah."

"Yes, Sir." Josiah spun on his heel with purpose, leaving the strategic group and the temple.

Malachi beheld the Celestial in his gaze, anger emanating from his glittering, dark eyes. Smoldering fury rode his voice as he spoke. "Celestia's contempt of the gods of the Nile and Mount Olympus only encourages them even more to consider joining the Seraph.

"The Seraph promise the gods respect. Respect which they do not receive from you or any of Celestia. Bia is a coup for them as she is the Goddess of Force and Power." He leaned in toward the Celestial being, his voice dropping to a low, contemptuous tone. "The way you saw fit to treat my soldier, who lays his life on the line on your behalf, sickens me." Malachi's eyes narrowed in his fury. "I blame the successful recruitment of the gods on your Celestial sanctimony as much as I blame Gideon and his viper's promises."

Katherine hissed in a breath at Malachi's daring comment, shooting a surreptitious gaze toward the Celestial. Rare goose-bumps covered her arms as yellow beams of light flared from the obscured eyes of the Celestial upon the being's obvious annoyance.

"You are indeed bold to express your opinion, Malachi. I warn you to tread lightly." The Celestial's contralto voice issued from her light-shrouded countenance, sounding as though she were speaking in a tunnel. "We existed long before gods, angels, and humans. We helped shape the creation of the Earth, Ether, and all in between." She paused as her light-suffused countenance pulsed. "There is much you do not, and will never, understand."

Malachi looked back down at the maps, his jaw working in vexation. He rubbed the back of his neck. "We shall await Josiah's plans, then finalize the mission and recover Artemis."

After taking a deep breath, Malachi brought Katherine and

the Celestial back into his gaze. "Do we want to consider bringing Bia back with us?"

"I believe we should, Malachi," Katherine said. "We may not be this close to her again. She has the potential to create strong leverage for the Seraph to be more attractive for other gods and deities to join with them. I believe I can capture Bia if you assign me a contingent of six warriors. That will free you to concentrate on recovering Artemis."

Malachi nodded and said, "I have no doubt you will be effective, Katherine. If you would agree, I will send eight men with you; men to guard all four corners, two to give you direct protection and a layer of reinforcements, and two to help secure Bia." He waited for her proud argument against two more men.

"This will be a difficult mission, Malachi. While we need to keep the number of warriors to a minimum to avoid drawing attention, I think it wise to take your additional men."

"I am in shock," a new voice arose in the gathering.

Malachi and Katherine turned toward the inflection they both knew so well. The golden archangel Raphael appeared, resplendent in his gilt armor, his snow-white tunic blinding in the desert sun as he joined in their circle.

"Who would have ever thought we would be witness to Katherine agreeing to one of our suggestions?" Raphael asked as he stepped into the circle about the table.

Katherine berated Raphael with a hot flash of her deep topaz, lioness eyes.

Ignoring Katherine's umbrage, he nodded in greeting to the luminous Celestial.

"Raphael," the ethereal white figure intoned in her empyrean voice.

Raphael turned and clasped Malachi in a warrior's embrace, then looked to Katherine and started a step toward her.

She lifted a finely arched brow, her eloquent, icy silence and stare stopped him better than holding her spear in front of herself could have.

He stepped back and said simply, "Katherine."

Malachi pulled a hand over his chin to wipe a grin from his face. *Some things never change*, he thought, including their rivalry and bond like that of siblings. He turned to the charts and drew in everyone's attention to the missions at hand.

As Josiah and his contingent of seven warriors converged on Bia's temple with skillful stealth, a deep, ferocious growling came from the west side of the temple. Josiah turned to his men and held his hand up before himself signaling the need for absolute silence. They proceeded to increase the care with which they moved, suppressing all disturbance. Voices carried as several humans spoke in hostile tones. The feral snarling grew louder. They drew in closer.

Josiah motioned for the other four warriors to cut through the courtyard and advance from the back side of the stone building, while he and his remaining three men would approach from the face of the temple.

They headed along the front of the temple, then spied around the corner to see Artemis and a large, agitated black bear. The massive ursine and the goddess were back to back, surrounded by hostile, uniformed fighters. The swaying bear challenged three soldiers, each pointing a spear at the threatening animal. Their eyes shone above cloth extending from olive green turbans, which obscured their lower faces. Bright green viper insignias on the turbans marked them as Seraph. Two other Seraph stood between Artemis and the temple with their swords drawn. Her bow and arrow lay discarded on the ground behind them. Rips in the skirt of her green chiton exposed her well-muscled calves and forest-hued boots. Bruises darkened her upper biceps. Dried blood dotted cuts from a bramble on her arms and her left cheek.

The Seraph with spears moved in toward the bear. The great ursine lunged forward and swiped a massive front paw armed with horrific claws. The bravado of the Seraph soldiers evaporated, and they stepped back.

Josiah caught Artemis's eye and that of his squad leader, who peeked out from the other side of the temple. He pointed to the two Seraph behind her and made a cutting motion across his neck.

"Let me go," Artemis snarled, her brows pulled together and her fists clenched.

One of the Seraph soldiers called out, cajoling, "Why do you fight us, daughter of Zeus? Your father cannot stomach the Celestials and the free-thinking they offer humans. If you bring your father to our side, both of you would have great power and be rid of that bitch, Hera."

Artemis curled her lip in disgust, her forest-green eyes heated with anger, "Your penchant to make humans into useless cattle sickens me. My father wants humans who make the choice to worship him, not mindless idiots."

The bear growled with menace in its throat and saliva dripping from its fierce jaws.

"You are at an impasse, traitors to Zeus. Let me go. You cannot win," she yelled.

"We cannot free you, goddess. We are loyal to Gideon and the Seraph. We will take our venom-coated swords to you without regret if you do not agree to come with us. Do not doubt we will fight to the death for Gideon to rid the world of the arrogant Celestials."

"So be it," Artemis said, solemn determination radiating from her eyes and set of her jaw.

Josiah and his three warriors, their swords already drawn, ambushed the Seraph facing the bear. The bear reared back. Josiah's other warriors attacked the Seraph soldiers threatening Artemis.

Artemis spoke with guttural words understood only by the bear.

The great beast leapt upon one of the soldiers and his spear.

Josiah and two of his men advanced on the other Seraph while the third kept an eye on the bear and his prey.

The warrior angels outnumbered the four remaining Seraph soldiers and made quick work of dispatching them.

Soon, the Seraph soldiers lay dead and scattered about, their weapons still grasped in their hands and their open eyes lifeless. Blood ran into the stream alongside the Temple of Bia.

The bear struggled to breathe as it lay wounded at Artemis's feet. She crouched beside the brave animal and laid her hands upon its massive body, murmuring as she stroked her fingers through the thick fur until the bear stilled. A tear fell from Artemis's eye which glistened orange in the setting sun as it rolled over the thick, dark fur where the bear's heart had beat only moments before. Artemis stood, waved her hand over the massive beast, and the bear's inert body faded away.

The Grecian earth cooled under the darkening skies. Stealthy in their soft steps and whispered conversation, Josiah and his commanders spirited Artemis back to her own temple.

Led by the disheveled goddess to her lavish throne of entwined trees and vines, Josiah handed Artemis her bow and arrows after she stepped onto the dais. The green leaves woven through her sovereign seat firmed and brightened, rustling as she sat.

With a wave of her hand, the thick woodlands which surrounded the perimeter of her temple murmured and thickened to obscure them from outsiders. Torches within lit of their own accord, their flames wavering in the balmy breeze.

She held Josiah under her intrepid, forest-green gaze. "I thank you and your warriors, Josiah, and my father thanks you. This shall not be forgotten."

Josiah nodded. "I know it frustrated Katherine that her mission to retrieve Bia from the Seraph proved unsuccessful. I, however, am grateful we lost none of our warriors in this battle, and Kratos did not follow his sister into the Seraph fold. Bia is now indelibly Seraph. She would have betrayed us, and any loss would have been in vain.

"As for your gratitude, it is appreciated, Goddess. But it is our duty to protect those not allegiant to the Seraph, at all cost."

"Indeed, it is our duty," Malachi's deep voice preceded his entrance into Artemis's temple. He inhaled with deep appreciation as he stepped into the midst of her forest. "Mother Earth is strong here, Goddess Artemis, and Sister Moon shines her favor upon us from the heavens above."

Artemis's smile shined through the grime smattered across her face. "The forces you command set a high bar for all oth—"

"'Mother Earth' and 'Sister Moon', Malachi?" The Celestial from earlier in the day appeared behind the warrior angel with malice in her voice.

Josiah turned toward the Celestial and blinked against the being's bright light.

"What of it, Celestial?" Malachi asked as he inclined his head in defiance.

The bright yellow beams shining from where the Celestial's eyes would be brightened. "What of it? It is blasphemous for a celestial being, Malachi. You are an angel..." she paused, "or have you forgotten? I believe you very well may have neglected to recall from whence you came, with as much as you make yourself familiar with the gods of Olympus." Her bright golden beams shifted to Artemis, then landed again upon Malachi. "And of the Nile."

"Familiarity? Blasphemous? You dare accuse me of blasphemy?"

"I more than dare, Malachi. I will be taking this to The Five." The Celestial disappeared, her imperious threat echoing through the temple after her bright presence had vanished.

Artemis stepped off her dais, tread over to Malachi, and laid her hand upon his greaves-encased, muscular forearm. "My apologies that you have been addressed in such a manner on my behalf,"

Malachi clasped her proffered hand. "Goddess, you have experienced enough distress this day. Do not vex yourself further. The Celestials seem intent to pass judgment on my communion with our Mother Earth, no matter what the situation."

CHAPTER THREE

450 BCE ~ Temple of Thoth, God of Judgement and Learning, Egypt

WARRIOR'S DISCIPLINE did little to disguise Malachi's tension. With each caged lion's stride, the pteruges extending from under his black linen cuirass brushed his thighs. He paced in measured steps across the floor of the Temple of Thoth with his hands clasped behind his back. It seemed to him eons stretched as he awaited news from Archangel and Diplomat Raphael. His long, dark hair—pulled back from his temples—lifted in the desert breeze like a sly raven shaking out its feathers. The overhead linen sunshades snapped out a rhythm in the hot, arid winds.

A swirling column of gilded flecks near Thoth's massive ebony and gold throne caught Malachi's eye. The regal Raphael solidified from the maelstrom of burnished motes. The dry, sand-imbued winds danced with waves of his flaxen hair and the pleats of his immaculate white tunic.

The continuous crackling of burning incense and rippling linen sunshades hummed under the hushed strain between the two warriors. The forlorn cry of a distant hawk echoed off the dunes, mirroring Malachi's disquiet.

Raphael's ethereal, intense blue gaze landed on the brooding Malachi.

Malachi broke the stare to release the tense bow of contention. He gave a brusque nod to the archangel he regarded as a brother-in-arms. Shattering the silence, the dark warrior turned to a heavy teak table, resplendent with a glistening bronze pitcher of water and a wide bowl overflowing with plump dates and red-green apples. Malachi poured them each a goblet of cool water. The sweet temptation of the fruit drifted about the table, mixing with rich incense.

Raphael stepped closer to take the offered goblet. Sunlight glinted off his golden scabbard and belt as he moved. The harsh edges of his austere expression softened as he sipped the deified, cool water under the desert heat.

Malachi eased his own dry mouth before setting his goblet down with a forceful clunk. Apples bounced in the bowl, and one rolled onto the table. He crossed his arms, his muscles bulging with tension and a deep scowl darkened his already grim expression.

"Tell me your news, Raphael," he demanded in a low voice as he prepared for the blow.

"The Five have spoken, Malachi. You are Earthbound and relieved of your command." Resignation churned in Raphael's eyes. "I have been instructed to assure you that your rank remains the same. They recognize your combined beliefs in the Elements, Mother Earth, and the Heavens cannot be altered; yet they cannot reconcile this with you as an angel. They openly state you are too valuable to risk losing to the Seraph. For as much as you think they cannot understand you, The Five have a deep respect for you, your honor, and your sense of strategy."

Malachi grunted in bitter acknowledgment. He rounded on Raphael, anger vibrating through his body. "I have planned and executed complex, successful missions for Celestia. I have served with honor and fortitude," he bellowed as spittle flew from his mouth. "I have legions of warrior angels who are loyal to and fear me."

The indignity burned into his soul, cutting through his accomplishments as a fiery sword. His face reddened. "The Five are a bloody sham, hiding behind the doors of the Great Hall. Their shriveled balls and edicts can go to River Acheron!" The word 'Acheron', carried by his wrath, echoed off the dunes about them.

Malachi's lips curled with frustration. He knew this was an affront he could do nothing about unless he joined with the Seraph. He had already decided he would burn in the molten River of Sorrows before switching allegiance to the soul-eating faction. Hot anger flowed from his cobalt gaze as he focused on the golden Raphael. "How bloody ironic that I wage war and maintain order so that humans can pursue free will, and the self-important Celestials take mine away!"

Throwing his head back, Malachi growled in pent up fury and tightened his hands into fists. Dropping his chin, he brought Raphael back into his sight and gritted his teeth as he ground out, "They prefer to keep themselves removed from the dirty side of defending the Heavens and Earth. The lily-white bastards disgust me. They are determining my fate at their whim, not my merit. This, this..." He sputtered in his deep anger. "This bloody missive only serves to validate my opinion of the vile, pathetic lot."

A paring knife lay next to the bowl. Malachi grasped it and stabbed the lone apple with a vicious strike. The fruit fell into halves on either side of the blade, the tip now lodged in the table. "Arrogant bastards, taking away my command," he snapped. The vibrating knife handle rang about his words.

Raphael's gaze slid from the resonating knife blade to Malachi. Persuasion entered his tone as he lifted his hands in supplication. "My friend, this is indeed a bitter dram to swallow," he agreed. "But we both know that you chafe amongst the Celestials and they are uncomfortable around you." Raphael strode closer to Malachi, his eyes imploring. "This is not a slight. The Five believe that as Earthbound, and a lone operative, you will be a more formidable opponent in our efforts to quell the growing reach of the Seraph. They acknowledge your command of the Elements and your alliances with the deities will well serve you and our fight against the Seraph."

Rather than placating him, Raphael's words wrought dark storms in Malachi. He heaved in great breaths as he fought for control. He stalked to Raphael, coming face to face with him, his rage overflowing. "They decided this? Without consulting me?" he asked with a sneer. His mouth worked in his agitation until he again found his voice. "As much as I know they abhor me, they still see fit to use me—just not in their pure, Celestial midst?

"I crafted and executed plans to meet their objectives! I led my warriors into battle and achieved great victories with minimal loss." Frustration radiated from him as an arrow quivering in its target. "Those cowards are casting aside all I have accomplished," Malachi said as he turned, again pinning Raphael with the daggers of his stare.

"What about my warriors?" he asked. "The Celestials act as though I and my men are obelisks to move about at their whim!" He snatched up an apple half and flung it with fury many leagues into the desert, where a sand-dwelling rodent would later find a sweet, cool feast.

Raphael moved closer to the warrior, hands open in the trust of brothers-in-arms. "Malachi," he said, "take heed. There are facets in this turn of events you can use to your advantage.

"To ease your concern regarding your men," Raphael explained, "Josiah now leads them at my insistence."

Malachi blew out a breath as he rubbed the back of his neck and paced. "Aye, he is an accomplished leader and strategist," Malachi said while he stared out over the barren desert landscape. He turned to Raphael, grudging respect warming his voice. "My men will be fine under him."

"There is another facet in their reasoning," Raphael continued. "The Five have expressed concern the Seraph may find an easy mark in you, with your frequent travels between Celestia and Earth and your mixed system of beliefs. You do fraternize with humans and the gods more than they prefer."

"Ha! 'Fraternize'?" asked Malachi. "How else do the fools think I can infiltrate and gather information to plan successful missions?" Malachi slammed the table with his fists and its legs skittered along the floor of the temple as the tabletop crashed to the ground, almost as if to dodge further rage. "Those damned Celestial bastards can go fuck themselves," Malachi cursed, his face sharpened with a sneer. He rounded on Raphael, ridicule lacing his words. "Or mayhap the bastards do not understand how to fuck."

Raphael coughed but kept his face expressionless as he countered, "Therein may lie a rub, Malachi. You are not steeped in decorum and celibacy." He paused as he looked at Malachi with sincerity in his gaze. "All truth, my friend, they—we—need your discerning eye."

"Consider this; given your strong relationships with the deities, your ease of movement on Earth, and your brutal cunning for these critical missions, I agree with The Five." He grasped Malachi's shoulder and said, "You are, indeed, one of the strongest, most strategic of warriors in this great war of eons."

Malachi's anger ebbed, his eyes now dark with pensive thought rather than hard with rage. Raphael walked to Thoth's gilded throne and sat. He rested his elbow upon his knee and stroked his red-gold beard while he gathered his thoughts.

"We all know—they all know—you are skilled, astute, and fierce." Raphael gave a rueful half-smile. The archangel stood and paced, explaining, "There has been much unrest. Seraph factions have taken more effective shape—."

"Raphael," interrupted Malachi. "The Seraph have been taking 'more effective shape' for eons. You are allowing yourself to be a vessel filled with Celestial drivel, only to sweeten it with your honey, pour the nonsense into a golden goblet, and expect me to drink of it."

A half-smile formed on Raphael's mouth. "Is that not what diplomats do?"

"Go bugger yourself, Raphael."

Raphael rolled his eyes and shook his head, then resumed pacing as he spoke, "To continue, The Five have determined, as Earthbound, you have a strong advantage and garner less chance of capture and torture than you would have traveling between the two dimensions."

"Hold there," snapped Malachi, incredulous. "They judge I am not up to the task to avoid capture were I not Earthbound?" he asked as insult hardened his eyes and the set of his shoulders. "They, who could not walk in my steps for a single tick of the sundial?"

Raphael closed his eyes and pulled his hand over his face.

"At ease my friend," Malachi sighed as he forced his anger away. "I know this decision is not of your making." He reached out and clapped his steadfast friend on the back. "I am not like you; I do not travel with grace between both worlds," Malachi admitted with reluctance. He placed his hands on his hips and turned to look out of the temple, up at the cloudless sky, and blew out a tense breath as he wondered out loud, "Mayhap, they are right." Shifting his gaze to the golden Raphael, his brows pulled together, he asked, "Just what have the bastards decided I will do as Earthbound?"

Raphael sat again upon the throne and leaned toward Malachi with his elbow perched upon his knee. "A duty I believe for which you are well suited, in spite of your anger at this moment. You are now an Immortal Guardian, my friend; well-prepared to protect that which would lend the Seraph great power were they to capture it and call it their own. Your first mission," Raphael said while he swept his hand across the temple with a flourish and his voice rang out with a regal air, "is to be Guardian of the Temple of Thoth, God of Judgement and Learning, Great Arbitrator of the Gods."

Malachi stared in disbelief at Raphael. "In the name of Zeus! You are bloody joking."

Raphael stared back in silence, his hand remaining outstretched.

"You are not joking."

Raphael stayed silent, his deep blue eyes searching Malachi's.

Malachi rubbed the back of his neck. "Thoth's temple needs a Guardian like the desert needs sand," he declared.

Raphael lifted a brow.

Malachi's eyes widened. "In the name of Zeus, bugger me," he said.

Unable to help himself, Raphael barked out a laugh. "I thought he tried that once, and you kicked his godly ass to the River Styx."

Too confounded to appreciate the humor and the memory, Malachi glared at Raphael with a fierce frown.

Raphael mugged a half grin, then shifted to a neutral expression as he continued with his explanation. "As we both know, Thoth is harshly unbiased. It would benefit the beings recruited by the Seraph, and the Seraph themselves, to have Thoth out of the way.

"The Five have determined that it is imperative that Thoth and his temple remain protected at all cost," Raphael said. His solemn golden gaze held Malachi's dark one, imparting the critical nature of Malachi's new role.

Raphael continued in his explanation, "Thoth is working to further develop a system of writing, and a method to teach the art of mathematics to humankind. Losing Thoth's academic advances for humanity would erode free will and be a boon to the Seraph…" His voice trailed off. He wrinkled his nose as a noxious odor wound through the temple. His blue-eyed gaze swept the space, then he turned his head both ways and sniffed to identify the source.

The warm desert wind strengthened and the faint, fetid pungency danced to the senses of both Malachi and Raphael. They exchanged concerned glances.

The unpleasant odor burgeoned to a stench of sulfured decay. Then, a putrid gust of air kicked ashes from the bowl of burning incense and dried fruit into both their eyes. They blinked to clear their vision with little effect.

Raphael shimmered as he raised his guard.

The strong need to retch pushed aside, Malachi readied for battle. Adrenalin pulsed through his warrior's muscle-bound body, which now hummed with preternatural power. Cobalt blue flames appeared at his fingertips.

Malachi threw one hand before him to ward off further assault and swept the other in an arc before his eyes, the blue licks of fire flaring as they came near the evil of the manipulated ashes. Debris fell from both his and Raphael's eyes. Their vision cleared as the muscular, undulating form of Apep—the malignant god of Chaos—materialized at Raphael's feet. The massive asp's sulfur-yellow body shifted from a wavering mirage to a palpable, slithering being. His serpentine body was thick as the columns and longer than the ninety cubits of the temple.

Raphael jumped back from the horrific creature, his eyes wide in alarm and mouth pulled down in revulsion.

Apep wound his long, broad form past the feet of Thoth's throne. A cold, evil whisper of reptilian flesh filled the air as he slithered past the hardwood. He coiled his lengthy body into a sinister and malodorous spire on the opposite side of the throne from Raphael. The spiraled viper towered over Raphael by at least a cubit and a half.

Apep, Raphael, and Malachi formed a hostile triad, each staring with antipathy ripe in the air.

Baneful, sulfured scorn radiated from Apep.

Malachi's jaw ticked and his body tensed, ready to cast his angel's fire.

Both Raphael and Malachi's muscle-bound wings materialized, peaked like snow-capped mountaintops behind their broad shoulders, the rustle of their leathery feathers almost swallowed by the desert winds.

Raphael's gilt eyes gleamed as a golden aura shimmered about him.

Malachi cleared his throat and spat to the side.

Apep turned his massive snout toward Malachi and peered with malice at the warrior angel, his sulfur-yellow eyes split by fathomless black pupils. His thick neck undulated as his head swayed from side to side. With a demon's hiss, out slithered his forked tongue, the reach seemingly endless. Near Malachi's face, the forked tip flicked before retracting.

Malachi leaned back and steeled himself, flinching as the ghastly, undulant tongue neared his face.

One last flick, then Apep fixed his eyes on Malachi and spoke. The serpent's voice, deep and born of the bowels of hell, wrapped the angel in its unrelenting malevolence. "Our sspiess have informed uss, angel, that Celesstialss no longer conssider you one of theirss. You would have great power with the Sseraph, Malachi the Fallen. Come, join uss. Be exalted rather than casst down as offal." Apep's deep intonation slid as shards of evil past the ears of Raphael and Malachi.

"Thiss one," Apep hissed as he gestured toward Raphael with a turn of his head, "is working to ssway you into believing the Celesstialss sstill hold you in regard." He raised his head and sneered, "Sss... Celesstialss hold no-one but themsselvess in regard."

Apep flicked his tongue at Malachi and said, "Come. Come, Malachi the Great, come where you are apprecssiated rather than maligned." His unblinking, foul gaze fixed on the dark-haired warrior.

Malachi drew in a deep breath through his nose, his unwavering, flaming cobalt eyes fixed on those of the serpent. He spoke through gritted teeth, "Apep, we note your invitation, but you speak half-truths."

"You think the Celesstialss do not?" Apep interrupted. The god threw his head back and hissed a hellish parody of a laugh. He lowered his head and extended his neck until his snout came within an apple's width of Malachi's face. Apep searched the warrior angel's eyes with a measured stare. His fetid breath washed over Malachi, lifting the angel's dark hair. Grunting, the asp pulled back and said, "I thought more of your intelligencsse, Angel." The last word issued forth from his mouth dripping with disgust as his baleful gaze moved over Malachi. Apep then spat at his feet.

"I would go to the Fields of Asphodel or the River Acheron before I joined with the Seraph or the likes of you, Apep," Malachi snarled as the cobalt flames of his eyes flared.

The serpent gave a menacing hiss, a sound many unfortunate warriors had heard before meeting a horrific end, and intoned, "So be it, fool. We intend to see you ssuffer; hear you beg for redemption." Apep pulled his head back, towering over his coiled body. The serpent moved his head from side to side, then lowered it near Raphael while still undulating and peered with malevolence at the golden archangel.

Raphael's powerful wings ruffled as his golden aura blazed.

Apep reared back and his hood flashed open as he opened his jaws wide. Saber-like fangs glistened in the desert sun, poised over the archangel's head.

Raphael moved with lightning speed to remove his sword from its scabbard but was stopped when Bia appeared and restrained his sword arm. Apep continued to eye him with a predatory light in his malevolent gaze.

Bia smiled with maleficence upon Raphael.

Malachi witnessed rare fear and desperation enter the unflappable Raphael's eyes. Sweat beaded on his forehead and his pulse beat in a rapid tattoo at his throat.

Just as Apep struck out at Raphael, Malachi manifested a fiery blue orb of energy between his hands, imbued with his intent. He heaved and cast it with great force at the asp. Molten blue sliced readily down through the viper's coils as though they were lard. A hissing sound emanated along with a foul stench as the orb cauterized the serpent's innards in its descent.

Apep howled, his head still surging forward as the blue-hot sphere cleaved his coils. The snake's hood retracted as the fetor of burned and decaying flesh filled the air. Apep's visage rotated away from Raphael as his massive head plummeted to land upside down with a sickening bounce with his baleful gaze on Malachi. Smoke spiraled into the dry, wafting air from his cleaved coils, the sulfur yellow scales now blackened at the edges.

Bia paled, her mouth agape, as she stared at the carnage. She whisked her gaze to Malachi, baleful hate emanating from her eyes, then aside to Raphael. A mask of repugnance fell across her face. She pulled away from Raphael as though he were a hot poker, then vanished. Where she had stood a moment before suddenly vacated, hot desert air blew past Raphael as it rushed to fill the void.

As the desert wind caromed about, strands of Malachi's hair fluttered alongside his face, appearing as unfurled raven-wing feathers. His gaze of cobalt flame was locked on the defeated reptile.

Apep's evil, saffron yellow gaze glowed with a malevolent light as it fixed on Malachi. "Sss, you will pay dearly for thiss, Fallen Angel. Mark my wordss," he hissed as his forked tongue flicked, lengthened, and curved toward Raphael. It came within a hand's breadth of the archangel's neck before Raphael jumped back.

With a burst of yellow light and odor of decay, Apep disappeared. A small pile of ash remained on the floor to the right of the throne.

Malachi drew an ethereal circle in the air and flicked his fingers outward over the ash. Desert winds scooped it up and dispersed it over the sands. With another flourish, he brought a cleansing gust of wind through the temple. The fire under the incense and dried fruit flared as Malachi's power flowed, and the air filled with pleasant aromas.

With a ruffle, Raphael's wings dematerialized. He sat on a nearby bench and let out a long breath as he rubbed the back of his neck. "A word to the wise: Don't be tempted to entertain the thought of a casual tryst with Bia. I know you like to play with fire, but she is much stronger than I ever thought possible. You may find yourself chained to the same rock as Prometheus."

Malachi laughed. "I may enjoy mutual pleasure with women of like mind, Raphael, but never of the Seraph. I am not a buck in rut." He picked two plump, red-green apples from the brass fruit bowl and shined one against the linen of his cuirass, then tossed it to Raphael as he flashed a cocky grin. He then polished the other and took a huge bite.

"By Zeus," Malachi remarked as he chewed. "How quickly

word of my banishment has traveled. Mayhap Thoth's temple does need a guardian after all, my friend." He cocked his brow as his eyes lighted with a mischievous gleam. "In fact, I now wonder if your Celestial ass needs a guardian, too," he laughed as he took a second bite of the sweet apple and juice ran from the corner of his mouth. He lifted the back of his hand to wipe away the nectar.

Raphael bit into the sweet, decadent fruit, then mused aloud as he chewed, "You know, the viper bite would have hurt like the fire of Hades, but I would have recovered quickly." He stood and retrieved his goblet.

Malachi shook his head. "No, I disagree," he said, taking another bite, "your Celestial ass is in definite need of a guardian!" A grin split Malachi's face while he chewed. "No time like the present to establish who is in charge."

Raphael's laughter died as his eyes widened, his gaze falling behind his comrade.

From behind Malachi, a deep and preternatural voice asked, "Is that so, angel?"

Malachi paused mid-bite, then yanked the apple from between his teeth and flung it out into the desert sand. He wiped his hands down the front of his armor and grasped the hilt of his sword at his scabbard. "As a matter of fact, my lord Thoth, it is so," he said with quiet menace as he turned to the source of the voice. Malachi glared at the tall, imposing figure with the head of an ibis and a dark, broad human-like body corded with muscle. Thoth returned a measured, unblinking gaze. His fierce, bird-of-prey eyes were blacker than kohl.

A cocksure grin split Malachi's swarthy, bearded face.

Thoth planted his hands on his hips, threw back his ink-black head, and gave a hearty laugh. The gold bands about his biceps glinted in the desert sun as he shifted in his booming amusement.

Malachi closed the space between him and Thoth, hand

slapped against forearm in a robust clasp. They pulled close and clapped each other's backs with sturdy affection. Malachi stretched his tall, muscular body to embrace Thoth, who towered over him by at least half a cubit. Thoth's imposing, dark, and powerful body gleamed as he moved, contrasting with the flawless white linen shendyt wrapped about his hips.

Thoth stepped away with a brusque nod to Raphael who stood near the greater god's throne.

The archangel gave a respectful half-bow of greeting.

Thoth again fixed his intent gaze on Malachi. "Apep and Bia dared to show their revolting selves in my temple, Malachi." His preternatural voice rumbled his displeasure. Thoth pivoted and paced. He slammed a fist into an open palm as he continued, "They risk much doing so. Something must be afoot!" He strode to his throne and sat.

Impaling Raphael with his intense black eyes, Thoth commanded the archangel's attention. "I have many questions, Celestial." He rolled the word 'Celestial' about in his deep, preternatural voice as though he had a bitter wine upon his tongue. "Why does the foul serpent show himself here? What brings you to the temple of a god your kind prefers to pretend does not exist?" His voice was dark and tinged with cynicism. Thoth then leaned toward Raphael, his vicious beak elongating as he cocked his head toward Malachi. "And, tell me why Malachi is now 'Malachi the Fallen'."

Raphael bowed his head in deference, then looked up and explained, "Thoth, I hold you and your purpose in the highest of regard." His voice remained even. "The Celestials acknowledge your unarguable objectivity in arbitration of the gods and other beings of power." Raphael paused as Thoth's beak returned to its prior length, although it was nevertheless menacing, then continued, "You keep order among the most preeminent of gods of both Olympus and the Nile. You meet the continual challenge without prejudice or flaw."

Thoth interrupted, "To the contrary, Raphael. My word is law; there is little 'challenge'. I maintain a balance with no favor to light or dark." He paused, then said, "Explain yourselves."

Raphael continued, "Malachi spends much time in the temples across the lands. He has developed strong and positive relationships with the gods. The Celestials have taken note, and admit they miscalculated the attraction the Seraph would hold for the more powerful. They have fostered a wide and robust following."

Thoth nodded. "The Seraph threat appears to have gained even more momentum and credibility. As much as I despise your pompous Celestials, the boundaries between Celestia, humankind, and the gods provide a much-needed balance. And, were the Seraph successful in their quest to enslave humans and twist their energy toward evil, the world would become like Acheron, the river of sorrow."

Having garnered Thoth's acknowledgment, Raphael dove into the crux of the matter. "Our spies and strategists have determined that your temple is at risk for infiltration, even attack. Apep's attempt to recruit Malachi and be rid of me only further confirms their machinations." Raphael paced as he explained. "Malachi is now assigned the duty of Immortal Guardian, with his current assignment to protect you and your temple. The guardians are honor-bound to keep watch over that which holds great power or knowledge, the misuse of which could bring great harm to the heavens, gods, the mortals, or Earth. The Five see strong strategic advantage to having Malachi here, in that you may draw many of the Seraph out, as your conquest would prove a coup."

Nodding as he listened, Thoth remarked, "I agree there is a strategic advantage to have Malachi take this assignment." He shifted his gaze to Malachi, who shrugged, unrepentant, and bent to snag another apple. He arched a brow while he polished the apple against his linothorax cuirass, then bit into it. Thoth sighed and said as he glared at Malachi, "But, to look at him now, I may have my doubts."

Malachi responded with an audacious grin as he chewed his apple.

Thoth waved a dismissive hand toward Malachi, then turned his attention back to Raphael. "Continue, Archangel," Thoth commanded as he motioned to a stone bench before him.

Raphael backed up to the stone seat and looked to Malachi.

Malachi nodded for him to continue.

Raphael moved his gaze back to Thoth's. "The strategy behind making Malachi Earthbound is the collective thought he will be more effective this way. The Five also feared he was at greater risk of capture with frequent travels, thus a secondary reason for his banishment."

Thoth peered down at Malachi and said, "You never did fit in with those whiter than gull-dung Celestials." Thoth said the last as though it were a bitter and slimy snail caught in his elongated, curved beak. "Truthfully, Malachi, your time and intellect were wasted with them." Thoth spat to the side as if to rid himself of the taste of the subject. "Hmm. I suppose I must ensure things are kept lively here for you. By Isis, we do not want you bored," he exclaimed, then leaned back in his throne and threw back his head with a hearty laugh.

Raphael gave a polite chuckle.

Malachi noted Raphael glancing back and forth between himself and Thoth. The archangel's face had the look of someone who found a piece of gristle while chewing but did not want to upset his host and swallowed.

Amused by the archangel's obvious discomfort, Malachi found unexpected pleasure with the turn of events at the behest of The Five and Thoth. It dawned on him he no longer needed to conform to the expected behavior of a Celestial. A grin split his face. "I have no doubt you will, my lord Thoth. I have no doubt."

Malachi turned to Raphael. "You have delivered your message, my friend. I have no intention of starting a revolt in Celestia. The Five may rest easy concerning my change in status."

Relief etched Raphael's face. "Thank you. I should take my leave."

Malachi moved to embrace Raphael, white and gold against black; their hearty claps rang through the temple. Raphael shifted his hands to Malachi's upper arms as he placed a kiss upon each of Malachi's cheeks. "My faithful friend," he said as he eased back and looked Malachi in the eye, then stepped away.

Raphael nodded to Thoth.

Thoth gave a regal dip of his kohl black head.

His gaze fixed on Thoth, Raphael shimmered as gold flecks danced around him, then he vanished.

CHAPTER FOUR

345 BCE ~ Temple of Thoth, Egypt

THOTH SLAMMED his fist upon the armrest of his throne. Linen sun blinds billowed, the bowl of apples and dates jittered on its table, and a lone apple rolled onto the floor. His thunder carried across the temple. "Your Celestials are nothing but a sanctimonious lot of idiots, Raphael. They are inept in their understanding of humans and gods."

Calm, Raphael maintained eye contact. He nodded, his expression remaining neutral. He ignored the lone apple which had stopped at his feet. He found himself a target of an exceedingly rare show of temper by Thoth, unbiased Arbitrator of the gods. Not entirely immune, it seemed, to the imperious Celestials.

Thoth's black eyes glittered with wrath. "Malachi has been here only five Risings of Sopdet and Harvests. The Celestials see

35

fit to send him already, in this mere drop of time, to watch over a philosopher?" he asked, then drew a breath. "Surely, they can find another Guardian to send from your legions of warrior angels?" Thoth brought his sharp, curved beak within a linen cloth's breadth of Raphael's face.

Behind Raphael, coveys of limestone pebbles rolled, and dust billowed from the temple structure onto the stone floor. Raphael's unflinching, ocean-blue gaze remained on Thoth.

Thoth peered at Raphael, his anger in palpable waves emanated from his massive, unyielding body. His black beak elongated and curved into a vicious hook at the end.

Raphael's aura shimmered, gold flecks darting about his body.

With a low, frustrated growl, Thoth leaned back and rested his right shoulder against the seat back of his throne. His beak returned to its original length, and he gave a negligent wave of his left hand. "You need not fear me, angel." The fury ebbed from his voice and countenance. "At least, not at this time." His voice shifted to subdued ice with the promise of future threat.

Not breaking eye contact with Thoth, in spite of the god's wrath, Raphael took a breath and responded, his hands open in front of him, "I realize the choice appears dubious, Thoth, my lord." He moved to stand before a stone bench, awaiting Thoth's permission to sit.

Thoth motioned to the bench with a casual wave of his hand.

"To your point," Raphael began as he sat, "the Celestials know they do not have an appreciation for the perspectives of the gods of the Nile and Olympus. In re-evaluating the progress of our alliance, they have determined a need to take such into account. You are in a unique position to arbitrate the grievances of the gods with an unbiased, broad perspective. They request that you consider communicating directly with them to offer more insight."

Desert winds punctuated the silence between the golden archangel and the enthroned, dark Egyptian god.

Thoth finally spoke, "I cannot give you an answer at this time, archangel. There is much I need to consider. Such as eons of Celestial disdain which will not simply disappear, my lack of faith they can come with sincerity to the table of diplomacy—against the need to indeed strengthen the alliance." He gave an impatient nod of his head. "Enough talk of Celestials. Tell me of this philosopher and why Malachi is needed."

"The Seraph view the confusion and fear caused by King Alexander's sieges as an opportunity. They make it known they offer protection from Alexander to those who would turn and join them. Aristotle is Alexander's confidante and advisor. If the Seraph take Aristotle out of the picture, chaos will ensue, and they will gain a sizeable advantage."

Thoth stroked his beak in thought as he listened. "Go on."

"Aristotle's philosophy is counterproductive to the Seraph rebellion. Celestia has determined it critical for Aristotle to have protection."

"That is all well and good for Aristotle and Alexander, angel," Thoth's voice was intonated with sarcasm. "Please, share with me how my temple will be protected."

"I believe you will find Katherine the Adamantine quite capable. She is one of our most formidable assassins and guardians, a Sekhmet lioness warrior of the ancients, and of the Nile," Raphael answered.

"'Quite capable', you say, Raphael? Hmm?" issued a low, contralto female voice from thin air near Thoth's throne.

Raphael scowled, and both of them looked toward the disembodied voice. Sea blue and silver coruscation filled the air in a tall column near Thoth's throne. Consolidating, the shimmer took on a dark, cinnamon-skinned female form. As she solidified, the silver tip of her dark blue spear shone in the sun.

Cinnamon hair, in scores of thin braids, pulled back from her temples, fell to the middle of her back. Her cerulean linen shendyt shone like the sea, and her polished bronze cuirass and greaves shone as if the sun itself stood among them.

"Katherine," Raphael intoned, curt yet courteous, with a nod toward her, "a grand entrance, as usual."

"Raphael," she mimicked his tone, then looked to Thoth. "Greetings, Thoth, my lord." Her nut-brown skin tone emphasized the shifting topaz of her eyes.

His daunting gaze upon the woman, Thoth's black eyes glittered while his beak elongated and again curved in an intimidating hook.

Unflustered, Katherine gave a brief bow of her head to Thoth, no attention given to his fierce countenance. The chest plate of her cuirass glinted in the sunlight as she shifted her gaze back to Raphael, dissecting him with her penetrating stare.

Displeasure seeped from Raphael as his lips turned down at the corners and he inclined his head.

Katherine tsked. "Come, now, Raphael. You archangels can be so strait-laced and stuffy."

Raphael peered at Katherine with narrowed eyes as he unrolled several maps. He took a deep breath, then looked down at the papyrus splayed before them. "I know you will handle things well, Katherine. Take heed, the Seraph are becoming more cunning and shrewd. Keep alert for the slightest divergence. Assumptions can be dangerous—"

He looked up in time to see her lips forming silent words, assumptions can be dangerous, as she mocked him. Raphael halted. He lifted his brows as the tops of his wings appeared and peaked, ruffled from behind his shoulders, in his annoyance.

Katherine returned his gaze, her lips turned up at the corners in a subtle smirk.

The moment stretched for an eon; the incense cracked.

Raphael's hard stare, heavy with authority, bored into Katherine's.

The archangel's fierce expression fell away, relenting without giving quarter. Raphael continued as nothing had transpired. "As I was saying, Katherine, assumptions can be dangerous. The Seraph, with their infiltrations, are making it more difficult to know friend or foe."

Katherine nodded and asked questions as she and Raphael went over the maps, the incident also behind her.

From his ebony and teak throne, Thoth watched the exchange with his chin and beak resting upon his right hand.

Katherine's head together with Raphael's as they discussed their plans showed a strong rapport, and their warrior's bond and mutual respect palpable.

Soon after, they pulled Thoth into the planning. The three preternatural beings discussed the elements and strategy of transition from Malachi's guardianship of Thoth's temple to Katherine. Together, they mapped out comprehensive plans of protection, fresh with Katherine's insights. The changing landscape of the fight against the Seraph led them to outline several contingencies—Raphael himself included as one of them as he made them both aware he could be called upon. Satisfaction imbued the air as they wrapped up their strategic session.

As Raphael rolled the maps onto their scrolls with meticulous care, he nodded to Katherine. In response, she spun on her heel toward the now redolent Thoth, her cinnamon braids swirled about her. The moment hung in balance. Her bronze armor glinted in the sun as she straightened.

Thoth's eyes found hers.

Her shoulders squared as she assumed an austere posture. Strength and prowess emanated from the lift of her chin, every curve of defined muscle, and her keen gaze.

Katherine the Adamantine raised her intrepid visage to

Thoth and said, "You have my word as a follower of Sekhmet and on the blood of the goddess that flows in my veins, I will guard Thoth the Arbitrator and his temple with honor and at all cost." Her declaration, resonant and sure, rode the desert winds and echoed off the dunes.

CHAPTER FIVE

332 BCE ~ The Lyceum, Athens, Greece

FROM A DISTANCE, Malachi watched the charismatic Aristotle command a presence over the attentive crowd, a crowd that gathered to hear him give his public lecture every afternoon. Aristotle's silver-haired head bobbed as he spoke and his white robes shone bright under the Athenian sun, rippling as he lifted his arms to add emphasis to his words. His sure voice carried through the white stone amphitheater.

The great tutor's mind, view of the natural laws, and ability to articulate complex concepts in simple terms never ceased to amaze Malachi. *I wonder if the Earth will ever see another like him,* he mused. He had developed immense respect for the philosopher.

Malachi remained on the alert as Aristotle charmed the crowd. There had been several assassination attempts over the thirteen years Malachi protected Aristotle, and he had thwarted all. Not without challenge, or close calls.

He had been effective in extracting information from some of the would-be assassins before they perished under his hand. The intelligence gained from them had often proven to be of high value to the Celestial and deity factions in the ongoing war.

The Seraph had made many endeavors to extricate these captured assassins before they shared sensitive information. Malachi's wards proved too strong for recovery teams to broach. Instead, he used the attempts as opportunities to study Seraph strategies and craft his wards to be more effective against their varying means. Raphael had shared with Malachi that Celestial intelligence had ascertained he cost the Seraph a substantial number of their most effective and valued operatives.

Malachi enjoyed knowing that as Immortal Guardian of Aristotle, he had decimated much of the Seraph's hopes for advance. It did remain at the back of his mind with each cut he made into the Seraph forces; Gideon would work to one day exact a high price from him.

The tone of Aristotle's voice signaled Malachi the great philosopher was drawing his public session to a close.

Aristotle concluded the lecture. He turned to move from the stage to enter the annex off the Lyceum.

The crowds surged, wanting to touch the philosopher's white robes and ask him questions about their own situations. Malachi strained to watch every movement about his silver-haired charge and keep his wards strong and sensitive to infiltration attempts. The few moments of Aristotle's journey from stage to annex were the most nerve-wracking for Malachi. He scanned the teeming crowd for signs of malice, or voids of emotion and thought, as assassins were often adept at masking all.

Once Aristotle made it to the main door, Malachi caught up with him using camouflaged, preternatural speed.

Relief flowed through Malachi as he and Aristotle reached the other side of the door and his strong wards of protection. They walked through the entrance hall and deeper into the house.

He checked and reset the daily protection wards over and through the compound for the philosopher. He changed them often to prevent the Seraph from learning how to get past his ethereal boundaries.

Aristotle spent his days poring through and coalescing the writings of prior great teachers, including Plato—his own teacher—and Socrates. Plato had also transcribed Socrates's writings. Aristotle wove the insightful words of many into a multi-faceted, complex, and seamless tapestry of philosophy, the breadth of which left Malachi in awe.

Sitting down to the mid-day meal with Aristotle and his wife, Pythias, Malachi, and Aristotle enjoyed shared laughs from the colorful antics of the morning crowd. Malachi caught sight of the statuesque Adelpha, Pythia's handmaiden, striding down the hall from Pythia's quarters to the kitchens. Her thick fall of burnished blonde hair piled high on her head added to her proud carriage. His admiration of her confidence, natural sensuality, and quick wit rose in the warm smile which stole over his stern countenance.

Adelpha stopped mid-stride as she caught his smile and warm glance. Mischief lit her deep brown eyes when she lifted the corners of her mouth. She broke off the shared moment with that feminine, sidelong look gifted to women, and returned to her business at hand as she entered the kitchen.

Malachi brought his attention back to his meal and dove with appreciation into his midday repast. He enjoyed the crusty, fresh bread paired with salted sheep's milk cheese and succulent olives while his mind wandered over Adelpha's lush curves.

"Malachi, your thoughts, if you will," Aristotle said as he interrupted Malachi's carnal musings.

Bread halfway to his mouth, Malachi struggled to clear the fog of his daydreams and bring his thoughts from his loins and food to the great teacher.

"If Socrates chose to drink the hemlock, did he commit suicide or was he executed?" questioned Aristotle, referring to the well-known trial and death of Socrates sixty-seven years earlier.

Contemplation took Malachi's gaze far away while he chewed. He swallowed, his Adam's apple bobbing, then shared his thoughts, "Plato wrote that Socrates postulated he did not hold wisdom, thus his wisdom exceeded others. He admitted his own lack of understanding. Plato also wrote that Socrates understood that if he did not accept the judgment of death from the courts of Athens, he would turn the citizens against the leaders of the city, and this would be of great detriment." Increased sureness imbued Malachi's voice as he arrived at his answer. He looked to Aristotle and said, "He accepted his execution. He would not have chosen to die without the judgment against him. Therefore, he did not commit suicide."

Aristotle nodded, "Most excellent perspective, my friend. You are indeed learning."

Adelpha appeared, and Malachi noted the affectionate smile Pythias gave her. It warmed his heart that Aristotle and his wife considered the girl family. Heat suffused his groin as he let his gaze wander over her.

Adelpha flashed a scolding glance to him.

Malachi worked to bite back a laugh.

Aristotle's voice disrupted Malachi's reverie. "I need to be on my way to study and categorize the seashells I collected this past week." He stood, stretched, and backed away from the table. "Many similarities and variations."

Over the past thirteen years, Malachi gained an appreciation for Aristotle's systematic method of defining elements of the natural world; examining and documenting cause and effect, which allowed him to arrive at consistent conclusions. "Would you be in need of my assistance, sir?" he asked.

"Not this afternoon, Malachi, thank you."

Malachi nodded, and from around Aristotle, he stretched to watch the sway of Adelpha's hips as she walked behind Pythias to the lady's quarters.

It seemed she sensed his eyes on her backside, as she turned around and flashed him a 'come hither' look.

He winked at her, enjoying how her smile deepened for a brief moment before she affected a serious expression and returned her attention to her task at hand.

Malachi fought a grin as he brought his attention back to Aristotle, busy adjusting his chiton and robes, disheveled from sitting. "I am sure you will enjoy the peace and quiet after the lively crowd of this morning."

The silver-haired teacher looked up from his task and smiled. "Indeed, I shall, Malachi," he said, then turned to walk to his study.

Eager to wash off the dust of the crowd, market, and streets, Malachi went to the baths. Hope filled him that Adelpha could spirit away from Pythias and join him. Together, they took great pleasure in opportunities to assuage their carnal appetites, well matched in their wit and proclivities. Malachi knew he could not foster a committed relationship with a mortal. He could not afford distraction from his mission by emotional involvement. Trusted women, who also found gratification in satisfying these appetites and did not have an eye on deeper emotional ties, had often become good friends through the years.

Adelpha, her place in Aristotle's household secure and having a strong bond with Pythias, expressed she found no desire to have a relationship which may interfere with her standing. She had seen this happen to many of her peers.

Malachi bent to unlace his greaves from his muscle-bound calves. He glanced up and caught her bronzed-blonde head peeking around the marbled doorway. A smile played at the corner of his mouth, aware he had his thigh muscles flexed, he kept them so for the benefit of Adelpha's discrete admiration.

He laughed inwardly as he caught her rolling her eyes at his overt display before she pulled her head back around the corner.

His greaves undone, Malachi stood and unfastened his black leather chest plate, then peeled off his leather vest; the muscles in his arms rippling with their contained power. His breastplate and vest now on the marble bench, but his loins still covered by the pteruges, he stretched. His massive chest and defined abdominal muscles gleamed with steam of the baths. Upon lifting his forearms up behind his head, he heard a sultry, feminine gasp. He lifted a knowing brow, enjoying their game, and dropped a hand to pass in a virile manner over the muscles of his abdomen.

"Adelpha, you might as well show yourself. I know you are there, dear girl."

A provocative feminine laugh came from the other side of the doorway. "You have discovered my game of hide and spy." Her lilting, playful voice preceded her tall and graceful form through the doorway, her rich brown eyes alight in her desire. The elegance of her thick, wavy hair piled upon her head, held in place with silk ribbons woven through the locks, emphasized her innate grace. Fine jeweled bronze hair pins scattered through her rich hair glinted in the daylight streaming through the unshuttered windows.

"Do you truly believe that you can hide yourself from me, Adelpha," Malachi asked with a warm sensuality as he took her hand and lifted the back of it to his lips. An appreciative gleam appeared in his raven-black gaze upon her eyes over her hand. He noted the blush which feathered through her cheeks and the swelling of her full, sultry lips as she pulled in a breath upon the touch of his lips on her sensitive skin, imbued with lavender. An urgent ache consumed him.

Her cream-colored linen chiton fell in graceful folds from where it gathered into straps on her shoulders. The linen was fine and soft, befitting her station as Pythias's personal companion. A white silken rope crossed several times over her waist in an elaborate pattern. The top of her dress, where it fanned from the shoulder straps, was pulled taut over her breasts. Her hardened and swelling nipples strained against the soft linen.

Malachi stood, turned her hand over and flicked his warm, skilled tongue over her sensitive palm as he stepped in closer to caress her breast with his other hand, then roll her nipple between his calloused thumb and forefinger.

Adelpha pulled in a sigh, leaning in toward Malachi.

Through the fine, gathered linen, he pinched her nipple, then gave a light tug, eliciting a hitched breath.

"Come," he said, "bathe this bone-weary warrior, Adelpha, rid me of the grime of the Lyceum crowd, then we will assuage your ache, hmm?"

Malachi lifted a knowing brow as Adelpha stepped away and walked around him trailing her tapered fingers over his well-muscled chest and back.

Her sienna brown eyes, warm with desire, moved up and down over his powerful physique while an evocative, feminine smile played at the corners of her lush lips. She stopped at his left arm and answered, "I would happily assist you with your bath, Sir." Her nose wrinkled as she sniffed while she moved to press her tall, graceful self along the length of his rugged warrior's body. Her mouth was at his left ear. "You do have the smell of the market on you," she agreed with a playful whisper, which grew to a throaty laugh full of warmth, lust, and promise.

His cock stood at attention and leapt in a rush of desire. Her lavender fragrance, mixed with the scent of womanly yearning, proved heady to Malachi. His right hand came up behind her head, he dug his fingers into her hair and crushed his mouth to hers, plundering. He felt her knees give out and caught her weight with his arm, pulling back from his passionate kiss.

"I must not smell that bad," he said, against her mouth with an intimate, carnal laugh. He deepened his kiss again, plucking the pins from her hair, wrapping the length of her thick blonde hair about his hand as he ravaged her sweet mouth, tasting her passion.

Her eyes fluttered closed as her head fell back.

Malachi curled his well-muscled arm about her waist and trailed hot, hedonistic kisses from her mouth down her neck, over the rise of her breasts. His close groomed beard rasped against her skin, bringing a pink blush. He pulled a breast free, plumped the mound in his calloused grasp, her nipple distending with her coursing sensual hunger. He captured her nipple between his teeth, tugged, then seized the swollen bud with his mouth and suckled, as he groaned against her breast.

She lifted her hands to either side of his head, worked her fingers into Malachi's thick raven-black hair, holding his head in place. Her head fell back and her cheeks became flushed with desire.

A kiss first upon the swell of her breast then another on her neck, he lifted his head and brought her out of her haze.

"Come, bathe me, Adelpha," he commanded, as he took her hand and pulled her toward the marble pool filled with steaming water.

His abdominal muscles rippled as he lowered himself into the steaming water, sighing with abject pleasure as the soothing heat enveloped him.

Adelpha climbed into the water next to him, still clothed, proper for a respected, revered servant. The linen of her skirts floated about in the water. She scrubbed his face, then his back, working the cloth over his entire body. Rivulets dripped over the curve of his shoulders and muscles as she bathed and rinsed his brawny body. She worked in deferential silence.

Rare relaxation and pleasure of the bath were evident in Malachi's typically harsh and austere visage, a smile tugging at the corners of his generous mouth and his obsidian eyes imbued with warmth.

Bending to wash his calves and feet, the top of her dress became soaked. Her dusky nipples showed through the wet linen as she stood. She raised her eyes to his face. Adelpha stepped next to him, lowered the cloth over his groin. Their gazes remained locked while she encircled his rock-hard shaft with her cloth covered hand, cleansing him. He snaked a hand to a globe of her ass, covered by wet linen and dug his fingertips into the rounded flesh. His cock swelled again.

He could see a moan threatened to spill from her; he bent to kiss her beautiful lips and coaxed the moan from her mouth into his. He lifted his head.

She shifted the cloth to his sac, Adelpha swirled the rough material with care, then moved to the sensitive area behind.

His eyes remained on hers, sinful pleasure coursing through Malachi.

She moved the cloth to the most intimate area.

His gaze boring into hers, daring her to break away as she cleansed him. A deep grunt rumbled through his chest. He grasped her wrist. "Drop the cloth. You are finished with my bath, Sweet Adelpha." His voice was low and smooth as warm honey, a contrast to the brute strength of his hand encircling her wrist.

The abandoned cloth floated down through the water. He set his hands about her waist, lifted her tall body, and sat her on the side of the pool. On the edge of the marble, Malachi set her heels, her wet linen draping over her bent legs. He pushed back the water-laden material back to bare her legs. Leaning between her lithe thighs, he grasped her tender flesh to partake of her nectar, his beard scraping over her delicate skin.

With his tongue he teased her tender bud.. He lifted both

hands to her breasts, pushed her wet chiton aside, rolled her nipples between his thumbs and forefingers and tugged. Malachi smiled with male carnal satisfaction against her sweetness, as her back arched and a deep moan escaped from her.

Adelpha splayed her palms behind her on the marble floor, her head fell back.

Malachi maintained a firm hold on her thighs as she writhed on the marble. She gave him the precious nectar he sought, her toes curling in sublime pleasure. He groaned against her flesh, the resonance pushing her over the edge.

A sunburst, she blossomed in a deep orgasm.

"Yes, my sweet Adelpha, that's it," he growled against her, his voice low and husky. He drew out her pleasure. She bit her lip, he knew, to keep from keening out loud. As he stood up in the water, he slid two fingers into her silken sheath. Male pleasure darkened his eyes, his gaze fixed on her flushed face, while her orgasm rippled through her, her feminine muscles contracting about his fingers. Her tension ebbing, he swirled his calloused fingertips, then eased from her.

Her bemused gaze remained on Malachi as he heaved himself out of the marble bath, moving over the strength corded through him. Malachi grabbed several of the linen towels folded and stacked on a nearby table and walked with confidence, unconcerned about his naked state, to a chaise lounge, his erection full and thick. He created a makeshift bed with the towels padding the lounge, then strode to Adelpha, every movement intrepid, masculine. Offering his hand, he helped her to stand, her legs trembling. She rocked on her feet to catch her balance, steadied herself with his hand. Malachi led her to the chaise.

Once Malachi helped her get comfortable on the chaise. He leaned over, placed his hands on either side of her head and nudged her legs apart with his knee. She drew her legs up as he settled between. A deep groan rumbled through him as he surged into her. Adelpha lifted her legs and rested her heels on the backs of his powerful thighs. His head lowered, he nipped at her shoulder with a soft growl. His cock twitched and swelled, his climax near.

She mewled, her hot breath fanning his ear as her femininity contracted about him. She dug fingertips into his shoulders.

A deep thrust, he remained as he released his seed, his head thrown back, ecstasy etched on his face, a groan of satisfaction rumbling deep in his chest. His preternatural essence shimmered a bare moment. He moved his mouth over her, kissed her hard, while drawing a deep breath through his nose.

"By Zeus, you are lovely!" he exclaimed, as he dropped his head onto her collarbone. A sheen of perspiration coated both of their bodies as they both took heavy breaths.

Malachi sensed her smile against his shoulder as she trailed her fingers over his back, slick with sweat.

"Not a bad way to spend an afternoon, Malachi," she said as she planted a kiss at the crook of his neck. "I do need to go and assist Mistress Pythias with her evening toilet before dinner."

"Of course, Adelpha." He lifted on his elbows, smiled down at her, withdrew, kissing her forehead. He stood.

Her eyes moved over him, a blush imbued her cheeks and chest.

Solicitous, he retrieved a towel for her. Malachi finished dressing, she wrapped up in the dry linen towel. His dark eyes on hers, he closed the distance between them, placed a tender kiss upon her cheek.

The next day, after Aristotle had given his morning lecture to the masses, he poured through *Electra*, by the Tragedian playwright Sophocles. He liked to review the master author's work as reference before revising his future lectures on Sophocles and literature.

Malachi studied Aristotle as they worked in companionable silence. The breeze wafted through the courtyard window, gently lifting the linen wall hangings about them.

The air palpably changed and the hairs on Malachi's neck rose. Whatever raised his alarm, the wards he had set over Aristotle's grounds did not contain it. In battle-readiness, his heart beat faster. He gave silent thanks Aristotle sat next to him. Having a niggling sense of periphery darkness, Malachi extended his senses to Adelpha and through Athens.

There, the market! Malachi sensed the terror riding on the shriek of Adelpha, who had gone to market with Pythias. He delved closer in his mind's eye. At an herb vendor, Adelpha's handbasket lay on the ground, dried herbs strewn about, sending a chill through Malachi. Adelpha stood in front of Pythias, her hands extended outward, appearing to guard Aristotle's wife.

Next to the discarded basket, a cobra weaved side to side, its hood extended, threatening the two women. Their Celestial guard lay dead next to them. *Dear Isis*, Malachi prayed. Pythias and Adelpha appeared as two startled women to the market crowd milling about, the magical cobra and dead guard invisible to humans.

Malachi cursed the Celestials for the frequent unpreparedness of the non-warrior angel guards from the Celestial ranks.

Trepidation grew in Malachi. This could only be the work of gods.

Malachi, filled with a driving need to remove Pythias and Adelpha from danger, also knew he could not leave Aristotle unattended. The Seraph had indeed set a lethal and malicious trap. Just how lethal became apparent as Bia materialized in the courtyard outside Aristotle's study. It took everything Malachi had not to leap in front of the philosopher and through the window to behead her.

Bia caught his eye, her lips tipped in a sly smile tinted with triumphant malevolence. She lifted glinting chains before her. Horrified realization filled Malachi; the metal links were of the same enchanted chain she used to affix Prometheus to the rock in the Caucasus Mountains for his perpetual torment. She tossed a meaningful glance to the studying Aristotle as she snapped the length of chain before her floating form, then back to Malachi, her maleficent smile deepening.

Malachi formed a call for assistance to Raphael, only to see in his mind's eye the goddess Artemis appear behind Pythias at the market. Artemis bent and let loose a mongoose from her hunter's satchel.

Malachi moved closer to Aristotle with his hand on the hilt of his sword and his eye on the goddess levitating outside the study window. In the market, the enchanted mongoose made quick work of the Seraphian cobra and relief flowed through Malachi. He stood, made as if to stretch, and moved between Aristotle and the window. Between his hands, he conjured a molten blue orb with Bia in his sight.

A scowl washed over Bia's face. Fury darkened her expression as understanding dawned: Artemis had foiled her plan. She glanced at the orb and vanished.

Malachi shifted his attention to Adelpha, Pythias, and Artemis.

Disgust shone through Artemis's tightened smile as she coiled the limp cobra and tucked the offensive reptile into a large pocket of her satchel. She imparted that the viper would be delivered to Thoth, to examine its deified venom.

With a chuck of her tongue, Artemis called to her loyal, fearless mongoose. The innocent looking warrior of an animal scampered into the main compartment of the bag, which Artemis then patted with affection.

Bowing, Malachi sent his gratitude for her intercession.

Artemis smiled, then disappeared into the crowds of the market.

Malachi watched from afar as Pythias hugged Adelpha. The shaken handmaiden crouched to pick up the strewn herbs and collect them into her basket as Pythias bent to help.

He knew his guard would now need to remain even higher, as the ante had been upped. Foreboding shadowed his heart.

CHAPTER SIX

181 CE ~ Temple of Thoth, Egypt

Earlier in the day, Katherine had made an offering of a beloved shield to the Ancients of the Elements, praying that her communion with the Ancients remained strong.

Roman Emperor Marcus Aurelius had died the year prior and great unrest grew under the rule of his son, Commodus. Tension spilled over into Egypt. The rise of Christianity in Alexandria siphoned believers away from the Greek and Egyptian deities. The Seraph took advantage and gained strength through the turmoil. The gods sought Thoth's arbitration more than ever, as the Seraph rebellion swelled.

Katherine knew Malachi had his hands full in Rome as disquiet flourished. The documented academic advances of humans were endangered as the systematic destruction of libraries gained popularity. Malachi worked to prevent the devastating loss of precious manuscripts written by the great academic investigators and philosophers.

On high alert, power thrummed through her mind, body, and soul as she walked the perimeter of the Temple of Thoth, setting wards of protection. The forces of Air, Earth, Fire, Water and Aether moved in concert with her while she molded their energy, casting forth ancient spells of protection. She had a strong sense of nearby unease, and the more she walked, the more she was sure she had perceived a shift in power this evening. There was something on the horizon watching, waiting for a moment of vulnerability.

She searched for Thoth's thoughts, his strength and essence unmistakable. Katherine could sense his location. For over five hundred years, they had coexisted; their relationship one of mutual respect. Katherine foiled all attacks on Thoth and the temple. She had eliminated several skilled Seraph assassins over the centuries. When she rested, she made it a practice to set far-reaching wards which provided an alert to both her and Thoth to any intrusion.

Pulled from her reverie, dark magic edged into the periphery of Katherine's psyche. The impression of a cold, jagged force—black with filth—raised an alarm. Katherine roused herself and used her mental senses to scout the periphery of the temple. She caught the bare wisp of a dark cloaking spell. Advanced and clever, its source perceived her discovery and receded as soon as it gained her notice.

She sought Thoth's essence and located the brilliant, harsh god. His mind opened for her, as it always did when she had a communique for him, and Katherine shared her visions of the cloaking spell and dark magic. She sensed his acknowledgment, then his abrupt disconnection.

Thoth had developed his own protections, to which she was not immune.

Katherine flinched, having never grown accustomed to his

terse closure. Even though she tried not to let it sting, it always did. She pulled herself from her reverie and turned to find the source of the cloaking spell. As she grew closer, she screened her own essence. Katherine maintained the facade of her vigil in the hopes the intruder would think themselves undetected and redirected her energy to casting spells of deeper protection. The Ancients rose to meet her call, and a faint blue aura shimmered about her as she worked. Sister Moon smiled upon the warrior in blue.

She stilled, thinking she had heard something. A scurrying sound to her left—with evil in its wake—sent a deep chill through her. Her spear now at the ready, she sent Thoth an urgent warning. She commanded a silence of the Elements and desert life about her. The air and earth fell still. Intent, Katherine listened.

A skirring crescendo signaled multiple beings were present. Other than this, she sensed nothing else of the dark magic of the intruders. Their craft must have been powerful, a thought that sent a fear of the unknown winding through Katherine.

Spear and shield held at the ready, she circled with sure footing. Her Sekhmet bloodline ancestors guided her senses. She heard the disturbance in the air as a blade wheeled toward her torso. Her rich fall of cinnamon braids flew out as she spun to block the blow with her shield, and she threw a high kick in the direction of the unseen foe. Her foot connected with sinewy being. The intruder cursed in Babylonian, a long-lost tongue, causing hairs on her neck to rise. Something ancient, evil, and lethal hunted her. She sent a call to Raphael for aid, and another urgent warning to Thoth.

Katherine made an entreaty to Sister Moon to shed light upon the darkened temple and her stalker. An ethereal glow suffused the temple and its perimeter, which partially dissipated the intruder's cloaking magic. She spied the glint of an eye, the shadow of a black limb, and flashes of weapons. Heart racing, she deliberately calmed herself to slow her breath to remain stealthy. A shadow appeared nearby, and a blade gleamed in the ethereal moonlight. Katherine spun toward the shifting shadow with a firm grasp about her spear. Flesh gave under the tip of her weapon. With a firm yank, she freed it as an agonal breath hung for a moment in the air, then the intruder's body thudded to the ground and was still.

The assassin's cloaking spell fell away, and Katherine's discerning gaze swooped over their countenance. The lower half of his face was obscured by a black cloth. He wore the black garb of a Babylonian soldier, and the green viper insignia of the Seraph on his sleeve appeared incandescent under the moonlight.

More sought her demise, and the capture or death of Thoth. She brought her attention back to the invasion and gauged her surroundings. A shadow at her right flank, the rush of air to the left. She shifted her spear to her shield hand and threw her heavy-bladed elemental boomerang toward the shadow, holding her shield behind her to deflect the blow from the other side. A mace clanged with some force against the shield, rocking her with the strength of the blow. She spun with her spear and stabbed the owner of the mace, meeting little resistance as the blade sunk into flesh. There was a gush of blood as she withdrew the weighty spear tip and a coppery smell permeated the night air.

In the same instant, the whir of the spinning boomerang sang to her, then came the unmistakable sound of the blade cleaving through flesh and bone. A head rolled to the ground, its unblinking eyes glinting in the dark, then the owner's body crumpled to the ground just behind it. The boomerang continued its song and gave off a flash of blue light, burning the gore off itself before returning to its mistress. She trilled a soft kulning of gratitude to the boomerang while it sang in victory, whirling around her once. Her hand up, the blade landed home with a solid thud in her palm.

She listened again for more opponents, reaching out with all her senses. Meanwhile, she gave thanks to Sister Moon for the stalwart aid and protection her shield and weapons afforded her. Katherine sensed Raphael nearing and sent a prayer of thanks to the Ancients.

Alarm rose as she heard the whoosh of a weapon cutting through the air from behind her. An unbearable pain blossomed in her thigh, just beneath her armor, then spread out to encompass her entire body. The burning was greater than the lava of Vesuvius. As a blur, she saw Raphael appear in front of her, then heard a thud behind her. A small flame of relief flared knowing he had dispatched her attacker. In agony, she fell to her knees as her vision darkened. Thoth's beaked, fierce visage swam before her as she pitched forward onto the hard ground. All went black.

Thoth and Raphael rushed forward to Katherine and turned her over with care. She had landed prone on her face without breaking her fall and blood poured from her nose. Her breath slowed and her color leached away to ashen. As an immortal, death should not overtake Katherine. Life ebbing from her made little sense to either of them. Raphael splayed his hand over her heart, bent over her head, and held his cheek near her lips. Her weak breaths fanned across his nose. He recognized the unmistakable odor of sulfured decay.

"Thoth," his voice thick with dread, "Katherine has been poisoned with the venom of Apep!" His eyes shot to the battle axe lying between Katherine and the assassin he had eliminated. "The yellow edging on the weapons," he gasped, his gaze locked onto the weapon.

His dislike of Celestials set aside, Thoth knelt on the other side of the Sekhmet warrior.

Raphael shifted his head out of Thoth's way, deferring to the deity's knowledge of alchemy and healing.

Thoth leaned his head down near her now blue lips, his beak pointed along the line of her sternum. He sniffed at Katherine's breath. The unmistakable, pungent odor of the Seraph poison filled his nostrils. Thoth's intense black gaze flew to meet the archangel's. Raphael's fear of losing Katherine, the one other warrior he revered almost as much as Malachi, etched his face.

"Time is short," Thoth said, urgency threaded through his deep, preternatural voice.

He looked about, assessing the weapons on the ground about them. "There is venom enough on the assassins' blades for me to make a serum, Raphael," he said as he lifted his eyes from the weapons back to Raphael. "I had devised a formula with the goddess Bia's cobra venom." Purpose imbued Thoth's deep timbre. "While I do this, work hard and fast, Raphael. Visualize the venom in her blood, blockade it while her heart beats. This will cleanse her organs of venom with clean blood. Do not stop," Thoth ordered, and continued, "Gather the venom you visualize from each area affected in Katherine's body and push it out through her left heel."

Thoth walked around Katherine. "I will create an exit," he said, unnatural desperation threading his voice as he bent to her still, cool foot and laid two fingers upon it. He murmured an incantation in ancient Egyptian, casting a spell to make the egress for the venom. "We both need to move with haste before the viper's poison overwhelms her and wins." His tone was insistent and uncompromising.

Closing his eyes as he splayed his hands over Katherine's torso, Raphael immersed himself. He became one with her beating heart and moving blood. *You will not die, Katherine!*

The venom appeared in his mind's eye as malevolent yellow serpents with glowing eyes. The deadly creatures wrapped themselves about her blood vessels, obstructing life-sustaining movement of blood, strangling her organs. Dismay edged through him to see the edges of her kidneys and liver had already turned deathly gray.

Raphael formed Katherine's blood forces into a massive army, organized into regiments to deploy to various areas. Raphael armed blood drops with appendages, which would choke or cleave the venom serpents. The archangel sent urgent messages to every part of her body for the blood cells to capture and herd the snakes to the chute at her heel. At his metaphysical level, the vicious invaders were larger than Raphael. Fear, a unique companion for Raphael, maintained a strong sense of the imperative for him.

While Raphael did his work at Katherine's side in a trance, Thoth moved at lightning speed, collecting the yellow venom with deft care from the blades into a ceramic pot. He brought the venom to his alchemy library and work area, where he distilled the toxin with expertise. Giving thanks to Isis, magic enabled him to set the correct temperatures in the distillation pipes and decanters without a wait for heating, the water reaching a boiling point on command.

From a scroll held open on a stand, Thoth reviewed his notes of the experiments with the venom of Bia's cobra, the properties of the poison and how he had made the prior serum; all simultaneously, while he worked. At the same time, he referred to his treasured Chinese alchemical writings to help ensure accurate crafting of the anti-venom serum. *By Isis, Katherine had saved my life, so my work for her shall keep the balance.*

Using great care, Thoth gathered the distilled and alchemized venom into a pot. He saturated thin strips of linen in the pot, stirring them about in the syrupy concoction with a pair of bronze tongs.

Deep in a trance, Raphael remained at Katherine's side.

A writhing, growing pile of serpents balled up at her heel, Thoth noted with disgust and satisfaction. One began extruding from her heel, squealing like a pig, then dropped with a heavy "plop" into the hideous mound. He gave thanks to Isis, noting Katherine's color had much improved, her breathing less labored. Glancing at Raphael, he noted the archangel dripped with perspiration in his desperation and metaphysical battle. Dots of blood mixed in with salty beads of sweat ran in rivulets off Raphael, staining his typically impeccable snow-white tunic with pink splatters and splotches.

Not desiring to interrupt the effective battle Raphael waged, Thoth kneeled with stealth at Katherine's head. He bent her head back, lifted her tongue and placed the anti-venom soaked linen strips under her tongue, knowing her body would absorb the serum with efficiency from there. Finished, Thoth sat back on his heels, and let Katherine's head and neck return to their natural resting position. With grudging admiration, he acknowledged the skill and fervor with which Raphael worked. Relief filled Thoth to see Katherine's body pink up where the anti-venom had traveled.

From inside Katherine's blood vessels Raphael became alarmed when he saw black serpents advance until he saw them annihilating the yellow serpents with destructive efficiency. Admiration, gratitude, and relief filled him for Thoth's quick work, the antivenom performed with targeted, pernicious grace. Raphael kept up his continuous assault and command of Katherine's life forces. His search and expel mission would not cease until he and the black serpent warriors had cast out all the venom.

From his place at Katherine's head, Thoth watched as the exodus of the yellow venom serpents went from a steady stream to a trickle at her heel, then none.

From inside Katherine, Raphael kept sentry, ensuring the antivenom spread throughout her, and hunted down any stragglers.

Thoth attempted to gain Raphael's attention without startling the entranced archangel. "Raphael," his voice was a firm whisper. "Raphael," he whispered again, louder. "Katherine is out of danger."

Pale and soaked with perspiration, Raphael blinked as he regained his mental footing in the corporeal world. His deep blue eyes focused on Thoth. He appeared confused and disheveled. Then he glanced down at Katherine and looked back to Thoth, who nodded once, a stiff affirmation. With a cry of relief, Raphael slumped over Katherine's belly, dragging in deep, ragged breaths, his back rising and falling.

"Angel, you had better get your sweaty Celestial ass off of me," said Katherine, her voice raspy. She grimaced and shifted her weak legs in her attempt to dislodge Raphael.

Raphael's face buried in her belly, he turned toward her chin. She attempted to move him off her and laughed. Rare joy shined through his expression while he rested his cheek on her armored stomach and looked up at her. The more Raphael tried to compose himself, the more laughter erupted from him.

Katherine lifted a weak hand to his head, ran her fingers through his sweat-dampened golden hair with rare affection. She swallowed, looked up to Thoth, then back at Raphael, and closed her eyes.

"Thank you," she whispered, her voice fervent and hoarse.

Thoth nodded, unable to speak. He found his voice trapped in his throat and an odd sensation of tightness in his chest.

Thoth stood as Raphael slid away from Katherine's belly.

Thoth shifted to stand at her left side, Raphael at her right. They both extended their hands. Katherine laid her hands in theirs, thumb woven with thumb. With a simultaneous tug, Raphael and Thoth pulled her to her feet, steadying her once she was upright.

After Thoth and Raphael assisted the shaky Katherine to her quarters to rest, Raphael did a thorough sweep of Thoth's temple and reinforced Katherine's already strong wards. He located Thoth in the courtyard. The god stood, his head tilted back, contemplative, gazing at the constellations and the moon.

Thoth let go a long sigh.

Raphael looked sideways at him. It was not the time to interrupt his thoughts.

Thoth's eyes remained on the stars. Finally, his voice carried over the sounds of the night, solemn and low. "I feared for her life, angel. I never worry for anyone. I cannot." He paused. "I did not believe I had it in me. It was a most unpleasant sensation; the band of fear, which is still tight about my chest. I cannot quite catch my breath and the weight of everything is heavy on my mind." His voice caught. "With sensations such as these, I cannot make unbiased decisions." Thoth's voice held a strong note of resignation.

Raphael stole a stealthy look at Thoth. Shock rose in him to spot an unshed tear in Thoth's black-as-night eye. He quelled his surprise, even his intake of breath at the sight. He understood the imperative need for Thoth to abandon these emotions and his heart ached for the stalwart arbitrator of the gods, a powerful god himself. But, not powerful enough to avoid the heart, it seemed. He regarded Katherine as a sister-in-arms, with whom he could be at the both greatest of ease or irritation in the span of minutes. He trusted her and her judgement in all things. Raphael remained quiet.

Thoth let another heavy sigh escape, while he grasped and acknowledged the unspoken pact of silence between him and Raphael. "I will go check on Katherine now, if you could plan to do so later this eve," he requested, a heavy heart imbuing his tone.

"It would be my pleasure to do as you ask."

Thoth ruminated over what he would say to Katherine once he saw her, as he made his way to her room.

He chose to enter in a physical manner, rather than materializing. After a swift, soft knock, he entered her chamber. His eyes sought the lioness warrior, then landed upon her sleeping form. He could not draw breath as the band tightened further about his chest. Unfamiliar and unwelcome tears burned once again, unshed. Watching her chest rise and fall with a regular rhythm, he gave thanks to Isis she was not cold and still.

Katherine's eyes fluttered open, a small smile crept across her when she saw Thoth. "If I did not know better, I would think you worry for me, Thoth," she said, fatigue overwhelming her as she spoke.

Thoth found himself unable to think, to articulate anything; something which had never happened to him over thousands of years.

Katherine's eyes widened, then she smirked as realization dawned of his discomfort. "Does the cat have your god-ass tongue, Thoth?" She expected him to rebuke her as was his way with everyone. Instead, his gaze remained on her, his eyes haunted with angst and… something else.

"By Isis, you are worried," she exclaimed, her heart ripping in two at the pain she saw in him. Thoth bent to her, sat on her bed of layers of linen fluffed between more layers on a wooden pallet, wrapped his arms about her to pull her close, her heartbeat now against his. He inhaled her unique, and now beloved scent, imprinting it upon his mind.

Her hands placed on either cheek, she expected to feel feathers. Instead, skin warmed her fingers. Katherine pulled away and looked upon a man's visage. Thoth, but different. His skin dark, his eyes black as kohl - Thoth's eyes. She pulled his face to hers and opened her mouth to kiss him, her tongue danced with his, burning his unique taste of power, desert, and knowledge into her memory. Her ears buzzed in what she knew was a cautionary, preternatural resonance as their individual magic mixed, each one's preternatural nature unsure of the wisdom of such a combination.

Thoth pulled away, his arms still about her, dragging in a

breath. His eyes searched hers. He spoke, his voice coarse and emotion laden. "I have not assumed a human form for thousands of years, since the greater gods deified me. I find myself overcome with gratitude you are still with us, lioness. Your warm kiss affirms that your heart beats and your mind works— that you are alive. Your touch and kiss are paradise, Katherine." He drew another shaky breath. "I am grateful you still walk among us. I thought we had lost you," he said as he leaned in to kiss her one more time, not unlike the parched man at the spring of the desert oasis vanquishing his thirst; drinking as much water as he is able for the next leg of his journey.

She moved her fingertips over his smooth, dark head, memorizing his human form. Katherine placed her hand on his face, taking in the peaks, valleys, warmth, and high cheek bones of his human visage.

His kiss stretched on through three cries of the wolf echoing off the dunes. The soulful sound wafted in through the window on the cool night desert breeze. Mournful, yet powerful, the mystic call captured their moment with perfection. Thoth tugged at her lower lip then soothed with a planted kiss, hugging her to him, in his want to be as close to her as possible. His hand splayed over her back, the other clasping her head to his. He moved his lips against her ear in an intimate caress. In a low whisper, he said, "Once you are recovered, I regret you can no longer stay here, lioness."

She nodded against him.

"You know that I cannot afford to be distracted by emotions such as this," he paused and pulled her closer to him. "Understand, Katherine, I would never hesitate to give my life for you." He wiped a tear from her cheek which had marked a trail along his thumb where he held her face to his.

"I know, Thoth" she whispered, her warm breath feathering past his ear as she planted a sweet kiss onto the outer shell. Turning her head, she kissed her tear from his thumb.

Pain filled her chest as deep dread overwhelmed her at the thought of pulling apart from him after over five hundred years of familiarity and trust. This revelation of love, brought by near death, would not be possible when honor bound by his duties. She hugged his vibrant, powerful form to her, wishing to Hades they could be mortal and free of their obligations.

~

Both Thoth and Raphael were lost in thought as they viewed the constellations in the crystal-clear desert sky, their silhouettes emphasized the difference in their stature. Thoth was tall and proud, and his dark skin almost blended with the night, while Raphael's shoulders were a half cubit lower than Thoth's.

"She sleeps," Thoth informed Raphael while his gaze remained on the stars. He heaved a deep breath.

Raphael turned his head toward the god, surprised, as Thoth did not share vulnerability; at least not with him.

The Egyptian deity's gaze remained on the stars. His eyes shone with unshed tears in the moonlight, revealing a rare expression of pain.

There was no need for words as the blessed silence hung between them. Sister Moon bathed the two beings of honor in her comforting light. Her teardrop fell to the Earth, fading away over the god and the archangel, now bound by an almost implausible trust.

With another deep breath, Thoth broke the silence and said, "My temple and I are in need of a new Immortal Guardian."

"I have the wheels in motion," Raphael whispered.

~

Thoth looked up as Raphael entered his solarium.

"We have dispatched Katherine to a location near Hadrian's

Wall, in Britannia. The climate there is ripe for Seraph recruiting. In truth, her seasoned, firm, and diplomatic presence is needed. There is much unrest between the Caledonians, Britons, and the Romans. Now, the Christians are filtering into the volatile mix. Katherine will have challenges set before her," Raphael explained while he paced, his white tunic bright in the sun.

"I am gratified to know that her prowess will not go to waste, Raphael," Thoth said.

"Katherine lets nothing go to waste," Raphael said, his flaxen hair and snowy garb contrasting with Thoth's dark countenance. "The Celestials have assigned another follower of Sekhmet, Naomi the Stygian, to you and your temple as Immortal Guardian. She has consistently trained hard and has proven herself a hellacious fighter in many battles and missions, Thoth. Her moniker is apt."

"Thank you, Raphael. Naomi will be a welcome addition to the temple. 'Born of the River Styx.' A fitting name, indeed," replied Thoth.

PART II

HONOR BOUND

1615 - 1938 CE
ENGLAND, ITALY, AND GERMANY

Men's vows are women's traitors.
—*William Shakespeare,*
from "Cymbeline"

Honor is not about making the right choices.
It is about dealing with the consequences.
—*Sophocles*

CHAPTER SEVEN

Tuesday, May 6, 1615 CE
Northeast Outskirts of York, England

DAPHNE PULLED the crate of twenty-one basil seedlings onto the waist-high wooden workbench and began the task of transplanting them into larger pots, three to a pot. While the chill of winter had kept spring at bay, the warm sunshine filtering through the glass ceiling panes of the orangery held the promise of summer and caused Daphne to perspire.

A moue crossed her lips as she spied a droopy basil plant, its leaves darkened and sad. As she mourned the seedling, she caught sight of Abbess Katherine entering the orangery. "Hello, Abbess," she said with her attention still on the herb. Daphne stroked two fingers down the length of the dejected plant. "Be stronger. Happy," she whispered with care.

The wilted basil transformed. Its green became more vibrant

and the stalk now stood strong. Daphne's smile widened. "That's it," she encouraged in a whisper.

"Child," Abbess Katherine intoned.

Daphne jumped as the abbess interrupted her ministration to the basil plant.

"If I did not laugh and work with you every day, Daphne, I would say you are about the devil's handiwork by the way you have with plants and animals. Please keep your wits about you," she admonished as she paused and stepped close to Daphne. Her black robes, veil, and white pinafore apron shifted as she moved. "I realize this is second nature to you," the abbess continued, "but others may be fearful of the skills you have. Pay mind." She grasped Daphne's chin and turned her head to be eye to eye with the Abbess, "Daphne..." she started, her face solemn and her dark bronze skin contrasting with the white wimple covering her hair and neck.

Daphne's heart skipped a beat as Abbess Katherine's topaz eyes flared.

"Promise me you will be more careful."

The abbess's grip on Daphne's chin tightened, her strong, slender fingers inescapable. Dread fissured through Daphne as concern swirled through the abbess's intense gaze.

"Terrible things could happen to you if the wrong people see or know what you can do," she said. She brought her face closer to Daphne's and her eyes grew as cold as death as she explained, "One cannot always tell who the wrong people are, Daphne." The abbess released her chin and stepped back.

Hot tears threatened to spill over, which mortified Daphne. At seventeen, she did not cry. Her heart pounded and nausea rose. "Yes, Abbess," slipped out as a whisper.

The abbess still stared into her eyes, holding her captive; then smiled, good humor filling her topaz gaze. "Now, let's finish getting these basil plants repotted," she said, her demeanor once again kind and warm.

Daphne took a deep breath and quelled the nausea. The scent of basil soothed her rattled soul, as they worked, their heads bent together. Thankful the air between them returned to normal, Daphne adored the easy affection which flowed between them.

While they worked, Abbess Katherine elucidated, "Daphne, while you need to exercise care, you have proven a strong acumen and an understanding of ethereal gifts. You persevere and are persistent. You have an open mind, keen observation, and methodical approach. All of these lend themselves to you advancing into a formidable alchemist and academic." She took a deep breath, then continued, "I do not want you to be discouraged by what I said earlier. I desire you to be careful," Abbess Katherine gave a wistful smile, "but I believe it is time we move you to a mentor under whom you would be safe to stretch your wings."

Confusion ran through Daphne. "Leave here?" she asked, her gaze now searching the Abbess's eyes instead of on the fragrant plants she held.

"Yes. You, your father, and I will work together to ensure you are comfortable and have an opportunity to advance your knowledge and acumen," the abbess replied and squeezed Daphne's hand. "You are capable of great things, Daphne. You have a rare understanding of the ethereal world about us, and a formidable, inquisitive mind. We shall not let it go to waste."

Fear and anticipation swirled in Daphne's psyche and heart. She reminded herself she trusted the abbess.

Abbess Katherine backed away from the bench and stripped off her gardening gloves. "Daphne, please finish cleaning up in here. I am going to check on Sister Anastasia and see how she is doing with her weaving. Your father will be here soon to collect you, dear."

Daphne nodded and said, "Yes, Abbess. I will make sure everything is tidy." Daphne turned toward the potting bench. A blue and black butterfly landed upon her left shoulder and flitted down to her open journal, landing on a detailed sketch of basil roots with meticulous notes made in Daphne's neat, tiny hand.

Daphne murmured words of affection to the fragile creature, which beat its wings in a slow cadence as in if response. Daphne slid her gray gaze up to the abbess, curious if she had witnessed this as well. Surprise leapt within Daphne to see tears had welled up in the abbess's eyes, which were fixed on the butterfly.

Abbess Katherine smiled through her tears. "Never mind me, child. You are like a daughter in many ways," she said while blotting her eyes with a clean corner of her soil-smudged, white apron. Her steps quick and sure, she turned and exited the warm and fragrant orangery through the narrow, wooden door.

Hearing the abbess's footsteps grow more distant on the flag-stones toward the abbey, Daphne pondered the tears in the older woman's beloved gaze. She sighed as she wondered at the sudden display of emotion. Shaking off the melancholy, she finished potting the basil and cleaned up the debris. Her stomach growled as she left the glass structure

Outside of the orangery, rays of the spring sun steeped the abbey courtyard in its hopeful light. The crocuses' deep purple hues peeked out from among muted shades of winter frost. The mouth-watering scent of fresh-baked bread wafted on the March breeze, calling her to the kitchen. She followed the same path the abbess had just taken, her steps quickening as she thought of butter melting on the still-warm bread.

The old, wooden-plank kitchen table had divots worn by hands and elbows over the centuries. For Daphne, while she ran her hands over the familiar table, the smooth and wide indents seemed to hold an essence of years of good cheer and laughter.

A succulent snack of cheddar cheese and Sister Madeline's fresh, crusty bread while she bantered and laughed with the good sister, buoyed her spirits. Joyous barking from Henry, the abbey sheepdog, carried to the kitchen from the front of the building, signaling Daphne's father had arrived.

With a wide smile, Sister Madeleine pressed treats for the Heatherton horses into Daphne's hands. Then the sister shooed her away rather than have the excited young woman stay and help clean the kitchen, which Daphne most often did.

Daphne planted a sweet kiss upon each of Sister Madeleine's cheeks, which were imbued with her familiar scents of rosemary and freshly baked cakes. Daphne's lavender skirts caromed about her as she sped through the halls. She flew down the front steps to greet her father—John Heatherton, a scholar and mathematician—and his black Hackney mares, which were beloved to her.

The pair hitched to Heatherton's wagon stomped and snorted; their huge, soft-brown eyes not letting Daphne out of their sight. She ran past her father, his arms held open in an unmet hug, to greet the excited equine pair. Both mares, ebony with white stars on their foreheads, pranced and whinnied while she kissed the white markings and the pair nudged her hands.

Heatherton shook his head as he lowered his empty arms. A bemused smile lifted his lips while he watched his daughter fawn over her beloved horses.

"You can smell the sugar and carrots, my pretty ones," Daphne said, affection lacing her voice. With a grin, she pulled the treats from her pocket.

Abbess Katherine exited the abbey, her habit flapping in the breeze behind her as she came down the steps like a raven stretching its wings. Daphne watched Katherine grasp John

Heatherton's hands with both of her own. He grazed a polite, chaste kiss of greeting on each of the abbess's cheeks.

The abbess leaned into him as he greeted her and whispered, "John, meet me in the abbey study once Daphne takes her horses to the stables to care for them."

John Heatherton gave the abbess's hands a gentle squeeze. "Daphne, dearest," he said, his voice deep and smooth, "take the mares to the stables for a well-deserved break, would you?"

"Of course, Father," answered Daphne. She nickered to the horses while she climbed onto the wagon. With a jingle of bridles, the wagon lurched once the mares had pulled enough to get its wheels turning. Daphne, adept with reins, drove the pair around the abbey to the stables.

Sister Madeleine settled Abbess Katherine and John Heatherton in the study with biscuits still warm from the oven and mugs of cold, fragrant cider.

"I trust all is well with Daphne, Katherine. You have not alerted me to any issues," John said with a hint of question in his voice.

Abbess shared her concerns while she paced. "John, no, no," she said with emphasis, "There are no behavioral issues with Daphne. I don't think there ever will be." She paused, grappling with her words. "However, her intelligence and thirst for knowledge will soon exceed what I can teach her." She looked at him, disquiet swirling in her topaz eyes, then continued, "Your daughter has many gifts. In working with her almost every day, the depth of her abilities surprises even me, John. Her powers of observation are unmatched by myself or anyone here. Daphne does figures in her head in seconds while the rest of us are struggling with an abacus, or chalk and board." The abbess's skirts and veil billowed as she turned. "With a simple touch, she heals plants and small creatures," she exclaimed.

Katherine stopped to sip the apple cider, then set down her pewter mug. "John," she said, her tone suddenly somber, "I fear others will notice there is something different about Daphne. You and I both know this may lead to her being accused of witchcraft."

John opened and closed his mouth as he went pale and his gaze grew somber, then managed to push out, "Yes... I imagine caution is warranted."

Katherine nodded, then brightened as an idea seemed to come upon her. "By Isis, John! Er... I mean, by heavens," she said as her eyes danced with victory. "I think I have the perfect solution for your unique, brilliant daughter. The renowned alchemist, Dante Santorum!"

John Heatherton blinked to clear his clouds of worry and asked, "My apologies. Who, Abbess?"

Abbess Katherine nodded and replied, "It is all a bit much to take in, John."

She paced about the study, her black skirts swirling around her legs as she moved. "Master Dante Santorum is an eminent western European alchemist, who subscribes to both the Paracelsus and Hellenistic philosophies in alchemical sciences." She paused and explained, "Paracelsus's line of thinking has developed over the past one hundred and fifty years. He espoused detailed observation and well-documented methodology in an effort to advance science and medicine with proven means." The abbess stopped in front of her pewter mug, toasted Heatherton with it, and grinned as she said, "The opportunity to study all of this, Daphne would adore."

Heatherton smiled back, then encouraged her, saying, "Go on, Abbess, please."

"Yes, yes," she replied, setting her mug upon the table with a graceful tap. Abbess Katherine strode to the mantle, then faced Heatherton.

"This may prove to be a challenge, as many alchemists and physicians vie to mentor with him, John. But, I know him well and will speak with him concerning the virtues of having our Daphne as a protege," she said with hope in her voice.

Then, she smiled and her eyes filled with a reassuring light. "I promise you, John, Master Santorum is honorable and would never think to take advantage of an apprentice. Dante is pure in his goal of advancing knowledge," Abbess Katherine said. "However, with our prejudiced times, I am prepared to send one of the abbey maids, Esther, with Daphne to serve as chaperone," she added.

John Heatherton took a deep breath. "I trust you, Abbess. If you judge Daphne should go, then she must go," he replied with trepidation riding his voice. Heatherton swallowed, his eyes searching the ceiling as he strove to take in all these developments. "I appreciate the lengths to which you have gone to place her with an accomplished mentor. What do you say we plan on having her go after she turns eighteen years of age? That is only five months from now." He shot her a grave glance, then continued, "I do agree if we do not get her moved, the results could be disastrous for Daphne, and beyond heartbreaking for us."

CHAPTER EIGHT

Wednesday, May 7, 1615 CE ~ York, England

ABBEY MAID ESTHER found herself fatigued maintaining a cloaking spell in the study during the conversation between John Heatherton and Abbess Katherine. Much to her chagrin, the abbess possessed admirable powers of discernment, requiring a great amount of continual concentration while also eavesdropping.

Esther relished that her unassuming appearance and mannerisms made her an invaluable spy to the Seraph and Gideon.

She had gained Gideon's notice when she connected Abbess Katherine and the formidable, legendary Immortal Guardian—Katherine of Sekhmet—as one and the same. This earned her a reputation among the Seraph as an observant and intuitive operative.

With each assignment, Gideon handed Esther increased

responsibility and discretion to handle matters as she judged best.

Gideon had set up an effective staging area in York for the Seraph rebellion to continue infiltrating London. Esther had proven her worth many times over, as people often overlooked an aging house servant.

Eager to inform Gideon of the intent to send Daphne to apprentice under Dante Santorum, Esther slipped out of the abbey. She needed to visit with a local baker with the stated ruse of purchasing rye and yeast for the kitchens. The stocky, red-haired baker—also a Seraph spy—communicated with Gideon through direct thought. Gideon had declared his hope of recruiting Daphne to the Seraph, recognizing her acumen and powerful gifts. Esther found it amusing to receive her instructions from Gideon through the flour-covered baker while he kneaded dough with his large and rough knuckles. The top of his linen, sweat-stained, and once-white hat flopped over his left ear rather than stand at proud attention. The heat from the wood-fired clay ovens was oppressive, even with the cool March air wafting through the bakery, the back door held ajar by a black and white speckled river rock the size of a man's work boot.

"You are to allow Daphne's apprenticeship to move forward, and to accompany her as a chaperone," the baker said with a gap-toothed grin. "Gideon expresses delight at the windfall opportunity of having a capable spy in Dante the alchemist's household." His tone turning serious, he added, "Gideon instructs you to meet with Vicar Tobias Matthews this afternoon."

The wily baker continued, "It's curious. Abbess Katherine has frequent dealings with the vicar. They both claim their meetings regard Anglican church business." The baker stopped his kneading and picked up a wooden paddle. He checked on his dough and removed the golden loaves from the large oven with the broad, smooth wooden tool. He talked as he worked. "Vicar Matthews acts as an operative for the Seraph. Abbess Katherine and Vicar Tobias Matthews appear to keep a wary eye on each other.

"The abbess has been here several centuries, the vicar only two decades."

"Why does the abbess allow the vicar to stay?" Esther asked.

He set the paddle down in a stand and began to shape the kneaded dough into loaves. "That is an excellent question. I suspect the abbess judges she has a good eye on the level of Seraph activities and incursion by keeping watch over the vicar. 'Better the evil you know, than the evil you don't', aye?" he answered. "No matter, I do not presume to understand how the mind of an immortal works," he said, then continued, "Neither the abbess nor the vicar have a desire to make local humans aware of their true purpose."

The baker handed Esther a package wrapped with string in a tidy bow. "Here is your yeast and rye for the abbey cook, Mistress Esther. Be on your way to see the vicar."

Esther made her way from the baker's shop to the red brick parsonage. A sly spell she cast in her wake assured she drew little notice as she walked past the gated houses and townhomes of the village outside of York. The white picket fence of the parsonage came into view as she crested a small rise in the sidewalk.

Each footstep closer to the house brought more in focus the cold, dark detail of the imposing black iron door knockers. Twin ouroboros, serpents symbolic of infinity, faced each other. Each damned to eat their own cold, metal tail for eternity. A chill slithered down Esther's back as a sudden, unbidden image leapt to the forefront of her mind—of the asps taking each other's tails and crossing over the door, making her escape from the inside impossible. Shaking off the vision, she raised her arm, hesitating over the black metal viper on the right and deciding against it, her hand curled into a fist to knock. As her clenched fingers moved forward, a cheery face replaced the painted wood of the door. "Oh!" startled Esther, not expecting the vicarage housekeeper in her linen mob cap, pressed white apron, and spotless gray dress to open the door before she even knocked.

"Oh, dear, Mum. You must be Mistress Esther. Do come in before you catch a chill. The vicar has been expecting you." The pleasant housekeeper stepped aside to make way for the still-surprised Esther.

"Yes. Well, umm, thank you."

"Follow me, Mum."

In his study, Vicar Tobias Matthews stood warming his hands before the hearth. He turned to Esther when the housekeeper announced her. In his black cassock, Vicar Matthews cut a dark, imposing figure with his height and broad shoulders. The length of his black frock undulated along his height as he turned. Her vision at the front door rushed back upon her. She worked to keep herself from fleeing the study while in her mind the specter of the serpents' tails crossed over the doors threatened to overwhelm her.

The vicar's gaze landed on her. If the front door's iron vipers were to have silver eyes, they would be like his, piercing and predatory. The white square of his Roman collar appeared stark against his olive skin. The ebony of his wavy hair blended almost seamlessly at his shoulders with the dark fabric of his clothing. To Esther, he seemed a black rat snake with the face of a human.

As soon as his housekeeper closed the door to the study, the vicar spoke, "You have news for me, woman." His deep, silky, voice reverberated about the study.

Esther dove into her report without preamble, "Daphne Heatherton is leaving the abbey to study alchemy under Dante Santorum. I am to go as a chaperone."

He nodded, then replied, "Good, good. This could work out

well for us and be a coup for the Seraph." He clasped his hands together, his eyes alight with machination. "We will have you in a most advantageous spot with the oak and Santorum. This is excellent news, indeed, my good woman," he said, dark delight laced through his words.

"Yes! Go, Esther. Go with Daphne," the vicar said with crafty enthusiasm. "Act as a solicitous attendant and chaperone. Give them no reason to question your presence," he ordered. A stern note entered the vicar's voice and his eyes hardened. "We must exercise patience," he cautioned her. "The right time will come to destroy the oak."

"It is my hope, Esther, to recruit the brilliant Daphne to our cause. That will require your patience, as well. By the time we see this through, she will join us," he paused and smiled like the viper readying to strike, "or die."

"Understood, Vicar," Esther said, nodding with her rheumy eyes on his while she yet clutched her package of rye seed and yeast cake.

"I would expect nothing less from you, Esther. Keep me updated, either in person or through the baker," answered the vicar. He turned back toward the hearth. "Now go."

Esther bowed and took her leave. A jaunty bounce to her stride, she headed to the abbey, relishing the spring air and changing tides. *Oh, the great joy I shall experience to take part in Abbess Katherine's comeuppance! I cannot wait to have the haughty bitch at my mercy, begging for her life.*

CHAPTER NINE

May, 1618 CE ~ The Annex, York, England

MALACHI ARRIVED IN YORK, relieved to be free of Rome.

For one-hundred and fifty-seven agonizing, long years, he barely tolerated the Vatican. The misguided actions and infighting between cardinals created a significant consternation for Malachi.

Even under his diligent watch, Seraph had infiltrated the Vatican. Worse yet, cardinals placed greater importance upon their machinations for power-mongering than on fighting back the Seraph advancement. This enabled further significant Seraph incursion into politics and the sciences outside of the Vatican, as well as prestigious institutions of learning. Malachi lost all patience for the Holy See and his court. Resentment filled him with the damage they had allowed, while so many others laid their lives on the line to fight the Seraph.

Disgusted with the short-sighted and self-serving leaders of the Church, Malachi engaged in shouting matches with several of the cardinals, leading to his unceremonious expulsion from the Vatican.

Raphael interceded and petitioned The Five to assign Malachi to a less volatile situation before Malachi brought even more perturbed Celestial attention to himself

Thus, Malachi found himself in York, in a too-quiet meadow, to watch over a tree. A tree. Isaiah the Ancient, a druidic oak whose galls produced discerning ink. Malachi had a hard time believing a simple oak held importance in the fight against the Seraph.

Disinterest filled Malachi, thus annoyance. He skipped a rock over the brook and watched as it tapped the surface of the water several times before it disappeared. The early summer, clear night proved to be a pleasant, if boring time to arrive as he shook the political and imperious dust of Rome and the Vatican from his armored boots.

An ethereal glow cast from the three-quarter moon suffused the glade. Starlight points glinted, scattered as though a sack of diamonds spilled open on the black velvet of the night sky. Moonlight shone off the ever-moving surface of the meandering brook. A water wheel near a stone annex at the back of the large house creaked as it turned, slow and steady, with the brook's flow. A deep thrum emanated from the massive, ancient oak rooted alongside a bend in the stream. Whorls in the bark appeared to share the oak's own story; deep gouges and gnarls pointed to missing limbs, attempts to fell Isaiah, and other inflictions of great damage. Yet, young, bright green leaves had started to unfurl from the buds of another spring.

In his assignments since Aristotle, Malachi rarely enjoyed his surroundings unless he had a warm and willing female companion. A small flame of hope now burgeoned that York may prove different.

Evensong of the meadow seeped away a measure of

Malachi's bitterness. Night creatures played their serenade, enhanced by the occasional call of a wolf or an owl. The never-ending murmur of the running brook provided background harmony.

The teasing breeze kept the night dew at bay and danced with his long sable locks.

Malachi's shadow, wrought by moonlight, mimicked his movements as he wove intricate Egyptian hieroglyphics onto the tablet of dark night. Spirits of antiquity called forth as he set wards to guard Isaiah while he gained much-needed rest. He gave thanks for the flowing water of the brook near him, ferrying spiritual energy for Ancients to come to him as he worked.

While he set his wards, Malachi reflected upon the mystery of how many years Isaiah had existed, and his current mission of Immortal Guardian of Isaiah the Ancient.

Raphael had explained, "Oaks produce oak gall apples, which form around wasp larvae." Raphael's impromptu botany lesson had bored him out of his mind. He laughed to himself, recollecting his attempt to look attentive while Raphael droned on. Raphael's eye roll and kick to his shin clued him in—he had failed miserably in feigning interest. Raphael continued anyway, "When boiled down and mixed with ferrous sulfate, the process creates a rich and prized deep purple, almost black ink.

"Isaiah's ink, once dry, glows iridescent in the moonlight if the person who wields the pen is true of heart for the good of humans.

"Malachi, at least pay attention to this part," Raphael had implored, exasperated. "This discernment has created high stakes for the Seraph for the past 1700 years with their spies and operatives planted through academia, religion, and positions of political and economic power. Their writing with Isaiah's ink would not, does not glow. Isaiah the Ancient provides an infallible means to root out Seraph operatives and spies."

Malachi reminisced over his knowledge of the Druids, Isaiah the Ancient as one of several enchanted entities associated with the Druids and mystical peoples of old. The Ancients, of which the Druids were part, had bestowed powers and enchantments upon these entities to provide balance and a means to combat the corrupt nature of humankind and the deities.

With the rise of the Seraph over the past two thousand years, pervasive corruption had gained momentum. These enchanted entities provided a means of detection of the Seraph operatives or protection from them.

Malachi recalled his initial assignment as Immortal Guardian for the fierce Egyptian deity, Thoth, and the god's resplendent temple. Thoth taught him of the many subtleties possessed by deities and preternatural beings. These nefarious and narcissistic traits had the potential to prove disastrous with beings enticed by the Seraph.

When Egypt fell to Alexander the Great, Thoth shifted into another dimension. The greater deity held considerable sway over the gods, but was no longer intertwined with the belief system of Egyptians or humankind at large. This freed Thoth to address more pressing issues in ethereal realms as the power and influence of the Seraph advanced.

Malachi brought himself back to the present. His wards in place, he knelt next to the brook, his leather waistcoat protesting while he bent to the ground. The night creatures silenced for a moment upon his disruption, then continued.

The fresh, sweet, and cool water called to him. He cupped his hands and drank from the running stream. Through the brook, he swirled his fingers and watched the dark glittering play of the moonlight over the water as it eddied about his fingers.

Ancients whispered their secrets, Sister Moon bathed him in her soft light. His mind clear, his heart no longer heavy, he stood, refreshed, and walked to stand next to the wise oak.

Respect for the ancient tree now flowed through him. Malachi laid his touch upon the rough bark of the venerable Isaiah, closed his eyes, and communed with the enchanted oak; that the old, wise oak may know and trust him.

Assurance and knowledge coursed between them; ancient talisman and Guardian.

Malachi opened his eyes and took in his surroundings. A stone block annex stood east of Isaiah. Its windows were now dark, the female and male alchemists who worked and studied within its confines gone for the night. Malachi could feel their essence and scruples. Dante Santorum, a skilled man of great acumen, mentored the astute woman, Daphne Heatherton. He sensed she possessed great, yet untapped ethereal potential. Exhaustion overtook him. He closed his eyes and blended with the oak, falling into a much needed, deep and renewing sleep.

CHAPTER TEN

Wednesday, April 20, 1622 CE ~ The Annex, York, England

FRESH SPRING BREEZES wafted through the open windows of the annex which stood at the back of Dante's country house. Embers glowed white-hot in the alchemy oven. Even with fresh air wafting in, the annex could become hot and stifling.

Essences of rosemary, lavender, melted metal, and burning wood created a cacophony of aromas which suffused the stone-walled workroom atmosphere. A moment stolen from her tasks to stretch, Daphne glanced out the window to the huge old oak and winding brook which had carved a deep channel through the glade's rich earth.

She resumed her labors at the waist-high workbench, her capable hands steady as she used a scale to measure out a precise amount of silver. Her muted, lavender-gray muslin skirt swayed around her stiff leather apron—splashed with silver and pockmarked from flying ash—while she moved from one end of the bench to the other.

After placing the metal into her crucible, Daphne added a quick note to her loose parchment. Her feather quill bobbed like a pigeon while she wrote. At the far end of her workbench sat her favorite mortar and pestle with dried rosemary, already ground to a fine powder, blanketing the bottom of the bowl. Dried and crushed lavender filled a small pot next to the rosemary.

Perspiration threatened to slide into Daphne's eyes. She blotted her forehead with the back of her hand. The heat brought a flush to her cheeks. Dante's hummed Scottish ditty lamenting a soldier's unrequited love drifted by and mixed with the rhythmic churn of the water wheel from the brook. Enjoying the moment, she took respite from the prickly heat, glancing over to her mentor.

Dante somehow fit his tall, gangly frame into a chair at their shared writing desk, which sat in front of a larger window to take advantage of the light from the sun and moon. His jovial nature shined through every jutting yet relaxed crook of his knees and elbows. Without fail, when working, he wore his black velvet academic's cap with a mink ball affixed to the top. His cap, set at a tilt, served well in emphasizing the precarious angles his body affected whenever he worked at the desk.

With her padded mitts and long, iron tongs, she removed the crucible from the oven, careful not to let molten silver slosh over the rim. She set it atop an iron hotplate to keep the metal liquid for a longer period while she worked with it.

With a small ladle, she measured and poured silver into lanolin and then added extracts of rosemary and lavender she had distilled earlier, stirring to ensure even distribution of the ingredients, lost in the concentration of her work.

The scratch of Dante's quill on the paper of his journal stopped here and there when he dipped the quill into his prized pewter inkwell, filled with Isaiah's rich ink. Daphne found great comfort in the sound of Dante's nib moving across the pages. She knew when he drew one of his beautiful, detailed illustrations by the change in the cadence of the scratching nib against the parchment. She stole a glance over at him. She could not help but smile as a light breeze coming in from the open window lifted the ends of Dante's wavy, brown hair from his shoulders. They appeared as sparrows ready to take flight.

Meticulous notes she had made with prior versions of the burn salve proved helpful as Daphne worked to combine the proportions she had calculated would give the effect she desired. With confidence, she amalgamated ingredients in the correct order with appropriate heat applied for the precious ointment.

While she stirred the fragrant lanolin mixture, her mind wandered to Dante's mentoring of her in how to make Isaiah's ink with iron sulfate, gum, and Isaiah's oak galls.

Daphne thought back to a year ago, once she and Dante had established a strong mutual trust. He took her to the glade near the old oak, carrying one of his journals with him. She recalled the night as though it happened yesterday. Dante spread a blanket upon the grass near the brook, not far from the oak. They sat together, under the shining moon.

Dante had opened his journal. Against the parchment, which appeared blue-white in the moonlight, the scrawl of Dante's writing appeared as though it could be plucked off the page and scattered to be part of the stars in the sky. Daphne's heart had almost pounded out of her chest when Dante revealed to her the ethereal magic of the ink.

Never selling the ink, Dante only gifted it, to keep Isaiah's ink pure in intention, he had explained. Dante went on that night to share stories of some people who avoided having their writing tested with the ancient oak's ink under the moon. Often, he would later find they had turned down darker paths.

A knock upon the annex door interrupted her thoughts while she stirred the salve.

"I will get the door, Daphne. You are occupied," Dante called out. He scraped the chair feet against the floor as he moved to stand, then groaned, his stiff joints getting the better of him.

"Northrup, Coughton, please come in," she heard Dante say from behind her.

A headache crawled into her skull as she clenched her jaw when she heard their names. These two alchemists made it apparent to her they were none too pleased about her apprenticeship with Dante, which had not gone to one of them.

"To what do we owe the pleasure of your visit, gentlemen?" Dante asked.

Coughton cleared his throat, and his eyebrows drew imperious mountains on his forehead as he lifted them.

"Well, yes. Word has spread Mistress Heatherton made a salve for the two boys who suffered burns when Natty Cornish threw the boiling water out her window," he said. He shifted his gaze from Dante to Daphne, his chest puffed out like a peacock's. "We are here to ensure you make the salve with at least some measure of skill and only for the purpose of healing the burns," he said, patronization dripping from his lips.

Daphne bit her tongue. It took all her willpower to swim past the bait. Her headache flourished while Coughton outright questioned her ability and integrity. She continued to stir her salve while casting glances at Dante for guidance.

Aware that most alchemists had little use for women practicing their craft, Daphne worked to keep herself above reproach. Some years back, King Henry VIII made it illegal for females to practice as barber-surgeons. She understood alchemists saw this as a parallel, justifying the exclusion of women from practicing the art and science of alchemy. King James had since passed yet another Witchcraft Act in 1604, increasing the peril for women.

"Come now, gentlemen," Dante said and smiled as he clapped both visitors on their shoulders. His laugh lines crinkled in his sun-kissed face. "Daphne is a most skilled alchemist, very capable of mixing an effective and pure salve for our young, unfortunate boys. I hear by way of Abbess Katherine, the salve Daphne made three days ago has been quite helpful in relieving the young lads' pain and hasten the healing."

Coughton glanced over to Daphne, then looked back to Dante, and countered, "It is our civic duty to ensure the woman knows what she is doing, mixing potions and the like."

"Potions, Coughton?" Dante's face hardened. "You believe my apprentice mixes potions?"

Coughton's face reddened. "Tis a natural conclusion to make of a woman," he argued.

"You don't say, Coughton," Dante said, offense strong in his tone. He strode over to the constant-temperature water bath simmering away on the iron plate on top of the oven. "Mary the Jewess, the first known Western alchemist, is credited with the brilliant invention of the water bath," he gestured to the elaborate contraption. "I do not know where we would be today without it," he said. He gave Northrup and Coughton a hard look, his glittering gaze moving between the two. "You think to question Daphne's skill and motive because she is female?"

Northrup and Coughton stared at Dante without speaking.

Hot tears welled up in Daphne's eyes. She kept her head down as she retrieved two ceramic pots with lids in which to place the salve for the boys. She would be damned before she gave these two sanctimonious idiots the satisfaction of knowing they had upset her.

To her consternation, Northrup moved behind her and stared over her shoulder while she spooned ointment into small pots. Scents of rosemary and lavender, fragrances of calm and healing, seemed to do nothing to break the tension. Her hand itched to shove the spatula into his eye. "May I be of assistance?" she asked, working to keep her voice pleasant.

"Hmm," a cryptic murmur issued from him.

Daphne thought to herself, *Even his grunts are slimy.*

She followed the track of his eyes to her notes and a lump formed in her stomach.

"What have we here?" he asked, with feigned surprise.

"Nothing of import, Master Northrup. A few notes jotted down," Daphne replied, trying to sound carefree. Down the small of her back nervous perspiration trickled. Bile rose in her throat. She did not want his vile hands on her notations.

Northrup walked the remainder of the way to the wooden workbench.

Daphne inhaled the soothing scent of her salve with each step he took, in an effort to quell rising nausea.

Northrup picked up her notes, turned to Dante, saying, "A most, um, elementary note of proportions." His tone held disdain, and he squinted his eyes. "Does Mistress Heatherton's scribble glow under the moonlight, Dante?"

Dante's expression hardened. He made quick work of crossing to Northrup, removing Daphne's notes from his hands. "Gentlemen, we ascribe to Paracelsus's concepts of importance in proportions in mixing of a curative as well as the quantity of an ingredient ingested or applied," he explained, while he set the parchment back onto the workbench. "To answer your question, yes, her writing is suffused with light under the moon."

"Very well," Coughton replied, dismissal imbuing his voice.

The men moved to take their leave.

Coughton turned and added, "Dante, while we are here, let us remind you of the Academics meeting next Monday at the Abbey." He turned to Daphne and doffed his hat. "Good day, Mistress Heatherton," he said, his tone clipped and imperious. He made a show of leaving her out of the invitation.

The chill in his voice gave Daphne a deep sense of foreboding.

Dante closed the door behind the two. "Daphne, I am sorry you had to suffer through that."

"Tis no matter. We know what we are about, Dante."

Dante replied, "Indeed we do. I do keep hoping they will change their minds as they recognize your talent. Yet, every time I see them, they seem all that much more intent to remain blind to your skill." He paused. "It maddens me. I would address it more strongly with them, but I fear that may bring even more dark attention upon you." Dante peered at Daphne, hurt and frustration swirled in his eyes, his face painted the dull red of deep anger.

"Tis no matter," Daphne repeated in a soft monotone while she stared off into space. Her desire to put the incident behind her fairly screamed from her flat, acquiescent response. She snapped to attention as her gray eyes flashed to his. "I have work to do, Dante."

CHAPTER ELEVEN

The Evening of Thursday, April 21, 1622 CE
The Annex, York, England

LIGHT in the alchemy annex shifted as dusk fell upon the day. She had not realized the passage of time until she noticed she was having difficulty making notations on her loose parchment. Daphne tilted her head back to stretch her neck. The prior day's conversation with Northrup and Coughton had been weighing heavily on her mind.

With a strike of flint against steel, Daphne lit the beeswax tapers on the desk. The pungent scent, beloved to her, permeated the air. She took an appreciative whiff as she rocked back on her heels to relieve her aching feet.

Chair feet scraped against the wood floor as Daphne pulled her well-nicked, ladder-back chair from under the shared desk. She spread out her quickly-scratched notes from the day and smiled at the familiar divots formed by Dante's elbow resting on the wood in the same place over the years. She ran her hands over the depressions and warmth wrapped about her heart. Fluid and graceful in motion, she poured her tired body onto the chair.

Daphne reached to the right upper corner of the desk, uncapped Dante's prized pewter inkwell and set the cap down onto a small ceramic tray. Confidence and sureness pervaded her movements as she lifted the quill from its pewter and wood holder and dove into reviewing her notes from the day to journal her findings. After yesterday's tension with Northrup and Coughton, diving into her thoughts and accomplishments provided welcome relief.

Alchemical observations of the day and her endeavors unfolded in her mind as she noted her proportions. Deciding how to best diagram the process, Daphne brushed the soft, curved feather of the quill against her chin while she organized her thoughts. Inspiration found its mark, and Daphne took her nib to the parchment of her journal with purpose, and the resulting sketch of the amalgamation process was flawless.

Moonlight spilled over her desk. The nib scratching through her journal gave her a strong sense of satisfaction while she plowed through her notes, coalescing them into flowing observations and clear instructions. A light metallic scent—produced by ferrous sulfate in Isaiah's ink combined with the fragrance of the burning wicks—permeated the air. A cherished and familiar aroma which signaled the end to a successful day.

At a stopping point, Daphne stared, mindless, through the window at Isaiah. The oak's leaves stirred under the moonlight in the spring breeze and shifted to varying shades of black, silver, and gray.

Amid the movement, a dark, shadowy male materialized in front of Isaiah. Daphne blinked her eyes. Rather than disappearing in her logical doubt, he grew more defined. Her heart rate doubled. Moonlight burnished the ripples of his formidable, muscular form. A fall of dark hair spilled over his shoulders in a cavalier fashion. She found it impossible to drag her gaze from his unexpected presence.

Fear and fascination warred within her as her pulse pounded in her ears. She set down the quill into its holder without taking her eyes off him.

Clarity reigned and worry for Isaiah's safety shot through her. She stopped and listened with her heart and mind. She did not sense Isaiah protest in distress of any sort. Daphne relaxed her guard, but her gaze lingered on the male figure as she remained still in hopes of going undetected.

His head whipped around. His gaze, blue as St. Elmo's fire, impaled hers.

Daphne jumped. Tears of fright welled in her eyes and she brought her hand to her gaping mouth. Daphne admonished herself to settle. The thought he may hear her pounding pulse terrified her. Fear of the unknown loomed in her mind. She postulated she now knew the frozen fright of the deer to be caught in the archer's sights.

He stared, unblinking.

Goosebumps raised along her arms. A chill crawled down her back as ringing overtook her ears. Daphne could not take her eyes from his mesmerizing stare. Unable to move, her hand rested upon her lips while her pulse continued to pound; this preternatural being had attempted to scrutinize her scruples.

Without warning, she could move her limbs. Her body jerked and she moved to catch herself in the chair, her balance thrown off-kilter by the sudden release. Daphne's fingertips fell from her lips.

Now lightheaded, Daphne grasped the front of her desk with both hands to keep from going into a faint.

His gaze remained upon her, his eyes now dark in the shadows, his back to the moon.

Daphne's head hurt as she tried to comprehend the furled wings and startling blue, illuminated stare she had witnessed.

Without preamble, safety and warmth bloomed at the crown of her head, poured over her body, and through her to her feet. Understanding dawned. He meant to ease her fear and panic. Daphne found herself unsure if she should be grateful for his care or offended at his presumptive actions. She wondered if this being caused the flames of foreboding which licked at her mind.

Strong in her belief of the mystic, ethereal nature of the world one could see and not see, Daphne recovered from her terror and surprise. Her inquisitive nature took over. She gathered his warmth together in her mind and turned it over to examine it. She smiled with triumph as she drew strength from it and gained confidence in her ability to deal with the winged male and his mystic power.

With deliberate motions, she moved the ball of energy from her psyche into her hands. Her cupped hands held it before her chest and pushed the orb of palpable energy back to the stranger. A momentary sense of regret fell through her from sending away the gentle and soothing warmth.

Patiently, she watched for his reaction when his magic returned upon him. Her lips curled in discrete triumph as she saw him still.

About the ethereal ball he cupped his hands and made a motion as though to toss the energy into the air, then tucked it into the "Y" of tree limbs of Isaiah.

Facing her, the interloper brought his hands together before his chest and made a small bow.

He cocked his head as though in thought and lifted a hand to Isaiah's trunk. The glittering obsidian of his eyes disappeared, as he must have shuttered his gaze. He nodded, then patted Isaiah's bark with what she interpreted as listening and affection.

Turning forward to Daphne, he smiled. His gaze flickered with the glow of blue light for a fleeting moment, then darkened. He gave a gallant bow as he rolled his hand at his waist with a flourish. The beginnings of wings ruffled from his back, then fell flush with his shoulder blades.

Daphne gasped, incredulous.

He straightened.

She could have sworn she saw a smirk cross his lips. Indignation leapt within her.

He disappeared.

Daphne stared at the now empty space in front of Isaiah. She wished to catch just one more glimpse of her mysterious stranger. She harrumphed. *Her stranger?*

With a need to ease her tension, Daphne lifted her right hand to the back of her neck and rubbed the strained muscles as she pondered what she had just witnessed and sensed. She sat and began to journal all the details she could recall of him, the reactions he seemed to elicit from her.

The air in the annex changed. Daphne stilled the quill midstroke. Ink bled from the nib into her journal page. Hair raised on the back of her neck and her arms.

"Good evening, Mistress Heatherton," a deep, well-modulated male voice poured from the darkness behind her, the accent unfamiliar to her learned ear.

Daphne edged her left hand to the jewel-handled quill sharpening knife. "What is your intent," she asked as her fingers curved about the blade. Her gaze straight ahead, she paid attention to her periphery. Into her throat her heart leapt as a male arm snaked past her cheek. A warm hand and strong fingers curled over hers, his muscular arm against the length of her arm. His hard chest pressed on her trembling shoulders.

"My intent is for you not to attempt to do me in with a quill sharpener," he said, his velvet baritone winding past the shell of her ear.

A hint of a smile threaded his voice. Her pounding heart slowed.

Stray tendrils of hair at her left temple rustled as he spoke. His warmth seeped into her shoulders, like a blanket heated at a hearthstone. Awareness dawned her well-being depended on his mercy. From where he stood, he could wring her neck.

She took a steadying breath. Isaiah trusted this winged, male creature. Daphne decided to take faith in Isaiah's judgment, even though fear coursed through her with his forbidding presence.

"A friend of Isaiah's should be a friend of mine," Daphne said with a calm she did not possess as she made her left hand loosen its grip on the sharp quill knife. His fingers, corded with his strength, stayed curled about hers.

"Mistress, you are wise to hearken to Isaiah's word. Our stately oak has judged the character and honor of creatures time and time again," he replied, his voice deep and silky, his accent pleasant but unfamiliar.

His strong hand unfurled, lifted from hers. His well-muscled arm peeled away from her own.

Daphne relished the sense of having her own space about her again. His proximity had been of extreme disconcert to her.

Her heart quieted, sounds of the night filtered into her consciousness. An owl hooted, crickets sang their summer song, the brook ran, and the water wheel creaked. Daphne took comfort in these things and used them as a balm to her soul while she gathered her thoughts.

With grace she did not know she retained, she stood without faltering and turned her back to the desk to look over this stranger.

His fierce bearing intimidated her, juxtaposed with gratitude that he now wore a cream-colored blouse, his torso no longer bare. Ribbons gathered the sleeves of his blouse at his wrists, and a short fall of ruffle extended over each hand.

Vulnerability threatened to be the victor. With a spine of steel, Daphne quelled her fear and cleared her head. "How do you know of Isaiah? How do you know his name? What are you called?" she asked this powerful creature of the Elements. "Why have I not seen you before?"

"Your heart is in this place, Mistress Daphne. You have good reason to ask me these questions and many more," he replied. "I am Malachi, an Immortal Guardian. I have been sent by heavenly beings to watch over the wise, old oak, Isaiah." He peered at her and continued, "My passage of time is marked differently than yours, Mistress. You are an Elemental being, yet you are mortal."

Silence yawned as Daphne stared at Malachi. She wondered if she would awaken from this incredulous dream.

She attempted to comprehend the words which flowed from this creature. Daphne made a conscious effort to be more observational, less emotional. It dawned on her the dark, fleeting shadows she had witnessed near Isaiah on various occasions and convinced herself were nothing were probably this dark, preternatural creature who stood before her.

She had witnessed wings erupt from his back… No, he had shown her his wings, however brief a moment. She continued to pin him with her measured stare, without a care that seconds ticked by, as she mulled over whether she should be terrified. Curiosity encroached on fright's borders within her mind. He had not murdered her… yet.

Curiosity won.

The pulse at Daphne's throat slowed, as her posture eased.

To Malachi's relief, she no longer looked like the rabbit about to flee the fox. He held his stance, his arms at his sides as her intent eyes moved over him, inch by inch.

Minute changes shifted through her expression while she scrutinized him. Her thoughts evolved with the changing light in her eyes. Tension ebbed from the room. The beauty of the countryside night seeped into its place.

Eagerness to learn took over Daphne's fear, "You have wings," she stated, more than questioned.

"Yes, they appear when I call them forth. Angel's wings."

"But you are not an angel?"

"I am what is known as an Immortal Guardian. I once commanded legions of warrior angels, but no more. I do remain loyal to the death to the same side as angels—it is complicated."

He blew out a breath. "I prefer Earthbound beings over Celestial beings, and the Celestial beings prefer that I not bring Earthbound rabble back around to them." He looked into her eyes to ensure he had not overwhelmed her comprehension. "It is a sore and complex topic between the Celestials and me. But I assure you, we both reside on the upper side of the underworld."

"I see, Malachi. Thank you for explaining what is obviously an uncomfortable topic."

"You are welcome, Mistress Daphne. You have nothing to fear from me."

She thought that an ironic statement as he appeared he could swipe off her head as a knife cuts through butter. "So you say, Malachi. Yet, I would be foolish not to be cautious."

He nodded. "Indeed, were I standing on the other side of you watching and listening, talking with a being such as me, I would also advise you to be cautious." His eyes warmed. "I do hope we will be able to share more of our thoughts and experiences in the future."

"I would like that, Malachi," she said, growing braver. "I must admit, I am curious." Thirst for knowledge pushed daring words from her mouth. "If I have nothing to fear, please allow me to examine your hand," she requested while she extended her own hand, her palm turned upward and open. To prevent her own hand from trembling, she concentrated hard on not showing her trepidation.

Daphne's eyes followed his right hand as he settled it into her outstretched palm. She still had the sense of being in a dream. Daphne flinched as Malachi's calloused skin contacted hers, the size of his hand overshadowing hers. A determined scowl crossed her face as she brushed aside her anxiety and ignored the pounding of her heart.

Warmth from his skin seeped into hers. Her shoulders relaxed with relief as she realized he did not have the marble cold of the dead.

He curled his long, strong fingers about her palm, trapping her hand in his. Daphne's heart again leapt into her throat.

Thoughts of a lamb tempting Fate by grazing in the presence of the lion came to her mind. Daphne brought her thoughts back to the present. Her curiosity, her need to study the world about her, again won over her fear. She lifted her other hand and stroked two fingers over the battle-roughened skin of his knuckles. She slid them across his hand to the underside of his wrist, and a smile lifted the corners of her lips when her fingertips landed upon the steady throb of his pulse. Daphne stared into his eyes, trying to see into him, his true intent. *Surely, this is a dream.*

Face to face, silence reigned in their perusal of one another. Candles bathed them with warm, flickering light.

Malachi worked to keep his face blank and not betray the surprise he experienced upon the welcome and pleasure which coursed through him with her touch. Male heat traveled from his entrapped hand to his loins and chest.

He had faced the most formidable of foes and circumstances as he moved through his centuries of existence. Yet, he now knew this woman could bring him to his knees if she so chose.

The line of Daphne's mouth softened as she became more trusting of this warrior before her. Her gray eyes lit with wonder she had this beautiful, amaranthine being under her intent study.

Malachi stood a head taller than her. A foreign and uncomfortable sensation of vulnerability moved through her; the breadth of his shoulders dwarfed hers. His fierce, battle-readiness radiated from him, yet her curiosity reigned.

She proved one of the most intrepid souls he had encountered in his immortal existence. Malachi chose to stay quiet and give this unique and brilliant woman the lead in this encounter.

"You feel very alive to me, Guardian," Daphne said, her voice somewhat breathless with her excitement and fervent hope he would not disagree.

"Is that so, Mistress Daphne?" he asked, as he lifted a male and arrogant brow, his warrior's imperious tone ringing through her.

A blush crept up Daphne's neck and into her cheeks, her face reddened under his intense scrutiny.

He stared down at her, she gazed up at him, while they stood toe to toe. His hand remained in hers, he did not attempt to disengage from her, as she feared he might.

Irony sunk in for Daphne that mere minutes ago his proximity terrified her, now she hoped he would remain at her side. Daphne found she had to school herself not to laugh.

"Here, Malachi, come to my workbench with me," Daphne requested. She turned to walk toward her work area, expecting him to follow without question.

Malachi laughed to himself, amused, but decided not to give her trouble and followed behind her.

Once at her workbench she released his grip and lit two lanterns. Flint fragrance permeated the air. She lifted his hand to set between the lanterns, taking liberty with no hesitation or fear in her movements. Daphne opened a drawer and located her disk magnifying glass.

She lifted it to her the right side of her face, her right eye now comically large to Malachi through the glass. He found himself needing to hold back a laugh.

Daphne stooped over his hand as she held a glass disk between her eye and his skin. "Hmm, hmm," a cryptic murmur as she perused over every sixteenth inch of skin with the glass. She paused and peered at the battle scars crisscrossed on his knuckles.

Malachi found that he was enjoying having her head over his hand, the gleam of the lantern light shining off her hair. He caught an enticing whiff of rosemary and lavender arising from her.

Daphne laid her hand next to his and moved back and forth between the two with her eye peering through the disk. She set the magnifying glass down then collected her parchment and workbench quill, her face holding an industrious expression.

Malachi watched her intensity and single-mindedness with a combination of admiration, amusement, and curiosity. She sketched shapes of her skin pores and his, making notations of differences and similarities. Daphne dipped her finger into water then flicked a drop of water onto the back of his hand, then hers.

A scowl crossed Malachi's face, his eyes darkened, taken aback by her boldness in doing this without his permission. Worry for her filled him as he realized she would take such chances in the name of curiosity. As she bent forward to examine how his skin reacted to the water compared to hers, he leaned forward. With deliberate, icy menace, he whispered, "What if I did not desire to have water dripped onto my person, Mistress Daphne? Woman, you are playing with fire."

Daphne gasped as his words sunk in. She straightened from peering upon his arm, her magnifying glass still grasped in her right hand. Her mouth opened and closed, tongue-tied as Malachi scowled down at her. Heat moved into her neck and face; she knew her cheeks had turned bright red under his scrutiny.

"You a—are correct, Malachi," she said as she tossed the magnifying glass onto her workbench as though it had burned her hand. The lens landed with a clatter, then rocked side to side. Daphne watched the rocking disk in horror, wishing she could hide away. It took what seemed to Daphne an eternity for the glass to stop making noise. The disk finally stilled. Her wide eyes moved to Malachi's. "My apologies," her mortified whisper drifted about them.

Sympathy moved him. Malachi took her hand and gave a gentle squeeze. "I am not offended. You are brimming with brilliance and enthusiasm, which I am coming to admire.

"None of us want to see anything regretful happen," he continued. "You would be wise to think about potential repercussions with those you pull into your investigations and experimentation. I am aware that Abbess Katherine has also cautioned you to this regard."

Suspicion clouded her face. Her embarrassment shifted in the blink of an eye to indignation. Eyes narrowed, she pulled her hand from his grasp. "Pray tell, how do you and Abbess Katherine know of each other?"

"Katherine and I have known each other a long time."

"Stop being evasive." Her gray eyes flashed with frustration and anger. "It is offensive to my intelligence." She stepped to trap him between her, the workbench, and the stone wall. "How long have you known Abbess Katherine? Or should I say 'Katherine'? I have a sense you knew her long before she was an Abbess. How long, Malachi?" she insisted.

Surprised she had maneuvered to corner him, he grasped her thirst for knowledge superseded all else, including her personal safety. He let himself remain cornered, not wishing to frustrate Daphne further.

Malachi took a few seconds to assess the risk in being forthright with Daphne. He decided to be honest without softening the edges, replying, "I have known Katherine for over two millennia."

Daphne felt her stomach lurch at his answer. She searched his eyes, which he kept unwavering on hers. "Over two thousand years..." her voice drifted off as she reiterated and let the unfathomable sink in. "Katherine and you have known each other for over two thousand years?"

Malachi nodded, his face blank of expression.

"How old is Isaiah?"

"No one knows. He has been here for over fifteen hundred years based on word-of-mouth history. Passage of time is different for Isaiah. He cannot discern his own age," Malachi explained, his dark, fathomless, yet warm eyes not leaving Daphne's.

A rueful smile crossed Daphne's face. "Somehow it is easier for me to accept that Isaiah has been in this glen for over fifteen hundred years than to think you and Katherine, and heaven knows how many others, have been living and breathing for over two thousand years." She sighed, rubbed her neck, then nodded, her cloudy eyes clearing. "Time is wasting in my pondering, so I shall set this aside and ruminate over it." Daphne's expression shifted to intent and purposeful. "I assume you are here to watch over Isaiah because of the properties of ink made from Isaiah's oak gall egg," she stated. "But would that place him in danger? How long has Isaiah had Guardians?"

Admiration rose in him for Daphne's skillful shift from the question of immortality. He pondered for a moment as to how much he should reveal and gave her credit for her intellect and open mind.

Malachi looked upon Isaiah through the annex window. "Known history of the Ancient Oak dates to the time of the Druids," he explained, glancing at Daphne. "'Druid' means 'knowing the oak'." He swung his gaze back to Isaiah and continued, "The Druids either discovered Isaiah's gift of discernment of those 'true of heart' for the good of all, or bestowed it upon him."

Taking Daphne's hand into his warm, strong grip, he imbued a sense of calm and control to their careening conversation. He led her to the window to look upon Isaiah as they spoke of him. They stood side by side, her hand on his warm forearm.

"That is murky, as the Druids left no written record," he explained. "They were highly respected. Caesar wrote that they could halt war between two armies with simple actions." He barked a rueful laugh with a sardonic lift to his brow. "Not even I can do that." Malachi looked down at Daphne, grinning at her eye roll, appreciating she had relaxed enough to enjoy his humor. He returned his gaze to Isaiah.

"Celestia has assigned Immortal Guardians to Isaiah since Rome invaded what is now England. The Seraph took the opportunity during the Roman conquests of Britannia to recruit many to its nefarious intent, which was around 100 AD."

Daphne's brows knitted together in confusion. "The Seraph?"

"Yes," he replied, his mouth lifting at one corner in a half-smile, as he stared out the window. Warmth entered his voice, imparting his sincerity. "My apologies, I neglected to remember that you do not know of the Seraph. That is a compliment to you, and a humble reminder to me," he said, respect for her threaded through his voice.

"I have no care for compliments and reminders of humility. I want to understand," she insisted, her clear eyes searching his.

His heart and mind paused in appreciation of her practical nature. Resolute, he continued, pulling his gaze away from her and back to Isaiah. "When Celestia, upon order of The Five, destroyed Sodom and Gomorrah with true fire and brimstone, all perished including innocents, children, and beasts of burden. Gideon, a fallen archangel, used the destruction to meet his ends. To draw others to him, he has constructed a cause of avenging what he touts as the merciless and unnecessary blanket annihilation."

"The Five?"

"Leadership of Celestia are the seats of The Five, named for the Elements Earth, Air, Fire, Water, Aether," he explained.

Her fine brows pulled together as she turned, formed a time-line, and attempted to apply logic. "The Five Elements rule Celestia? The Fifth being Aristotle's Aether, which he wrote of two thousand years ago? Yet, The Five made an edict concerning Sodom and Gomorrah, many generations before Aristotle?" she spoke out loud, while thinking this through.

"Yes, Aether was revealed to the brilliant, ethical Aristotle, who I had the pleasure of guarding for several years."

Shock crossed Daphne's face as her jaw dropped open. "You knew Aristotle? 'Breathed the same air as him' knew him?" she exclaimed. Her ears rang while the unbelievable hammered at her. She vacillated between acceptance and disbelief. "You knew Aristotle?" she repeated her question, knowing she was being redundant, but could not help herself.

He nodded, bemused, attempting to remain sympathetic toward her plight of incredulity as he worked to tamp a chuckle.

"Do you know what I would give to have one-half hour with him and his mind?"

Admiration that her mind placed the potential of being with Aristotle over giving credence to the one-thousand-seven-hundred-year time frame wound about his heart and mind. "I judge myself fortunate to have been witness to his thought processes, ruminations, and teachings," he said.

Malachi smiled, his dark eyes warm as his gaze moved over Daphne, taking in her open and attentive demeanor. "Gideon, vocal in his feigned revulsion at the death of innocents, gathered power-mongering followers and gods who had fatigued of

Celestials regarding them with disdain," he further explained, looking to Daphne.

She nodded for him to continue.

"I agree that Celestial leadership is distant and assuming. I would also argue that the Greek and Egyptian gods have human faults, behaviors, priorities, and most detrimental: pride. Thus, the gods of Mount Olympus and the Nile, while possessing ethereal power, are closer to humans than Celestials," he said. A rueful smile crossed Malachi's face. "Though, most deified beings would be hard-pressed to admit such."

"Word traveled through many realms that an archangel broke off from Celestial authority. The response garnered exponential strength, if you can imagine," Malachi continued, peering at Daphne, satisfied to see she remained enrapt in his telling. His gaze wandered back to the Oak. He continued with his explanation, "Previous rebellions had germinated outside Celestia with beings who did not yield much sway outside their own realm. Gideon was and is different; the answer to several millennia of hope for a way to oust Celestials as prime rulers of the Heavens and Earth."

Malachi walked to the workbench and picked up a quill, situated loose paper, and sketched as he resumed the telling of events. Daphne remained quiet and intent on his every move and word.

"The gods and demi-gods you read of in Greek and Egyptian mythology exist," he said, his somber gaze imparting the truth of his words. "That is how their presence is so strong and persistent in literature, their legends and tales of woe remain everlasting.

"They are, indeed, woeful beings as they take prideful falls," Malachi explained.

"This is so much to ponder, but it is all fascinating," Daphne said, while she walked to her desk.

Pensive, Malachi retrieved the quill then continued, looking down as he sketched Isaiah the Ancient, "Power adulterates people, gods, and even Celestials. Power, of all things, has the most ability to taint all touching it.

"The Seraph, as the rebellion has come to be known, has proven successful. They are surreptitious in their infiltration of every government, religion, and influential political organization. Gideon's leadership has evolved with the Seraph movement, supporting the evolution of the Seraph as something to be feared by the heavens, humans, and gods," he finished his explanation. A soulful sigh erupted from him, his frustration with all he had been through apparent to Daphne.

Restless, Daphne stood and crossed to the workbench. She peeked at Malachi's drawing. Her eyes lit in amazement while she looked over his sketch of the oak and ethereal phantoms hinted upon in the shadows cast by moonlight. Malachi had captured the flowing movement of the brook near Isaiah, and the glinting water in the soft rays of the moon. That this preternatural, terrifying, larger-than-life warrior had just made this beautiful ink drawing struck her as incongruous.

"Your sketch is remarkable, Malachi. It appears I could reach out and touch Isaiah's bark and run my fingers through the stream."

"Thank you. I obtain a great deal of enjoyment from sketching," he replied while his eyes probed hers. He saw no fear. He sensed her appreciation of the sketch and the incongruity. They had come far in their trust in one another in a short time. A foreign sensation squeezed about his heart. He brushed it aside.

"Back to the Seraph," Malachi continued, "Celestials have surmised the Seraph were instrumental in the spreading of the Black Plague. The plague quelled the burgeoning renaissance of knowledge and advancement of science. Our operatives tell us the Seraph gained many footholds in village governments and churches.

"Immortal Guardians have spent exceptional time and effort

identifying these infiltrations, then eradicating them." He smiled, pleased to see he had not overwhelmed Daphne. Her eyes remained clear and rapt on him and his telling of the tale.

"Are you ready to hear of Abbess Katherine's work here, or do we need to save that for another conversation?" he asked, taking care, an unusual tactic for his battle-hardened approach.

"Abbess Katherine?" Daphne questioned, having to reorient herself. She blinked. "Oh, yes, Abbess Katherine, and you having known her for two thousand years..." Her voice fell away as she shook her head while taking it all in.

"Our chat has indeed made me much more comfortable," Daphne said while she glanced at the candles, noting how far the wax had dropped.

Malachi's intense gaze followed hers to the flickering flames.

Daphne sighed, wanting to hear all the information, yet not desiring to hear any of it since her understanding of the world had already been upended this night. She knew she would be alone, not having anyone with which to share her fears or celebrate this incredible fork in the road.

Daphne peered at Malachi. "I believe this is a good time for me to understand the abbess's purposes at the abbey. But then, I believe it best for me to ruminate and reconcile things a bit before we delve much deeper," she answered him. A wry smile crossed her face. "Such as two-thousand years deeper," she laughed.

The warmth and promise of her laugh wound about Malachi's heart as an enchanted vine.

"You might agree, Malachi, that I have already had to make the unfathomable fathomable," she said, her voice imbued with hints of the rich colors of her humor.

Malachi surprised himself responding to her laugh with a chuckle of his own. Rare to laugh, yet she had coaxed one from him with nary an attempt. He sensed himself pulled down an unfamiliar rabbit hutch and on unsteady metaphorical ground.

"Fair enough, Mistress Daphne, the telling of Abbess Katherine's story, then no more for tonight," he agreed.

Daphne's expression illuminated with excitement and curiosity. She stood, her gray gaze pinned on Malachi, tilting her head to the side. "Yes, thank you, Master Malachi. Or would it be 'Immortal Malachi?' 'Ancient Malachi?'" A mischievous spark danced in her gaze

Realization dawned she had needled him. Her increasing comfort and familiarity with him filled Malachi with unexpected pleasure, "'Ancient Malachi', Mistress Daphne?" he asked, affecting a severe tone, "I think not," he replied, the laughing warmth in his eyes belying his stern, warrior's voice.

Her warm laugh poured over him like honey, sweet and pure. "What else would you have me call a person over two-thousand years in age? 'Ancient' is an accurate description for something of antiquity. You don't agree?" she asked, with a grin.

He grasped her hand.

Their eyes flew to each other's, the flash of strong attraction gripping both of them. Silence hung between them, neither willing to break the enthralling gaze.

The battle-hardened calluses of his sword training and the strength in his hand both intimidated and made her want to know more.

He lifted her hand to his lips, not taking his eyes from hers, and his warm breath danced over her knuckles as he spoke. "I do not agree," he replied, lifting her knuckles to his sensuous, firm mouth to place a kiss as light as a butterfly's upon her lavender and rosemary scented skin, his gentle touch intoxicatingly incongruous with the preternatural warrior aura about him.

Heat coursed through her belly and traveled to those secret places she had never paid much mind, her studies far more important to her. Her lips parted as a blush bloomed as the fairest rose in her cheeks. Enchanted, she could not take her gaze off his dark eyes which held forbidden promises. Desperate to partake, she ached to understand her need to have his touch upon her and wrap herself within his dark sensuality. She hoped he would never let go of her hand.

For Malachi, the sense of belonging with Daphne was foreign. Yet, he smiled, gave her fingers a gentle squeeze with his sword-roughened hand, then let go and broke their gaze.

Daphne shook off the sense of being bereft, her hand no longer held in his. She clasped her hands together and refocused, her thirst for knowledge taking priority. "The night grows old, Malachi. Tell me of Abbess Katherine," she reminded him.

"Hmm, Katherine, yes. She came to York about three hundred years ago, around 1320. There were a lot of rumblings in York as the Seraph had built a strong presence. The Celestials assigned Katherine as Immortal Guardian of Isaiah the Ancient and the abbey. The abbey is central to the folk of York and a strategic place from which to keep watch over Isaiah the Ancient.

"Katherine worked to become well established at the abbey. With the advent of the Black Plague, the townsfolk found Katherine and the abbey a blessing. Those were dark and desperate times. Many people, often entire families, found themselves locked away and left to die for fear of the disease spreading. Terrible things happened in terror of the disease itself and through black-hearted, power-mongering people taking advantage of the horrific situation."

Daphne's rapt gaze did not move from Malachi while he recounted the plague and Katherine's work in York during the plague.

"Katherine provided refuge for many children whose parents had perished. She brought food and water to the sick and the convalescing she discovered through physical or ethereal means.

Many people would have died without her assistance, as no one else would dare go near them."

"Katherine saved many people from cruel fates," Malachi's voice dropped to a low, somber tone. "She gave many dying parents solace in their children would be safe and have their needs met."

Malachi walked to the window, unsettled and unable to stay still at the workbench. Intrepid and ethereal strength emanated from him as he moved. He stared out at the steadfast Isaiah.

Daphne eyed his broad back. Her hands itched to touch from where she supposed his wings sprouted. Curiosity caused her mouth to water with almost undeniable need to explore Malachi's skin at the tops of his shoulder blades. Moving to be closer to him, it seemed she walked through Elemental currents. The air about him thrummed. Against the desk she leaned, nestling her hands between her posterior and the desk edge to resist the temptation to touch him.

Malachi continued, seemingly unaware of her distress in her curiosity, his far-away gaze lost in recollection, "Katherine is lion-hearted, and a stealthy, skilled warrior. She has taken many an enemy's life with only a spear or her own hands.

"She acted with exceptional courage in those dark times. Katherine maintained a strong line of thought with me over the two years the plague ran rampant, to avoid leaving Isaiah unprotected if something happened to her." He turned, his dark eyes bored into Daphne's gray ones, and continued, "Our Abbess is very much the fierce Guardian. I have seen her fell warriors of legendary acumen, skill, and strength while remaining unscathed.

"She puts much energy into maintaining a facade of learned gentility and humility as the abbess." His gaze freed hers as he laughed and shook his head, adding, "Katherine is probably one of the least humble people you will ever meet! Her ability to blend in with the local population yet be effective as a Guardian has amazed me through the centuries. But I digress.

"Katherine has done exceptional work in keeping the abbey thriving for three centuries, an eye on Vicar Tobias, who is of the Seraph, and maintaining watch over Isaiah The Ancient."

"Three centuries? The Abbess has been here three centuries. Three hundred years?" Daphne asked, a laugh of disbelief escaping her mouth. "Give or take a few years, I am sure."

Malachi peered upon Daphne, wondering if she had fatigued. He realized, with a start, he could not read her, as he could most humans. Brushing aside the thoughts until later, as to what that might mean, he asked, "Would you prefer to continue learning of Katherine's time in York now, or another time?"

His thoughtful question freed her from her apprehension. Daphne flashed him a sharp glare, sudden resentment rising toward her shattered view of her once insular and comfortable world. She captured his gaze and held it as she searched his soul for dark intent, finding none, she freed him.

Disconcerted and caught off guard by her psychical strength, a rare occurrence for him, Malachi almost reeled from the force. He had to work to keep his balance once she released him from her mental scrutiny.

Vexed, she eyed him, her brows furrowed, and said, "I am already this far down the path of your madness concerning Abbess Katherine, you might as well take me the rest of the way."

Upon her sharp tone and dry humor, Malachi fought back a laugh. He worked to navigate Daphne's changing seas of emotion and epiphanies; a challenge to which he proved unaccustomed. He did his best to imbue his voice with sympathy. "I realize that these revelations are causing an imbalance in your heretofore balanced world, Daphne."

Her eyebrows furrowed more, her eyes shifted to steely flint, vexed, as awareness dawned.

Malachi fought back a laugh.

Indignant, she huffed and said, "While I believe you see nothing untoward with new imbalance in my previously predictable world, I find your patronization distasteful; an insult to my intelligence."

Her umbrage licked with guilt at his heart. "Touché, Daphne," he replied and dipped his head in a regretful bow. "My sincere apologies. Be assured, I hold you in high esteem." Warmth imbued his obsidian eyes while he spoke. He returned his gaze to Isaiah.

Malachi continued, "Returning to Katherine's story, she has managed her continuous presence in such a way as to not raise suspicion with the local folk or the church. She has taken various surnames through the years. The wards she has set about the abbey and its records have strengthened her illusions.

"The Celestials garnered information from valid sources that Gideon has moved into the area, which Tobias has readied for him. This may prove to be an opportunity to trap Gideon.

"Katherine has a need to devote her attention to the abbey and Vicar Tobias while I focus my attention on the Oak and the town of York. Katherine and I often work in concert, even apart from each other, the whole being greater than the sum of the parts," Malachi explained.

"A lovely sensation, Malachi," Daphne agreed, "One I do enjoy when I am free to commune with nature." She gave a wistful sigh. "I do not often share these thoughts with people. Abbess Katherine warned me away from involving people other than Dante and herself in my abilities for fear of being accused of practicing the dark arts."

With a level stare, Malachi reaffirmed the abbess's warning. "You have a pure soul, and I sense strong abilities in you. Abbess Katherine is correct, you want to avoid people other than Dante, Katherine, and myself having any realization of what your abilities entail. That path is fraught with men and beings of nefarious motives."

Vehemence rolled off Malachi as he stared her down with his glittering, obsidian eyes. Insistent fervor imbued his voice, catching her off guard. Without thought, she raised her hand to her throat and edged away along the desk two steps further than she already was from his imposing, dark, and intimidating form.

A bolt of guilt reamed through him as Daphne stepped away, pale, her eyes as wide as proverbial saucers. The sensation unfamiliar and disconcerting to her. He found himself assailed by sensations and emotions which he had not, until now, experienced over his immortal existence. She continued to look at him as though she were a cornered rabbit. His heart ached as he did not desire to bring her fear or discontent. Regret flowed through his words, "Daphne, my apologies for alarming you."

His deep voice, which he dropped to a low whisper, floated about her.

"Beings?" Her voice was a hoarse whisper as comprehension dawned of the tide of a paradigm shift, into which she found herself pulled.

Malachi nodded, then reiterated, "Beings." His face was solemn. "I believe we have talked enough of all this, Daphne. It is overwhelming. Let us take a refreshing walk to Isaiah and the brook, then get you off for a spot of supper," he suggested.

He held the crook of his arm out to her in invitation.

Daphne looked over Malachi, her recalcitrance evident in her pale expression.

He patted the crook of his arm, and cajoled, "Daphne, please come. It is a beautiful night. A walk will help both of us clear our heads."

Daphne pushed herself away from the desk. Reluctant, she gripped the crook of Malachi's arm. He cupped his warm hand over hers, gave a brief, affectionate and reassuring squeeze. His strong, calloused, warm hand remained over hers. They stepped out into the night air, Malachi leading the way.

Equanimity seeped into Daphne as Malachi drew himself back to walk alongside her while the balmy night air steeped her in calm.

Tension eased from her grip on his elbow. Moonlight filtered through her gray eyes. Awe overtook him. He knew this moment would remain imprinted on his mind for eternity.

As Daphne neared the oak, she noted an energy about Isaiah she had not sensed before. The air surrounding the tree hummed low and thick. She reached out her free hand, bringing it closer to the oak's bark. A welcoming vibration strengthened more the closer her hand came. She pulled her hand away, then moved it closer again. Delight crossed her face and alighted her eyes as she proved her silent hypothesis true.

Malachi found himself again held hostage by her happiness. "Isaiah has always had this energy, Daphne. You did not have prior reason to pay attention. You now know of Isaiah's conscious conversation. Isaiah is also reaching out to me as he and I are old friends."

A smile turned up the corners of Daphne's mouth as she sensed Isaiah's affirmation to Malachi's statement of friendship. An owl gave its haunting and beautiful call, rounding out the moment with perfection for Daphne. Contentment entered her body and mind as angst departed. The warmth of Isaiah's approval curled about her and moved her to place her free hand along on his trunk and beautiful, craggy rivulets. A greeting spoken in ancient Celtic, so low she wondered if she heard it, whispered past her ears. A shiver of enchantment spiraled down through Daphne as she realized she heard Isaiah's salutation.

Malachi lifted his hand to Isaiah as well. Isaiah gave a warm surge of energy, expressing his pleasure in being touched by both Daphne and Malachi.

Compelled by the moment, he bent toward her and placed his firm lips upon her soft mouth as he captured a sweet kiss. His lips curled in a smile as he felt her mouth open under his and her intake of surprise. He kept still, letting her become accustomed to their touch.

Her lips moved the slightest bit under his, capturing his in a kiss and she turned about the table in her adept manner.

Malachi remained inert, content to have Daphne take the lead.

Daphne leaned in closer, pressing her lips more fully to his.

Shocked to sense the warmth of her tongue slide along his mouth, his breath hitched.

Daphne savored his male and earthy essence. While her lips lingered on his, she breathed in his unique, male scent. Heat licked deep within her. Appreciation that he gave her the lead only served to increase her sensual enjoyment of the moment. Her level of comfort with him increased with every breath.

Caution tossed aside, she leaned deeper into Malachi, instinct leading her to open her mouth further under his, the sweep of her tongue no longer tentative, but taking delight in his unique flavor.

Heat rushed to Malachi's loins and he resisted the urge to fold her in his embrace, as he wanted this exploration to be on her terms. He gave fervent thanks to Fate Daphne returned his kiss.

Her cool, capable hands landed on either side of his face.

His heart stilled.

Her hands pulled his head down to plant his lips more firmly against her, her fingers slid into his hair.

Wonderment and warmth poured through him. Lust teased the edges of his enthrallment. He rubbed his calloused hand over her upper arm as he savored her. His tongue danced with hers, her piquancy now seared in his brain. He rubbed his thumb along her upper arm where his hand rested.

Daphne sighed into his mouth, digging her fingers into his hair, against his scalp, as she pulled him yet harder against her mouth.

Esther peered out Daphne's bedroom window searching for Daphne on her way from the annex for her supper, as darkness had fallen. *What's this? Daphne walking side by side with a man? Kissing?* Her lips curled in a conniving smile as nefarious light entered her eyes.

Cloaking spells took a great deal of energy for a woman of her advanced age, but she gambled the information gathered would be worth the cost to her. Neither Malachi nor Daphne seemed to note her spying upon them from the window of Daphne's bedroom. Isaiah appeared to be oblivious as well, she noted with calculating satisfaction. Her gnarled fingers dug further into the drapes hanging about the windows.

Daphne had never kissed a man—or anyone—with passion. Her ever-logical, curious mind examined the warmth coursing through her and found this most pleasant. Wishes filled her for the kiss not to end. She had only met him, but she sensed on an ethereal level she always had known him. His tongue swept over and around hers as she leaned into his strong warmth. She decided she wanted to keep him there and moved her mouth to take him in even further. She again inhaled his masculine, earthy scent. A sigh of pleasure bubbled up from her feminine core, swirled higher, and escaped as a sweet wraith from between her lips. She softened against him, giving the lead back to him.

Her subtle acquiescence hit Malachi like a bolt of lightning. He tamped down the conquering warrior within, pulled her close to him, wrapping his arms about her, his hands splayed across her back. Isaiah set a wave of approval about them; Malachi imprinted this moment, the air thick with Fate. At a crossroads, he did not hesitate to choose which path to take.

Malachi shifted his lips from hers and placed a sweet kiss on Daphne's forehead, a chance for them both to catch their breath. His lips stilled against her skin; contentment flowed through him. He inhaled the now treasured scents of rosemary and lavender which imbued her essence.

Reluctance to have the kiss end fissured through Daphne, replaced by a sense of being cherished as he placed his beautiful lips on her forehead, his well-muscled arms wrapped about her.

"It is a lovely night, and we shared a beautiful kiss, Daphne," he sighed, his breath edged by angst. "I am compelled to be honest and tell you our kiss was the most moving kiss I have experienced in all my years, Daphne."

Her heart skipped a beat hearing his admission. She had thought their kiss moved heaven and earth for her because of her inexperience. She found she could not breathe, to know that their shared kiss affected this powerful, mystical being as much as it did her.

"I found the kiss most enchanting, Malachi," she whispered, her voice fanning across his neck. Relief moved through her they were not looking upon each other. Otherwise, conversation would be a thousand times more difficult.

His low, masculine laugh moved against her forehead and he hugged her tighter. "I could tell, Daphne. Your enjoyment added to my enjoyment of our kiss." He pulled away from her forehead and chucked his finger under her chin, lifting her gaze to his. "It is late, my beautiful and gifted alchemist. You need to get your evening meal and some rest. You need to be fresh for working with Dante on the morrow."

Leaning down, Malachi placed a brief, chaste, and sweet kiss upon her passion-swollen lips. He smiled down at her. "I need to check the wards I have set."

The sincerity in his dark gaze gave her pause. She lifted herself onto her toes, mimicked him in placing a sweet chaste kiss upon his lips, which curved up in a delighted smile under hers.

"Good night, Malachi."

Breaking away, she turned and walked to the main house.

Esther moved away from the window where she had been peering upon the couple from the shadows. She hurried to the kitchen, careful to be light of step, to prepare an evening meal from what Cook had left for Daphne.

Malachi watched as she made her way, admiring her purposeful stride. Hope lit a flame within his cynical soul. Once Daphne was through the main door, he released a breath he did not realize he had been holding and turned toward Isaiah. He sensed the wise oak's deep hum of approval rippling about him. Affirmation was an unfamiliar companion to Malachi, thus his welcome of it guarded.

CHAPTER TWELVE

Friday, April 22, 1622 CE
The Annex and Town, York, England

THE SUN PEEKED through the shutters and nudged Daphne awake. Recollection of the blissful flavor and silk of Malachi's kiss brought her fingers to her lips. She rubbed her fingertips along the soft skin, wondering how her kiss felt to Malachi.

Memories flew through her mind, swooping like a raven. Conversation snippets, her trepidation then curiosity, his enigmatic presence winged through her thoughts. *Malachi! An Immortal being! I touched, walked with, kissed an Immortal being!*

Daphne sat straight up in bed with her heart in her mouth, questioning her sanity. Filled with curiosity, she bounded out of bed and picked up her hand-held mirror. She pouted, patted her cheeks, turned from side to side, then stared at her own eyes. Nothing looked different, yet she felt different. A whole new world opened for her.

Questions ran rampant through her mind. The surreal nature of the prior night bombarded her thoughts. Even last night, she wondered if she had dreamed everything. It had seemed real as she ate her cold, waiting dinner last evening.

Last night, Daphne feared she would have a hard time sleeping, yet her fatigue from her long day yesterday had won and she had slept hard. In the mirror, she looked into her own eyes and searched their depths. Clarity of thought gazed back from her gray eyes. Both a relief and terrifying when she considered how much her understanding of the world and time had shifted in twelve hours.

With care, she set the mirror down, opened a shuttered window, and looked upon the old oak. Celtic words, in a low, deep tone, rumbled through her unbidden. Fear of the unusual snaked up her back. Daphne quelled her unease, then listened with heightened senses to Isaiah to better understand his earthy, ancient language.

"One does not always know who the wrong people are," he echoed the abbess's warning from some years back.

The cautionary words slammed back into Daphne full force and terrified her, coming from the oak word for word. The ethereal connection took her breath away.

Clear as a cloudless sky, that day came back to her, when her father and the abbess had decided she needed to leave the abbey to study under her now beloved Dante.

A deep sense of foreboding shivered through her.

Esther bustled into Daphne's room and smiled at her, interrupting her somber reverie. "Good morning, Miss Daphne. Master Dante says there are visitors in the Annex this morning. He would like you to come visit with them," Esther explained as she laid out one of Daphne's lavender and gray working dresses, along with a muslin shift and gray bodice.

With a deep sigh, Daphne rekindled her curiosity and set about getting washed up and dressed for the day. Esther assisted her in securing her chestnut hair in her snood. After wishing Cook a good morning, she enjoyed a quick breakfast of fresh bread and cheese. As Esther bent to clean her dishes away, Daphne exited the kitchen to walk to the annex.

Esther's gaze followed Daphne's progress down the walk, her rheumy eyes betraying her sly thoughts. She ducked into the kitchen with Daphne's dishes and asked Cook if they needed rye seed. Cook took Esther up on her offer and handed her shillings from Dante's food coffer. Excited to pass on her news to the baker, Esther found herself light of foot as she made her way to the bakery.

Brisk morning air cleared Daphne's thoughts as she set her mind ready to tackle the day working alongside Dante. Of late, Dante had not been answering her questions for her. Instead, he had her search for the answers herself—review of their journals, his library of references, or her experimentation. Days stretched longer without Dante's ready answers. Instead, she found herself more self-reliant and critical in her thinking. She was gratified to see how far she had come, yet understood the quest for knowledge never ended. Each proven, or disproven, theory always led to more questions.

The familiar creaking of the water wheel and wafting wood smoke greeted her as she neared the annex. Conversation among men drifted through the open windows. Daphne listened as she stepped to the door. At least three men were talking, including Dante. She steeled herself for the subtle scorn she unerringly experienced when around her male alchemical peers. This happened even though Dante had made his deep respect for Daphne quite apparent to the alchemy community.

Daphne had apprenticed for several years with Dante, which spoke volumes of the regard he had for her. But, the invitations for academic events had Dante's name penned on them, never hers. Her male peers did not go out of their way to enjoy a conversation with her if they ran into her at the apothecary, blacksmith's, or the glass blower's shop. Chatter dropped off when she and Esther would enter an informal gathering of fellow alchemists in a shop, then pick back up behind them as they left.

Ruminations put aside, Daphne grasped the bronze door handle and pushed open the door.

The threshold of the annex seemed to divide Daphne's world between welcoming and disparaging. The fresh air of morning tinted by wood smoke gave way to the cold wall of disdain thrown up by Alchemists Francis Coughton and Elias Northrup. They wore matching dark scowls, both sets of eyebrows deepening at the interruption of their private audience with Dante Santorum. Their daggered, hostile stares ignored, Daphne took the higher road and greeted them with a gregarious tone. "Good morning, kind Sirs," she said, even though she found the word 'kind' a challenge to utter without gagging—especially after their encounter two days ago.

"Good morning, my dear Daphne," Dante said, his fond and intelligent gaze on her as she closed the door.

Francis Coughton opened his mouth, then closed it. He moved his lips again, pushing out a reluctant-sounding greeting. "Yes, er, good morning, Miss Heatherton."

Elias Northrop gave a simple nod, looking back and forth between Coughton and Daphne.

Daphne smiled with sincerity at her mentor and said, "Good morning, Dante."

She swept her eyes back over the visitors and wondered how she did not freeze to death in their presence.

"Northrop, Coughton, and I were just debating the principles of proportions in creating salves and tonics, Daphne," explained Dante. "These fine gentlemen have done some reading of Paracelsus and dosing after their visit two days ago to become more familiar with the concept."

Turning back to his guests, he said, "Daphne and I have found that having a consistency in proportions and preparation methods has allowed us to replicate salves with similar and optimal effectiveness."

From the brass wall hook, Daphne retrieved her apron and looped it over her head as Dante continued to chat with Northrop and Coughton. After rolling back her sleeves, she secured the cuffs with bands about her forearms. She retrieved her loose notes from yesterday and journal from her desk, determined to get to work with or without the presence of the hostile interlopers.

On her way across the worn oak floor to the workbench, she heard Dante espouse the virtues of her journaling style. Her heart leapt into her throat. Her journal was her soul—she did not want their rude gazes or pawing, irreverent fingers to fall upon her sacred notes and drawings. She lifted her eyes to Dante, glanced to the two interlopers, then back to Dante. With a sinking heart, she realized his face shined with pride. It dawned on her Dante wanted to show off his protege.

Daphne continued to the waist-high work bench. She opened her journal to her latest project: the burn salve. She held loose parchment notes of the progress she had made yesterday on formulating the salve. Her bile swallowed, she worked to keep a neutral expression. Daphne spread her pages across the worn surface of the workbench and opened her journal. Northrop and Coughton flanked her, their faces dour with skepticism. Daphne described the process she used to create the burn salve; her notes, observations, and methodology written upon the loose sheets, then documented in further detail—along with sketches—in her journal.

Angst pushed aside, Daphne delved into her passion for her craft. Northrup and Coughton's expressions shifted from world-weary dubiousness to attentive as they bore witness to Daphne's acumen and methodology.

Dante caught the men exchanging meaningful looks behind Daphne's back and found himself filled with a deep foreboding. He deigned to interrupt them, saying, "Daphne and I do need to get the day started, gentlemen. We have much to get accomplished, but I have had a most enjoyable morning with you."

Daphne looked up, rather startled by the abrupt conclusion to which Dante had brought her exchange with the alchemists. Aware Dante had sound purpose behind every action and word, she remained quiet.

With profuse thanks to the alchemists for their time, Dante ushered them into the brisk air while lauding the beauty of the morning. Closing the door, he leaned his back against it and sighed, his face drawn with frustration.

Puzzled, Daphne asked, "I thought things were going well. I believed Northrop and Coughton had arrived to the point of giving me credence for my abilities."

"Yes, they did, but they were none too happy," Dante replied. "It is unfortunate, but you are a menace to them, in their minds, with your innate understanding of the world and your ability to articulate it so well."

Daphne backed away from Dante toward the workbench to blink away her tears. Rage filled her.

Concerned, Dante watched with angst-filled eyes as Daphne's straight back expanded and contracted like a fireplace bellows while she heaved breaths and tried not to cry. The aquamarines in her snood glittered with her movements, reflecting her righteous anger. He jumped as Daphne slammed her hands down upon the workbench.

"By heavens, Dante, I will work hard and prove the lot of them wrong," Daphne promised, her cheeks suffused with red in her ire.

"I have faith in you, Daphne, to do that and so much more. You have a brilliant mind and soul, my dear. You perform head and shoulders above everyone else," Dante said with absolute confidence.

Calm and purpose washed over her. She collected herself. She sensed Malachi behind this change in her mood, and that made her smile.

Deciding there was no time like the present to let Dante know she had met Malachi, she took a breath and prepared for his reaction. "Dante, I met Malachi last evening."

"The Guardian," he replied solemnly.

"Yes, the Immortal Guardian of Isaiah."

"I see." He paused. "What else did Malachi share?" Dante asked, suspicion threading his voice.

Daphne paced as she recounted the highlights of the conversation. "He talked of Katherine's time at the abbey and her assistance to the townspeople during the Black Plague. The impact Sodom and Gomorrah had on the archangel Gideon. The birth of the Seraph, the Seats of Five." Stilling, Daphne looked Dante in the eye. Her gaze piercing his, she added, "That he watched over Aristotle. Aristotle! The Aristotle! Dante, I cannot believe that I am saying this, but I believe him!"

Dante's emotions ran the spectrum while Daphne shared these tidbits of information. He became more and more perturbed with Malachi for sharing all of this with Daphne without him present.

"I see," said Dante again, cryptic, almost silent.

Daphne had predicted Dante would not be pleased, as he had not broached the subject of Malachi himself. Already in this far, she decided to press on, saying, "I can now hear Isaiah speak."

A rueful smile crossed Dante's face. "I had hoped to introduce you to Isaiah myself when the time was right. This may have been a fortuitous meeting between you and Malachi. It is past time you were made aware." He stopped and fiddled with his cap a moment, his eyes closed, then peered at her, warmth and worry churning together in the sparrow brown of his gaze. "What is done is done," Dante said with resignation. With a defining clap, he clasped his hands together, changing the atmosphere of the annex. "We have a busy day ahead. Let us get to work."

A smile tipped the corners of Daphne's mouth. She agreed, "Yes, indeed. Our lists are long."

Time slipped by for Daphne as she concentrated on collecting distilled, concentrated rosemary into a glass flask for a new batch of the burn ointment, to mix with the silver slurry she had amalgamated. The annex door opened and closed, then heavy footsteps walked up behind her. She jumped as she heard Malachi's deep voice from close by, almost dropping the flask and the precious essence of rosemary with it.

"Good afternoon, Dante and Daphne," greeted Malachi. "My apologies, Daphne, I did not intend to startle you."

Daphne kept her eyes on her task, putting the interruption to the back of her mind as she replied, "No matter. I did not drop the flask. Now, if I had, you would find yourself doing this instead of me."

Daphne smiled as she heard both Dante and Malachi laugh, her eyes still on the rosemary essence dripping into the flask.

"Hello, Malachi. It is good to see you," Dante greeted him from the desk, his head remaining down as he kept his attention on his writing.

Pleasant surprise filled Malachi as he took in how little Daphne and Dante allowed his presence to interrupt them, leading to a sense of comfort. He leaned against the workbench and crossed his arms in front of his chest. Content, he watched Daphne's efficient, skilled movements and easy interaction with Dante for some time.

Daphne set to mixing her essence of rosemary with lanolin and the slurried colloidal silver, paying him no mind.

Lifting a small pot to his nose, Malachi took a whiff. The pleasant fragrance of the balm surprised him. "May I try some?" he asked.

Nodding, obviously distracted, Daphne handed him a clean cloth and a small wooden spatula. Malachi scooped just a bit of the balm out with the spatula, then spread it over his arm.

Daphne noted with some superstitious relief the silver in the balm did not burn Malachi.

Humor danced in Malachi's obsidian gaze, with which he speared hers. One side of his mouth quirked up. "Look," he exclaimed in mock surprise, "my skin does not smoke with the silver on it!"

Heat flew to Daphne's cheeks when she perceived, embarrassed, Malachi had voiced her old-wives-tale fear the silver would burn him. Her jaw flexed as her ire bloomed then rose. Daphne harrumphed, rolled her eyes, and scraped the salve off Malachi's arm with the spatula; none too gentle. She wiped the instrument off with a rag, making a point to ignore the imposing figure hovering over her.

Worry filled Dante's eyes as he watched the interaction between Malachi and Daphne. With a cough, he signaled for Daphne to get back to work. "We shall see you later, Malachi, I am sure."

Malachi moved to leave the annex. His purposeful walk slowed with each step as he neared the exit. At the heavy wooden door, he stopped and fiddled with narrow-necked green and brown glass saddle-flasks of various sizes on a nearby shelf.

Trying not to smile, Daphne turned back to her loose notes. The pieces of parchment made for a satisfying sight and sound as she tapped them onto the workbench and made a neat stack.

The door closed behind her as Malachi finally took his leave.

She found her mind wandering through the day while she worked with Dante.

Over the stone threshold, Esther stepped into the bakery and peered about for the proprietor. Her footsteps creaked on the warped wood floor. The baker looked up while kneading his dough and nodded. He called one of his assistants over and instructed her to take over. With a wipe of his hands on his white cloth apron, he motioned Esther into the back of the bakery.

She went straight to the crux of the matter. "The Guardian and Daphne have eyes only for each other. I witnessed them kissing under the oak last night."

"Excellent, Miss Esther!" exclaimed the baker. "I am sure Gideon and Apep will both be pleased to hear this news. Not only do we now have them all in the same vicinity, but Malachi's heart is also becoming wrapped into this." His eyes sparkled with anticipation. "Revenge shall be sweet for Apep. Indeed, I shall report your news to Gideon and Vicar Matthews. Keep me apprised of any new developments."

"Thank you," Esther replied. "I serve the Seraph, and look forward to the tide turning for them. Once Apep eliminates Malachi and the oak, Katherine should prove easier to kill."

"That is our common goal, Esther. Here is the rye you told your cook you would purchase for your household."

"Thank you," Esther said with a grin. She pocketed the coins Cook had given her and left the bakery with rye in hand, her stride light and purposeful.

Golden light filtered into the annex as the day came to an end. A bat swooped near the window and Daphne watched with delight as the skilled acrobat chased an evening meal. Crickets began their serenade as the annex door swung open. She sensed a warm and welcome presence behind her.

"Hello, Dante," Daphne said, her eyes not leaving the bat.

"Hmm. I do not believe I am Dante." Malachi's deep voice filled the room.

Irritation rifled through Daphne at having her enjoyment of the evening—and her journaling—interrupted by this being who seemed so human even though she knew he was not. She remained at the window, staring out but unseeing.

Vexed, Daphne turned toward Malachi, only to see his gaze fixated on her. "What is wrong? Do I have an ink smudge on my face?"

"No," he answered, then paused, appearing to have a need to search for words, "the gold of the sunset behind you, framing you—" his voice and the awe imbuing it drifted away.

Her eyes flashed upon his face, then moved up and down his length as though he were a specimen not doing as expected.

"I have disturbed you, Daphne. My apologies," said Malachi.

Taken aback to see hurt in his eyes, she paused as regret pricked at her conscience. She had thought him incapable of feeling angst. Not sure what to say or do, she eyed him in silence.

He looked at her, his hand still on the handle of the open door.

"You will let insects in. You may stay, but close the door," she both admonished and gave him permission in the same breath. The internal thoughts of absurdity at this almost made her laugh out loud.

Nodding to her desk, her tone clipped, she added, "I was just about to journal, if you would like to sit with me and see what I worked on today." Adding a purpose-driven, dramatic sigh, Daphne made his imposition upon her privacy known; she admitted to herself she did not realize just how sacred this time was to her, until now.

Malachi moved a chair next to the desk, taking care to be quiet as a mouse. He had no desire to conquer as the warrior. Instead, he decided to respectfully observe in hopes of losing the status of an interloper. In silence, he watched her work in earnest as she rewrote the notes into her journal. With skill and ease, she added small illustrations. The way her mind worked, the conclusions and calculations she did without difficulty, made his head spin. His admiration for her—already high—increased tenfold.

Never before attracted to the scent of leather, Daphne found the fragrance wafting from Malachi more than appealing. Whenever Malachi shifted in his seat it would drift, tantalizing her senses. She found appreciation grew for his silent presence and genuine interest in her work. She had assumed he would find her journaling boring.

After some time, her neck and fingers stiffened. Daphne decided to take a brief break. "I need to stretch a few minutes and give my hand a break from writing," she explained while rolling her shoulders.

Malachi saw relief flow into her face, easing the furrow between her brows. He lifted a brow, crossing his arms in front of him. "Not a surprise at all. You have been at it for quite some time," he said. Malachi motioned a hand toward the pile of note papers Daphne had already journaled from. "May I?"

Her eyes closed, she opened them to glance at his hand. "Yes," she answered in a whisper, her lids falling shut again.

Stealing a peek, Daphne watched his eyes track over her pages, his expression inscrutable. This needled her. She moved her head back a bit to catch a glimpse of the page currently in front of him. She slammed her half-open eyes back shut when he lifted his gaze toward her, but not before she caught the glint of amusement.

"Daphne, I would not be honest if I did not share that I am most impressed," Malachi said. "I am privileged to have a glimpse into how your brilliant mind works. How the pieces of the puzzle fit together for you." He smiled as he added, "And, your illustrations are beautiful, with incredible detail."

"Thank you," she replied, as her eyes darted about the room, seeking some distraction. She pushed her chair back and the feet scraped against the wood floor, sounding thunderous in the silent annex. Daphne stood up, arched her back, and let out a groan of relief. With a glance at the seated Malachi, she said "My apologies, I forgot you were sitting there." She turned her back to him, arched again, then lifted her arms above her head as she once again stood straight.

Amused at her unsubtle reference to him interrupting her time and space, Malachi did his best to bite back a laugh, as he knew it would do nothing but get her ire up. "By all means, continue. Do not let me get in your way."

She turned back to him—looking down at him, he thought, rather like he was an ant.

"Oh, trust me, Malachi. I will not abide you getting in my way," she said in a tone imparting she would not tolerate interruption. "You will be the first to hear about it." Standing next to him, while he remained seated, the thought crossed her mind she much preferred this over peering up at him. While tall herself, he towered over her.

The door to the annex opened and Dante entered. He looked over to the desk. Surprise, then a scowl, crossed his face as he saw Malachi with Daphne.

"Good evening, Dante," she greeted her mentor. "I am taking a brief break from my journaling. There is much to transcribe after all of our work today," she shared. "How are you this beautiful evening?"

"I am well, Daphne. Cook saved some dinner for you. I figured you had a lot to get documented," Dante said as he shot a pointed glance toward Malachi. "I hope that Malachi has not been a distraction."

That Dante was not pleased to see him there with Daphne became plain. Malachi knew that Dante would not have concerns about him taking advantage of Daphne, so he wondered on what Dante's displeasure centered.

"Oh, no, Dante. I made it clear to Malachi that he had to let me journal in peace, without interruption. Truth be told, one would have thought he was a mouse tonight."

Malachi lifted his fist to his mouth; hopeful he had turned a barking laugh into a polite cough.

Dante looked from Daphne to Malachi, his brow furrowed in his dubiousness. "A mouse?"

Her hands clasped behind her back, she nodded, stood on tiptoe, and rocked back on her heels. "Yes, quite so. A mouse."

Malachi watched the fond exchange between Dante and Daphne, appreciating the ease with which they bantered. He was startled to realize he longed for the same ease with Daphne.

"I have heard Malachi called many things. 'Mouse' was not among them, until now."

With a sidelong glance to Malachi, Daphne said, "Stranger things, Dante."

"Daphne," Dante called.

To Dante she looked, a fond smile crossing her face. "Yes, Dante?"

"Consider enjoying your dinner now, then come back and finish your notes. The break will do you good—refresh you." His tone made it obvious he brooked no argument. A rare thing for him, to tell Daphne what to do.

Daphne looked to him, confusion swimming in her eyes. She

decided not to argue, and agreed. "It has been a long day. I do believe that is what I shall do. Thank you."

Both Malachi and Dante watched her leave. Dante looked out the window, ensuring she made it to the house.

Now standing and looking over Dante's head through the annex window—at the upper level of the house—Malachi spotted Esther's gray hair as she peered out Daphne's bedroom window. Her eyes landed on his. They stared at each other for a moment; she startled, he suspicious. His hackles raised. She backed away, disappearing behind the drapery.

Malachi grew in his unease with Esther every day.

"Malachi," Dante said.

"Yes?" he replied to Dante with respect, looking him clear in the eye.

"I have a great deal of regard for you, Malachi," Dante began. "And, I have come to think of Daphne as a daughter, as well as a protégé. I would give my life for her without even thinking about it."

A sinking sensation filled Malachi. He despaired that he could not be free of what Celestia and Fate demanded of him.

"Death, pain, and destruction follow you, Guardian," Dante said. "Do not let such touch her." Dante's gaze bored into Malachi's. "However, I shall not interfere with her choices. She is a grown woman."

Under Dante's scrutiny, Malachi chafed. He rounded on Daphne's mentor. "I would never place her in the way of harm," he said. Then he went on the offensive, his eyes flashing his ire. "I fear for her safety, considering the alchemists who envy her place at your side and her obvious abilities. She runs circles about them, and they know it," he warned. He stepped closer, imparting his frustration that Dante was putting Daphne at risk of harm, yet not acknowledging that peril hung over her neck. "I see and sense the dark, deep resentment these 'learned men' harbor toward her," Malachi hissed with disgust. "I have worry they will use nefarious means, without conscience, to be rid of her."

"You have a point," Dante admitted. "But I see the chaotic darkness which follows in your wake." He advanced on Malachi, his own eyes somber and hard in his angst. "Don't let it touch her," he warned.

The two men stared at each other, neither willing to back down.

The door swung open. Daphne's face fell from anticipation to irritation as she looked between the two men. The tension in the air thick, swirling with anger. With a harsh look to both of them, her gaze moved from alchemist to angel. "Whatever has both of your hackles raised, cease or I shall refuse to be around either of you," she said, anger rolling from her.

She swiped up her journal and loose papers she had not yet copied, then turned on her heel. Regally, out she swept, slamming the door behind her with her righteous anger. Both men winced.

Dante's gaze pinioned Malachi's, his enmity falling from him in waves. From between his clenched teeth he ground out his words. "Do not let the bloodied soil of your battles touch any part of her, Angel."

Malachi lifted his chin and looked with irritation upon Dante and his sanctimonious ire. "Keep her safe from your witch hunters, Dante."

"We understand each other, then?" Dante asked, subtle hostility in his tone.

"Yes," replied Malachi, quiet anger imbuing his response.

"Leave. I have work to do, Malachi," Dante said, dismissing him.

Dismissed by a mere mortal, dull red suffused Malachi's face. Yet, he knew there would be no winner in this conversation. He decided to ignore the slight: he had to deal with mortals in their world, as a part of it, and he was learning.

"Very well," he said, his voice clipped and cold. He demate-rialized before Dante, deciding a show in power would be response enough.

Daphne stalked up to her bedroom, lit candles at her desk, then wiped her hands down her face in frustration. With a huff, she sat down and spread out her notes, irritated at having to relocate over the posturing of two men.

"You are journaling here tonight, Miss?" asked Esther with surprise in her voice.

"Oh!" Daphne jumped, having not heard Esther come up behind her. Her hand at her throat, she recovered. While the old maid stared back at her, she pondered an excuse—as she was not sure how much Esther knew of Malachi. "Yes, Dante did not want me around noxious odors he feared may form with the work he planned on doing this evening," she explained, then looked back down at her papers, intent on sorting them.

"Is there anything I might get for you, Miss Daphne?" Esther asked, her eyes boring into the side of Daphne's head as her venomous hatred poured from her gaze and wrinkled frown.

The malevolence streaming toward Daphne crawled over her skin. Daphne peered at the benign expression of the old maid. Confusion crossed her face as she questioned if she imagined the malignant wave. Sensing nothing now, she attributed the animosity to her distress from walking into the disagreement between Malachi and Dante.

Daphne's suspicion had been rising regarding the maid's intent. She decided discretion would work more to her favor. Her expression schooled, she threw a glance the maid's way, she answered, "A cup of tea would be lovely. Thank you, Esther."

Once in the kitchen, Esther contemplated placing a spell upon the tea to make Daphne ill, then decided against it. Daphne would be on the alert for just such a thing now. Esther realized her error in not masking her contempt. She was angry at herself for letting her true nature show in her hatred of the girl everyone seemed to love.

As evil intent stole over her elderly countenance, her nose and chin sharpened. She thought about the comeuppance the chit was soon to have and the soul-rendering heartbreak Dante, Malachi, and Katherine were about to suffer. She hummed a cheery ditty, picking up the mug of tea to bring to 'innocent' Daphne.

From his hiding place in the shadows of the kitchen, Gideon grimaced. Esther had been an accomplished spy, until now. She almost gave away the game tonight, as he witnessed firsthand while cloaked in Daphne's room. Once they recruited or eliminated Daphne, they would need to dispatch Esther. "A pity," he mouthed to himself, then faded away.

CHAPTER THIRTEEN

Wednesday, June 1, 1622 CE ~ The Abbey, York, England

KATHERINE AND RAPHAEL both received a message from Malachi with a request to meet him at Katherine's abbey.

Raphael appeared, his dress classical angel. Katherine rolled her eyes as he materialized, throwing a look down upon the greaves laced up his calves and his pleated white tunic.

"You do not approve, Abbess?" the golden-haired Archangel asked, moving his hand with a flourish in front of his pure white clothing. "I am not sure how much room you have to talk in your black habit and white wimple." He raised his knuckles to his lips to keep from laughing out loud while the abbess glared at him, her lioness topaz eyes fierce. He asked, "Tell me, do you take flight down the halls with your veils flying out behind you?"

She glared at him. "At least I have the sense to blend in, instead of resembling a Roman centurion. You look ridiculous."

"I see abbess-hood has encouraged your humble and kind nature," Raphael replied.

Katherine opened her mouth, ready to catapult a retort. Before she could launch, Malachi materialized. He sported a cream linen blouse with ruffles spilling over his wrists with black leather waistcoat, overcoat, and breeches. "Raphael, see here." Her eyes moved over Malachi with matriarchal approval. "Malachi may have a privateer look to him, but he has the sense to appear contemporary."

Malachi rolled his eyes in irritation at Katherine, then scowled at both her and Raphael. "Has there ever been a time when the two of you have not bickered?" he asked, wondering how two such accomplished beings could be so childish with each other.

"Yes, when she was almost dead and unable to talk. As soon as I revived her, she insulted me," Raphael replied.

"You were lying across me, covered in sweat," exclaimed Katherine.

Malachi's eyes widened, he looked askance at Raphael.

"For heaven's sake, not in the way you are thinking, Malachi." He looked to Katherine, chiding her, "Stop with the dramatics and innuendo. It is unbecoming of an abbess."

"Enough!" Malachi bellowed with perturbed impatience. Decorative brass plates sitting on a bookshelf behind Katherine rattled against the wood.

"Yes, my apolo—"

"Quite sor—"

Katherine and Raphael tried to apologize over each other's words.

"Enough," Malachi growled again through clenched teeth. Awkward silence ruled the moment.

As he paced, Malachi explained, "I require your joint counsel." He stopped and turned, ensuring they were both paying attention. "I am just going to say it." His dark eyes searched both of theirs. "I believe I am falling in love with Daphne, and I believe it is mutual."

With a viper's hiss, Katherine's eyes narrowed to slits. She said in a low and threatening tone, "You better not have laid a finger on her."

Raphael pulled his hand over his face in obvious frustration. "She's mortal," he cried out.

"I have not touched her," Malachi replied, paused, then added, "yet."

"What do you mean, 'yet'?" asked Katherine, her face reddening. "You dog."

"She's an adult!" exclaimed Malachi.

"You are an Immortal. You can influence her thoughts." Katherine jumped up and reached for Malachi's neck. The lioness protecting her cub.

Raphael stepped between Katherine and Malachi, then faced the latter with condemnation hardening his ice-blue gaze.

"I cannot influence her thoughts," Malachi's solemn whisper thundered through the study.

Anger fled from Katherine's face.

Raphael's brows lifted as he turned, making a triad of the three of them.

In rare surprise, Katherine brought her hand to her heart. She stared at Malachi, eyes wide. "Oh heavens, Malachi," she said, breathing out the words in a shocked whisper.

Raphael remained quiet.

"To anyone else, I would say this can come to no good," Katherine said, raising her clasped hands to her chin. "What are you going to do?" she asked, worry threaded through her question.

Malachi paced, agitation in every step. "That's why I asked both of you to meet me," he said. He turned and caught Raphael in his sights. "You. Archangel. You have not said a word," he snarled in his frustration. Then turned it to an insult befitting a brother-in-arms, "Tell me your thoughts, Cretin of Celestia."

The silent pause grew heavy and mournful as Raphael's ache for Malachi became palpable in the air of the abbey study. He lifted his somber gaze to Malachi. "You already know the answer," Raphael replied while he looked at his fellow warrior angel and peered into his soul. "The question is whether you are strong enough to do so."

"Bloody damn it all!" Malachi thundered. He looked to Katherine with desperation. Fathomless black pits of anguish formed in Malachi's eyes.

Katherine sucked in a breath. Her gaze remained glued to every move he made, every nuance which crossed his face. She glided like a black phantom to Malachi, and laid her hand upon his forearm.

Raphael's gaze did not leave Katherine.

With quiet grace, Katherine spoke, "Sometimes, the path is not predestined. I am not sure if we are meant to stop this union or bless it. When you first broached the topic, I believed there was no way in Hell this should happen between the two of you." She flashed her topaz eyes to him. "Malachi," she paused and sighed in resignation, "I believe you need to let your heart guide you."

She looked to Raphael, then back to Malachi. "We need to remain neutral and not sway you."

Raphael threw his hands up in frustration. "You cannot be serious, Katherine."

She held up her hand, her palm facing Raphael; one of the few beings in all realms who could make such a motion toward the archangel and escape unscathed.

"Raphael, do you know without a doubt what is supposed to happen?" Katherine asked, imparting her sincerity. "If Malachi could influence her, the answer would be simple—he cannot enter a relationship with her."

She paced, then rounded back on Raphael, the folds of her veil and habit flying out. "I cannot ignore that Malachi is unable to influence or read Daphne, a mortal. To me, that twist of Fate is very telling."

Raphael shook his head as he rubbed the back of his neck, his tension getting the better of him. He replied, "I still believe this is an angel's folly and beyond dangerous to Daphne."

"I agree, Raphael. This path together is fraught with danger for both of them—in particular, Daphne," responded Katherine. "But who are we to make that decision for Malachi and Daphne, when he does not appear to have an unfair advantage over her? Where affairs of the heart and mind are concerned?"

Malachi could not take his eyes off Katherine, her words ringing through him. Hope kindled while fear snaked up from deep in his belly to his heart. He wondered if he and Daphne were on an inexorable journey orchestrated by Fate.

Raphael looked to Malachi, regret churning as dark clouds in his eyes. He said, "You know where I stand, my brother."

Malachi shifted his gaze between Katherine and Raphael. Even though he did not receive clear counsel, he had shared his burden, which brought a measure of relief. Malachi looked up, imploring the heavens, then became disgusted with himself for doing so. He brought the unintentional prayer to an immediate halt, abhorring the thought of asking Celestia for anything—of large or small consequence.

"Malachi," came Katherine's voice from behind him, "if you do pursue a relationship with Daphne and she is agreeable, I believe you owe an explanation of your intentions to Dante and John Heatherton, her father."

Malachi grimaced, then replied, "I shall take your words into strong consideration, Katherine." He looked to both his confidantes with angst and sincerity in his gaze. "Thank you." He bowed, then dematerialized.

Pools of anguish gathered in Katherine's topaz eyes as she looked to the archangel. "I do believe things will get painful and ugly, Raphael."

CHAPTER FOURTEEN

Wednesday, June 1, 1622 CE ~ Outskirts of York, England

AFTER ANOTHER RESTLESS night's sleep and a quick breakfast, Daphne made her way to the annex. A headache lingering at the back of her head and a sense of malice licking at her heels had become constant companions. In response, she now worked to keep her wits about her and her eye on Esther.

The once well-ordered and insular world she knew had disappeared, its absence a continual intrusion into her thoughts. Her blooming relationship with Malachi and Dante's displeasure added to her turmoil.

While she enjoyed Malachi's attention, part of her wished she could turn back the clock and never let this unfold with him. Yet, she was drawn to Malachi like a moth to the flame.

With the fresh air of the crisp, chilly morning, her headache eased. She veered off the path to the annex, headed to Isaiah and the water wheel instead. She had a need to align her thoughts and rid herself of the chaos swirling in her spirit even if for a few moments.

As Daphne stared unseeing into the brook, the creak of the wheel and babbling of the water proved soothing and hypnotic.

In his mind, Malachi searched for and found Daphne at the brook. He cringed as he sensed her angst. A dark aura pulsed about her, then dissipated. It dawned on him she had rid herself of discord. "Very good, Daphne," he whispered while watching her from afar, unwilling to disturb her. His fists clenched as he realized he wanted nothing more than to be part of her life. Yet, his duty and the far-reaching consequences of pairing his immortality and her humanity could not be ignored.

Tears burned his eyes, surprising him. His mouth pulled down in a grim, self-deprecating smirk, as he left Daphne to her reverie. Unresolved silence hung turbid in his wake. Into woods opposite the annex he walked, taking in the soothing quiet. He needed to set his mind to examining his wards guarding Isaiah, analyzing attempted incursions.

The bells on the annex door jingled as Daphne entered. She was surprised to see Dante at the desk this early in the day instead of the workbench.

Dante motioned to the chair near him. "Daphne. Come, sit."

With a puzzled look for the unexpected variation in their workday Daphne joined him.

"I would like you to consider joining me to see Abbess Katherine today," he requested of her.

Daphne searched his eyes, her stomach twisting into a knot. "Go on," she said, her tone clipped.

His jaw stiff and his voice unsure, Dante dove in while his hands played with a nutcracker. "I know I said I will respect your judgment, your decisions, including those involving the warrior angel. But, I believe you would be wise to ask for counsel from the abbess where Malachi is concerned."

Daphne stared at Dante. She vacillated between anger and deep affection. It occurred to her, once she looked past her indignation, speaking with Abbess Katherine may be to her advantage.

The silent moments while Daphne digested his suggestion stretched into a tortuous eon for Dante.

"I believe this is a good idea, Dante," Daphne agreed. "Thank you. I should like to join you today."

He smiled as he took her hand, relieved, and said, "Daphne. You are many things to me—a strong apprentice, already an accomplished alchemist. The daughter I never had. Most of all, a beloved and respected friend."

Her throat closed with emotion as her eyes welled with tears. With the heel of her hand, like a child, she wiped them away, then cradled his cheek with her gaze on his. "You are a mentor, like a father, and a dear friend to me, Dante," her voice a whisper.

Their ride to the abbey was pleasant and filled with banter. A rare, carefree morning, their spirits lifted with a balmy breeze accompanying them on their journey. Wildflowers in bloom waved to them in bright colors from the side of the road. They both knew they would cherish this time, their ride together, no matter what transpired.

Katherine had sensed them coming and why. At the entrance, she called out a greeting as the horses pulled up, filled with happiness to see her beloved Daphne.

As Daphne came around to hug her, Katherine kissed both her cheeks then held Daphne's face between her hands, exclaiming, "Look at you! A beautiful, formidable, intelligent woman. You do my heart proud, Daphne, my love."

"Thank you, Abbess. I have tried to be what you laid out as expectations of me," replied Daphne as she laid her hands over the abbess's. "It is wonderful to see you, Abbess. It has been too long."

"Indeed, child, it has," Katherine responded. She looked to Dante and Daphne. "Come, let us go in, I have cider and scones waiting for us."

Once seated in the study, refreshments enjoyed, Katherine looked to Dante. Her face neutral, she asked, "Please share to what I owe the pleasure of your visit?"

Dante looked to Daphne; she nodded.

"The Guardian of Isaiah," Dante said with obvious irritation.

"Malachi?" asked Katherine, wanting to be sure.

"Yes. He and Daphne seem to be developing an affinity for one another," Dante replied. "I do respect Daphne's ability to decide on her own behalf."

Dante glanced at Daphne, then turned his gaze back onto Katherine and explained himself. "I believe you can better explain the potential complexities of such a relationship better than I could, and with less emotional investment."

"Ah, I see," said the abbess, her wimple bobbing as she nodded her head. "There are indeed many complexities here, and I shall be frank," she paused, "one of the largest being that Daphne is mortal, and Malachi is not."

Katherine turned her intense topaz gaze to Daphne. "Malachi is not a gentle soul. He has played a part and been witness to bloodshed, war, atrocities, and treachery.

"He is loyal. He does not sway from duty, no matter how it pains him. And, believe me, his loyalty and sense of duty cause him pain. He feels much maligned by Celestia, yet knows no other way than to support that order in our universe, as we know it. I am confident he would never betray Celestia or Earth for the Seraph, or any other faction."

Fascinated by her beloved Abbess, Daphne listened, then said, "I know you are immortal, a Guardian as well, and a fierce warrior."

Dante remained quiet, listening.

Katherine replied, "Yes, that is true. But we are not here to talk about me. You need to have your eyes and heart wide open to the understanding that any road with Malachi will not be an easy road, Daphne. You need to decide if the scales balance the joy you would have at his side, against the inescapable angst you also would have.

"I cannot presume to understand the greater machinations at work here, what Fate has in store. I will not interfere. The decision must be yours and yours alone, my dear Daphne," Katherine said, laying the decision at Daphne's feet.

Katherine stood and walked to the cold, dark hearth. She kept her back to them a moment, then turned. Her expression somber, her eyes compelling in their lioness golden topaz, other forces at work in her contemplation. "I will share that Malachi also came to me for counsel. I said the same to him which I am saying to both of you." She looked at Daphne, then to Dante. "I have decided not to interfere."

Dante, turning his hat in hand, nodded pensively.

Daphne and Dante left in melancholy silence, their ride back one of mutual introspective quiet, each lost in their own thoughts.

Back at the homestead, Dante sent the wagon and horses with one of the footmen. He turned to Daphne. It seemed a great canyon stretched between them. The bleak and awkward silence hung like a cold rain between them, which neither knew how to banish. Dante cleared his throat and said, "May I suggest you freshen up, have a bit of refreshment, then let us get back to work."

Daphne's heart broke a little with the uncertainty which burned in Dante's eyes. "Yes, that is a good idea, Dante."

Before she could leave, her thoughts again dragged her away. The Daphne that left this morning for the abbey was a different Daphne than who returned. The realization that she may have a great responsibility with Malachi's heart weighed upon her. She did not desire to add one more disappointment, insult to him. In her eyes, he had a lethal strength and ferocity about him, she also saw his heart as vulnerable and the most fragile of glass.

She continued to stare off into space.

"Daphne, did you hear me?" Dante asked.

Daphne shook herself out of her haze, blinking, and shifted her gaze to her mentor. "Yes. My apologies. Yes, I did," she replied. Sighing, she moved toward the house. "Refreshment and work sound like the best order for this day, Dante. I shall meet you in the annex soon."

She turned to walk to the house, the wind tossed her loose tendrils of chestnut hair, her aquamarine beads sparkled in the early afternoon sun. Great, yawning sadness filled Dante, as Daphne seemed to have the weight of the world on her shoulders.

Work! Yes, work, intellectual challenge shall get this day moving the right direction and ease our gloom, she thought to herself, determined to shake off the melancholy.

Unease filled Daphne when she entered her bedroom and Esther's rheumy gaze moved over her. Esther was up to no good; Daphne knew it in her bones.

The world about Daphne now appeared in different colors and facets than before visiting with the abbess this morning. Something inside her had changed… a new awareness. Everything appeared, smelled, and sounded different. The old souls of the house whispered their secrets to her. The floorboards showed her the grand oaks they once were, and she wanted to weep. They comforted her with their shared enjoyment of being part of the house and near Isaiah. Exotic spices from far-away lands floated past her in the breeze. With conscious thought, she tamped, controlled the noise and the cacophony of sights, sensations, scents, and sounds.

Esther blinked and lifted her hands to her heart as Daphne read her cold, black soul. Daphne sent her a stern warning to watch her step. Esther's eyes widened, then she curtsied and left, leaving a chill draft in her wake.

Daphne let her newfound power course through her. She was sure Katherine had unlocked this for her, but she pondered over why. Her mind sifted through all sorts of possibilities, then she let it go as she remembered the Abbess's words: *I cannot presume to understand the greater machinations at work here, what Fate has in store. I will not interfere.*

She washed the dust off her face and neck, which helped her to feel much like her old self; the melancholy also scrubbed away. Her quick lunch of apples and cheese tasted of heaven, the earth, and sun—perfect. A new world opened for her, one she embraced while she walked to the annex, a world where she found she could control how much or how little she would hear, see, touch, smell.

The beloved aromas of her and Dante's alchemical ventures washed over her as she pushed open the annex door.

Bemused, Dante watched her float about as she worked, almost glowing. Something had slotted into place within her. He was not about to question it, as that was part and parcel of the mystical elements of alchemy. Instead, he enjoyed being witness to a transformation.

An hour into work, all hints of heaviness dissipated. Pursuit of knowledge and working together brought them both great satisfaction.

Companionable silence soon filled the annex.

"By Jove, it worked!" Dante called out.

Daphne jumped, almost dropping her glass flask partially filled with a measure of hydrochloric acid upon Dante's exclamation.

Excited for him, she set the flask down, hurried over, and looked. She jumped for joy for him. "The slurry!" she called out, celebrating. "You were able to keep the ingredients combined for your wound salve."

"Yes! Yes, Daphne, yes."

She hugged him, his treasured, unique scent filling her.

The door opened, the bell jingled, and Malachi stepped in. His battle-hardened presence filled the room. "Greetings, my friends. I decided as Guardian, I should check on what you two are cooking up."

Daphne's eyes flashed to Dante, her heart in her throat, awaiting his reaction.

"Malachi! I have just made a huge advancement in a salve I have been working on. Come see," Dante said, calling him over.

Relief moved through Daphne in waves. "Hello, Malachi," she greeted him.

Malachi moved more into her view as he made his way to Dante. She had a sudden, strong vision of mystical ravens swirling about his head as he fought a fierce battle. They blended into his raven black hair, giving him their stealth, fortitude, and acumen to augment his own as sweat and blood sprayed around him as his sword clashed. The ravens sent by Hades. Hades? The mythological Greek god? She closed her eyes, turned back to her work, and pondered it away to contemplate at a later time.

"Malachi, what say you we enjoy a walk after I journal tonight?" Daphne asked, compelled to do so but not sure why.

A smile warmed his obsidian eyes. "I would be pleased to join you for a walk in the beautiful night, Miss Heatherton," he replied.

Her belly did a flip, his deep voice like warm honey to her. She could not help but let her artful woman's smile tip the corners of her mouth.

Her smile was not lost on Malachi.

A blush rose to her cheeks. She huffed and turned back to her distillation project, the liquids bubbling away and precious drops collected from the ends of long, twisting tubes.

CHAPTER FIFTEEN

Evening, Wednesday, June 1, 1622 CE
The Annex, York, England

With haunting, forlorn calls, the mystical owl made her presence known. Malachi strolled with Daphne along the stream as they discussed the recent discoveries she had read of in the healing arts.

Malachi shared with Daphne of the many methods he had seen come full circle over the millennia, and how it appeared humankind was on the cusp of several discoveries which would advance alchemy, astronomy, and medicine by a significant amount.

A mournful shudder rippled through her. Daphne paused, then whispered, "I would love to study medicine at Oxford, or anywhere." Tears welled in her eyes, appearing in the moonlight as flawless crystals. "Even though I know I am more learned and astute than most men, I cannot because I am a woman," she said, wiping the angry tears away with a trembling hand.

"It is such a bitter pill to swallow. If I voice my objections or press my case, Dante and the abbess fear I will bring unwanted attention to myself. And I risk accusations of witchcraft by men who would use those means to be rid of me." Daphne took a shaky breath. She stared out over the moving brook, its ripples reflecting the moonlight. "My apologies for my melancholy, Malachi." She saw that he, too, stared out over the brook. It seemed the two of them searched for answers in the dark of the glade. "I should not have gone on," she said as a tremulous smile crossed her face.

Malachi took her hand and clasped it, imparting comfort. "It is not right that such is the way of things, Daphne. I admire your intelligence and skill," he said, then let go of her hand. "I have no doubt you would make an excellent physician." He searched her gaze, his own intensifying. "I fear that Dante and Katherine are correct, and it would be best you do not press the issue.

"I can relate to how all of this has affected you." The night breeze lifted his hair as he spoke, evoking images of the dark raven—solemn, contemplative, and fierce. "In my long life as a warrior angel, the Celestials have never accepted me. All despite being one of their most feared and effective warriors, respected by legions upon legions." He turned away, his inability to speak further thunderous.

Night air, thick with his palpable pain and humiliation, swirled about Daphne. Her heart broke.

"Celestia cast me from the heavens, barred from ever returning. Not a disciplinary decision, or so they told me. The expectation remained for me to perform, lead, and sacrifice without question," Malachi explained while hot indignity rode the burning wave of his admission. He curled his hands into fists and continued, "I am not unsullied enough to be around them. Yet, I am to fight for them; be placed in peril." He turned to her.

"And lead others to their death for them." His bitter words and angst hung in the air.

Isaiah murmured, the tree's deep tones mixed with the bubbling of the brook.

Daphne marveled she did not hear the resonance of the oak a few days ago and could now recognize it plain as day. Her heart ached for the tormented, courageous warrior before her. A wolf howled in the distance.

Malachi levitated a flat stone from the ground to his hand. Between his clenched teeth, his face pulled back in a grimace, he ground out, "Sanctimonious bastards!" He hurled the stone, fierce, efficient, and graceful in his movements as tension released from his body. The fluid motion was breathtaking for Daphne to witness. The stone skipped down the brook, seeming to her to go on forever, hearing eons of delicate taps on the water.

Daphne stepped over to him and grasped his hand. She spun him to her and laid her other hand upon his cheek. Her gray eyes searched his stormy, dark eyes. "You do know of what I speak. Of the hardship of falling in step with the expectations of those around you," she said while she stroked her thumb along his cheekbone. "I do so out of fear and respect to Dante and Katherine. You do so out of obligation and a sense of honor and have done so far longer than I can even imagine."

Malachi raised his calloused hand to cover hers, dipped his head, and captured her lips in a tender kiss suffused with admiration, warmth, and respect.

Daphne, inexperienced but not naïve, knew this was different. She sensed their time was limited. She human, he Immortal. Fate would not smile upon their union.

A vortex of emotions roiled through her. His kiss sublime, he tasted of the forest and the stars. His warrior's resilience and intrepid strength attracted her like a moth to the light. This kiss, this moment needed to go on forever. She made a conscious choice at that moment to know and revel in everything with him, about him.

As the evening breeze played at her skirts and his hair, she stepped to align her body with his, pressing herself against him, both of her hands now on either side of his face. His eyes searched hers, as she plumbed the depths of his. Reverence, regard, embers of passion reflected in his gaze.

The owl called as her thoughts coalesced into sentences. The elements of night beckoned to her soul. Her tone and words, sure, yet soft, washed over him while she searched his face as she spoke, "I want to know all of you tonight, Malachi. I desire you to know all of me." She pulled his head down to hers, pressed her lips to his. Her tongue slid between his lips; she sighed into his mouth as she savored his essence, something she craved in the short time she had known him. Her tongue parried with his, shifting into a timeless dance. His woodsy scent surrounded her as he became her world.

Malachi's heart skipped and stomach flipped as comprehension dawned. Passion's heat flowed through him. He tore his lips from her kiss and tamped his surging lust, kissed the top of her head and lay his cheek against her forehead. Her beloved, unique fragrance of rosemary, lavender, and molten metal drifted about, imbuing for him the aromas of the nighttime glen. Awash in wonderment of the openness and trust this incredible, strong, and brilliant woman showed him, he imprinted this moment in his heart to stay with him into eternity. Her acceptance and admiration moved mountains in his soul. Bitterness carried within him for centuries crumbled.

"Daphne, are you confident?" he asked. He knew the answer, he could feel her assent, but part of him had to hear her say this out loud.

She ducked out from under his chin and looked up into his eyes. "I have never been surer of anything in my existence, Malachi," she said, sincere and confident.

Unshed tears burned in his eyes.

Daphne watched with fascination as a tear escaped, glinting in the moonlight, traversing over the crow's feet about his eye, to his sun-burnished cheek. She lifted a fingertip to the drop, lifted it from his cheek, placed the crystalline angel's tear on her lips. Her tongue flicked, pilfering the precious bead.

He groaned, crushed his lips to hers, swept her mouth open with his tongue, leaving no part of her soft, warm open mouth untasted.

Daphne's knees buckled with burgeoning wanton desire. Malachi caught her weight, his kiss deepened, her hum of pleasure fanned his carnal fire.

She tugged his lower lip into her mouth, Daphne feasted on his warrior's essence and nipped his tender skin. He groaned as he dragged her hips hard onto him, ground her over his erection, then chuckled into her mouth, saying, "You know very well what you are about, my sweet. Hell-bent on us enjoying each other to the fullest."

Low and deep, he growled as he delved into the warm crook of her neck. Her answering shudder of delight sent him careening into burning desire.

"Malachi, yes!" She shoved her fingers into his hair and pushed his head over her chest to an aching breast. She arched her back and offered herself up to him.

"Everything about you is passion and elemental beauty, my love, everything," he murmured, reverent. Slipping his hand inside the neckline of her dress, he pinched her nipple between his battle calloused thumb and forefinger and rolled it, as he tugged the neckline of her dress down with his teeth, his primal growl of passion baptizing her carnal hunger.

About her bowed waist he held her firm with his other arm, bared both breasts to the moonlight and drew her nipple and areola into his hot mouth, suckling, while he tugged on the other swollen berry.

Molten sensual heat erupted deep in her belly, she bucked her hips, groaning out loud as her hips lifted again in a timeless invitation.

"By Isis, you taste of the sun and heaven, Daphne," he whispered around her swelling breast.

Pure adoration burned in his gaze, as he took in her voluptuous arousal.

Eyes half-open in her haze of desire, she watched his heated, carnal gaze traverse over her. His raven black hair fell forward onto her chest, Isaiah watched over them, his branches silhouetted by the moonlight. She closed her eyes and seared this memory into her brain.

"I don't think I will ever taste enough, get enough of you, Daphne, my love," said Malachi, emotion deepening his words to her.

After setting a tender kiss upon her plumped breast, Malachi helped her to stand up straight. "It is too beautiful a night for us not to make it part of us coming together." His deep, silky whisper washed over her, adding to the lushness of the moment.

Shucking his black leather overcoat, he spread it over the soft ground, the scent of leather mingling with the night breeze and further stoking the hot embers of her desire.

The sight of Malachi's honed, broad, and strong warrior's body moving as he prepared a bed for them, fanned her woman's lust and wonderment. She thought herself the most cherished woman in the world.

With admiration, she witnessed the skill and ease with which he set cloaking wards about them to screen them from prying preternatural or human eyes. Malachi's ethereal power domed about them. A smile of anticipation tugged at the corners of her lips, to enjoy this powerful man she loved.

Once done casting his spell, Malachi turned to her.

Her breath held as his gaze, heated with desire, burned a trail of passion over her. Pure predatory male satisfaction imbued his face as his eyes burned over her exposed breasts.

Daphne shuddered then gasped as lust flared in her womb and nether lips under the masculine heat in his obsidian gaze. His dark eyes lifted to hers, Malachi held out his hand, she placed hers in his, then stepped over to where he had lain his cloak. He turned her around. She hitched in a breath of anticipation of his fervor and touch, molten desire flowing again to her feminine sex.

Malachi's strong arms reached around from behind her and down to the laces of her velvet bodice; his warm firm lips teased her neck sliding down to her shoulder. Her head fell back upon his shoulder with an indulgent, sensuous sigh escaping from her swollen lips.

With a growling low chuckle in her ear, his dexterous fingers grappled with the loosed laces of her bodice, then he spread the front plackets apart, his broad hands brushing along her chest and belly. For Daphne, this evoked images of his eventual spreading of her nectar-laden femininity. Flames of aching want leapt deep within her.

The lower edge of her bodice held in his firm grip, he tugged it up and over her head as she lifted her arms.

Daphne's heartbeat whooshed in her ears, her nether lips pulsed and a core of heat bloomed. After he set the bodice aside, she felt his hands land at the small of her back, where her skirt laced together. She groaned with need as he tugged her skirt down over her hips, anticipation of being undressed for Malachi bringing her arousal to flow like molten lava from her core out. Impatience to be rid of her clothes heightened her desire. She wriggled her hips to hasten the shedding of her skirt.

Malachi chuckled against her derriere. Daphne groaned. He leaned over, his shoulder brushing the back of her legs while he unlaced her boots. Sensual lightning flowed up her leg, through her body where his shoulder brushed hers.

Malachi shifted behind her to stand, then grasped the hem of her shift.

Her stomach did a flip and heat rushed to curl deep within her belly, when cool air moved over her thighs and stomach as he lifted the muslin fabric. Embers of yearning leapt; flames of hunger licked at her femininity. Unfamiliar, yet sublime tension pulled at her threads of desire.

She turned and looked down over her shoulder at the male behind her, the man about to become her lover. Her heated gaze moving over his raven's hair, high cheekbones, broad shoulders, muscular arms as he folded her skirt. Her gaze caught his, his soul in his dark eyes. She could not tear her gray gaze from his, enthralled.

He could not draw a breath, entranced by the vibrant, brilliant, undressed, self-assured woman standing before him. Her gaze over her shoulder evoked images of the marble statue of Aphrodite in her temple, and Aphrodite herself. Daphne's clear, gray gaze held no doubt, only burning desire. He found himself humbled in her presence and by her inner strength, femininity. Her lips tilted at the corners up in the age-old beguiling smile of women who knew they held a man's heart. The cold hard, cynicism about his soul crumbled.

There were no words between them, a strong connection flowed between them, as sure as the air she breathed.

Sensual, elemental sexuality smoldered in her gray eyes and evoked a surge of predatory fervor through his core. Between his hands, he clasped her jaw, kissed Daphne hard and deep, leaving no corner of her mouth untouched. Her knees buckled as she groaned into his mouth. Her hands and fingers splayed over his powerful biceps. Behind her knees he hooked his arm and lowered her down upon his cloak.

Her eyes half-closed with the haze of passion, she lifted her hips in invitation. He bent and kissed her palm, nipping the middle. She hissed in a breath, lifting her hips again with a mewl of need. Malachi smiled against her palm, her beauty beyond anything he had before witnessed. He let go of her hand, whispering, "A moment, my Love."

Malachi made quick work of shedding his leather armor and clothing, then laid down next to Daphne, his gaze focused on hers, a searing smoky gray which moved him heart, mind, and soul.

Propped on his elbow, he leaned over her. Malachi planted a kiss on Daphne's smooth, bare shoulder, then brought his mouth to hers, savoring the sweetness of her lips. Rosemary, lavender, and molten silver mingled to greet him. Evening breezes caressed them both as the brook ran alongside, providing harmony to the melody of the creatures of the night.

Malachi growled as he lifted his head from her sensuous kiss. His gaze moved over the length of her body, every curve, every dimple. He found himself afraid to peer too close at this moment; it seemed of beautiful, gossamer glass that might shatter into a thousand shards were he to handle it too much.

Fascinated by the subtle play of expressions across his face and light in Malachi's eyes, Daphne could not take her eyes off his visage. As his hand stroked over the planes of her body, light shifted in his dark eyes, the set of his stern mouth softened, all reminding her of rolling clouds in a storm-ridden sky. With him, she found a deep level of comfort, contentment yet sensual tension.

To Daphne it seemed she had stolen a slice of paradise, she was not about to let it go.

Her elemental voices whispered this time had an end. She

decided whatever lay on the other side would be worth grasping this moment with her warrior angel. With that she lifted her arms, wrapped her hands over his shoulders, and pulled Malachi down to her full-lipped kiss, her eyes looking into his dark, hardened soul and rejoicing in the light she saw breaking through chinks in his armor.

His shoulders blocked her breasts from the moonlight as he leaned down to return Daphne's fevered kiss, holding his weight away from her.

A hum of pleasure escaped from Daphne, she bent her leg at the knee and let it fall out to the side in an age-old invitation. He swept his hand down the length of her, Malachi parted her nether lips and ran his fingertips along the silky, slick edges. Daphne gasped then lifted her hips and mewled in need. In his carnal answer, he eased two fingers inside her channel. He watched her face, pleased to see her eyes widen then blink at the sensation of his fingers swirling about in her hot, pulsing core. Even if he tried, he would not have been able to stop the smile which stole into his lips, "Daphne," his deep whisper caressed her ear, "this moment shall be forever burned into my soul, my mind.

"Everything about you is beyond heaven," he said as he lowered his head, slanted his lips over hers, savoring her kiss. She ground against his hand, purred into his mouth, "Dear Isis," he rumbled against her cheek.

His deep voice reverberated through her chest, heightening all the sensations he evoked. She lifted her hands to his shoulders, as she clenched her silky canal about his fingers, keening.

"Patience, Daphne. Enjoy, savor," he admonished, with love, as he brushed his kiss down her cheek to the crook of her neck, nipping and tasting her essence. Restless, she lifted under him, as she clenched her nether muscles about his fingers.

Malachi smiled against her neck, relishing the sensual creature within her. A fervent wish this moment could go on forever lit a candle in his soul. He inhaled her precious essence as he journeyed his lips to the rise of her breast, swirling his tongue just before he reached the dusky rose areola.

Desperate to have her nipple in Malachi's hot, knowing mouth, Daphne keened, arching her back, while she shifted again to bring his surging fingers deeper into her feminine core.

With adoring mercy, he laved attention on one breast then the other.

The cool night air edging over her silky folds heightened the wondrous sensations he evoked. Daphne bucked against his fingers, her ache, need deep and hot as she teetered at the precipice, knowing she would plummet over the edge at any moment.

His cock jumped as his eyes swept over the sheen of perspiration over her body, rivulets, glistening like diamonds, beading between her breasts.

Heat coalesced into a tidal wave of sensation. Her feet tightened, her toes curled, then her vortex spun out. Waves of physical and emotional sensation crashed through Daphne as her body peaked. She found her breath difficult to catch, as aching, carnal pleasure coursed and pulsed through her.

"Yes, Love, yes," Malachi rumbled low and soft in her ear, almost a purr as he watched her back arch and a flush spread over her body.

Daphne willed Malachi to look at her. He lifted his head, her gaze holding his as her orgasm coursed through her.

Malachi nudged her knees apart with his own, his eyes peering into her soul, capturing her every emotion and reaction. He settled between her legs and smiled as the weight of her heels rested on the backs of his thighs. His weight rested on his elbow and brought his hands to her face. With his thumbs he stroked her hair above her ears. Poised at her entrance, her heat filtering over the tip of his hard, hot shaft. He looked into her soul through her gray eyes as he entered her and thought to himself that he had never seen anything as beautiful.

Her world was him, only Malachi, her gaze pulled into his hypnotic, obsidian eyes. Passion and restrained savagery danced about in his deep, glittering gaze. Her core stretched to accommodate him, the sensation at once strange and right. He plunged, buried to the hilt. She tightened herself about his width and laughed as his hiss moved over the shell of her ear. She took his length more deeply into her with a shift of her undulating hips. Daphne thought she could drown in his worshipful eyes, while he held her in his arms.

"Hmm, you enthrall me, Daphne, my love," Malachi said, then he moved his mouth over hers and swept her mouth with his tongue as he pulled back then fully surged into her. Retreating, he surged again, setting a rhythm. All the times he had been intimate with a woman, none were as wondrous, as with Daphne. He found the keeper of his heart, the soul mate he never thought existed for him. Heated desire centered in his loins, he quickened the pace, driven by his carnal need.

Daphne gazed upon him with smoky, sultry passion as his pace and intensity increased.

He grunted as she grasped his cock with her muscles as he retreated, she tightened again as he surged. Malachi dropped his head and dug his teeth into her shoulder, pounding hard and fast, his back arching up.

Through the slick perspiration covering his back she dragged her fingers, savoring his masculinity, Malachi's intensity stoked her own.

A haze of carnal heat billowed as he surged. Her woman's core gripped about him as his girth increased.

Daphne's head fell back, her chest arched up to him. She rode the wave while he drove into her one last time, hard and deep. He threw his own head back, his Adam's apple a blatant reminder to her of his overt masculinity.

He lifted himself over her flushed body, extending his arms. The dam broke in his release. He growled low and deep, his triceps bulging. Beads of sweat trickled down his sloped back as he plowed one last stroke into this sensual, giving woman.

Clenched about him, she held his cock tight within her, a sensual enchantress, reveling in the spell she had cast over her warrior angel. She floated down from a haze of desire, giving a languid stretch. Perspiration had pooled between her breasts, beautiful drops of passion.

Malachi sensed his heart rate decreasing. He dropped his head to her shoulder, nipping her skin, imbibing her salt, growling low and possessive as he did so, her essence surrounding him, in every way possible.

He aligned his lips to her ear. "I could stay here forever with you."

Her heart skipped a beat as his words sank in.

Malachi traced her jawline with a kiss which he skimmed to her lips, ran his thumbs over her cheekbones. Shifting his weight onto his forearms, he laid his head in the soft hollow just beneath her collarbone. He closed his eyes, indulging in their sensual haven.

In the afterglow, she basked and floated, relishing this state she did not know existed, until now. She skimmed her fingers along his muscular back. Under her fingertips she discovered rough skin arched above his shoulder blades. It came to light this could be from where his wings emerged. Fascinated, she walked her fingers along the patch of rough skin on either side of his back, found the path taking her fingers between his shoulder blades. She glanced down at his profile, noting that he seemed to remain relaxed, his face smooth. Along the curve of his shoulder blades, she paid more attention to texture, attempting to understand how his wings hid and how they emerged. She stole another look at Malachi's expression and had to keep a laugh from bubbling up at Malachi's raised brow and the uplifted corners of his lips.

She stayed her course, slowing, even more, to take in each bump and ridge into account. Malachi was not lodging any protests at her exploration. Indeed, he seemed to enjoy it.

Never having had allowed someone to touch his wing ingresses prior, Malachi surprised himself by allowing Daphne to have free rein.

Isaiah gave a low warning of time passing into night. The owl called; her cautionary word added to that of the ancient oak's.

Malachi kissed Daphne's collarbone, reluctant to move, reluctant to end their intimate time together. "My love, it is time for us to return to the world outside."

With feminine resplendence, she lifted her arms and stretched like a sensuous cat, then kissed his cheek. "I suppose we must, my warrior." She smiled against his hair and groaned with loving regret as he slid from inside her.

Malachi stood; she placed her hand in his and he helped her up. Solicitous, he retrieved her shift for her. Her lack of shyness as she lifted her arms to let him slide the soft muslin down over her nude body brought him marvel and wonder.

Daphne stood with her back to Malachi. She smiled as she felt him tug the ribbons as he laced up her skirt.

He found himself relieved she could not see the grin of pure joy on his face at doing so. These emotions were foreign to him, he found himself hesitant to reveal all to her that which he was not quite sure he could yet reveal to his cynical self. He kissed the back of her neck as he gave one final firm tug to her skirt laces and his heart skipped a beat as a lilt of laughter escaped from her upon his playful tug.

Daphne turned to face her warrior angel. Her eyes moved with deep appreciation over him, relishing all of him—his reason, care, mordant nature, sharp wit, and preternatural qualities. Their time together proved to be wondrous to her—passionate, yet imbued with respect and love. She did not feel in the least self-conscious, but admired, desired, cherished.

She stepped to him, lifting her hands, pulled his head down to bring his lips to hers, her fingers playing in his raven dark hair at the back of his head. "Thank you, Malachi, my warrior, for a night from heaven."

The crickets and the brook filled the silence while he watched her walk back to the house.

With a tug of drapes back into place, Esther backed from Daphne's bedroom window and readied to help Daphne prepare for bed. Suspicion rose within her; sure a cloaking spell hid their activities. She could not see either for quite some time and doubted Daphne would stray far from the house.

The wistful, satisfied expression on Daphne's face combined with her womanly walk gave Esther a strong sign Daphne and Malachi had enjoyed intimacy. She rejoiced, knowing the more Malachi and Daphne entwined, the more pain Gideon and Tobias would bring to Malachi.

Daphne may prove a convenient Achilles Heel for the guardian.

Daphne let herself into the house, humming, closed the door behind her with a soft click. She trod with light footfalls up the steps to her room. Distracted as Esther helped her ready for bed, she collapsed into her bed, a deep sleep soon overtaking her. Her sense of being well-loved ribboned through her thoughts, heart, and dreams.

Malachi went to his quarters he had built in the glen, hidden from prying eyes by his wards. He set the wards he used for respite about Isaiah and also placed wards about Daphne. His brow wrinkled upon picking up a dark edge near her. The more he scrutinized it, the more it retreated, disappeared. He searched again for it, finding nothing. Concern pecking at him, he set another layer of wards about Daphne. Satisfied he had established more than adequate protection about Daphne and Isaiah, he fell into a peaceful sleep, rare for him.

CHAPTER SIXTEEN

Thursday, June 2, 1622 CE
Outskirts and Town, York, England

IN THE COOL, early hours of the morn, fog slithered about Esther's form while she made haste to the Baker's. The mouth-watering aroma of fresh baking bread became more pungent as she drew closer to the bakery. More appetizing to her was the news she had to share with the baker. The time to strike drew upon them. Esther relished her part in the machinations to destroy the oak and Malachi.

The bell suspended from a bracket at the top of the door gave a merry jingle as she stepped into the bakery with her dark plans. Esther almost always had a hard time holding back a laugh at the cheery sound of the bell, knowing the baker was part of The Seraph.

With hurried glee she made her way back to the ovens, the kitchen quite warm after the cool of the morning air. Baker looked up from sliding fresh loaves off wide wooden paddles onto cooling racks. An eyebrow arched beneath the band of his floppy white hat. "Good morn, Mistress Esther. You appear as though you are most anxious to share news."

Esther, bubbling with joy, stepped close to the wide wooden table laden with warm loaves, then closer to the baker. She said, "I have strong reason to believe Malachi and Daphne had biblical relations last eve. Whether or not they actually did, the Guardian is more than enamored with Daphne, thus quite distracted. I believe now is an optimal time to set our plan into motion."

The baker smiled and said, "The Seraph appreciate your diligence, Esther. You are indeed earning your place of honor amongst them once York is overtaken and the oak gone. I shall make Vicar Matthews aware of your observations. Believe me, you will know when we set the plans into motion."

"I shall wrap fresh bread for you. Dante's Cook will appreciate your early morning journey. Still-warm bread with breakfast this morning would be most delicious, hmm?" A conspiratorial expression and tone gave his words a dark twist.

Esther smiled and agreed. "Baker, indeed, you are quite thoughtful." A dark edge curled about her words.

Headed back to Dante's home with her aromatic package, Esther looked forward to seeing life unravel for Dante, Daphne, and Malachi.

CHAPTER SEVENTEEN

Monday, June 6, 1622 CE ~ York, England

WITH A SLY LOOK out the window, Tobias turned and set his teacup down upon the matching saucer on the mantle and said, "I think we will have plans for a fine trap for the Guardian and the Oak, Gideon. Encouragement of fear in the town Elders of that female chit alchemist practicing witchcraft is a stroke of brilliance. It will not be in the least bit difficult to spark the rumor and fan the fires, Gideon."

With an evil hiss of a laugh, Gideon nodded. "When she is arrested to be tried as a witch, we will have created a great distraction for Malachi. A sublime opportunity to move in for the kill.

"Let us consider that Daphne could be of great use to our movement, Tobias, if there is a way to spare her. But her death would also bring insurmountable heartbreak to Malachi," he said with certain joy.

Gideon continued, "We shall see how this plays out. The oak will die for certain. Daphne Heatherton's fate has yet to be determined." He nodded with self-affirmation and steepled his fingers. "Imprison her as a witch. If we rescue her from a witch's trial, she may see us as saviors. Thus, advancing our opportunity to recruit her into the Seraph. If she perishes, it will break Malachi." He looked to Tobias Matthews with a hunter's gleam in his eye. "Either way, Tobias, we win this battle."

"I agree. When should we set our wheels in motion?" asked Vicar Matthews.

"The sooner the better, I believe at this point. You could send a note this afternoon requesting Northrop's and Coughton's presence tomorrow morning to discuss a 'matter of some importance'. The short time constraint will impart urgency," suggested Gideon.

"I am interested to see how Northrop and Coughton will start an investigation. If they will take it upon themselves or get others involved from the outset," Tobias voiced his thoughts out loud.

With a harsh tone and gaze, Gideon instructed, "Keep control of the situation, Tobias. Ensure that Northrup and Coughton begin the investigation on their own. Use discretion to avoid a mob - which could be messy and over which we would lack control. Keep me apprised.

"Also, strategize on how to keep Katherine in the dark as long as possible. Otherwise, she will do her damnedest to thwart all of this. It is dangerous to underestimate her and her prowess."

"Understood, Gideon. It will be as you say."

"Yes, Tobias, or there will be a heavy price exacted—from you," Gideon warned. A whirlwind of dark gray ash, reminiscent of the destruction of Sodom and Gomorrah, obscured his tall, Stygian form. A mere moment later, all traces of him and the ash disappeared. Tobias stared at the void where Gideon had stood, a fission of fear feathered about his soul. He needed to ensure that he remained in his good grace.

Sitting at his desk, Tobias penned letters to Northrop and Coughton, requesting their presence at eight o'clock on the morn or to inform him in short order if not able to make the appointment. He sent his footman post-haste to hand-deliver the letters.

The conundrum of Katherine gave some thought and he decided that his best course of action was to admonish Northrop and Coughton to be subtle in heating the embers of suspicion of Daphne Heatherton with the other Elders, as to not create a mob or town panic. Katherine, none-the-wiser, should stay put. He held hope she would catch wind of the happenings late into the game and swoop in too far behind to rescue Daphne Heatherton.

At eight o'clock in the morning, sharp, the vicar's house-keeper showed both Northrup and Coughton into his study. Seated at his desk, Matthews gestured with his hands to the two chairs opposite his massive oak desk. He steepled his fingers, appearing deep in thought, as he awaited both Elder alchemists being seated.

Once settled, they looked to him with anticipation.

"Gentlemen, thank you for coming on short notice. I have a matter of a delicate and confidential concern to discuss with you, to ask your counsel and to express my worry," Matthews said, springing his trap.

Hats in hand, they both nodded.

"You both are familiar with Daphne Heatherton, the apprentice to Dante Santorum, I am correct to assume?" he asked while he noted with inner satisfaction that a scowl crossed each gentleman's face upon the mention of Daphne. "It is blasphemous for a woman to be practicing the art and science of alchemy as she does!" Matthews exclaimed.

Both men nodded, a zealous glint of righteousness revealed in each of their gazes.

"As charitable as I am, I have looked the other way. Santorum is her mentor and he must see something of worth there." Tobias gave a dramatic pause. "Looked the other way... until now. I saw Ms. Heatherton at market last week. She was holding an apple, appropriate for a temptress. I bore witness to the apple multiplying into two in her hand. She paid the farmer's boy for two apples. No matter, she conjured an apple."

With dark fascination, they leaned toward him; both Northrup and Coughton gasped.

Coughton took the bait. "Conjured, you say, Vicar?" he asked.

"Yes," confirmed Matthews, with a solemn nod of his head and glee in his Seraph heart.

"You are certain the girl did not pick up two apples to start, Vicar? I am not doubting your word, I desire to ensure I heard you right," Coughton asked, while he shifted in his seat, squirming. "This is a serious charge with grave consequences."

"Of course, Coughton. I am not offended you are proceeding with caution, considering the nature and potential outcome of what we are discussing," Matthews cajoled him.

Northrup spoke, "She is of exceptional skill with the alchemical arts. How could a female be so without the assistance of a dark source? I have known of no other like her." Righteous zeal grew in his voice, his eyes coming alight, as he pointed a shaking finger heavenward.

"I agree, but we must stay with fact, Northrup and not conjecture," Tobias said while he worked to refrain from rubbing his hands in glee. This was going better than he had expected. Both men were playing right into his hand.

"I have also witnessed a wilted rosebush bring itself back to bloom under her touch," he added, hammering another nail into the coffin. Northrup and Coughton's eyes did not leave him as he spoke.

"I realize that we have not brought accusations such as these about in our fair city for quite some time. We have a responsibility to proceed with caution. We do not desire a mob effect, nor do we want to start mass-hysteria and have finger-pointing occurring between neighbors and townsfolk out of fear," said Matthews, with feigned concern.

Both Northrup and Coughton made intonations of hearty agreement.

"To that end, we must proceed with discretion, my good gentlemen."

Coughton cleared his throat, then asked, "What are your thoughts, Vicar, on how we should proceed?"

"I have pondered that myself. I welcome any strategy you may have, as this is a matter of some delicacy." He looked at both Northrop and Coughton as though he held them in the highest esteem, then continued, "Tell me what you think of informing the magistrate of our suspicions and paying an unannounced visit to Daphne and Dante? Place them under a line of expert questioning without a chance to prepare. Let us see how the unnatural female reacts to having her back up against a wall. I think we may have a solid case if she defends herself and Dante with means of magic, with reputable witnesses of learned men."

"That is a most excellent plan, Vicar. I believe that the three of us could agree on a few pointed questions," Coughton said with a tone of great self-importance.

His lips itching to curl into a grin of triumph, the vicar kept his expression and tone somber and sincere. "Our good man, Dante, may need to be freed from her spell."

"Yes," exclaimed Northrup. "How else would he be amenable to mentoring a female as he does and defend her acumen?"

The Vicar pulled a sheet of parchment from his desk and dipped his quill into the inkwell. "Let us put our list together of questions, while we are gathered, gentlemen, and this is all churning in our collective minds. No time like the present. We can always add additional thoughts as they make themselves known."

Both men tumbled the remainder of the way into Tobias's trap. Gideon would be pleased.

CHAPTER EIGHTEEN

Wednesday, June 8, 1622 CE ~ Outskirts of York, England

SURPRISED TO HEAR a knock at the door, Dante set down his iron tongs and crucible, then stripped off his padded gloves as he strode to the door. On the other side was Northrop and Coughton, attempting to appear as though they were not straining their necks to peer into the annex behind him.

"Hello, Coughton, Northrup," said Dante as his eyes searched both of theirs, at which point they could not meet his gaze. "How might I be of service to you fine gentleman?" he asked, his palms now sweaty about the padded gloves.

Northrup cleared his throat, took a deep breath. "Is Mistress Daphne available," he asked, his face turning a dull red, "that we may have a brief audience with her, Dante?"

"I shall go to the house to retrieve her from the library," Dante replied. He turned the padded gloves over in his hands and asked, "May I inquire as to what business you have to discuss with her?"

The silence stretched on. Dante cleared his throat and spoke. "Mistress Daphne and I collaborate. Anything you have to discuss with Daphne should involve me as well, my good friends."

He then stepped past the two men and peered at them, then directed, "Come to the house with me, gentlemen. I will have Cook bring you refreshments. Daphne and I can meet with you in the parlor."

Coughton and Northrup looked at each other, then Coughton replied, "We had hoped to speak alone with Mistress Daphne."

Dante replied, "Surely, you would understand that it would not be proper for me to allow Daphne to meet with you two gentlemen by herself." He paused and smiled, the corner of his mouth twitching a bit, then said, "While I realize you would not be improper with our fair Daphne, rumors do take on a life of their own. My house has a staff who gossip at times." Dante coughed, then went on. "I am sure you would agree it is for the best."

In his peripheral vision he spied Malachi giving him a stealthy nod from behind Isaiah. A measure of relief sifted through him. He forced a smile onto his face, his gaze still on his unwelcome visitors, interjecting before they protested his presence with Daphne. "Let me go find Daphne for you."

Dante stepped out of the annex. Northrup and Coughton, having to step back, pulled shut the annex door behind him. He realized his oven gloves were still in his hands. No matter, act natural, he coached himself.

In the library, he looked about. "Daphne," he whispered.

She looked up from the book of constellations and heavenly bodies. Her smile of greeting faltered; his urgent tone and worried gaze was apparent. "Dante, what is the matter?" Her pulse escalated at the fear emanating from him. She could sense something dark had entered the house—in addition to Esther.

Dante took her hands between his and dove into the goings-on with a clipped whisper. His words were spoken in rapid breaths, and his gaze was intent on hers as he imparted his perceived gravity of the situation. "Northrup and Coughton are here. They have asked to meet with you in private. Under the guise of propriety, I have refused a private meeting and did not allow them an opportunity to argue. We cannot put off meeting with them, as it will make whatever is going on worse." He squeezed her hand. "They are in the parlor. I have alerted Malachi, as I fear they will find reason to accuse you of practicing witchcraft."

Daphne's eyes widened with fear, then she blinked tears back. Her heart in her throat, she trembled as she grasped Dante's hands. "I fear Esther is part of all this."

"I am not sure what to do, but Malachi is aware something is afoot." He gave her a reassuring smile. "You and I play off each other well, we can use that to our advantage.

"Let us go. We should not keep them waiting any longer." He let go both her hands, grasped one, and set it upon the crook of his arm, giving her a pat of encouragement.

Daphne walked into a den of lions. With a regal lift to her head, she imparted a confidence she did not feel. Each predatory cretin, she greeted with a courteous dip of her head. "Hello, Mr. Northrup. Hello, Mr. Coughton." She turned and backed to the settee. The hungry lions sat in wingback chairs opposite to her, licking their chops. Dante stood at the cold hearth.

"Gentlemen, you said you had questions for Mistress Heatherton?"

Northrop looked to Coughton, then to Daphne. He had the appearance of someone who had a bitter beetle fly into his mouth and could not spit the distasteful creature out, despite trying. "Mistress Heatherton." He steepled his fingers then laid his hands on the armrests, appearing restless. "Well, yes," he paused, and shifted in his seat, looking to Coughton, again, who simply nodded his head. Irritation darkened Northrup's face. He flattened his expression and looked again to Daphne. "There are concerns you receive assistance from the darker ethereal realm."

Dante, who had been by the mantle, moved to stand next to Daphne, and asked, "Northrup, what are you implying?"

Coughton interjected, his tone petulant, "To be plain about it, Dante, the good Mistress Heatherton is in collusion with the devil. She is a witch."

Her hand to her throat, Daphne gasped. She opened and closed her mouth, unsure how to respond.

Dante, standing next to where she sat, put his hand down in front of her face, signaling her to be quiet. Fury poured off him in waves.

Daphne swore she saw the parlor pulse with his rage.

Silence reigned as Dante made it clear he thought Northrup and Coughton foolish.

Daphne gave thanks for his presence and righteous ire. Shock moved through her when he spoke, his normally affable tone cold and deadly.

"Pray tell, gentlemen, why would you come up with such a theory?"

Northrup gathered up the courage to speak. "She's an alchemist, and she is a woman."

"Yes. Daphne is an alchemist and a woman. What about it? Mary the Jewess was a woman and one of the first alchemists. Have you lost your minds?"

"She has you under a spell to make you desire to apprentice her," Northrup rushed out his words.

"What? Daphne has me under a spell?" he sputtered in his wrath. "This is the best you can come up with?"

From the hallway, Esther eavesdropped. Her lips curled in a

smile of malice, reminiscent of a shark. She concentrated on a porcelain decorative pitcher sitting on a side table and made it fly toward Northrop.

Coughton yelled, "Ho!" He jumped up and swung his arm out to stop the pitcher which halted in mid-air short of his arm. It hovered in place, then dropped, landing with an ominous clatter on the wooden floor. The pitcher split into several pieces, the largest one of which rocked on its curved back.

Daphne, in shock, stared at the broken pitcher.

"Witch!" Coughton cried out, with the fervor of a fire and brimstone preacher. He pointed a wretched, curved finger at Daphne. "Witch!"

His face red and dark eyes burning with fury, Dante looked to both Coughton and Northrup. "The girl is no witch! Your machinations to rid her are evil and misguided." Spittle flew from his mouth as righteous vehemence poured forth. "Your feeble souls shall regret this black treachery!" Dante heaved in a great breath, then shouted, "Get out of my house, now! Out!"

Ceramic knick-knacks on various shelves through the parlor rattled as Dante's furor thundered.

Coughton and Northrup looked at each other, then peered at Dante with confusion and terror in their eyes.

From the corner of her eye, Daphne caught the top left of Esther's forehead pulling back around a hall doorway. Anger and validation fountained from her. That's the cursed witch! The old crone Esther had made the pitcher fly! She knew this as sure her heart was pounding in her chest. She gazed with trepidation at the two idiots, she had once thought intelligent, staring at her with slack opened mouths. With a split-second decision to bring the crone back before her accusers, she dashed past them. As she had feared, they tried to stop her, attempting to grab at her dress, only to find their hands blocked by an invisible wall of sorts.

Malachi! Relief flew through Dante's mind as Coughton's and Northrop's grasping claws grabbed at the air, sensing he had stopped them.

Daphne ran into the hall, hurrying after Esther's skirts and apron ties rounding a corner. She sprinted, rounding the curve of the hall, and caught a gather of Esther's skirt in her fist, nausea rising as she touched the treasonous old woman. "Stop, witch!" Grasping at the shoulder of Esther's muslin shift with her other hand, she brought the old, gray woman around. The malevolence shooting from Esther's gaze, while expected, shocked her in its ferocity. Esther's teeth came as a rabid raccoon at her hand clasping the fabric of the old maid's dress at the shoulder.

Daphne wrenched Esther, throwing the vicious, bared teeth off their mark in the nick of time, then moved her hand down the struggling woman's shift-covered, bony arm.

Diabolical in her snarling and frothing at the mouth, Esther struggled to break free as Daphne hauled her toward the study. Esther flailed her boney elbows, hips, and knees, trying to break free.

Strands of Daphne's chestnut hair had come loose from her snood; perspiration dotted her forehead and hairline as she fought to propel the crone into the parlor.

Surprise rounded Northrup, Coughton, and Dante's eyes.

"Tell them! Tell them you threw the pitcher, old woman," Daphne ground out the words from between her clenched teeth as she shook the old woman from behind, her fists clenched in the back of the crone's dress.

Dante watched with fascinated horror as Esther rolled her eyes back in her head, screaming, a partial red handprint appearing on the crone's shoulder where the dress had pulled away. "Help me! Get me away from the witch. Her hands are burning me. Help! She is making me go mad," Esther cried, her voice shaking with distress. A subtle odor of burning flesh permeated the parlor.

Her teeth bared, Daphne shook Esther again, commanding her, "Tell them, you black-hearted bitch! Tell them!"

Esther moaned and appeared to have fainted, Daphne still holding onto the crone's shift and skirt as the old woman's body drooped from where Daphne held onto her.

Coughton and Northrup broke from their enthrallment of horror and extricated the old woman from Daphne's grasp, their gazes moving with concern over the crone and condemnation over Daphne.

Silent rage rose from Daphne as Esther opened her eyes, obscured from Coughton and Northrup, aiming a maleficent gleam of triumph at Daphne.

Sounds of the front door opening and closing filtered through the house. Relief filled Dante as Abbess Katherine entered the parlor. Katherine's quick, assessing gaze took in everyone, landing upon Coughton and Northrup carrying Esther to the settee.

Northrup looked up from the old maid. "Thank heavens you are here, Abbess! We have a most distressful situation," he said, relief in his voice.

Katherine moved forward to the old woman, her veil billowing, "Yes, I see, gentlemen, and Daphne. Dante, please get some cloths dampened with cool water for Esther."

"Daphne, child, are you unharmed?" asked the abbess while she looked with obvious concern to Daphne.

"Her?" bellowed Coughton. "Abbess, you are asking this one of evil-doing if she is unharmed? I rather think you should ask such of me, Northrup, and the old woman!"

Katherine stood at her full height and looked over both Coughton and Northrup as though they were misbehaving students and she were the schoolmistress. "I am concerned that you both have made a judgment of a serious charge with little fact. I had thought much more of the two of you."

"The pitcher! It flew!"

Abbess Katherine turned to where Coughton pointed, and the shattered pieces of the pitcher stared back at everyone.

A shrewd gleam moved into the abbess's eye. "Gentleman, you are alchemists of the esoteric philosophy. I know you use incantations to move objects and practice transmutation of materials. Do not believe for one minute I will hesitate to bring my concerns to the higher courts of York regarding the dark arts you practice to achieve your results."

Both Northrup and Coughton paled.

"How do you know, without a doubt, that it was Daphne who cast the pitcher?" She took the cold cloths from Dante, blessed them with the sign of the cross and a whispered prayer, then laid them upon Esther's forehead and arm.

Esther's eyes flew open and she howled in agony. The cloths flew from her person across the room, livid red rectangular marks left behind where they had laid. She sat up and growls like those of a cornered rabid dog poured from her. She laid baleful eyes on the abbess. Katherine stared upon the old woman with virulent disgust, as though she were a slug leaving a trail of mucous across the floor.

Esther's growls quieted as she rocked in place, humiliated, her plan rounding back to haunt her.

Daphne had witnessed the flows of energy as Katherine made incantations over the rags, heating them and caused the hot rags to fly off Esther. Quiet with her knowledge, she watched the scene unfold—thankful the abbess had taken matters into hand.

"Do you now believe that it was Daphne who threw the

pitcher, gentlemen?" The last word expelled from Katherine's mouth as though vomited.

Mouths opening and closing like fish out of water, feet shuffling, Northrup and Coughton glanced at Daphne then Abbess Katherine.

"Abbess, I think it best Coughton and I return to town."

With piercing topaz eyes, the abbess agreed, "That is a good idea and I suggest you act with discretion, gentlemen."

In the foyer, Dante swung open the heavy oak door with the bronze oak-shaped door knocker.

The two alchemists left without a backward glance, no further words uttered.

Discretely, Dante watched the hatted gentlemen make their way to their carriage. Coughton unhitched the horses, patting them as he did so. A rueful smile curved Dante's lips, witnessing the kindness Coughton showed. The jangle of harnesses and bridles sounded as the two alchemists made their way to the drive then drove away post-haste.

Dante spun on his heel and peered at Katherine, who stood next to the scowling Esther, her game found out. "What to do now, Katherine?"

A dark, predatory grin took over Katherine's expression. She bent over, grabbed the front of Esther's bodice, and shook her. "Who put you up to this, crone?"

Malachi strode in, glancing at Esther with contempt. "I smell Tobias all over the old woman."

"What shall we do with the treacherous bitch?" snapped Dante, his wrathful gaze moving between Katherine and Malachi.

His hands on his hips, Malachi blew out a troubled breath, his gaze somber. "I fear we have forced Tobias's hand. He has set inexorable wheels into motion, his or… Gideon's hand. In either case, they have forced ours. Tobias will not sit for long on what Northrup and Coughton will relay to him of their visit with us.

"Esther's fate will unfold without intervention on our part." His face hardened and his eyes glittered as he speared each one of the three with the fire in his gaze. "I fear Esther will be the least of our worries. We need to prepare for any eventuality." Malachi's piercing visage held them each prisoner as he let the gravity of the situation sink in.

He looked to Katherine. "I lay my sword that Gideon will expect you to be here, Sekhmet. He will launch an attack on the abbey soon to pull you away from here in a flurry."

Katherine gave a curt nod. "Aye, Angel. I agree. We need to remain one step ahead." Her abbess habit, rather than at odds with her strategy of battle, appeared as fierce as her visage. "As for Esther, we can secure her to the heavy desk chair until we see what unfolds."

"I concur."

"Dante and Daphne, let us speak of our collective resources and how to manage the next few days, as I sense they are critical."

With wide eyes Daphne, let out a shaky breath and sat down on an ottoman, the events of the past thirty minutes sinking into her thoughts and psyche.

"I will take the crone to the outhouse. I want no soul to empty her chamber pot."

Esther gave Katherine a baleful glare.

Katherine bent, grasped Esther's arm and the nape of her shift, and hauled her to a standing position. She dragged the old woman out of the room, to the glen outhouse.

Daphne stared after the duo. Relief replaced the tension in her face, her brow easing. She snatched her now cold tea and gulped it.

Dante gave a soft chuckle. "Here, girl, I have some courage in a bottle for you."

He poured a dram into the teacup she held in her hands. A rueful smile graced his face. "Quite the afternoon for you, Daphne. This is for sipping, not gulping."

Daphne lifted her brows, her eyes on his, and took it all back in one swig. "Ah." She closed her eyes as the warmth of the spirit moved through her. *Courage in a bottle, indeed,* she thought as her knees shook a bit less.

"That hit the spot, Dante," she said as she wiped her mouth with the back of her hand, feeling much less off-kilter. "A half dram more, if you please."

"Are you sure?"

She shot him a sharp look. "I would not have asked if I were not."

"Yes, of course." He poured a half finger more into the bottom of the fine bone china teacup. "My apologies, Daphne."

With blank parchment spread onto the desk and inking a pen, Malachi encouraged a swift and strategic plan. "Let us give some thought into handling whatever comes our way to our best advantage."

Daphne and Dante gathered about the desk.

Upon bringing Esther back from the outhouse, Katherine moved the chair to the hall outside the parlor, where they could watch the crone. Katherine ensured she would not overhear their plans, setting wards against sound.

Malachi and Katherine secured the snarling, wriggling Esther to the chair.

Back in the parlor, Malachi gave Daphne a long, searching look. He took her hand in his, interlacing their fingers, announcing, "We will return in short order," stealing her out of the parlor, past the baleful Esther. He dragged Daphne into the kitchen. His heavy, muscular arms about her, he hugged her to him, inhaling every fiber of her essence.

His deep shudder reverberated through her.

Daphne tilted her head back from his shoulder and peered into her warrior's visage. His eyes dark with fierce concern.

Malachi lifted his hands to either side of her face, pressed his mouth to hers then overtook her with his sweeping tongue. Her kiss, made of wildflowers, sweet mountain springs, and moonlight, could bring him to his knees. I cannot lose her! Not now! He ground his mouth against hers, as he dug his fingers into her hair through her snood.

Daphne sunk into Malachi's kiss, losing herself. She let all her weight rest on her solid and strong Malachi. He tasted of sandalwood and courage,

Daphne brought her hands to either cheek, holding him as he was holding her. Her world was only him—his strength, his angst, his carnal nature, his love for her.

Malachi encircled both of his warrior's hands about her wrists. Pulling away from the kiss, he planted his lips on each of her hands at the base of the thumb. The aquamarine beads in Daphne's snood shimmered, freckling reflected sunlight onto the wall and ceiling. The dots moved in an intricate dance, appearing as the constellations of the gods to Malachi.

He laid his forehead against her raised hands. "I would give my life for you." His husky whisper somber and heavy with emotion.

Daphne pulled their joined hands lower and grasped Malachi's shoulders. Her eyes searched his, "Malachi, I love you."

He captured her lips with his. Visceral emotion wrapped itself about his heart and gut, a warrior's love. The vulnerability she created in him was both heaven and hell.

From her waist to her derriere, he slid his hands and pulled her hard against him, a fervent wish filling him to bring her within him to protect her for all time. Bloody Zeus. If I ever lost her…

He broke their kiss, moving his mouth across her cheek to her ear, a heartfelt caress as he tasted her ethereal light. "Daphne," he breathed into her ear, his cheek against hers, the infinite depth of his devotion wrought in his low voice, "I love you as I have never loved another, place, time before, in all my centuries of existence." He paused, swallowed. A tear rolled down between their cheeks. He could not tell if it belonged to him or her. "If ever anything happens to you, I am not sure I would survive it. I am terrified of what we have and yet grateful to Fate for what we have together," he kissed her temple, then continued, his whisper falling across her ear, "All of my existence, I have moved forward without fear. I find I can no longer do such. Dread fills me that something will happen to you." He paused, again. "There will indeed be a time in my future when I will be without you, my love, as you are mortal. We shall cross that bridge when we come to it." He held her tight.

Daphne hugged Malachi to her, overcome, unable to speak.

Esther's heightened growls interrupted their reverie as she worked harder to strain against her ropes while Katherine tightened them.

Reluctant, they broke apart, each searching the other's soul with their gazes.

On the way back to the parlor Malachi noted with no small measure of satisfaction that Katherine had the crone well in hand.

The old woman, now foaming at the mouth, sat secured to the chair snarling as a wild animal.

Leaning close to Esther's ear, Katherine affected her lioness growl, her tone low and menacing, "When Gideon gets his claws on you, crone, I will not have one ounce of pity as he tears you to shreds for the unwise attention you brought onto yourself revealing these powers to mortals. Your pride got the better of you, old fool!"

With lightning speed, Esther stretched and turned her neck to get her mouth near the abbess. Snapping her vicious teeth at Katherine like a rheumy mongoose.

Standing upright, fierce determination in the grim set of her lips, the Sekhmet glowed through her lioness topaz eyes. Katherine tore two strips from her black habit veil. The sound of the fabric rending proved ear-splitting in the small space of the hall.

Malachi, Daphne, and Dante looked up from the desk, drawn by the sounds.

Katherine turned her battle-ready gaze onto them, a feral smile crossed her face as she made the strips taut in her hands.

Daphne gulped, then pushed aside the feathering tentacles of sympathy for Esther. She turned back to the desk, her eyes on the plans.

Katherine stuffed a wadded cloth into the crone's mouth, avoiding snapping teeth. She crooned as though she were feeding a baby. The predatory light in her eyes shone, as though she were a cat toying with prey, while she took delight in Esther's distress. With certain satisfaction, she drew a gag across Esther's mouth, giving a solid yank to tighten it before she tied it behind the gray tangled head of hair. She stepped back to admire her handiwork. The black swath created a disturbing parody of a smile across the crone's jaw. Katherine tapped her fingers on her chin, as if considering a purchase at the market. "Hmm, if I had my way, I'd take you to the borders of Elysium and let Chimera peck away at you a bit at a time."

The crone's eyes grew wide above the gag and she struggled harder against the restraints.

Katherine set more wards about the hallway to keep Gideon or Tobias from probing the crone's mind once Coughton and Northrup got to Tobias.

The crone sensed the dome forming over her and struggled with futility against her bindings.

Katherine tsked to Esther, shaking her head with feigned sympathy, a wicked glint in her eye. She imparted to Malachi what she had done to safeguard against further treachery from the trussed-up crone, then disappeared, her destination the abbey.

Malachi stared out the window, his eyes moving over the stalwart Isaiah with deference and respect. The ethereal fingers of Fate had wound themselves about Isaiah's trunk and branches, the oak's shudders imparted to Malachi.

CHAPTER NINETEEN

Thursday, June 9, 1622 CE ~ Outskirts of York, England

EVENING FELL. The creatures of the glade remained silent, sensing unrest. The moon shone bright. Gaps in Isaiah's rustling leaves appeared as earthbound stars, pinpoint reflections of moonlight. The leaves themselves shimmered as the moth's wings in the shifting breeze.

Perspiration ran down Malachi's back, soaking his hairline as he toiled to set strong wards about the house, annex, and Isaiah. He also used care to set wards over the brook—to protect their water source.

He reached out to Raphael and informed the archangel of his suspicions, in the event they found themselves in need of immediate reinforcements.

Malachi searched for Katherine in the ethereal realm.

Fearful of interception of their communication by a powerful Seraph, Katherine sent Malachi a brief message confirming she had no active engagement at the abbey. With a clean break, she shut down her communication with Malachi once he signaled that he understood.

The Earth hummed and the annex seemed to breathe. Near the water wheel, Daphne sat upon a stone bench. Anxiety had her on tenterhooks. The air held foreboding of a challenge against dark, powerful forces. Dante and Malachi had convinced her she would have increased safety, outside with them. Isolation in the house or annex, while attempting to hide, had a good chance of holding more danger for her.

To pass the time, Daphne started to journal describing the events of the past day. Under the moonlight, her ink glowed, her figures and script appearing to hover over the parchment.

Gagged and tied to a chair set against the exterior wall of the annex, facing Isaiah, Esther growled around the cloth muffling her mouth. Burning rage poured from her cloudy eyes upon her captors. Malachi preferred her in plain sight, preventing her from causing further harm or chaos.

The jangle of bridles and clop of hooves raised the alarm of interlopers approaching.

They waited. The pause at the hitching post never came, and the breeze stilled.

From around the annex, Northrup and Coughton arrived with Tobias and the magistrate in Coughton's carriage. Coughton held the reins.

Northrup alighted from the carriage, the vicar behind him. Grave concern filled the vicar's somber eyes and straight set of his mouth.

Coughton exited the carriage, then turned to assist the magistrate while Northrup guarded his back.

Vicar Matthews, in his black cassock and pome-topped hat, approached Dante, the magistrate walking alongside him.

"Good evening, Master Santorum," Vicar Matthews greeted Dante. He drew a deep breath, appearing to gather courage.

Anger rising, Dante realized Vicar Matthews was putting on a show of somber, concerned citizenship for the others. "Northrup and Coughton had a most interesting visit today, based on what they shared with the magistrate and me."

"For your protection, Master Santorum," the magistrate began, his voice full of righteous vigor and his eyes alight with a zealous desire to save souls from evildoers. "I believe it best if we bring Daphne Heatherton and her maid, Esther, back into town with us. We must keep the good people of York safe from their dark influence."

His gaze, filled with a fanatical zeal, moved over Daphne, who was seated on the bench. "Mr. Northrup, if you please, stand with the good Mistress Daphne." Sarcasm imbued the word 'good'. "Take care not to look into her eyes, lest she cast a spell over you, Northrup."

Dante gasped. "Hear now!"

Tremors overtook Daphne as the magistrate's words fell upon her incredulous ears and Northrup's shadow fell over her.

With an obvious show, Northrup did not allow his glance to fall on her.

Turned about, Magistrate looked for Esther. "What have we here, Santorum?" He looked to Santorum; his eyebrows raised. "You have already captured the crone for us?"

Mad growls escaped from around Esther's gag and her eyes burned with fury as she pulled against her bonds, her chair rocking.

Fury and accusation blazed from Dante's eyes as he looked from the magistrate to Coughton and Northrup. "You betray the good Mistress Heatherton, and you betray me, you bastards." An icy promise of vengeance imbued every word he hissed.

Fearful of falling out of Dante's good graces, Northrup and Coughton made feeble protests. They shared the goal of getting the woman away from him, not alienating themselves from him.

"Silence!" Vicar Tobias Matthews hushed the misgivings of Northrup and Coughton.

"She is only a woman, for heaven's sake," Northrup whispered to Coughton.

Malachi almost revealed himself upon Northrup's whisper of ignorance.

The group of the five walked near where Daphne sat. Dante made sure he stayed between Daphne and the interlopers.

Daphne paled, aware the vicar, Northrup, and Coughton intended to have her arrested.

Malachi watched the scene unfold from the other side of Isaiah. He sensed Vicar Matthews probe for his presence and deflected it. Relief provided a brief balm as he did not sense recognition from Tobias Matthews.

Dante rounded on Northrup and Coughton, anger and disgust emanating from every pore. "Let us witness how true your heart is to the good of humankind as you journey down this ugly path of accusation!" The two stood facing him, not moving. Dante continued, "If your intentions are pure you have nothing to fear."

With shaking hands, Daphne tore blank pages from her journal.

Dante turned and took the parchment and quill Daphne held out to him. "Both of you, sign your names." Dante's gaze moved over them. "What you intend to put Mistress Heatherton through is far worse than bloody writing your bloody name on a piece of paper." He shoved the journal and quill at them. "Now, do it!"

Coughton gulped.

Northrup looked at Coughton, then back at Dante.

"Go on. Sign your name!"

Anxiety filling his eyes, Northrup took the quill and paper. He looked around Dante at Daphne; her letters remained incandescent on the sheets she held.

Repugnance sifted through Daphne, watching Northrup's fingers curl about her quill. She had some satisfaction upon seeing him pale and gulp while staring at her glowing writing.

Within Northrup's grasp, the parchment wavered. He handed a sheet to Coughton, who looked at the parchment as though it were a viper about to bite him.

"Go on, write your name, Northrup. You should have nothing of which to worry," goaded Dante as he stared at the alchemist. Vengeful intent rose like lava in Dante's eyes.

Daphne shifted from sitting on the stone bench to standing, unsteady on her feet. The events unfolding seemed surreal, unsettling, like a bad dream. She moved to Dante's side, between him and Isaiah.

Under the now bright moonlight, Northrup took Daphne's place on the cold stone bench. His hands shook as he whispered a prayer Isaiah's ink would glow. Daphne had left her open journal on the bench, the ink stunning in its iridescence.

Against the paper, the quill nib scratched as Northrup signed his name. A weak glow showed, then the incandescence sputtered, only to disappear. He glanced at Daphne as tears welled in his eyes. One fell, landed on the parchment, and bled through the ink. It appeared as a splatter of dark blood. "No, no," he wailed, a mournful whisper while shaking his head. Northrup stood, holding back a sob. He could not look Dante in the eye while he handed the quill to Coughton.

Unwavering, Daphne took in every movement made by Northrup and Coughton with abhorrent fascination.

Coughton sat, the stone bench also his writing surface. He moved the quill with confidence across his piece of parchment torn from the journal, the scratching of the nib as loud as the call of ravens. All eyes were on the parchment. No letters glowed or even sputtered. Nothing. "There must be a mistake, something wrong with this batch of ink." Incredulity masked his face.

Condemnation hot in Dante's dark eyes as he stared down upon Coughton, his lips curled in revulsion.

Furious, Coughton moved the quill over the parchment, ending with an angry scribble. He turned and caught Daphne's stare. Finger crooked, he pointed at her, shaking in his righteousness. "You! Witch. You write something." His voice rang with disbelief and desperation.

Daphne grasped the quill from Coughton's hand with trepidation. She looked up to Dante, he nodded. Daphne moved her hand with surety across the parchment. As soon as she penned them, her figures glowed with majesty and richness.

Coughton and Northrup both gasped.

"Rubbish," bellowed the vicar and bent to tear the parchment from under Daphne's hand.

In the shadows, an icy fear wound through Malachi's warrior gut, his battle instinct raised an undeniable alarm. Something is very wrong—more than just this bloody mess.

Malachi revealed himself and clamped his battle-scarred hand across the vicar's wrist.

"Unhand me, you Devil's spawn!"

Malice threaded through Malachi's low growl, "The Devil is not the enemy here, Tobias." Malachi spat to the side, then returned his vengeful gaze to the vicar. "You are the spawn of Gideon's twisted machinations!"

Malachi locked his obsidian gaze on Tobias and twin cobalt flames flared in his pupils.

Daphne gasped.

Northrup backed up a step.

Tobias spit in Malachi's face.

Ferocious wrath thundered across Malachi's expression, and his grasp on the vicar's arm tightened.

"Unhand me—," the high-pitched shriek of a wild animal caught in the wicked claws of a steel trap flew from Tobias's mouth as he twisted his body in an unnatural manner. He bent forward and twisted his shoulder back to extricate his arm from Malachi's grip.

The sickening crunch of bone splintering resounded as Tobias fell to his knees, sobbing and screeching.

∼

Terror filled Daphne as the horrifying scene unfolded before her. She had lain with the vicious, vengeful creature grasping the screaming vicar's arm. Bile surged at the back of her throat and her pulse pounded in her ears as she dropped her parchment. It drifted, floating side to side, the incandescence of the ink winking with each flutter. Once the sheet landed, the glowing ink upon the parchment glared upwards, accusatory eyes on all present.

∼

Malachi loosened his hold on Tobias's mangled arm. He stood, then looked with abhorrence down upon the rolling, blubbering vicar. Bared teeth glinted in the moonlight as Malachi hissed.

The vicar's useless limb drooped, the skin turning dark at the point of injury, thick blood seeping in rivulets around the exposed splinters of bone.

Judge and jury in his gaze, Malachi lifted eyes glittering with sparks of cobalt born of fury to Northrup and Coughton.

Their feet riveted to the ground, Northrup and Coughton found it impossible to move back from the massive raven-haired Warrior who had pulverized Tobias's wrist to an unrecognizable pulp with a single hand.

Retching, Daphne turned aside, emptying her stomach of its contents onto the ground. She heard Isaiah rumble low, reaching out to her in her distress. The acrid taste of vomit in her mouth disturbing, she longed for a sip of water. The running brook called to her, spoke of its refreshing waters. She glanced at the shimmering, moving waterway a tenth of a league to her left, and found herself pulled toward the stream.

Stealthy, not wanting to bring attention to herself, Daphne walked to the brook-side, knelt, and bent over. She gave thanks to Mother Earth and Sister Moon for the cool water while she slid her hand in sideways to decrease the amount of sound the rushing liquid would make against her skin. With cool water, she patted her cheeks and relief flowed through her. After a quick glance at the gathering about Isaiah, she threw caution to the wind and rinsed out her mouth with water she caught in the briefest of moments in her cupped hands.

Warning hairs on the back of Malachi's neck spiked, a rush of primal fear frissoned through him.

A mere moment later, the thick, sickening odor of sulfur permeated the night air. Apep's saffron yellow body coruscated, solidifying as the immense serpent's long yellow body slithered along the ground and spiraled up the Oak's barked trunk. Isaiah's wave of fear slammed into Malachi like a tidal wave. Malachi imparted to Isaiah that he would free him.

Vicar Matthews, his pain dulled with the appearance of the viper, spied Daphne upstream and Apep's tail snaking toward her. With a whispered incantation, he cast a spell, shifting clouds over the moonlight and obscuring the glen upstream to mask Daphne's location and predicament from Malachi and Dante.

Malachi glanced down the length of the inexorable, winding snake. The night now absorbing all in its Stygian domain about the glade. Apep's tail disappeared into the yawning darkness alongside the running stream. With his preternatural sight, Malachi tracked up the endless length of the asp never reaching the end of the tail. The distressed oak pulled Malachi's attention back.

Apep hissed, loud enough to echo about the glade.

The malignant whisper of his hide against Isaiah's bark seemed as loud as thunder to Malachi while the serpent wrapped his body about Isaiah's trunk.

The asp's maleficent yellow eyes, split by jagged, fathomless black pupils, bored into Malachi each time he coiled up around from behind the tree, his fork tongue flicking with a hiss of malevolence.

Slack-jawed stood Dante, the magistrate, Coughton, and Northrup behind Malachi, incapable of thought or action as they witnessed the great asp materialize and wrap about Isaiah.

Now silent, the pain in his arm forgotten, Tobias enjoyed quiet glee over Daphne's impending fate. Like a crab, he scrambled backward away from the group. He rolled over, stood, and stooped, holding his crushed arm sheltered against the fold of his belly. With awkward, loping steps, he scrambled to get away, before Malachi erupted with rage.

Now refreshed, Daphne started to stand. The night had grown pitch dark. Without warning, a malleable, icy cold, and strong appendage wrapped about her bent waist. Deep, heart-stopping fear filled her. She sobbed in fright, fighting to get loose, her sobs escalated to blood-curdling screams as she struggled. Desperate, Daphne whipped her body about to slacken the hold, while she tried to work her hands under the coiling appendage to break free.

The scaly cold strength grew tighter the more she struggled. Warmth ran down her leg as she lost control of her bladder.

Daphne wailed in terror as the appendage lifted her over the inky black running water. Her eyes grew wide as saucers, streaming tears over her face. Her mouth yawned opened, her horrific screams erupting.

∼

Daphne's soul-chilling cries pulled Malachi's attention back to the brook. Icy fingers of paralyzing dread squeezed about Malachi's heart, gut, and mind. The earth dropped from under Malachi's feet as his fear abolished the vicar's cloaking spell and the moonlight made the malevolent monstrosity of the situation apparent.

Dante's desperate battle cry as he ran toward Daphne broke Malachi of the bonds of panic.

Bark snapped and Isaiah's trunk creaked as Apep's coils tightened about the ancient oak. "My vengeancsse is your regret, Angel," spat Apep as he hissed, his forked tongue flicking out toward Malachi. "I ssmell your fear." The asp laughed, the sound deep, inescapable, soul chilling.

Apep's head thrown back in victory, his fangs glinted in the moonlight with drops of syrupy venom suspended from them. The giant asp lowered the screaming Daphne into the water with his inescapable, coiled tail. Her screams evaporated as the cold, rushing water covered her head.

Ruthlessly, Apep strangled the gasping Isaiah and held Daphne prisoner under the water in the grip of his cold, reptilian tail. To torment Malachi, Apep brought her up out of the water just long enough to keep her alive as he choked life from the oak. From within, his yellow eyes and fathomless pupils lit with the delight he took in rending Malachi's soul.

Fire consumed Malachi's gut and heart, the pain greater than a thousand-fold of anything known before to him. Apep forced his hand, forced him to choose. The outcome now written on his cold stone tablet of regret, as his resolve solidified, while his heart and soul cried out in agony. As much as he implored the heavens and begged the gods, the outcome would not, could not change. In desperation, he called for Raphael.

Daphne's screams and sobs of terror rode over the desperate battle cries of Dante as Apep's tail again lifted her from the water, then slammed her down and held her under again.

Against Apep's horrifying, unrelenting hold Daphne struggled for her life, her screams of terror and sorrow of abandonment riddling the air.

While hot tears streamed down the chiseled planes of his warrior's face, Malachi employed millennia of discipline and resolve. He manifested an orb of his angel's molten fire between his cupped hands and readied to cast it, every second of time ticking by a hellish eternity. His brawny, muscular wings appeared and ruffled at his back. Angst rose from his soul, caught as the sharpest, longest burrs in his throat.

Isaiah wept. He sensed Malachi's choice. He would have rather died. The ground trembled about his roots as he keened with lament.

Helpless, Dante watched from the shore, Daphne's desperate gaze on his. He witnessed Death enter her eyes. "No! Daphne, No!" He fell to his knees while Apep lowered his tail into the water, her head going under as Dante's knees hit the ground.

All of his ethereal power imparted to the orb, Malachi petitioned the Elements of Earth, Air, Fire, Water to lend their force to the molten cobalt.

The orb pulsed and hummed, increasing in diameter as the Elementals amalgamated their dynamism into the molten cobalt.

Sweat tinged with blood ran in heartbreaking rivulets down over the planes of his tormented face. Unchecked tears streamed from his eyes as he raised the churning, humming cobalt globe over his head and heaved, a battle cry heard leagues away as he cast it with great force upon the viper god's massive yellow body. The molten seething orb thrummed low and lethal as it sailed toward the bulging, muscular body of Apep, the Egyptian god of Chaos. The great asp's eyes widened with horror upon hearing the stupendous power bombinate through the cobalt.

Intent to bring about the ancient oak's demise before the orb would cleave him, Apep strained with all his might to strangle Isaiah. Bark and wood splintered. Isaiah groaned and gasped, low and archaic, under the serpent's force.

Isaiah's leaves drooped and darkened as he bowed, his pain and grief audible, palpable.

The glen rang with Apep's screech when the churning orb bit into the first coil. His head, with its pointed snout, whipped to no avail to where the orb cleaved through the great serpent's three yellow coils wrapped tight about the ancient oak. Monstrous screams of agony and anger shook through the ground and Isaiah's leaves. In the throes of agony, the serpent's neck undulated. As life left Apep's body, his head dropped like a large boulder to the ground, the dead weight landing on the side of his pointed snout with a stomach-churning thump. The snake's jaws remained open, his mouth a foul, black abyss framed by dull fangs coated with thick, drying, muddy-yellow venom.

Devoid of life, the massive asp's heavy tail stilled in the brook, his shrieks now silent, as were Daphne's.

～

Her body lay trapped beneath Apep's hulking tail. Her hair floated in the cold, dark water of the running brook from under the tail. Over and again, her pale lifeless hand caromed with the current against the yellow asp's scales.

At the shore knelt Dante, his hands covering his face. His woeful weeping rose above him to Sister Moon, who wept with him, holding him to her in her gossamer embrace of mourning ethereal light.

Vicar Matthews looked about. He rotated his once-crushed wrist, working out the stiffness where he had healed his arm during the melee. A malevolent light of glee shone from his dark eyes as he turned in a circle, surveying the grief and destruction about him.

His gaze landed upon the old crone, still tied to the chair; her skirts and disheveled gray hair trembled with the fearful shaking of her cowering body.

The vicar's joyous light shifted to baleful while he took in her cowering form. He concentrated his maleficent energy on her, wishing gone her offensive fear, poor judgment, and rheumy eyes which peered at him over her gag.

Vapor rose from her person while he smote her, then her body crumpled, collapsing down upon itself.

Pungent smoke from the charred body drifted on the night breeze through the glen effecting the long, searching, gnarled fingers of the crone.

Coughton, Northrup, and the magistrate remained speechless, their eyes glassy with shock. Disgust crossed the vicar's face to see Northrup's breeches stained dark with urine.

Stench of the cleaved serpent mixed with the acrid odor of the smote crone overpowered the air. Coughton and the Magistrate bent to the side and heaved, the sound of their vomiting compounding the wretchedness of dark, irrevocable grief blanketing the once happy glen.

~

Low, creaking notes of Isaiah's grief intoned the funeral hymn to Dante and Malachi's lamentation, souls torn asunder. The leaves of Isaiah's proudest, most stalwart limbs now brushed the ground, the oak bent in sorrow and injury.

To the right of Isaiah, a shimmering golden pillar manifested, solidifying into the Archangel Raphael.

Falling to one knee, Malachi bowed his head, sweat and blood-soaked lanks of his hair obscured his face. His gray-white wings heaved with his back as deep sobs wracked his body, his spirit shredded.

Ten feet from Raphael, a vortex of gray and black ash appeared. A tall and dark figure coruscated, draped in a black cassock, a parson's hat shading the chiseled face beneath the brim.

Raphael pushed forth the name from his tongue in a quiet, menacing tone, "Gideon."

"Archangel," Gideon intoned. Preternatural pleasure glinted in silver eyes shadowed by his wide black brim, while he surveyed the destruction. His gaze passed over the grieving Malachi. "It does my vengeful heart good to know that the Fallen Angel will suffer for eternity with the death of his love falling square onto his weak shoulders."

Gideon stepped to stand behind the sob wracked, kneeling warrior. With disdain, he stared down over the broken guardian. He leaned over, the brim of his parson's hat now alongside the crown of Malachi's head. The cleaved, dead asp lay stinking before them. His whisper slid past Malachi's ear like a soul-eating wraith, "Had you joined the Seraph, Malachi, you would be holding her in your arms and kissing her warm mouth."

Pausing, his breath blanketed Malachi. "Instead, her cold, dead mouth is kissing the obscene, reptile skin of Apep."

Disgust dripped from his words, as he stood straight, "The stench of your sweat, blood, and self-pitying grief revolt me, Angel." Gideon spat onto the ground where Malachi's scabbard tip rested, as to rid his mouth of the taste. He turned toward Apep and waved a hand over the halved, rotting serpent. It and he disappeared.

For once in his existence, Raphael found himself unsure of what to do. Unable to swallow past the knot caught in his throat or draw a deep breath, he canvassed the devastation and cloud of deep grief which had overtaken the glen. Grunts combined with weeping echoed off the annex stone wall. Raphael spied Dante struggling against the current to lift Daphne's dead weight and wet clothes out of the running brook.

A sense of purpose filled him, and he laid a firm hand on Malachi's shoulder. "We need to help Dante get Daphne out of the water, my brother. Now."

Malachi's eyes focused as he lifted his stricken eyes to Raphael. He shuddered, then nodded. He stood, gathered his wits, sharpening them to a singular goal.

Malachi ran, his feet pounding against the ground. He stilled at the shore. An unbreakable vine of thorns wrapped itself about his heart and lungs while he watched Dante toil and grapple to lift Daphne's lifeless and pale body from the buffeting water. Into the cold and dark water jumped Malachi and he strode against the current toward the weeping Dante.

With the splash of water, Dante looked up. His eyes lit upon Malachi as firebrands. "You! You stay away! You did this!"

Malachi halted. The chill, inky current pushed its inexorable weight onto him as it rushed past his calves. Moonlight cast everything in shades of black and gray. A dark grimace, a tragic parody of a grin, cut across Dante's face as he wept and struggled against the flow and slippery bottom of the brook to lift Daphne.

Daphne's upper body drooped in Dante's arms, her cloth-covered legs and hips bobbed, tugged by the moving water. The heavy, waterlogged fabric of her skirts swirled in the currents. Dark strands of hair adhered to her still, pale face. Her closed eyes and unmoving lips spoke volumes.

Raphael waded in and hugged his arm about Dante's shoulders.

It crossed the back of Malachi's cursing mind that Raphael had never offered personal assistance to humans. Frustration and pain rose as a fervent wish he could be the one with his arm about Dante. Instead, he stood in the water, helpless and abhorred.

Bitter and desolate, Malachi watched as Raphael leaned in and whispered words into Dante's ear. Dante nodded, then his head fell back and he keened, the wrenching wail echoing through the glen.

Isaiah's low moans of grief and pain wafted up the water to wind about Malachi.

A sword of anguish cut through Malachi's heart, he again fell to his knees, his head in his hands, cold water and rocks unnoticed. The water rushing past Daphne's body eddied about him, splashed up and ran down through his hands with his tears.

Raphael brought his lips close to Dante's ear and spoke over the rush of the water, "Dante, there is a reason for everything. I have asked The Five for intercession on Daphne's behalf. We must maintain the balance. Understand. We shall see what The Fates and The Five will allow."

Dante nodded, listening, his lips quivering in grief, his arms trembling with the struggle of holding Daphne's body half up out of the current.

"For now, we will work together to get her out of the water."

Dante's grief sliced anew with Raphael's words, as he keened, his head back.

Raphael's battle-hardened heart ached; he tightened his arm about Dante's shoulders. Deep fatigue had set in Dante's muscles and they needed to get this done.

For this moment, in the continuum of time and his entreaty for intercession, Raphael needed this labor to be of his blood, sweat, and tears; mixed in with Dante, Isaiah, and Malachi's grief.

"I am going to let go of you and move to her legs." Raphael slid his arm from Dante's shoulders and fought the swift water to get to Daphne's pale, cold feet floating to-and-fro in the current, her boots taken away by the inexorable brook. Raphael traced his hands up her cold leg and found the backs of her knees. "Dante, once I get her legs lifted out of the water, I will be able to get my arms under her hips. Just hold her steady, my friend."

With a shuddering breath, Dante nodded, widened his stance, and tightened the hook of his arms under Daphne's upper arms. He held her cold back firm against his torso. He could still feel the warmth of Raphael's embrace about his shoulder, buoying him.

Along the length of Daphne's legs, Raphael sidestepped and kept his hands under her limbs, ensuring he had caught her wet skirts along each length of her legs. He intended to avoid the resistance of the wet fabric dragging in the moving water. Raphael cradled her hips in his arms, her skirts now held secure between her body and his. He lifted her, taking a substantial amount of weight from Dante.

Immediate relief crossed Dante's face when Raphael assumed a large portion of the weight of Daphne's body.

Raphael looked at Dante and asked, "Are you ready to make our way to the shore, or do you need to rest more?"

"Let us proceed," Dante answered, his voice a low, determined rasp.

Raphael nodded once, grunting as he hefted Daphne's hips more against his torso, firming his grasp.

Grim pallbearers, they progressed as one, with measured cadence, toward the shore. The cold, moving water and slippery stream bed fought them with each step. Crickets' song their funeral dirge, moonlight their chapel candle.

Malachi strode out of the water and moved along the side of the brook to stand where they would step ashore. He set his feet wide apart, prepared to keep his balance. As Dante's heel hit the sloped shoreline, Malachi bunched the nape of Dante's doublet, helping him to stay steady. He hauled Dante up the angled shoreline as Dante struggled to keep his hold on Daphne.

Dante now on the shore, Malachi grasped the shoulder of Raphael's vest, pulled him up onto the solid ground. Dante moved back as Malachi dragged Raphael up over the muddy bank.

Desperate to lay his hands upon his love and to help, Malachi traversed to the opposite of Raphael and Dante. His stomach twisted into a deep knot when his hands came into contact with her cold and hard body, devoid of life. Determined not to weep, he hitched a shuddering breath. The bitter and painful blade of duty cleaved his heart knowing her eyes would not hold the warmth of laughter or love again.

Raphael regarded both men, they caught his gaze. He nodded his head once. They genuflected in unison, lowering her body to the soft, dewy grass.

Through the glen echoed the mournful call of the owl.

Isaiah sighed, the sound low, pained, and rumbling.

The three men moved to standing, each stared down through their grief upon the lifeless body of the brilliant alchemist.

A vortex formed near Raphael. Whirring, humming murmurs of the Ancients imbued the swirls.

Thoth materialized. His Ibis beak and fierce black gaze pointed toward Daphne's body.

Hope flared within Raphael. Thoth's appearance meant intercession was at hand, one way or another.

Katherine materialized behind Northrup, Coughton, and the magistrate. She kept her gaze off Daphne's body and focused her energies on getting the mortals out of the way and unable to recall what they had witnessed here.

"Gentlemen," Katherine called. All three started at hearing the Abbess's voice behind them. Northrup, Coughton, and the magistrate all turned to greet her. Katherine smirked as she glanced down at Northrup's urine-stained breeches.

He squirmed like a worm trapped under a magnifying glass with bright sun.

The black veil of her habit framed her intense, lioness gaze, which moved with measured deliberateness to each of theirs. "I believe it is time for you gentleman to take your leave." She nudged her chin over to where Daphne lie, then returned her gaze to them, now accusatory. "As both the crone and Daphne are dispatched, you have no further need for a witch hunt, gentlemen." She gave the magistrate an imperious nod. "I am confident, you agree, Magistrate."

Uncomfortable under her probing gaze, the magistrate gathered his wits, a challenge with all he had just witnessed. "Well, um, yes," he coughed and answered, "quite so, Abbess, quite so."

"Thank you, Magistrate.

"Before you take your leave, gentleman, please humor me a moment and look up to the moon."

All three looked up to the moon, compelled to do so by Raphael and Katherine working in concert. Once their gazes were turned upward, Katherine and Raphael washed their memories of Apep and all preternatural events and powers to which they had been witnesses. Raphael added compulsion to depart from the glen, annex, and house post-haste.

Released from the memory scrub, Northrup, Coughton, and the magistrate jumped into Northrup's wagon, urging the horse team to pull the wagon down the drive quickly as possible, the bridles and reins jingling as they did when the gentlemen arrived on this fateful night.

Katherine caught Tobias peering at the lifeless body of Daphne with certain joy in his gaze. With a Sekhmet war cry, she shed the habit from her person, her blue and silver armor took its place. She bore down on Tobias.

Fear replaced triumph on Tobias's face as the Sekhmet Warrioress advanced on him, growling low and lethal.

Fierce, predatory lioness anger burned in her topaz gaze as it moved over his face. Driven by righteous anger and grief, Katherine lobbed her spear at his chest. "You Seraph bastard," she shouted as he dodged the spear. It landed point down in the dirt behind him, the high end of the spear vibrating in the quiet, somber night of the glen.

Katherine pulled her boomerang loose and shrieked a battle cry. Tobias raised an ineffective wall of protection. The boomerang found its way around Tobias's ward and sliced without mercy into his upper arm. The limb fell to the glen grass, its fingers still wriggling in shock.

In disbelief, his mouth gaped while he lifted his good hand to the spurting wound, with a fruitless attempt to stem the blood flow.

A mystic kulning permeated the glen as Katherine called back her loyal boomerang.

Mouth still gaping open, his gaze on the intrepid, kulning Sekhmet, Tobias fell to his knees, then pitched forward landing with a solid thump on his face and torso. The returning boomerang whooshed and glinted over his head just as he pitched.

Molten blue flashed over the boomerang, purifying it of the malevolent gore before it landed with a solid thud in her palm.

His dark rich life's blood continued to spurt, escaping his body with diminishing force each pulse. A clotting, coppery lake formed about Tobias's stump and torso, his severed arm forming a macabre island.

Upon Tobias's piteous mewls, a vicious grin split Katherine's vengeful expression.

A black vortex appeared over the moaning Tobias.

Thoth growled, "Gideon" in his deep and preternatural tone.

Katherine jumped back, landing well away from the periphery of the vortex.

A cloud of ashy dust enveloped Tobias, his arm, and blood. A black void flashed out, then inward, taking all immediate sound with it. The air about Katherine and Tobias having an unusual absent quality. The void disappeared, in a pinpoint, taking the moaning Tobias and his spilled blood with it.

Katherine took no time in running over to Daphne. She pushed Raphael out of her way, fell to her knees, keened as she reached up to Daphne's face, traced her fingers over Daphne's eyes, cheeks, lips. She laid her head on Daphne's chest and wept, great heaving sobs, digging her fingers into the wet cloth of her dress.

A heavy, warm hand landed upon the back of her shoulder.

Katherine grasped, wrapped her own hand tight about the comforting touch.

"Katherine."

Thoth's low voice resonated through her, his preternatural voice rich and omniscient. The memory of his murmur a distant shadow from another time of grief. She ignored him and continued to weep over her beloved Daphne.

"Katherine, I realize you grieve, but time is short." His hand tightened on her shoulder. "I need your help to pull everyone together. Now, Katherine, for Dante and Daphne."

Cognizance dawned that Thoth had something of great import to discuss; she did not take offense. She gathered herself together, sniffling long and loud as a deep shudder moved through her. Katherine brushed her fingers over Daphne's cold, still cheek one last time.

She grasped Thoth's extended hand he held next to her shoulder and stood.

Katherine explained to Dante in hushed tones the need to accept Thoth's appearance and give Thoth the respect due a greater deity and to listen with care to the imperative nature of his message.

Malachi and Dante stood on each side of Daphne's body. Thoth stood at her feet, his deep, black gaze moving between them. "The Five have heard Raphael's entreaty for intercession," said Thoth. He was solemn, nodding toward each man as he intoned their name. "They will allow you the opportunity to save Daphne's essence, with conditions. The balance must be maintained."

Relief, gratitude flowed through Malachi. He staggered back a step, overcome with emotion. Malachi pulled his hand down his face and chased away the overwhelming urge to weep, time was of the essence.

Dante bowed his head in thanks. His shoulders shook with silent sobs.

Thoth continued, his voice low, ringing of ethereal aristocracy, "To maintain the balance and allow this intercession to move forth, here are the conditions:

"Dante and Malachi, you must work together to save the alchemist's essence—one cannot do more than the other. There must be a cooperative effort." With his fierce, depthless Ibis eyes, Thoth regarded both men. "I suggest you leave your blame here and move forward with a sincere understanding to work together."

Dante swallowed hard, then nodded.

Malachi whispered, "Yes." Hope formed a small crack in the black ice which encased his heart and soul.

"The alchemist will not return here, to this time. Her essence will be born into women who accomplish great advances in knowledge. She did die before her time, this will right that imbalance.

"She will not know you, Malachi, Immortal Guardian, when she crosses paths with you. You cannot lose, then regain without paying Fate a tribute of true pain.

"When you find her, it will be up to you to win her back, if you wish to do so. You will know when your destiny again intersects with the alchemist's."

Again, Thoth paused. "Do you both understand?"

Dante turned to Malachi, looked him in the eye, searching his grieving soul. "Yes, we understand, Thoth," he said, not taking his eyes off Malachi.

"Good."

"Dante, you are mortal. You are not to speak of this again or write of it, with anyone who is not present here and now.

"Understand, Dante, you will be in the realm of the gods in

your attempt to rescue the alchemist. The Fates will afford you protection from the gods. The other dangers you face in your rescue will be real and may cost you your life. Do you understand?"

Dante answered, his face and voice solemn, "Yes."

Thoth turned to Malachi, "If Dante dies, you will lose both him and the woman. Do you understand, Angel?"

Malachi shifted his intent glance to Thoth. "Yes, Thoth, I do," Malachi responded. He turned back to Dante. "I do understand," he said, as he nodded, holding Dante's gaze in his own.

"Malachi, you will not have your preternatural powers in the Underworld, nor will you have protection from other gods or their creatures. Take heed."

Thoth's imposing Ibis visage peered at each man, then intoned, "May Isis be with you.

"You have two Earth hours, started from when I gathered you together," Thoth explained. He then held both of his arms before him. Looped hemp rope appeared on each outstretched arm. Thoth motioned to the ropes with his fierce beak.

Malachi took one length and handed it to Dante, then took the other looped length for himself.

CHAPTER TWENTY

Thursday and Friday, June 9 and 10, 1622 CE
The Veil Between

ONE MOMENT DANTE had been standing over the dead body of his beloved Daphne, the next he was in a surreal landscape.

Steam erupted from geysers dotted all around. Pools of mud bubbled up, belching like a deep, low bullfrog call as the thick mud bubbled and popped. Eyes peered from the various rock formations and walls. The air smelled ancient—a distinct aroma of old, sacred places. Off in the distance echoed the sound of a swift river.

"Dante!"

Dante turned. Malachi stood with gold light emanating from behind him, appearing as a halo about the Warrior Angel.

"The Underworld?" asked Dante.

"Yes. It would be smart for us to pay homage to Hades

before we go hunt for Daphne," Malachi suggested. "His throne should be near the golden light."

"We only have two hours! Less!"

Desperation shined in Dante's eyes. He paled as he peered down the long length of a cavern they would need to traverse to get to where Malachi thought Hades' throne sat, not entirely sure, either.

"Trust me, Dante, if we pay homage and thank him for his hospitality and the opportunity to save Daphne, things will go much better for us than if we don't and he becomes perturbed." Malachi's eyes searched Dante's as he tried to impart the importance of tribute to Hades.

"Very well," Dante assented. "This is your realm." Reluctant trust threaded through his voice. "I shall follow your lead."

"Ah! A most wise decision, Dante!" A booming voice rang out behind them.

Dante jumped, yet again, startled, then whirled about.

There sat an immense, shirtless, broad, and bearded man upon a grandiose throne. The ornate, carved ebony back rose high above his head. A mane of his beard and hair surrounded his face. Locks stuck out in every direction, a dark lion-like deity upon the throne of gold and ebony. The gilt arms had scales carved into them, the ends curling into deadly dragon's claws, its ornate feet shaped as lions' claws.

To the right of and just behind Hades, stood a tall, regal woman. Long, wavy, dark hair spilled over her bosom and back. From her shoulders draped an elegant, white chiton, the waist cinched by an elaborate crisscrossed series of gold ribbon.

"Malachi is right, you are better off to pay homage to me." Hades laughed. "We gods do obsess over homage and tributes," Hades said, then mugged a shiny, toothy, self-serving grin. His expression sobered, and he peered at Dante. "You followed protocol, despite the desperate nature of your circumstances, human. I brought myself to you, rather than you having to come to me. I understand your time is precious."

"Thank you, Hades, um—my Lord," said Dante, awkward in speaking to a greater god.

Amusement at Dante's discomfort played across Hade's face. His intense gaze shifted to Malachi.

Malachi bowed before the throne. "Hades," he said. Then he nodded to the woman, and added, "Persephone, it is my pleasure."

"It has been some time, Angel," Hades intoned, his dark gaze moving over Malachi.

"Yes, Hades, it has. I thank you for your assistance." With great effort, Malachi attempted to keep emotion out of his voice. The one person he loved in thousands of years of existence had died a terrifying death, because he loved her. Responsibility weighed heavy on him; grief held him captive in a hopeless, cold darkness.

Hades intensified his gaze, peeling back Malachi's defenses, examining the broken, emotional being Malachi had become.

The lump in Malachi's throat built, the band about his chest tightened. Hot tears trekked down his cheeks, his angst about to overwhelm him.

Persephone intervened, curling her hand over Hades' shoulder. "Hades, my sweet, let us allow Malachi and Dante continue on their way." Her gaze fell on the warrior angel, and she said, "I am sorry for what you and Dante have been through. Hades is pleased to be of assistance, Malachi. In light of all the missions and guardianships you have carried out with success over the years to eradicate those pesky Seraph. It is the least he could do."

Malachi found himself taken aback to see the abject adoration which beamed from Hades' face as he glanced up at Persephone.

Hades clasped the hand she had upon his shoulder and squeezed it with affection.

"Yes, my dearest Persephone, quite so."

"Malachi, Dante, I know you are both anxious to be on your mission. The sun dial's shadows grow long. You have given me an admirable tribute, trading pleasantries with me despite the imperative need for attention to time to rescue your sweet Daphne."

Dawning realization rapidly replaced confusion in Dante's sharp alchemist's eyes. Now they stood on the shore of a raging river. The roar was immense as swift water poured over boulders. Lanterns suspended in mid-air shone light through the cavern. Had desperation not overwhelmed him the levitating lights would have filled him with wonder.

Malachi gave thanks to the gods and Hades for the illumination. The spray of the fast-moving water set as dew upon his bare skin. The River Styx!

"There!" Malachi cried out.

Dante spun to look where Malachi was pointing. In the rushing river bobbed Daphne, pale, holding on to a piece of lodged driftwood as the never-ending, rapid water splashed up into her mouth and nose, almost drowning her over and again. She coughed and sputtered; exhaustion had etched deep lines into her face. Malachi had already started to scout the shores of the River Styx from where Daphne hung on to the tree limb and downriver from her.

While scouting, Malachi noted occasional black glints in the rushing water. He looked over to Daphne. While the swift, cold, and powerful water took its toll on Daphne, the mysterious black glints did not appear to bother her. Thank the Heavens and Isis for small favors!

Dante and Malachi, with great discipline, concentrated on scouting for stalagmites strong enough to handle a rope and Malachi's weight. Time ticked away and Daphne grew paler and more fatigued by the second. The cold, swift water roared past, the spray biting into them with its chilled grip.

Upriver, Malachi looked for something they could use to their advantage. Hope burgeoned as he spotted a rock shelf which extended at least two-thirds across the river.

Stalactites extended down past the level of the rock shelf from the cavern ceiling. He thought they might serve to make it across the rest of the way. Several strong-looking stalagmites had grown up from the cavern floor on the opposite side of the river.

He headed back to Dante and reported what he had found and his strategy. "There is a rock shelf up-river which will get me more than halfway across the river. Several stalactites hang down beyond the shelf, which I can grasp and swing from one to the other to get to the rest of the way to the other side with a rope."

Worry grew in Dante's eyes, the shadows underneath darkening. "I am concerned the stalagmites may prove too slippery for you to grasp, but I don't see another option. We, you, are just going to have to make it work." A tear escaped as he spoke. He trembled.

Malachi grasped both of Dante's shoulders, determination flowing through him and into Dante, and said, "We will make this work, Dante. We have to make it work."

Dante nodded in silent agreement, as he wept without sound.

"I am going to tie one end of both ropes to me, Dante. You secure the other ends. If I fall, I hope I will float down, dead or alive, to Daphne. Then you can pull us in, using me as a raft of sorts.

"If I don't fall and make it to the other side, I would like us to secure the rope on either side of the river just past where she is hanging on, then loop the other rope around the strung rope and secure it to Daphne and me. You would haul us in with your end. What do you think?"

"I don't think we have any other options."

"Then, let us get to work, Dante."

With him, Malachi took both rope ends and made quick work of climbing the rock shelf. Dante held onto the other ends, in the grim possibility that Malachi may fall. Dante would still have the rope and not all would be lost.

Up close to the stalactites Malachi could see the slippery slimes shining off them. He would do his damnedest not to slip off and fall. He took his dagger from inside his boot, shored off a good bit of his hair, and wrapped the dark locks about his hands to give him a solid grip on the slippery rock formations. With a glance down, he saw Dante peer down the river then look back up at him.

Dante nodded that he was ready.

Fear shoved aside, grim determination in its place, Malachi took a leap of faith, leaning out from the rock shelf. He thanked the Heavens and Isis when his hand grasped the first stalactite. His hair wrapped about his hand gave him a good grip.

An arm's length ahead was another long stalactite. Swallowing deep, he pushed his feet with some force off the rock ledge and swung to grab the intended stalactite. He secured his grip about it and closed his eyes for a moment to give fervent prayer of thanks.

Dante stood on the shore, his eyes glued to every deliberate move Malachi made, other than frequent quick glances to Daphne. Malachi swung his feet to-and-fro, gaining momentum.

Dante winced as he watched Malachi let go of one formation, then fly his body as an acrobat through the air while still holding onto the last stalactite. He staggered in relief as Malachi clasped the final stalactite.

Malachi fought the pain and muscle fatigue as he grasped the last formation. He looked down at his Daphne. Desperate yet determined, she held onto the log despite being almost overwhelmed by the swift, inexorable water. He renewed his resolve to make his body do what they all needed him to do. Blood seeped from between his fingers and down his wrist. Twisting and sliding on the stalactites had sloughed skin from his hands. No matter; he could ignore it for now. He held hope the River Styx would take the blood as a tribute and give some relief to Daphne.

Malachi's feet dangled over the river. His arms and shoulders trembled as he strained to hold his weight. Grasping the narrowing stalactite had him in agony. Fear for Daphne and Dante, and his discipline surged burst of energy and purpose through him. He pushed his pain and fear aside, just as he had trained to do for thousands of years. With care, Malachi swung his legs to gain momentum yet not disrupt his perilous hold on the stalactite. He cast a glance at his brave Daphne—still alive—her eyes closed, concentrating on holding on to her precious tree limb. She worked hard at staying alive in the cold, swift water.

He heard a splash. An overwhelming pain exploded in his ankle. Malachi looked down to see a black creature, its preternaturally large mouth surrounding the ankle of his boot with several long and pointed teeth embedded in his boot. A horrifying fish-eel combination. He did not want to think what the vicious, toothed fish would have left of his ankle if he did not have on his armored boots. *My dripping blood must have attracted them.*

～

Malachi glanced down at Dante to see if he also had noted the creatures. Fear had made Dante's eyes black as night. He watched Dante swallow. Malachi nodded to him and continued his journey, ignoring the beast hanging onto his ankle by its teeth. He had no choice.

Checking on Daphne, surprise jolted through Malachi to see the water actually parting for her, giving her relief. *Of course! The Elements! Dante!* Shifting his gaze to Dante, the alchemist stood there in deep concentration, making hand motions. Malachi gave thanks.

The rest did Daphne some good. Color had started to come back into her face, and she did not struggle as much. Now, though, he could see her tears and his heart shattered yet again.

Not to be distracted, their time short, he eyed a smooth part of the shore not covered by stalagmites. To gain momentum, he swayed his legs, then found the sweet spot to swing through and let go. With a prayer to the Celestial God and to Zeus, and a growl of determination through his deep grimace of exertion, he directed his body with all his mental and physical might. All his millennia of existence flashed through his mind as he flew through the air, as mortal. 'Thump!' He landed right where he had hoped. His knees bent and he wobbled as he worked to catch his balance. With a glance down, he noted, with disgust, the eel creature still hung on. Malachi ignored it.

He hurried over to stalagmites extending up from the cavern floor, just a few feet downriver from Daphne. Time ticked away along with Daphne's life force, adding to his urgency. He scouted robust formations to which secure the rope. Hope leapt within him to spot one. Malachi looped one rope over the sturdy stalagmite, winding the rope about it several times. He wiped away blood-tinged sweat, then fashioned a harness for him and a loop for Daphne with the other rope, making it so it wound about the secure rope and he could move along it with Daphne in tow while Dante pulled them in.

His vision focused on Daphne for a moment. He noted with deep thanksgiving that somehow the rushing water was splitting to run on either side of Daphne while she hung on. Pride and admiration for her will and inner strength flowed through and buoyed him.

Malachi shifted his focus back to the ropes and harness. He extended his body out over the raging water while he tested the mobility of the harness across the secure rope. Another viciously toothed black creature jumped, aiming for his arm. He jumped back, quick enough to avoid a bite, the fish grazing his leather armor with its vicious teeth.

Re-examining the situation, it dawned on him the creatures were not attacking Daphne. Thoth's words rang through his head: Dante will have protection from the gods, you will not. If these creatures were of the gods, they may not attack Dante. Malachi looked over to Dante and willed Daphne's mentor to look at him, praying Dante would sense his mortal mental push.

Malachi watched Dante's eyes reluctantly move from Daphne to him. He held his arm out over the water. A vicious eel-fish jumped and arced, its jaw snapping as it aimed for his limb. He snapped it back, the creature only feasting on air of the Underworld before slicing back into the rushing water.

Pointing to Dante, Malachi then hit his own arm.

Dante aimed his own index finger at his heart and mouthed the question, "Me?"

Malachi nodded.

Dante glanced at Daphne. Then swallowed and shut his

eyes. He took a deep breath and opened his eyes, then dashed to the edge and held out his arm. Nothing.

Dante gave a thumbs up to Malachi.

Malachi nodded, then lifted the harness and motioned it toward Dante. He tried not to grimace when he saw Dante's eyes get as big as saucers.

Imparting a warrior's fierce stare, Malachi clamped one hand over the other wrist and pushed them forward, with force, showing strength together.

Hope's flame burgeoned within him when Dante did the same. Malachi noted a warrior's aura flicker about Dante and knew then the man had the ancients at his side, whether he knew it or not.

Malachi manipulated the ropes to slide the harness and loop over to Dante. Sweat broke out over his forehead as he did his damnedest to send Dante mental energy and determination, *Do or die.*

Eyes intent on Dante, Malachi watched to ensure the alchemist secured the rope well about his waist and the tightrope across the river. Dante had the same grim determination set through his face, body, and movements that he had seen in his men before they entered a great battle.

Malachi closed his eyes and prayed for Dante to Katherine's warrior goddess, Sekhmet, who accompanied great warriors into battle.

Dante wrapped his feet and arms about the double rope strung across the raging river and began making his way to Daphne. No black eel fish jumped to attack him.

Malachi could see beads of blood form where the rope dug into Dante's skin. The alchemist proceeded, without stopping to look, his eyes locked on Daphne.

After what seemed an eternity to Malachi, Dante had made it to Daphne. Malachi intently watched, his heart pounding at his throat, as Dante worked the loop for Daphne under one arm then the other. With a bob, Daphne started to be taken by the current, the loop not yet fully under her second arm. Malachi grunted, his teeth clenched as he inched forward, moving in concert with Dante. He gave a victory growl as Dante grasped the neck of Daphne's gown and somehow shoved the rope under her arm, his face bright red and pulled back in a deep grimace as he did so.

Malachi caught Dante's gaze as Dante looked up at him. He gave Dante a hearty nod of reassurance while he maintained his grip on the rope, now holding the weight of both Dante and Daphne.

Malachi started to feed the ropes to slide in their loop about the stalagmites on either side of the river. He exercised pure determination, for each pull, each effort to keep the rope moving and not running away with the force of the swift water. Every muscle in his body strained to get Daphne and Dante to shore. His hands dripped blood, the rough hemp rope merciless in digging into his hands, flaying them. Each inch closer to the shore Daphne got was worth his pain a hundred-fold. His heart pounded. Malachi found himself praying to the Celestial God he had forsaken, Sister Moon, The Five and Isis. The weight of Daphne, Dante, and the river pulling on Malachi became almost unbearable. Every sinew strained, his muscles cabled as he heaved and held steady, heaved, held steady. He threw his head back, beads of sweat rolled from every pore of his body. A grimace cut across his face, spittle flew from his mouth as he put every bit of his being into saving Dante and Daphne.

Malachi could see the strain of every one of Dante's muscle's working in concert to maintain a grip on Daphne as they inched their way along the rope, the loud, rushing water hungrily tugging at Daphne. Fierce and intrepid determination slashed across the alchemist's face. *Almost, Almost!*

Dante and Daphne were now only a few feet from the safety

of the shore. Malachi gave a mighty battle cry and forced a great heave upon the rope as he did so.

His war cry echoed through the Underworld. It reached Persephone's ears. Chills traveled through her and she grasped Hades' hand in prayer that Daphne would make it. Hades squeezed her hand back, finding he had the same hope in his heart.

Malachi's massive tug allowed Dante to get his feet onto the shore. Malachi watched as Dante grasped Daphne by the back and neck of her wet dress and hauled her onto the shore. They both fell sideways onto the muddy bank. His knees buckled as Daphne's pale body contacted solid ground. He could see Dante trembling from across the river.

In gratitude, Malachi fell to his knees and wept in deep heaving sobs, his tears mixing with his blood. He sat back on his haunches and wept as he gave thanks while Dante cradled Daphne. Malachi watched as Daphne opened her eyes, turned her head toward him. Her solemn gaze fixed on him from across the river.

"I love you," Daphne mouthed to him.

Then she disappeared from Dante's arms.

"Thoth! Raphael! Daphne's body has disappeared!" Katherine called out in shock. One moment it was there, the next it was not. While she examined the area of flattened grass, where Daphne's corpse had lain, two shimmering, silver-gray columns appeared on either side.

In an instant Dante appeared, stumbling, appearing off kilter and dizzy. He sat down and put his head between his knees.

Malachi then solidified, much more graceful in his stance.

Katherine ran over to Dante to check on him, crouching down.

Dante hugged her tight. He called out to all, "We did it! Dear God, Malachi and I did it!"

Katherine held and rocked him as he trembled.

Looking at his hands, Malachi opened and closed them. The hair wrapped about them gone. He reached up to feel his hair, finding it to remain shorn where he had cut it. He smiled at Dante as Dante shared the news. "Yes, Dante, we did accomplish what we set out to do. You fought better and with more courage than any immortal I have ever witnessed, and I mean that with all sincerity. You have my gratitude. Forever."

Katherine looked over to Malachi. She gasped. "Malachi, your hair!"

Malachi lifted his hands to his hair. Other than the shorn pieces, he felt nothing different. "What? Tell me!"

"You need to go look. It is not terrible, Malachi, just unexpected."

Not having the heart to look at his reflection in the smooth water of the brook, he decided to go to the annex in search of a looking glass.

Painful heat built up behind Katherine's eyes while she watched Malachi take the stone path to the annex. Sorrowful realization Daphne would never walk that same path to the annex she loved constricted about her chest.

"Katherine."

Thoth's deep whisper bumped into her melancholy musings, like a boat nudging the docks in dark, calm waters. *Simply more grief from a time best forgotten.*

"Katherine."

Now she realized the intrusion to be real. Katherine blinked tears from her eyes and brought herself to the present. *Thoth never whispered.* Dread filled her that he intended to resurrect the past ghosts of emotions she had fought long and hard to put to rest. Steeling herself with a deep breath, Katherine shoved aside her grief and trepidation. She mentally slid on her warrior's mask and brought the tall, dark god into her sight. "Yes, Thoth?" she asked in a whisper with deliberate tones.

A pause stretched on, as his black, fierce Ibis eyes held her intrepid Lioness gaze captive, barely.

Thoth blinked, then spoke, his low timber filling the space between them, drowning the crickets and pre-dawn bird song, "There is not a day, a rising of the sun, which goes by where I do not think of you."

She let another pause sift between them, then solidify, establishing distance.

"We both have our obligations, Thoth," her whisper sure. She lifted a brow beneath her wimple. "And tonight we have witnessed the folly of tempting Fate," she said, with quiet solemnity.

Katherine looked out over the brook, then brought her gaze back to a being who showed her his heart centuries ago only to shutter it away in that same ancient moment. Her tone changed to that of one talking with a fellow abbess. "Thank you for your intercession. I shall always be grateful."

Thoth searched her eyes. He then squared his shoulders, lifted his beak, making a proud profile. "Of course, Abbess," he replied.

Malachi spied Daphne's papers stacked on the desk, waiting for her journaling, and walked over to the desk.

He stroked his fingers over her neat writing and smiled. Dear Isis, he wished he could take part of her with him. Wistful, he read what she had written: her plans for the next day and a list of tasks. This was precious to him, but nothing of import to Dante.

He folded the paper and tucked it into his vest, near his heart.

With a brief glance out the window, he caught a flash of white in his reflection. He had forgotten that he had come into the annex to find a looking glass, or something which would serve as one. On either side of his head, the hair at his temples had gone white, appearing as pale stripes running along either side of his head with his hair pulled back.

His mourning was now a mace which pounded and shredded his heart over and again. He took a deep, shaky breath. He found he appreciated the white stripes of hair. He had been to hell and back, and it showed.

Malachi exited the annex, deciding it would be a long time before he could go back into that building which held so much of his true love.

Upon return to the group from the annex, Malachi noted that Dante had regained his footing. Thoth approached both Malachi and Dante.

"You are an accomplished and exacting alchemist, Dante. And, a believer of dosing, are you not?"

Dante nodded, his face still pale.

"I am a founder of Alchemy and am pleased to meet one as accomplished as you are in the art. I wish it were not under these difficult circumstances. I shall make it a point to convene with you at a more opportune time."

Dante nodded to Thoth, regret mixing with fatigue and pain reflected in his eyes. He replied, exhaustion threading his voice, "It is my honor to meet you, Thoth, sir. I, too, wish it were not under these circumstances. I do hope we will have an opportunity to talk in the future." He then looked to Katherine. "Has anyone notified Daphne's father?"

"Yes, Dante. Cook has gone into town to give Heatherton the message." Katherine continued, explaining the arrangements they had made. "Raphael has fashioned a casket and the mirage of a body. Northrup and Coughton will agree with whatever we say happened. The story we put together is that our poor Daphne found herself caught in the weeds in the brook and the current overtook her."

He nodded relieved Katherine had taken care of the details. "Thank you," Dante said. Tears flowed over the ravines of exhaustion lining his face.

Katherine's heart broke for him. "Heatherton will arrive sometime this morning. I am sure you and he will have much to share and talk about. It may help to share your pain with him.

"Oh, yes, we will have the casket buried at the abbey cemetery. We can all be there," said Katherine. "In interesting developments, the goddess Artemis has taken it upon herself to watch over Daphne's grave and discourage curiosity seekers." Katherine looked to Dante, wonderment in her face. "She says she owes Malachi and has a need to protect Daphne's memory from further insult. The Celestials have assigned a Guardian to take Tobias's place as Vicar, as we have been unable to usurp that seat until now. That is the one good thing which has come out of all of this."

Thoth, imperious and towering over all present, spoke, "Malachi, I wish you well in your search. Katherine, Raphael, Dante, Malachi." Thoth nodded to each. "Be well." A black column of swirling motes overtook him, then disappeared into a pinpoint of nothingness.

CHAPTER TWENTY-ONE

Monday, July 11, 1622 CE ~ Outskirts of York, England

RAPHAEL FOUND Malachi facing the brook—the damn brook—communing with the wounded Isaiah. He knew that Malachi found comfort in the Ancient Oak.

He stood behind the solemn warrior. "Malachi," he said, a fervent wish in his heart that his friend would be able to have less heartache. "I am to brief you on your new Guardian assignment."

Malachi continued to commune with the tree.

Raphael sensed the pause in Malachi. The moment suspended in the air between them; waiting to fracture and fall to the ground, broken.

"I am at the ready, Raphael," Malachi responded without turning around, his words almost swallowed by the perpetual running of the water.

The moment, instead, drifted down the stream, Malachi's indifference almost more deafening to Raphael.

This time there was no grousing, no assumption it would be a terrible place. Raphael recalled when Malachi had been sent to York and the fuss he had put up being assigned to guard Isaiah the Ancient. Raphael found himself hoping for the insubordinate Malachi to be back, rather than the acquiescent. He prayed this new assignment would be healthy for Malachi.

Restless for change, Malachi yearned for somewhere to go. Everything reminded him of Daphne. While no one had been holding him in York, he did not feel free to go until he had a reason. He did not have a place to go until he had a reason.

Raphael walked to Malachi's side, his eyes on Malachi's profile, "The Five have assigned you to the University of Bologna."

Nothing.

"At Bologna, a little more than two decades ago, Gaspare Tagliacozzi successfully developed reconstructive nose surgery for disfiguring wartime injuries. You have seen first-hand how these surgeries have failed horribly.

"Tagliacozzi's techniques set off a firestorm of medical and surgical advancements at Bologna. Now, the surgery and medicine programs at Bologna are evolving in size and acumen, proving them attractive and vulnerable to Seraph pilfering of medical and scientific talent."

Malachi turned to Raphael, "Are you bloody serious? The Five want to send me to a University? And you are going along with it?"

Hope burgeoned within Raphael's heart. He fought to keep a smile from sneaking onto his face and had to cough. With a glance at Malachi, he noted a lifted brow. He shrugged his shoulders and replied, "Who am I to question The Five?"

"You. You, as my ally. Or so I thought," said Malachi

"They have their reasons, Malachi, for wanting you there.

There are no small stakes at Bologna. I believe they deem you capable after your time with Aristotle and countless other academics. Dante, Rome... well, forget Rome, as that did prove rather disastrous."

"You are not helping to press your case, Raphael. Your skills as a diplomat are sadly lacking at this moment."

"Well, yes," Raphael pressed on. "To give you background, we have established that surgical techniques and understanding of medicine are evolving at a rapid pace at Bologna. Our intelligence has shared that the Seraph have infiltrated and recruited various members of the faculty of the University. The recruited faculty members are then shunning giving knowledge to the common people. Essentially an effort to send commoners back into the dark ages, to gain the Seraph more power over their fate.

"The Seraph are recruiting knowledgeable and skilled physicists, physicians, and mathematicians with promises of power and wealth," explained Raphael, "to the 'Academics of the First Order'."

Disgust crossed Malachi's expression, and he replied, "Working with Dante and Daphne, discussing with them Paracelsus, I have gained a deep appreciation for how critical scientific methodology is and advances in medicine are to all." Malachi's back straightened and his expression cleared. He gave Isaiah a hearty pat.

"I will remove the stench and influence of the Seraph from this place of learning," said Malachi, his demeanor one of purpose for the first time in months.

Raphael continued, "Our intelligence identified six professors and doctors of philosophy loyal to the Seraph who are working at siphoning away talent, but we suspect there are more. You will have your work cut out for you." Raphael stopped and asked, "Is this all making sense so far, Malachi?

Malachi lifted a sardonic brow.

"I will take that as a 'yes'," Raphael said, relieved to see some sarcasm back in his brother-in-arms. He paced as he reviewed more points of Malachi's assignment.

"I will give you a list of all the Bologna professors and assistant professors, and from where they hail. Malachi, as your friend, I request there are no shouting matches this time around. We believe enough time has elapsed since you left Rome, that your reputation should not precede you," Raphael said. "The University of Bologna practices division between Church and Academia, but there are still some ties with Rome. Many of the academics are sponsored or introduced to the university by cardinals."

"Understood, Raphael."

CHAPTER TWENTY-TWO

Tuesday, January 3, 1623 ~ The Abbey, York, England

"KATHERINE," Raphael spoke as they met in her study at the abbey, "The Five have issued their request, rather than order, that you carefully consider an assignment to Isaiah the Ancient as Immortal Guardian. They acknowledge that this may be an assignment with difficult emotional ties."

"I have given leaving the abbey consideration, Raphael. I believe it is time." She turned her piercing lioness gaze to him. "But, Isaiah," she sighed. "I would like to accept the assignment of being Isaiah's guardian, provided Dante would allow me to learn under him and I may stay at his home. I have a strong drive to carry on Daphne's legacy and continue to work to advance the presence and validity of women in the sciences."

Raphael nodded, and agreed, "The Five have indeed planned well, then. They will be pleased. I had consulted with Dante in light of Celestia's request. He, too, would like to see

Daphne's legacy continued and would enjoy your company as a comfort to him, in his time of grief." Solemnity took over his neutral expression, and he added, "There will be more attempts on the oak's life, as Apep proved unsuccessful. They may be more formidable than Apep—the Seraph are determined. I am confident you are more than capable of meeting any challenge they may place in your way, Katherine of Sekhmet," Raphael said with deep respect, then continued, "When you are ready to leave the abbey, give word and we shall ensure a smooth transition."

"Thank you, Raphael. Please thank Dante for me," said Katherine.

"The Five are assigning Naomi the Stygian, as the new abbess. She is well known to you, Katherine. I will have her come to you for a briefing before the month is out."

CHAPTER TWENTY-THREE

Wednesday, February 16, 1732 ~ University of Bologna, Italy

WHISPERS ECHOED through the halls of the Palazzo Poggi, home of the Bologna Academy of Sciences, drawing Malachi through the darkened, stone labyrinths. Ahead he noted flickering candlelight reflected from around the corner, along with the hushed voices of a man and a woman. A woman? In the Academy of Science? In his one-hundred and twelve years at the university, he had yet to hear a woman's voice in the great halls except for the occasional female tourist.

Tendrils of the stench of Seraph wound about Malachi. They were anemic, yet enough to warrant further stealth. He cast a cloaking spell, ensuring his footfalls remained silent and he was one with the shadows.

Without disturbing the silent air about him, Malachi moved to spy around the cold, stone corner of the hall into an open area of wide, slanted writing tables. A woman stood among them, her profile toward Malachi, her long and dark hair tied back. She leaned over a table and scribbled with fervor. Her hand appeared to not be able to keep up with her thoughts. Her eyebrows were drawn in heavy concentration as a professor of the academy spoke to her in Italian. He stood, in Malachi's full view, at the side of the woman's table. The woman gave the professor a scathing glance of profound irritation, then resumed her scribbling.

The professor became more emphatic, frustrated by her reaction, and he said, "I say, Signorina Bassi, that you—as a female—would be welcomed by the Academics of the First Order. They would appreciate your brilliance rather than question its origins."

The woman penned more figures, then stepped back and steepled her fingers as she fell into deep thought.

Malachi's heart pounded in hope and he broke into a sweat. *Could this be Daphne, come back?* he wondered. His grief and search for Daphne had been constant companions, and this Signorina Bassi was the first spark of hope he'd had in over a century.

The female looked to the man. "Movement of water is fascinating, do you not agree, Professor Castellani? Attempting to apply hydraulics to equations is a challenge indeed."

"Have you not heard one word I have said, Laura?"

Malachi heard the threat in the man's voice and understood then the odor which emanated from him. He now knew he had come across a Seraph operative, though not a strong one. Possibly a recent recruit who could be turned back.

"Professor, Bologna should accept my intellect, whether I am a man or a woman. I am choosing to fight this battle here and to earn my Doctor of Philosophy and a professorship, right here, rather than choosing the path of least resistance. If I choose to acquiesce and leave Bologna, I do the other women who have been working to advance in the sciences no favors.

"Please, Professor, refrain from interrupting my studies further with your attempts to pull me away from your university. I can only think you want me gone because I somehow threaten you. I would prefer that we be colleagues and work together, here."

Admiration of her artful handling of a difficult situation made a strong impression on Malachi as he continued to watch the exchange from the shadows. He spied Castellani's face shift from indignant to defensive to welcoming in the space of one minute or less.

Castellani would bear close watching. Bassi appeared to have called him off for the time being. Malachi would bet the Seraph would continue to work at recruiting the brilliant Bassi.

Heavy footsteps tread the hall from behind Malachi.

"Signorina Bassi, I have come to escort you home," a deep male voice called.

Malachi remained undetected in the shadows of the hallway as a tall, burly manservant walked past him toward Bassi and Castellani carrying a lantern.

Relief crossed Laura Bassi's face. "Just in time, Hugo. I am tired." Turning to Castellani, she added, "I look forward to working more on understanding hydraulic principles with you, Professor."

"Of course, Signorina Bassi," said Castellani, warm and gracious, as he bowed.

Laura Bassi laid her papers full of formulas and theories in a portfolio and tied it closed. After Hugo picked up the secured bundle, Laura laid her hand upon his arm and took her leave.

Malachi watched her disappear into the darkness of the night; he wanted to follow her. The flickering candlelight pulled his attention back to Castellani. His congenial expression had shifted to a calculating and predatory stare as the brilliant woman walked down the hall with her footman.

Strategy, a familiar and welcome friend, joined Malachi. He

now had bait in Castellani to catch the bigger Seraph fish at Bologna. He also desired an introduction to Laura Bassi, and Castellani could accomplish this for him, as well. Malachi conjured two steaming cups of fine black Chinese tea. "Hello, my friend."

Castellani jumped and turned. "Who the hell are you?"

"You might say I am a night watchman of sorts for these hallowed halls."

Castellani looked Malachi up and down, suspicion burning in his gaze. "I have never seen you before." He narrowed his eyes and asked, "Are you newly employed by the university?"

"Come and enjoy this cup of China's finest, Professor," invited Malachi. He placed a mug into the flummoxed professor's hands, enjoying the intentional confusion he had established. "To answer your question, I am employed by one who heavily endows this institution of learning." Malachi lifted his mug to the Professor, then took a sip, commenting, "It is quite good.

"Now, I have a question for you, Professor Castellani. Why would you want Signorina Laura Bassi to become a student of the Academics of the First Order?"

Castellani decided to take a sip of the tea and said, "This is indeed superb, Signore— my apologies, I appear to have forgotten your name."

"You did not forget it, Professor. I did not yet share it," Malachi said, deliberately keeping the Professor off balance. "You may call me Malachi. Now please, answer my question." He stared at Castellani, compelling him.

The professor took another sip of the rich, sharp black tea and seemed to ponder. "I don't know why, Malachi, but it seems to me to be most important that Signorina Laura Bassi join. She is one of the most astute people I have ever known."

Malachi walked around the seated Castellani as he interrogated the professor. "Who spoke with you of Signorina Laura joining this First Order?"

Castellani appeared confused, seemed to think for a moment, then replied, "No one, Signor Malachi."

"I have never heard of the Academics of the First Order," said Malachi as he continued to circle Castellani in a predatory manner. Candlelight cast his menacing shadow on the stone walls. "Pray tell, how long have they had their charter and what venerable scholars have lectured in their hallowed halls?"

Sweat beaded on Castellani's forehead and at his temples.

"Have a sip of tea, Professor," said Malachi, his gracious tone at odds with his searching stare, "and think about your answers. Concentrate."

"Yes, yes!" Anxious to please his inquisitor, Castellani picked up his mug with a shaking hand, tea sloshing as he sipped. He took a deep breath and appeared to calm a touch.

"Better?" Malachi asked. "Good," answering his own question with a nod. "What facts do you know of the Academics of the First Order?"

A perplexed look came across Castellani's face, genuine confusion clouded his eyes. "I do not know."

While Malachi read Castellani, the dark stain of Seraph attempted to hide its presence from him. Under that stain, Malachi sensed a vulnerable, good man. "I believe if you think about it a little harder you will be able to recall. Have another sip of tea. It will clear your mind."

Suspicion again crossed the professor's face. "Is there something in this tea, Signor?"

A half smile crept into Malachi's harsh expression. He answered, "Nothing but pure tea leaves, the finest from China, my friend. So pure that it is purging your soul and mind of the nefarious cobwebs planted there by another of impure motives."

"What say you, Malachi?" asked Castellani as he shot to his feet in a panic.

"I shall tell you while you drink more of this tea. I will even trade mugs with you, if you prefer, to prove I have no ill intent."

The professor's eyes darted from Malachi's face, to his own mug, and to Malachi's mug. Seconds ticked by, the longcase clock down the hall counting them with loud clicks echoing through the silence. At last, he sat and took a long swallow of the tea, belief in Malachi appearing to win at this moment.

With a measure of relief, Malachi sat across from Castellani and began his explanation. "A man without good motives seeks to prey upon the brilliant Laura Bassi's fight to obtain rightful academic recognition here at the university and seize it as an opportunity to recruit her intelligence to advance his own cause.

"You will see the truth of this, because you will find little recall of your conversation of the gentleman who attempted to recruit you to help him get to Signorina Bassi."

Anger narrowed Castellani's eyes and pursed his lips. He pulled his hands through his hair. "I feel terrible I tried to convince Signorina Bassi to go with them."

With reassurance, Malachi squeezed Castellani's shoulder, and he sensed the last of the inky veil of confusion and coercion leaving. Castellani was not playing at being a double agent. "We have stopped it in time. But now you can identify for me the one who put the clouds in your head and stole your free will, Castellani. This is how they work, one reason why what they do is so wrong. It is not by your choice. It would not have been by Signorina Bassi's choice either, once she came into their circle."

Castellani nodded. "Yes, yes, of course I will help."

A conspiratorial light entered Malachi's eye; he did enjoy these turns of the tide. "You must not let on that you are onto the game, Professor. Figure out who this person is over the next two days who wishes you to lure Signorina Laura Bassi to them. I will come to you when you next light a candle in this room." Malachi withdrew a shilling-sized piece of obsidian from his pocket and pressed it into the academic's hand. The stone vibrated in Castellani's palm while Malachi instructed, "Keep this stone with you, Professor. If you get into trouble before you can get here to light a candle, rub it, and I will come to you." Although Malachi would watch Castellani and know if he were in trouble, Malachi judged the stone would place the professor more at ease acting as a freshman agent, and in control of the situation. It would enable Castellani to be more effective and less likely to be found out. He removed his own hand from the stone.

Castellani rubbed his thumb across the stone and took a sip of tea, appearing thoughtful. "You have made this a most interesting night, Malachi. I am still wondering whence you truly come, but you appear to have the admirable Signorina Bassi's interest at heart. No harm will come to me or her, for both you and I to work at keeping her at Bologna. I thank you for pulling from me the fog of which I had been unwittingly infected."

With a slight bow at the waist, Malachi said, "It is my pleasure, Professor. I do have one small favor to request."

Castellani gave Malachi a sharp glance, some of the goodwill falling away. "And what might that be," he questioned, his tone lacking the warmth and charity it had a few minutes prior.

"A brief introduction to Signorina Laura Bassi. She is fascinating and reminds me of someone I once knew and admired." Malachi's heart pounded in dread Castellani might turn him down.

With a laugh, the professor's goodwill resurrected. "I had a fear you would request an honorary degree or credit for having taken a lecture. I would be more than pleased to introduce you to Signorina Bassi, especially in light of what you have approached me with here, tonight." He clapped Malachi on the shoulder.

Malachi found himself startled to enter into camaraderie with this academic, where rare and genuine happiness filtered through a tiny, unexpected crack in his mind's armor. With warmth, he grasped Castellani's hand and shook it. "Thank you, Professor."

"My pleasure. A strong grip you have there, Signor Malachi. The calluses of a practiced swordsman, if I am not mistaken," the Professor noted while he grinned at Malachi. "A life some of us may romanticize, but do not understand the true cost. The swordsman and, may I deduce, the spy."

Pain gripped about Malachi's heart. His wounds reopened. He kept his angst hidden and his grip strong about the Professor's. "Good night, Castellani."

"Yes, I do have an early lecture, Signor and need to take my leave. I shall keep you posted. My footman would be waiting for me by now. Good night."

"Until we next speak, Professor."

Professor Castellani wound down his lecture on the phenomena of galvanism. While the lecture hall emptied, a board member of the university—Giussepe Caliguri—approached him.

"Cardinal Bellisario will be most displeased if Signorina Bassi has to face the challenges of being admitted to the University of Bologna. Yet, Cardinal Lambertini seems to be intent on making this happen, Professor Castellani," said Caliguri as his dark, Roman eyes pleaded with the professor.

"What if Signorina Bassi prefers Bologna, Signor Caliguri?"

"You must convince her otherwise, as we have been speaking of, Professor. You agreed it would not be in her best interest."

Castellani tipped his head and looked at Caliguri. He decided to play along. "Of course, Cardinal Bellisario's Academics of the First Order would indeed allow her to study as she chooses. I shall speak with her, again, directly, at morning lectures.

"Signore Caliguri, could you arrange an audience with Cardinal Bellisario this evening, so that I might be fresh in my information to Signorina Bassi?"

"Excellent idea, Castellani! Yes, in my study, after dinner tonight, say seven o'clock this evening?"

Pride in Castellani's performance made the corner of Malachi's mouth twitch in a threatened half-smile, from his cloaked perch in the shadowy, upper seats at the back of the lecture hall.

A dour butler opened the door to Signore Caliguri's well-appointed townhouse to admit Professor Castellani. Cloaked and traveling along with Castellani, Malachi noted the breath-taking, ornate carvings in the wood accents and the lifelike frescoes. He sensed Castellani's attention wander, distracted by the opulent decor. Malachi mentally nudged Castellani, who then reached into his pocket and fingered the obsidian from Malachi as he followed the stiff manservant.

Relieved, Malachi imparted his approval that Castellani had brought himself back around. The butler led the professor to the study and pushed open the heavy oak door with brass filigree hinges. Malachi sympathized with Castellani, hearing his heart pounding in his ears, the thumping increasing as the gazes and preying smiles of Caliguri and Bellisario turned toward him, their twin toothy shark-like smiles brightening all the more as the door swung open.

"Greetings, Professor Castellani," said Signore Caliguri. "Please make the acquaintance of Cardinal Bellisario."

Bellisario held out his hand with Cardinal's Ecclesiastical ring and Castellani genuflected toward it. Disgust rippled through both Malachi and Castellani. Malachi lent Castellani willpower. Determination to go through the motions on behalf of Laura Bassi flowed through Castellani and won over the distaste threatening to overtake him. He laid his lips for the briefest of moments upon the cold, metal ring and said, "Greetings, your Eminence."

Bellisario looked upon Castellani with approval lighting his eyes. "Please rise, my son," he intoned, his red cassock and cape appearing to Malachi as majestic crimson blood flowing about him.

Castellani nodded. "Thank you, Cardinal Bellisario." He stood and said, "I understand that we share a common interest in Signorina Bassi."

"Yes," the cardinal replied. "Very much so, Professor. She is a remarkable woman. I fear Bologna would lay to waste her acumen, as they would prefer to shove her in a dark corner. Whereas, with the Academics of the First Order, she will be respected and praised for her work and intellect."

Castellani and Malachi had devised a strategy earlier how they would bait the trap for the Cardinal. Castellani, at his most diplomatic, forged ahead with their plan. "Your Eminence, I will share with you what Signorina Laura Bassi said to me when we discussed the advantages the Academics of the First Order could bring her. For Bassi, this is not just about her, but about the doors she may be able to unlock for all women."

Cardinal Bellisario peered at Castellani with intent. Malachi saw the flick of the silver tongue of Gideon's influence in the Cardinal's eyes.

Castellani continued, "While I see the benefit of her joining the First Order, she feels it is her obligation to her fellow female would-be academics to forge ahead at the University of Bologna."

The Cardinal drew himself to a fuller height, his robes deepening in their scarlet color. "Professor, it is imperative you convince her otherwise."

They had sprung the trap, the Cardinal's true allegiance becoming evident.

Caliguri appeared distressed. "Cardinal, please allow me to get you a glass of port," the university board member suggested.

The Cardinal whirled on him and said, "Yes, Caliguri. A most excellent idea! Could you leave us for a moment while you locate some wine for our gathering?"

The strong wave of suggestion Cardinal Bellisario poured over the University board member had Castellani shoring up his defenses.

Malachi noted from where he hid that Bellisario fairly vibrated with Seraph power.

As Caliguri hurried from the study the Cardinal turned on Castellani, then advanced toward him. He seemed to grow taller, his robes a deeper crimson. "Laura Bassi will indeed benefit herself and all women intellects by joining the Academics of the First Order, Professor," Bellisario said as he advanced another step, Castellani's back now against a settee. "You men of learning have no appreciation for intelligent women. We shall not waste their intelligence out of fear, as your peers do, Professor."

Castellani bent backwards to avoid the now looming Cardinal, whose robes appeared to swirl of their own volition. "It is most unfortunate that such is the way of things, Cardinal. Signorina Bassi desires to be an agent for change."

"She must not, she must come with us," thundered the Cardinal as he raised his arm over the professor's torso and a ruby-jeweled dagger appeared in his hand. He arced the dagger down toward the professor.

At that moment, Malachi appeared and stayed the Cardinal's arm with his sword. "Signorina Bassi has chosen not to come with you, Cardinal Bellisario," he said with clipped, quiet lethality.

The Cardinal laughed. "This is rich, indeed. You! Who are

you to talk, Malachi the Fallen? You, who let your woman of science die for a tree, of all things," he said with an aristocratic sneer.

Malachi steeled himself not to jump to the bait.

Port in hand, Caliguri began to enter the study, balancing a tray with three glasses and the wine. The oak door slammed shut of its own volition, pushing him back out and the lock turned under an unseen hand.

Castellani watched the key rotate, his mouth agape in disbelief, then shifted his wide, terror-filled gaze back to the sword and the dagger; the latter barely held back by Malachi's sword.

Malachi jumped back and lunged again toward the Cardinal with his sword, not giving Cardinal Bellisario a chance to stab Castellani. "Get back to your viper's nest, servant of the Seraph."

Bellisario stared at Malachi, cunning darkening his eyes and the crimson of his robes. "You truly believe Laura Bassi will be better off with the weak-willed men of Bologna? Weak men who will see her as a threat and want to keep her under lock and key? Gideon will uplift and praise her!"

"Yes, he will," agreed Malachi, "and he will have her use her knowledge to further enslave the human minds, as Gideon has of the other people who serve him."

The Cardinal turned, his robes flaring out as a roiling sea of blood and made a lethal throw of his dagger at Castellani. Malachi leapt and stopped the dagger's point with his sword just before it entered Castellani's chest at his heart. He then lunged at Bellisario.

Enraged, Bellisario screamed as a column of swirling red motes started at his knees, then climbed higher up his legs as he made to vanish.

Malachi lunged and impaled the Cardinal with the end of his blade, making a sickening sound like one might hear at a butcher's table as the sword slid through Cardinal Bellisario's innards.

The Cardinal arched back, gurgling as blood frothed at his lips. The red motes continued to travel upward as the Cardinal attempted to use his remaining life force to escape. Even as the motes rose, Bellisario's spilled blood blended with the front of his crimson robes.

With lightning speed, Malachi withdrew his sword from the Cardinal's belly and swiped the tip across his neck.

A parody of a smile appeared in Bellisario's throat as it was slit open. His eyes rolled back in his head as his body—from the knees up—crumpled to the floor. The lower limbs which had disappeared in the red motes did not re-materialize.

Terrible, unearthly screeching came from a hollow distance, as though through a tunnel, then grew closer. Malachi jumped in front of the terrified Castellani, his glowing sword held before him.

Gargoyles appeared; scaly, hunch-backed, and dark gray. They ignored Malachi, intent only on the Cardinal. Malachi and Castellani watched in fascinated horror as the creatures wrenched Cardinal Bellisario's writhing, crimson soul from his body.

The scarlet wraith twisted and gyrated, desperate to escape their clutches.

The gargoyles secured the Cardinal's essence in a silver net. The largest one waved his hands and Bellisario's dead form disappeared, including his spilled blood. They muttered and argued amongst themselves.

Malachi watched with amazement as one of the gargoyles pulled the apparently disembodied lower limbs of the Cardinal from an unknown realm, then banished them as well. It appeared Cardinal Bellisario had sold his soul. To whom or what, Malachi did not know—or care to know.

The gargoyles vanished with their bounty.

Malachi found himself relieved none had bothered to take notice of him or Castellani.

The oak door opened. Malachi cloaked himself. Caliguri walked in carrying a bottle of port and three glasses on a tray, confusion clouding his face. "I say, Professor, that door seems to have locked me out." He looked about the room. "Where is the Cardinal?" he asked.

Castellani lifted the port from Caliguri's tray, answering, "I believe he found the need to leave, Signore Caliguri."

Caliguri set the tray down, looking about, flummoxed. "But I did not see him leave."

The professor poured them each a glass of port with shaking hands. Gingerly, he served the board member, managing not to slosh any wine over the rim of the glass. He lifted his own in a toast, "It has been a most unusual night, indeed, Signor Caliguri. But I am most pleased to have had the opportunity to better make your acquaintance." He clinked glasses with Caliguri, and swigged back his wine, only to pour another glass and down it.

Caliguri took a healthy gulp of the dark red port, then looked around, remarking, "Most unusual, indeed, Professor."

Castellani cleared his throat and said, "Signore Caliguri, I am now of the belief the Cardinal had nefarious motives for our esteemed Signorina Bassi. We should think about joining forces, Signore, and see what we can do about convincing the others at the University to allow her a full professorship and a Doctor of Philosophy. There is no question she is deserving."

Caliguri peered at Castellani. "Nefarious, you say? I am not surprised, really. I am quite relieved he is gone. The air here is lighter, cleaner with him out of my home." He lifted his glass. "A toast to Laura Bassi!"

Disguised as a dark Moorish academic, Thoth's eyes remained riveted to the woman speaking, defending forty-nine theses to the members of Bologna's Academy of Sciences to earn her Doctor of Philosophy from the University of Bologna.

Malachi had never seen Thoth this entranced by a human before.

"She is indeed exceptional," Thoth whispered to Malachi, bending his head from his formidable height to Malachi's ear.

Laura Maria Caterina Bassi spoke with confidence, knowledge, and poise. Thoth and Malachi both watched and listened, transfixed.

While Malachi enjoyed the eloquent Bassi at the podium, before the amassed crowd of scholars, he relished their more personal time together as she and Castellani debated many of her theses.

Heartache warred with admiration. Bassi did not hold Daphne's essence. Yet, he could not help but be in awe of her intellect, her depth, and her ability to articulate her theories.

Here with Thoth, bearing witness to a momentous instant in history, Malachi gave thanks for this portion of his path. Thoth's words from that black night over a century ago came back to him: Her essence will be born into women who accomplish great advances in knowledge.

His search would continue.

CHAPTER TWENTY-FOUR

Tuesday, July 12, 1938
Kaiser Wilhelm Institute of Chemistry, Germany

UNDER THE COVER OF DARKNESS, Malachi mustered all his ethereal energy and all he could gather from the Ancients, casting wards to blanket the activities within the office of Doctor Lise Meitner at the Kaiser-Wilhelm Institute for Chemistry from the prying and all-seeing Nazi Gestapo intelligence. He wore the brim of his dark gray crushable fedora pulled low, obscuring the glint of his eyes from those who may be watching from afar through binoculars.

Irritated by the stiff twill which rubbed against his neck, Malachi yanked loose his tie and breathed a sigh of relief, his concentration remaining unbroken. Out of habit, his grip tightened about the hilt of his sword, nestled under the flap of his dark gray trench coat. He garnered strength and comfort from the proximity of his blade.

In from the Netherlands, under the guise of nuclear fission experimentation, Dutch Physicists Dirk Costner and Adriaan Fokker gathered with Otto Hahn and Lise Meitner at Meitner's office, to plan Lise's escape. Her flight needed to happen within the next forty-eight hours—as soon as Malachi received the go-ahead. Time and opportunity seemed to hang in the balance, just out of reach, and the stakes were high. The air remained thick with tension, making it a challenge for the scientists to "act natural", as they had been instructed over and over.

The lilting laugh of Doctor Lise Meitner drifted his way, carried on the summer evening breeze. Head of Physics at the Kaiser Wilhelm Institute, and an Austrian Jew, she found herself in imminent danger; now that Germany had annexed Austria just this year.

The imperative nature of Lise's escape maintained a grim, sharp edge in all they did. Humor forced for the sake of the discerning and suspicious Gestapo, the group did their utmost to appear as science peers enjoying each other's company, rather than on a mission.

Malachi met Lise two weeks ago. Raphael sent him from Albert Einstein's side in the United States to the Wilhem Institute in Berlin, the precarious situation ripe for Seraph recruitment attempts. The operation maintained a "dark" status—the fewer people and Celestials in the know, the better. Meitner and her expertise in the fledgling field of nuclear energy could prove a huge coup for the Seraph.

Malachi thought back to how hope had burgeoned for him in his search for Daphne during the first week with Lise Meitner. He paired himself with the physicist while she journaled her notes; her brilliance pouring forth as she moved about from her atom splitting lab to her blackboard to her journal. Lise's banter with Otto Hahn reminded Malachi of Daphne and Dante. Malachi glued himself to Lise's side and soaked in her aura while he, Lise, and Otto awaited word of permission for Costner and Fokker to enter Germany under the guise of conducting nuclear experiments at the Kaiser Institute. This would be a show of German "good will" toward the science community in these contentious days. Each passing second waiting for word on the Dutch scientists' visit seemed like the heavy swing of a large pendulum ticking away Lise's freedom and, possibly, her life. Every night of the past two weeks, Malachi had listened for and readied to fight off a Gestapo raid.

The more time Malachi spent at Dr. Meitner's side, heaviness seeped around his heart as he discerned the luminous and determined physicist did not hold Daphne's essence. The weight did not distract him from his task of working to ensure her silent and successful escape from Nazi-run Germany.

Hairs stood on the back of Malachi's neck, pulling him back to the present. The sound of muffled soldier's boots treading on the ground in a stealthy manner not-so-far-off echoed from the building in front of him. He materialized with a cloaking spell near the source of the disturbance to discover two Sichereitsdienst SS operatives preparing to break into the Institute some distance from Meitner's office.

Shadowy laurel bushes waved in the summer night breeze about one-hundred feet to the south. Malachi threw the sound of someone walking through the brush that direction. The second SS operative jogged off to check the perimeter near the bushes.

With lethal stealth, Malachi stole up behind the first operative, the taller of the two. The man worked with some expertise on picking the lock to the Materials delivery bay in the moonlight. Malachi found himself impressed at the operative's talent —in the dark, no less. Cold and silent, Malachi slipped a leather strap over the operative's head to encircle his neck, fast as quicksilver, and cut off his circulation without harming him. The man blacked out in seconds, unaware of what had just happened, assuaging Malachi's conscience. Malachi shrouded the now-still figure in the shadows, gagging and binding him with expediency. He waited in the darkness of the breezy summer night for the second operative to return.

The second operative jogged back with stealthy steps, turning his head as he looked for his partner. Like a phantom, Malachi glided up behind the unsuspecting agent then squeezed him until he went limp from lack of oxygen. Binding him hand and foot, Malachi also gagged him. He tucked both unconscious men into the back to the delivery bay. He then set wards to ensure they would remain unconscious for some time.

Malachi located their vehicle. Affecting the first operative's voice, he radioed a message to their command that Lise Meitner and the Dutch scientists continued to work late into the night. He received orders to stand down and keep watch, just the response for which he had mentally pushed. Malachi then briefed Raphael on the events thus far with a silent communique.

At five o'clock in the morning, Malachi took Lise and the two Dutch scientists to her home to freshen up and wait for word. To all appearances, the trio of accomplished physicists had been up through the night collaborating, which corroborated with the radio message sent to the agents' command a few hours prior.

Dawn lightened the sky. Malachi received telepathic word from Raphael to proceed with haste. He pulled the car around the front of Dr. Meitner's home. Fokker, Costner, and Meitner tumbled in, while morning bird songs proved the world kept turning no matter what was happening in one's life.

Dark circles under Lise's eyes showed stark in her pale face. Tears threatened to spill over as Malachi pulled away. Lise craned her neck and looked through the rear window of the car at her home. "My work and notes, my photographs, mementos, clothing—all of it left behind," she whispered. "I have ten francs in my purse. Ten francs! Otto gave me this diamond ring which belonged to his mother, bless his heart." She lifted her left hand, showing her ring finger. "In case I needed a bribe.

"This is it, all I have, now."

"Lise, it will be okay. I feel it in my bones, or I would not be here," said Doctor Costner as he hugged her to his side, his arm about her shoulders.

Doctor Fokker grasped her hand and squeezed it. "Lise, Doctor Meitner, you need to look like a happy scientist when we go through the checkpoints; not so shaken, or you will certainly give up our game to them," he admonished her, the warmth in his tone surrounding her in his confidence.

"Yes, Adriaan, of course you are correct, as always. Thank you, both, and Malachi."

They arrived at the first gate. Malachi handed everyone's papers through the window to the guard at the checkpoint, along with a gentle mind push to not really see Doctor Meitner's name on the documents. The guard shuffled through the credentials twice. Confusion drifted across his face. Malachi sent him a thought he had a sudden need to urinate.

A distressed look of urgency came over the guard's countenance. He shoved the papers back into Malachi's outstretched hand and waved them on. Malachi tossed the soldier a pack of German cigarettes as he drove through.

Relief flowed through the car. Fokker hugged Lise and kissed her on the head. Costner shook Fokker's hand and patted Malachi on the shoulder.

Malachi's heart sank as he spied the long line of traffic for the second checkpoint. He slowed as he came to the back of the queue. It edged forward. The brakes to the car creaked as Malachi brought the car ahead another twenty feet, then stopped. The pattern repeated. Creep forward, stop. The hot sun beat down. Flies darted among the long line of cars. His heart sank when he noted guards walking along and checking the cars sitting in the queue.

Malachi dared not look at Meitner in the rearview mirror. Lise did an admirable job keeping up the light banter with her Dutch colleagues.

The line began to move, and the guards stopped checking vehicles in line two cars ahead of them.

Malachi's nerves stretched taut as they drew closer to the gates. He maintained his mental push, straining to keep a balance, so the officer would not sense something off as Malachi tried to smudge Doctor Meitner's name a second time for the gate guards.

Malachi resisted the urge to shift in his seat to alleviate the tickle from the sweat rolling down his back. The hat band of his fedora became itchy, dampened with perspiration. Costner brought up a debate of caramel versus chocolate over a sundae.

These guards, in their wool uniforms, closer to the border, proved cranky in the hot sun with the long line of cars. They were not easy to sway. "Please tell me again, Fraulein Meitner, why you have permission to go to the conference in Amsterdam, and why the document for that is not here?" For the third time, the gate agent questioned Doctor Meitner and looked over her papers with his head shoved in the window of the car and his dark, beady eyes moving over Lise as though she might be prey.

Malachi, now desperate, called upon the Ancients. The air in the car changed. A low murmuring filled the interior of the vehicle while a whirlwind disturbed the maps lying about the inside of the car, lifting and teasing their corners.

A look of terror entered the gate officer's eyes. He yanked his head out of the car, cracking his crown on the window frame. "Go! Just go." He waved Malachi on, frantic now to have them gone.

Lise kept her eyes closed once through the checkpoint.

Fokker and Costner's visages had turned pale and they did not speak a word. Malachi did not answer their unspoken question.

They got five miles down the road, well past the border into the Netherlands. Malachi looked in the rearview mirror at Lise.

She caught his gaze. Dr. Meitner bent her face into her hands and broke into sobs.

PART III

IMMORTAL LOVE

2014 TO PRESENT DAY
UNITED STATES OF AMERICA

Love will find a way
through paths where wolves fear to prey.
— *Lord Byron*

CHAPTER TWENTY-FIVE

Friday, September 26, 2014 CE
Cornell University, New York, USA

OAK TREES DROPPED their bright red and gold leaves about Laurel while she grappled with her heavy backpack and hurried to her chemistry lab at Cornell University. A tardy entry into the lab translated to three hours of being glared at with disapproval by Doctor Sour Wine. The professor actually spelled her name Sauerwen, but "Sour Wine" better fit her less-than-sunny disposition. Laurel found herself drawn to the oaks and for them to be of particular comfort to her. She never could put her finger on why. With a hard push on the door of the Chemistry Building, against the vacuum created by the autumn winds blowing between the campus buildings, the door gave with a 'whoosh'. Oak leaves swirled and danced around her, following her into the hall. Her light brown ponytail blew across her face. Laurel spit the hairs out of her mouth and glanced up at the clock above the lab door, letting out a breath of relief. She'd made it on time from her job at the library to chem lab!

At the lab station, she worked to catch her breath, inhaling quietly through her nose, attempting to be subtle and not draw attention to herself. The more one flew under the radar with Doctor Sour Wine, the better, in the graduate Bio-Molecular Engineering program.

Chem lab got underway and Laurel soon found herself immersed in the graduate organic chemistry lab. A place where she could play all day, if she were allowed.

"Hey, Laurel," her friend, Melanie, called out after her, as they were leaving the three-hour long lab, "you gonna come for the darts tournament tonight?"

"I wish I could, Mel. I have the calculus papers to grade for Doctor Vioral."

"I hear ya, Laurel," Melanie said, nodding, her cafe au lait complexion and burnished brown curls striking in the fall sunlight. "You need your bread and butter. Tom will be disappointed, though. He loves it when you are his partner, 'cause he wins, and that man is a sore loser. You hit that bullseye like no other. It's almost like you wish those darts to that bullseye every time."

Laurel laughed, "Nah. It's just dumb luck."

With her warm brown eyes, Melanie gave Laurel a soul-searching look. "So you say, Laurel. But there are days I wonder. Like today. That Bunsen burner lit itself before you really even hit the ignition."

"Melanie, you are full of shit!"

"I am not, I am a Baptist. I'm keeping my eye on you and your Bunsen burners from now on, girlfriend."

"You do that, Mel, and I hope you think my Bunsen burners are cute," laughed Laurel. "Have fun and stay safe tonight, Love."

"I will. You too, Laurel. Those calculus problems can jump out and bite you, if you're not careful, you know."

"Ha! Very funny. Go have a cold one for me, Mel."

Laurel thought about what Mel had said about the Bunsen burners as she walked to the bus stop near the chemistry building. She had an awareness of sometimes knowing things before they happened and wishing a moving object would go a certain direction and it suddenly would. She had always chalked such events up to coincidence. Now she wondered.

She had also known for several years she possessed a talent for discerning what ailed people and animals with a simple touch. This she attributed to astute assessment skills and an ability to pick up minute details. *Oh, for heaven's sake*, Laurel laughed at herself, *What a bunch of bullshit! Calculus papers pay better than ruminating over this conjecture, even if it were true. Unless, of course, I could actually bring myself to hustle at pool and darts. Hmm, maybe that's a thought.*

"Come on, slow-poke," Laurel said to Tom, during their morning hike near the breath-taking waterfalls of Buttermilk Falls State Park.

The rushing water sent spray and prisms into the fall sunshine. Dancing droplets brought to mind her dream last night of being in a centuries-old alchemy lab, with the bubbling, boiling water, and steam for the distillation processes. The vivid nature with which she recalled her long dress moving about her as she removed a crucible from an ungodly hot oven had unnerved her. She could still feel the heavy, yet supple leather of her apron which protected her shift, skirts and laced bodice. Laurel tried to set aside the feeling of disquiet the all-too-real dream had raised.

A headache with which she had awoken this morning

loomed at the back of her head. With a roll of her shoulders and a mindful listen to the falls, she chased the pain away and kept walking. She looked back to see Tom *still* trailing behind her.

Laurel inhaled, appreciating the fresh air and the invigorating pace she had been maintaining. Taking a break while she waited for Tom to catch up, she stared into the rushing water and had a sudden feeling of being terrified of it, yet she loved it.

Laurel took an uncharacteristically cautious step back from the boulder's edge.

Tom's voice broke the nightmarish musing.

"I'm coming, Laurel. I am not in as good of shape as you. And, I am sorry to admit I have a bit of a hang-over." His parents' Chinese dialect drifted in and out of his American accent.

Laurel loved listening to Tom talk. This time she loved it even more and the distraction it gave her from her unbidden fear.

She laughed, and said, "Both are your problem, not mine, 'Dart Boy'. If you want to hike with me, as you insist you do, you had better train more to keep up." She resumed hiking, thankful poor Tom could not see her grin.

"You have no mercy, Laurel. Honest to God, I had no idea you were so fucking cold hearted—oh shit!"

Laurel's heart leapt into her throat when she heard the panic in Tom's voice. She turned just in time to see his arms flailing as he tried to catch his balance. He slid, his efforts to stay on his feet fruitless as he went down on a slippery rock, twisting his ankle. She swore she watched him, and his tall body go down in slow motion. She gave thanks he did not appear to bump his head.

"Oh, oww! Motherf—Ggg... it hurts." Tom grimaced as he rocked, holding his ankle.

Laurel scrambled over to him.

"Did you hurt your elbow, Tom? Or hurt anything else?"

"You mean besides my pride and my ankle, Laurel," Tom asked with a self-deprecating laugh, as he rocked to-and-fro, holding his ankle, in obvious pain. "No, I don't think so. But my ankle hurts so much, right now, I am not sure if I can tell if anything else is hurt."

"Let me see, Tom," Laurel said as she crouched down next to him. Her ponytail slid from her back to alongside her neck when she bent over him. She pushed his hands out of the way and probed his lower leg, ankle, and shoe-covered foot for obvious signs of injury. He hissed in a sharp breath here and there as she hit a few tender areas. She wanted to smack him for being a ninny but restrained herself. Not finding anything too concerning, she held her hands over where he had been holding his ankle, to offer comfort.

"Laurel?" Tom said her name with a question riding on his voice and a strange tone, "Laurel." He said her name again, with more emphasis.

She looked over at him, eye-level, still crouched, and imitated him.

"Tom."

He cocked his head and gave her a hard stare, his typical mischief gone. "I am being serious."

"So am I, Tom. What?" Mild exasperation threaded through Laurel's voice.

Tom hesitated. "I don't know how to describe this, and you will think I have gone over the edge." He took off his cap and jabbed his hand through his straight, thick dark hair. "Christ." He blew out his breath. "There is humming and warmth under your hands. The pain in my ankle is gone," he said while he looked at her. "I am a Mechanical Engineer. This shit does not happen. But it just did. I fucking felt it."

Laurel felt her pulse pound in her ears and her stomach knot. *What the fuck? Just play it cool. We'll figure this out later.* She looked at him like he had no clue what he was talking about, and felt a tiny bit guilty. "What 'shit', Tom? I held your ankle. It happens to feel better at the same time. No big deal."

"I am telling you, Laurel, I felt something!"

"Yes, Tom. You felt your poor, untrained ankle twist, and your ass—and your pride—hit the ground. Sheesh! M.E.'s! One has to explain everything to you guys in concrete terms."

"Whatever. Give me a hand up. I think I am okay, now. I need to get home and train so that I can keep up with you, Bunsen Girl." Warm, teasing sarcasm graced his deep voice.

"Melanie said something to you!"

"She's seeing things you make happen, Laurel," Tom insisted. "By the way, are you up for darts, tonight," he asked her, a hopeful look on his face.

"No."

"No?" Tom reiterated while he tested weight on his ankle.

"I have saved your sorry ass enough for one day. I am tapped out."

"Laurel, indeed, you do have a heart of stone."

"There are worse things to have. I'll take having a heart of stone. Let's go, Slick."

Butterflies invaded Laurel's stomach while she struck a match, the pungent scent filling the air. She leaned over from her sofa and touched the lit match to the wick of the pillar candle in the center of her coffee table. The wick sputtered, then caught, its light clove scent rising. *You are such an ass, Laurel, for even thinking that you might have some kind of crazy psychic telekinetic thing going on.*

Whatever. No hurt in trying a simple experiment.

I can't believe I am arguing with myself. Let's just do this and prove that it is all coincidence.

The candle flame flickered, bathing Laurel in its warm light in her small living room. The cinnamon and clove smell proved comforting, reminiscent of apple pie. Laurel focused on the flame, thinking of it growing larger. The room brightened as the flame increased in size and turned from yellow orange to bluish. "What?" she whispered to herself, then the flame dropped to its former size as soon as Laurel removed her full concentration from it. Her hands on her thighs, she focused again on the flame. It grew to the size of a beer bottle in a bare moment, the flame again blue. Laurel raised her right hand and passed it near the flame. Warmth radiated from it, bathing rather than burning her hand. She wondered if the flame would avoid burning only her or other things, or if she could control the heat, as well.

Retrieving a wooden spoon and a glass of water from the kitchen, Laurel ventured into her spur of the moment experiment. These seemed the best tools of opportunity, her best tool to test her hypotheses and avoid setting off the smoke alarm, or worse yet, the sprinkler system for her apartment complex.

Laurel set her smart phone on record and propped it up on a couple of books on a chair opposite of her. She tested and made adjustments, ensuring everything she wanted was captured in the frame.

Back at her seat on the sofa, she had a sense of stepping into a place where she had always belonged. Laurel found herself surprised that only intrigue filled her, not fear.

"Growing the flame," she whispered to narrate for the recording, feeling a bit silly. She then pushed past the sense of embarrassment for the sake of accurate documentation. The flame grew and turned bluish. "Right," she said as she moved her head to the right, and the flame moved with her. "Left." She did not move her head, but the flame moved to her left as commanded. "Center," she said with a whisper, and the flame came back to its resting place. She passed her hand through the beer-bottle sized flame, her eyes on the flame. "It only feels warm to my hand," she explained in a soft, factual voice for the video. "Now, I am going to see if the flame will follow my commands for heat on the handle of this wooden spoon. I do have a glass of water here, for safety."

Her gaze on the flame, she lifted the wood handle end to the flame. "Do not burn the wood." The air only held the scent of the candle. Laurel could not help but smile. She found herself split between just plain having fun with this or grappling with what many would call impossible. She also felt conflicted between incredulity, and a sense of rightness. She surprised herself not experiencing any sense of panic. She continued to hold the wooden spoon in the intense flame, the wood remained uncharred. She turned the handle toward the smartphone so the viewer would see the lack of blackening.

Laurel decided to prove the wood had not been wettened prior to her experiment. "Scorch the wood, but not too much. I happen to like this spoon." A light smell of burning wood permeated the air. Visible smoke rose from the flame and the spoon handle, the wood now darkened with a scorching shine in the middle of the spoon handle. "Stop," Laurel commanded out loud. The smoke dissipated, even though the spoon handle remained in the flame. "I am observing that I do not have a need to place the spoon handle in water at this time. It is no longer burning.

"This is one of the more interesting evenings I have had at home, alone."

Laurel got up and turned off the video recording, and pulled her hand through her ponytail. "Okay, now what?" she asked herself, one of the few times in her life she found herself at a loss for an answer.

On Sunday morning, Laurel spotted Melanie through the window of the coffee shop sitting at their favorite table as she rounded the sidewalk corner just before the entrance. Pushing the glass door open, Laurel savored the rich, initial moment of entering her favorite little cafe. For Laurel, the faithful jingle of the brass door-top bell heralded the velvety aromas of various fresh coffees, the sound of the steamer and the stories the burnished old wood floors imparted to her whenever she walked into the cafe. Warmth for all the senses always surrounded Laurel in this grand, old place.

A distant look on her face, Melanie made notes as she read something on her laptop and did not see or hear Laurel approach. She jumped, startled, when Laurel pulled out her chair. Laughing, she said, "Hey, girl, you just scared me out of this applied mathematics problem. I am ready to tear my hair out."

"Sorry. I don't do windows or Applied Math, Mel. And thanks for the coffee, babe," Laurel said as she took a sip. Mel ordered it just the way she liked it. She tossed a look at the counter and saw Tom had on the 'Apron of Pain' today. She lifted her mug to him with a smile. He mimicked throwing a dart, then a teardrop sliding down from his eye with a fingertip. She played an air violin. He tossed his towel over his shoulder with a grin and spun away to help the next customer.

"Well, shit, Laurel. I'll text Cutch and see if she can lend me a hand later today with this problem, it's driving me nuts. So, what's the scoop and what's this video you could not send me, but wanted me to see?"

Over the rim of her cup, Laurel whispered, "Melanie, this video I took of myself. In a million years, I would not send this to anyone. I don't care how trusted they are. Hell, I probably would not even send it to myself, Melanie. You're gonna think I'm crazy, fucking possessed, or took a shit-assed special effects course." She took a sip of her coffee. "I can tell you, I did not take a special effects course, and I am kind of freaked out."

Melanie's eyebrows came together, and she started to laugh.

"Laurel, you are the most evidence-based information person I know. This combination of words coming out of your mouth is not yours." She stared at Laurel. "Oh, for God's sake, just show me the video! How bad can it be?"

With Laurel's double earbud adapter, they both listened and watched the video Laurel had taken the night prior.

Melanie sat back in her chair and stared at Laurel when they were done watching the video, her tan fingers encircling her mug. "Well, shit, Laurel." She narrowed her warm brown eyes and peered at Laurel, asking, "Are you sure you did not use special effects? I mean, I am not saying you are making this stuff up; but to actually consider this is real, well, is kind of mind boggling, Laur. This is a joke, right?"

Laurel wrapped her ponytail around two fingers, a nervous habit, while she listened to Melanie's questions, then answered with a soft laugh rifled with sarcasm. "Mel, I wish I had that good of a sense of humor and film-making talent to play this kind of joke. I am afraid that is really me. And when I say 'afraid', part of me is downright shitting myself, the other part is thinking this could be cool as hell."

"Yeah, well, there is that, too, Laur," said Melanie, the practical mathematics whiz, her gaze intent on Laurel's. She thought a bit, then sat back in her chair and smiled. "Relax, Babygirl. You have no reason to have to want or need this... this crazy shit you just showed me. The world will be your oyster when you graduate. My thoughts are what you have here is a legit part of you which we don't yet understand. You are not possessed or crazy. Just learn about it all organically.

"But, and this may or may not be a big 'but', you control it, don't let it control you. If you sense yourself careening out of control, call me, we'll find some voodoo priestess my Auntie Marie knows in Savannah and go talk with them. Or I can take you to the Physics department - they'd have a field day with this talent of yours," Melanie said with a wink. "Otherwise, this stays between us, Love.

"Deal?" Melanie asked, her coffee cup raised.

"Deal," replied Laurel, clinking her cup with Mel's.

The Seraph science talent scout, Sarah Grayson, shut her laptop. With her earbuds and digital voice recorder, she appeared as though she were transcribing notes from a lecture. The voice recorder picked up just about every word of Laurel and Melanie's conversation with its enhanced microphone.

York Targeted Technologies had talent scouts making rounds through top-notch engineering schools throughout the world. Sarah had the Northeastern Coast of the US, a hotbed of exceptional engineering universities. Laurel Heatherton would be a home run with her psychical abilities and biomedical engineering acumen.

Laurel had caught Sarah's eye last spring at Cornell. She had logged Laurel into the York Targeted Technologies scouting database so that her banking transactions could be tracked, thus Laurel's proximity could be determined, if she moved. Serendipity favored Sarah for her to catch this gem of a private conversation between Melanie and Laurel today.

In flawless Jimmy Choo heels, which matched her dark red suit, Sarah stood, her dark, long, and thick hair, gleaming with health and wealth, flowed to midway down her back. She glided over to Melanie and Laurel's table. "Ladies, forgive me for inter-rupting, but please let me give you my business card." With smooth, eloquent efficiency of movement, she slipped two vellum business cards from her sleek silver case and handed one to each Laurel and Melanie.

"We are always on the lookout for formidable female minds, ladies. Check us out online, feel free to give me a call anytime. I don't want to interrupt your Sunday morning any more than I already have."

And then she was gone, almost into thin air. Her expensive perfume lingering behind.

"Laurel," Tom said her name, now standing at her table.

"Tom, I don't have time for darts tonight."

"No, Laurel. Please, listen. That chick in the red suit was spying on you. She was listening to what you and Melanie were talking about, taking notes. So not right."

Laurel burst into laughter.

Tom looked confused, "What?"

"If she was listening to me, Tom, trust me, she is going to think I am batshit crazy."

"Well, hell, Laurel, I already know that. Along with the fact you have a heart of stone. 'Off your rocker and cold-hearted'— the future of genetic engineering."

"Hey, if it gets me a pair of those hot Jimmy Choo heels, I'll take it,' said Melanie.

"Hell to the yeah, Sister," replied Laurel, high-fiving Melanie.

"God, shoes. I hate talking about shoes unless I am designing equipment to manufacture them. I am getting back to work." Tom paused. "But seriously, Laurel and Melanie, be careful. I am telling you, that 'Jimmy Choo shoe' bitch transcribed everything Laurel was saying."

Laurel pinned him with a look, panic riding up her back. She asked, "How do you know, Tom? Did you read what she typed?"

Melanie caught Laurel's fear and stood next to her.

"Are you kidding me, Laurel?" replied Tom. "I could not see her screen from that far away. But I am telling you, that it was as plain as day to me she was watching you two, listening to Laurel and typing what Laurel said."

Melanie peered at him, "And not what I said?"

He slammed his towel on the countertop, "You know, with you two, 'no good deed goes unpunished'. When Laurel talked, she typed. Okay?"

"Tom," said Melanie, with a sly light in her eye, "I do think you are sweet on Laurel."

"No, I like the way she does Integers."

"Right."

Laurel took pity on Tom. "Hey thanks, Tom. I do appreciate the heads up." She called over to Melanie, "I will catch you later, girlfriend. Thanks for everything." The bell jingled as Laurel pulled open the door and left the store.

"I know you like her, Tom."

"Melanie, I do like her. But I respect her more than anything. This may sound weird, but I know she is not meant for me. So, I'll enjoy being on the same darts team as her." He grinned at Melanie.

Parked on a residential side street about three miles from Cornell, in quaint Ithaca, Sarah Grayson reported in as directed. "That is right, Mr. Augustine, Laurel Heatherton," Sarah spoke into her cell phone from the leather driver's seat of her silver BMW while she reviewed the information from her database on her laptop, set atop the center console of the car. "Graduate student, Bio-Molecular Engineering." Sarah took a sip of her coffee.

"Excellent! Ms. Grayson, you have outdone yourself," replied Gideon Augustine, shadowy chairman of the board for York Targeted Technologies, a biological pharmaceutical company which had developed three successful immunologic drugs.

YTT served as one of Gideon's many front operations for the Seraph. Several housed successful and legitimate businesses, his coffers well-endowed. This allowed hundreds of his operatives to hide in plain sight and attain positions of influence through the world in board rooms, lobbying firms and government. "You cannot let Ms. Heatherton out of your cyber sight. If she is who I believe she is, you have tripped over a rare diamond, indeed."

Sarah set her coffee into the cup holder. "She does seem very bright, but what advantage would she have over another of the same from Harvard, Mr. Augustine?" Sarah asked while making notes in the Louis Vuitton planner open across her lap.

"Ms. Grayson, if you ever presume to question me again, you shall regret it like you have never regretted anything before in your life," Gideon ground out over the phone, the menace traveling over the network with ease.

Sarah's hand froze. The pen timbered from her now stiff and useless grip onto the planner, then rolled onto the rubber car mat. Sarah's mouth moved like a guppy as she gasped ineffectively for air, her face pale against her dark hair and red matte lipstick. Her wide eyes unblinking.

Her body jerked, released. Sarah dragged in a huge breath.

"Do I make myself clear, Ms. Grayson?"

Smoothing her voice, while the rest of her trembled, she answered, "Yes, Sir, Mr. Augustine, you do. Very clear."

CHAPTER TWENTY-SIX

Thursday, April 9, 2015
Cornell University, Ithaca, New York

MALACHI COULD NOT HELP but look around in wonder during his tour of the Cornell University Campus, the air electrified by an astounding level of pulsing curiosity, drive, intellect, and acumen.

Isaiah Technology Securities and Malachi Jacobs, CEO, won the contract at Cornell University; the job to test the level of adaptive and cloud-based security for the University's Information System and make recommendations for infrastructure security improvements. The stakes were high for Cornell to protect the ongoing research at the university and thwart hacking. From grades to high-tech engineering research, the IT security overhaul had been Board approved.

The Cornell CIO and CFO both communicated to Malachi that Isaiah Technology Securities received the contract award related to the respect and credit Malachi gave the Cornell designers of current IT security. This, along with the collaborative nature of his thorough plan, the non-proprietary, forward-thinking, and cost-conscious infrastructure bolstering suggestions Malachi outlined in his proposal. His reputation for thoroughness, discretion and continuously evolving expertise also helped.

In his centuries-long search for Daphne as an Immortal Guardian, the evolution of Information Technology and the need to provide ever-evolving security in IT provided a serendipitous way for him to grow a business in which he excelled, search for Daphne and serve as Guardian to several high-stakes industries, thus the development of Isaiah Technology Securities, with a premier, cutting edge and pristine reputation. To Malachi, landing the Cornell contract meant he had finally attained the credibility he had strived to achieve.

Right now, Daphne's absence seemed more profound and palpable to him. He knew she would be proud of this accomplishment.

In her honor, he intended to ensure ITS maintained or improved upon current momentum, quality, and integrity. He planned to continue to be particular about who he decided to contract with and hire. Malachi also planned to avoid stretching thin the company resources in chasing profits, choosing quality over quantity, even though he had 'advisors' coming out of the woodwork advising him to do otherwise; sniffing commissions, he was sure. One slip up could cause irreparable harm to the company's reputation, only to lose it all. He had no problem telling these hound dogs to get the hell out of his way.

The Director of Hardware Support, John Harding, brought Malachi on a walk-through of genetic engineering labs. Malachi had asked to see, again, first-hand, the workflow of the students and faculty in one of the higher-stakes areas.

At a workstation sat a young woman with a large screen in front of her, images magnified via a laser microscope displayed on the monitor. Malachi's gaze landed upon this woman. She paid him no attention, in deep concentration, and he found he could not pull his attention away. His line of vision moved between her and the large monitor she studied, before keying information into a desktop to the side of the microscope. Her light brown ponytail shifted with movement; tension painted a study in deep thought across her facial features.

"We are experimenting with the use of a laser microscope to study the splicing of pre-messenger RNA molecules," John explained. "What you are seeing up there is happening real time."

Malachi had the sense he should be awed by what John just shared, instead it seemed as though someone had punched him in the stomach, and he had ringing in his ears. "Who is using the microscope?" he asked.

"One of our grad students, and they have to reserve time to use it," John said.

Malachi tried not to growl out loud, and instead sound polite. "I mean what is the name of the person using the microscope?"

John gave him a quizzical look. "I really don't know, and is that relevant to your current information needs, Mr. Jacobs?"

Malachi panicked when he realized he crossed a line for business boundaries for his personal agenda. He thought fast, and said, "I thought it would be a good idea to look for her IT signature tonight, and trace where it goes and what doors the reservation portal might open. Examine all of that area for hacking vulnerability."

John's face lightened, and he gave a small laugh. "They use paper on an old-fashioned clip-board to block out laser scope time. But what you say has a lot of merit, Jacobs. I think we should consider changing to a unique identifier on-line login to use the scope for tracking and tracing purposes."

Malachi nodded and smiled, thanking Isis he had dodged that bullet. Nevertheless, frustration mounted that it appeared he would not be able to obtain the girl's name without appearing wholly inappropriate. He could not afford to lose this contract, either.

Malachi struggled to appear nonchalant while he attempted to probe her thoughts, find more about who she was.

He inwardly jumped when he sensed her slam shut the metaphysical door on his curiosity. He had not expected this girl to have picked up on it or react as she did.

John looked at him with expectation, half-turned and ready to start walking to another area.

Malachi knew he had already pushed the envelope of polite business boundaries here. He pasted on a pleasant smile, and his heart tore in two while he said, "I am ready if you are, John."

The four-hour block she had for the laser microscope had slipped away like quicksilver. Time-pressed anxiety nibbled at her psyche as she worked at capturing the digital images of the RNA assembly process at the molecular level.

Two male voices encroached on her concentration, irritating her. This would surely slow her down. They had better not stop to ask me any questions, she crabbed to herself, as she jammed a pencil into her ponytail.

A chill went up her spine as what she could only describe as 'filaments of cobwebs' formed a bridge between her and one of the men. A taller man with dark hair pulled back in a ponytail of his own, dressed in a charcoal gray suit with a black shirt and some sort of drab, black and gray striped ties—she really did not care. The psychical bridge came about without her doing or permission and that irritated her even more. *Dammit!* She needed to get her work done and her precious time at the laser microscope grew shorter by the second. Laurel slammed shut her mind from him and his cloudy, cobwebby bridge to make best use of the precious forty-eight minutes she had left.

CHAPTER TWENTY-SEVEN

Present Day, Late March ~ Seattle, Washington, USA

THE CHISELED PLANES of Malachi's face reflected blue and gray from the three large monitors from which he worked. Once again, he ran his self-designed diagnostics on the three HTML files. He took screen shots of the discrete and well-hidden data miners he tracked and preyed upon. Lining up screenshots side by side on a larger monitor above his three regular screens, he highlighted the diagnostic alerts and mining hacks. Sure enough, he had identified a signature, thus found the trail of the mole who had stolen information from the CAR-T biomedical research firm. The predator in him snarled. He would track down this motherfucker IT minion of Gideon's.

The sneaky-assed firewall breach methodology had Gideon's foul stink all over it, as well as his sharp, intricate web espionage signature. Malachi now had what he needed. The secure phone line activated, he reached out to his CIA IT Bio-Chemical Warfare Security contact.

The thrill of the hunt had a sweet, victorious flavor. Beyond that, Malachi found himself scared shitless. Gideon's potential goal for developing this type of technology could prove disastrous and deadly to thousands of people. Biological or genomic warfare designed for a targeted portion of society. Malachi wondered just what was Gideon's endgame—a negotiation tool or a device of mass destruction? Malachi had recruited some of the top minds in the field of predictive science and had them working on it.

Gideon had also grown savvy with IT and genomic technology. He put Malachi through his paces to keep up with him on a discreet and undetected basis.

While on interminable hold, waiting for his CIA contact, Malachi took a swig of the pre-requisite coffee which formed the pulsing blood of IT. As he savored the fine arabica grind, Malachi reflected on what brought him to this point.

Ryena Wickerham picked up the line.

"What the hell, Ryena, I don't have all fucking day."

"Cool your jets, Malachi. I was briefing the Secretary of Defense."

"I will let it go this time, Ham." He grinned as he practically heard the eye roll on the other end. With another swig of coffee, he dove into relaying to her what he had discovered while he hit send for the file of amassed screenshots and analyses coming her way.

CHAPTER TWENTY-EIGHT

A Monday in April, Present Day ~ Seattle, Washington, USA

THE HIGH-RESOLUTION, large monitor screen for the electron microscope Laurel Heatherton used revealed consistent genomic abnormalities which occurred on a regular basis for the high mortality lung cancer she studied to conquer. Doctor Heatherton worked to find a protein expression marker.

Their research had brought them to the cusp of a breakthrough. She could taste it. The question remained, why? Why did these gene mismatches occur for this type of cancer? Once she or her team figured that out, they would be able to develop an inhibitor to prevent it. She predicted solving this mystery would lead to several wider discoveries.

With sure, scripted movement of her stylus she made notes in her electronic journal on her touchscreen laptop. The background for her journal had the look of old parchment, something she had always favored.

When she completed her doctorate various bio-chemical and genomic research firms had wined and dined her to excess in their efforts to recruit her. The salaries and relocation packages offered to her were nothing short of outrageous.

Well-published in her Cornell University doctoral candidate collaborations and possessing an uncanny intuition regarding the next line of cancer and autoimmune research, Laurel found the pharmaceutical companies clamoring to hire her.

Her current employer, Pacific Pharmaceuticals, had promised her she could devote thirty-five percent of her work time and lab resources toward what she wanted to research, provided there were no initial copyright issues. That freedom to do research clinched the decision for her, more than any monetary reward.

Laurel turned from her large monitor when she heard the "whoosh" of the sealed doors opening. Two people stepped through the double airlock doors in disposable white clean-room coveralls with hoods and booties, which matched her own. The lint-free garb served to prevent contamination of specimens and electronics, which could ruin a multi-million-dollar experiment.

Her CEO Victoria Ferguson had a tall person in tow. *With Victoria, a force to be reckoned with, that would be a literal "in tow"*, Laurel thought to herself with an inner grin.

She could not see the face belonging to Victoria's tall companion. The clear plastic visor sewn into that bunny suit's hood pointed up to the very boring ceiling for some reason.

Victoria's beautiful, dark-skinned visage brightened when her gaze landed on Laurel. Laurel despised interruptions and did not enjoy being shown off as one of the 'prize acquisitions'. She tried to wipe the scowl from her face but found her brows returned to being furrowed as soon as she stopped concentrating on it.

Victoria's eyes sparkled as she made her way across the lab, signaling Laurel's grousing had not escaped notice.

With a better look at the pair of interlopers, now that she acquiesced to interruption, Laurel had a hard time not laughing out loud at how much the visitor dwarfed Victoria by an almost ridiculous ratio. Despite the difference in height, Victoria pulled along the tall, white-garbed 'abominable snowman' by his gloved hand. His strides long and loping along the spotless, filtered floor, he kept up with the energetic, unstoppable CEO.

"Laurel, is it okay if we interrupt you?" Victoria asked, not really offering her a choice. She just made it sound like she did, in her irresistible South African dialect. As always happened before Laurel could agree or disagree, Victoria continued with the intrusion in Laurel's workday, when she toured VIP's around the facility.

Laurel did not think it would matter if she said, "No. I prefer not to be interrupted." So, she carried on with the "show the prize" game and smiled, answering, "I would love to meet your visitor, Ms. Ferguson!"

A genuine smile beamed from Victoria's face, emphasizing her high cheekbones. "Mr. Malachi Jacobs, please let me introduce Doctor Laurel Heatherton, one of our most accomplished and prolific researchers."

Laurel wanted to climb under a rock. The heat of a blush moved up her chest into her neck with the effusive praise. Sweat beaded on her forehead, which she could not wipe away with the bunny suit in the way. She had a sudden, desperate need to itch the crown of her head. Instead, she swallowed her lumps and set down her stylus.

"Doctor Heatherton, Mr. Jacobs owns and runs operations for Isaiah Technology Securities, a comprehensive Scientific Information Technology Security firm, hired to find vulnerabilities in our information system security."

Turning toward the tall visitor to greet him, a bolt of a disquieting déjà vu shot through her as she met his dark and intense gaze through both of their face guards. She thought his eyes widened a bit when they landed on her. Then, to her surprise for such a robust man, he turned pasty under his olive complexion. She extended her gloved hand. "It is good to meet you, Mr. Jacobs."

"The pleasure is mine, Doctor Heatherton," he said, with an unusual but pleasant pronunciation threaded through his deep and smooth voice.

To Laurel, he appeared to have recovered as he gave her a firm handshake with their glove-covered hands. An odd warmth seeped into her skin as he grasped her hand. She chalked it up, in the back of her head, to having worked several long days in a row.

She could not quite place his unique continental accent. To her sensitive ear, he had an Old-World flair in his speech.

Malachi continued, "I have left my cards on your desk outside the lab. I would like you to call me with any ideas, concerns you may have where you think Pacific could be vulnerable for data incursion or theft." He glanced down at her tablet. His eyes shot to hers, surprise in his gaze, then he shuttered his reaction. "I look forward to hearing from you, Doctor Heatherton."

He smiled down at the petite, indomitable Victoria and said, "We have interrupted Doctor Heatherton. I think a planned meeting might work well to go over her everyday patterns of IT usage."

Laurel sensed his urgency to get out of her lab, or away from her. Some people have issues with claustrophobia in the white garb. Jacobs did not appear the claustrophobic type. He seemed to have a more personal need to get out of her lab as soon as possible.

Whatever, she thought. She needed to get her work done. It suited her fine to have him gone sooner than later.

"Of course, whatever you think will work best, Malachi,"

Victoria answered him, making obvious her willingness to meet his requests without argument.

An hour later, an instant message popped up on her computer screen to accept one of three dedicated meeting times Mr. Jacobs offered her. The time requested seemed inordinate, which included a tour of her lab for Mr. Jacobs, causing her to groan. She did not look forward to the interruption to her routine.

With a glance at her schedule, she selected a time for the next day and answered. Before she blinked, another ding sounded, signaling her meeting time confirmed.

The man wastes no time, except mine, she complained to herself.

To Malachi it seemed he had taken a boot to the gut and a knife to his heart when he laid eyes on Doctor Laurel Heatherton. Dizziness threatened his equilibrium and his ears rang when her voice feathered through his mind, then thundered through his soul.

Victoria's forthright nature helped to keep him focused in the lab. He had developed a great amount of respect for Ms. Ferguson's business savvy and her understanding of the human psychology as far as running the pharmaceutical company. He now understood why the board of Pacific Pharmaceuticals had expressed complete confidence in her.

Before he met Doctor Laurel Heatherton this afternoon, he preferred not to have Victoria drag him in to interrupt her. Doctor Heatherton appeared to be immersed in intense thought and work on the lab visual monitor, on which he first caught sight of her. He himself appreciated quiet and lack of distractions when involved in complex thought processes, since developing and running his Technology IT Security Company.

Now he was thankful that Victoria had insisted he meet

Doctor Heatherton with her at his side. It kept him from becoming a blathering fool and gave him an excuse to keep their unanticipated meeting short.

Adrenaline rushed through him. *He had found Daphne.* When he glanced down at Laurel's tablet journal in the lab, what he saw made him sure of it. She journaled the same meticulous way of Daphne's, in a similar handwriting. *Cornell!* He had also run into her that day when touring the laser-scope room at Cornell University. It seemed his heart might pound out of his chest.

Of course! Fate had indeed played a joke on him and made it all so damn obvious: the shared last name of 'Heatherton', and Daphne had been transformed to the laurel bush by Zeus to allow her to hide from the over-zealous attentions of Apollo.

He had to restrain himself from reaching out to grab her and hug her tight to him back in the lab. His hands itched to reach out and touch her. He laughed to himself as he considered the shock and offense which would have taken over his meeting with Doctor Heatherton and Victoria Ferguson had he given in to the driving need to clasp Doctor Heatherton to him.

Anticipation and fear brimmed over while he obsessed about meeting with her tomorrow. This would put his warrior's discipline to an ultimate test, to appear impartial and professional.

Now, it seemed he had indeed tripped over his love, or rather, Fate had tossed him into her path and made sure he knew it.

CHAPTER TWENTY-NINE

The Next Day
Seattle, Pacific Pharmaceuticals Conference Room

DISCOMFORT SIFTED THROUGH MALACHI. His palms dripped with perspiration. Had he been in battle, he would not have been able to grip his sword. How could he greet her if his handshake were as wet as the fountain in the lobby? Malachi wiped his hands down his fine chinos, as he adjusted the position of his laptop for the hundredth time.

A shadow darkened the light shining through the half-open door to the conference room. His mouth turned dry; his pulse pounded in his ears. He took a quick sip of water from the crystal glass the receptionist had given him.

She stepped in. His love. Her gray eyes were Daphne's eyes. *Act normal, for Zeus's sake!* She reached out her hand to shake his.

No paper gloves separating the skin of their hands.

It took everything in him not to tug her into his embrace, kiss her to kingdom come.

He wrapped his fingers about hers, his ears buzzing, somehow pumped her hand up and down and articulated, "Hello, Doctor Heatherton," without freezing or stuttering over the words.

Gratitude and relief filled him when she let go of his hand then pulled out a chair to sit across from him at the conference table.

It took Laurel a few moments to gather her thoughts. Caught off guard by his deep voice of velvet, imbued with the unique accent, and his fierce, warrior-like appearance. He had been much less imposing yesterday, dressed in a white bunny suit. For the first time, she noticed he had gleaming long black hair with well-angled sideburns cut in, the hair pulled back to the nape of his neck into a sleek ponytail, and the most curious streaks of stark white hair along each side of his head starting at his temples.

Laurel finally found her voice, deciding he could not be any more intimidating than the panels she had to stand before to defend her theses. "Mr. Jacobs, I have made several notes with my concerns regarding information security. Would you like me to dive in, or is there something you would like to review or discuss first?"

"By all means, Doctor Heatherton, please go ahead. I will ensure we cover all necessary information for my assessment of the vulnerabilities you may have in your work environment."

Laurel found herself thinking Mr. Jacobs a unique combination of expertise, barely contained ferocity and intuition. He made it clear he knew what he was doing. Despite his apparent disquietude, she had every confidence in him.

A lot of thought had gone into her list, it had become extensive the more she had reviewed how she conducted her daily activities and communications.

Malachi relaxed as they discussed a subject he knew inside and out, and in which he and his firm had extensive expertise. They even traded jokes here and there. He appreciated that he and Doctor Heatherton were becoming more comfortable with each other as their meeting passed.

He and Laurel set a date for him to shadow her in her lab. They left the conference room to tour the lab now, so that the day he shadowed her and her assistant, he would already be familiar with the equipment and the room.

After entering the double-door airlocked anteroom, they both suited up. With a whoosh the second set of doors closed behind them. Laurel led Malachi about her lab, now eager to show him her instrumentation, multiple monitors, documentation systems and how the gene-splicing technology worked.

"Doctor Heatherton, I am looking forward to observing you work tomorrow and another day when you will be engaged in activities different from those of tomorrow. This is all beyond fascinating."

"You might find yourself bored out of your mind, Mr. Jacobs. Some of this is arduous and slow," she replied. She found she looked forward to his return. She enjoyed his companionship more as each moment passed.

"Until tomorrow, Doctor Heatherton." Malachi shook her hand, then left through the airlock.

Laurel surreptitiously watched as he shucked the bunny suit, making sure he tossed everything in the correct bins. She wanted to find something wrong with how he did things. It disconcerted her how agreeable he had been.

Relief flowed through Malachi as a tidal wave, thankful he had gotten through their meeting, and even made sense when he spoke.

He blotted his forehead with the cotton handkerchief he insisted on having every day, even though his housekeeper informed him handkerchiefs are "antiquated," to which he thought, *if you only knew.*

"Tobias, we are so close I can taste it." Gideon turned from his executive office window overlooking the city of Seattle. The gray clouds churning in the skies reflected the silver of his long hair, secured neatly at the nape of his neck and framed by well-groomed sideburns. He brought the dark-haired Tobias into his sterling gaze. "Our biological—negotiator, shall we say, is on the cusp of being well modulated. I have our best researchers devoted to it."

Tobias nodded as he listened, a black leather portfolio open before him, taking notes. He looked up upon Gideon's pause. "I know you have funneled immense resources toward this project, Gideon. I agree it is worth the investment you have made. You have indeed designed a versatile, powerful, yet indiscernible weapon. Genius, Gideon, genius in advancing our cause toward world order. The chaos which exists today, as it stands, is disgusting and beneath us," Tobias said as he rubbed his aching arm, through the fine wool of his dark gray suit jacket. The pain which throbbed deep, where it had been once severed by the Sekhmet bitch never left him, only increasing his thirst for vengeance.

Gideon glanced from Tobias's face to where his hand massaged his arm, then back to Tobias's dark gaze, "You shall get your retribution, my friend." A predatory grin, highlighted by his high cheekbones and slicked-back hair, crossed Gideon's countenance, "We have many well-placed operatives, Tobias. With a bit more patience, we will soon be able to make our move. We are entrenched in trusted positions everywhere, in every corner of the world." He again looked out the window, his hands placed in his pockets with lethal elegance. Innate power and entitlement emanated from him and in his carriage. "It has taken much longer than anticipated, thwarted as we have been. This will make our victory all the much sweeter.

"There is one issue in our biologic arsenal masterpiece, for absolute accuracy in its use, which keeps eluding our researchers. I may have found a most sublime solution." He again pinned his gaze on Tobias's, triumph flared a brief moment in his eyes. "She will be able to resolve the issue without difficulty. Her name is Laurel Heatherton."

Through the day, Laurel found her thoughts straying to Jacobs. This surprised her, to find herself attracted to this man. She had had very few relationships in her life, not for any reason other than she preferred her work and research to dating. Men often ended up telling her they found her cold and rude. She did not intend such, when she was with them. She just found herself anxious to get back to her lab or writing papers. In her mind, she did nothing wrong.

Sex had been the same. She found herself thinking of solutions to problems while she engaged in physical intimacy. Her, few-and-far-between male partners were not enamored of how easy it seemed for her attention to drift from their ministrations.

She brought her mind back to the present. Sarah Grayson, a genomic and bioengineering recruiter whom she knew from Cornell, had been after her to interview for a position she promised would be lucrative. Insistent that this undisclosed firm had an exceptional interest in her, she agreed to meet her for a dinner meeting to discuss the nature of the offer and the work.

Laurel thought that if nothing else, their discussion may give her fodder for another research time allotment negotiation with her current firm. She explained to Sarah during each of her several phone calls that she found herself satisfied with her current position. If she did decide to leave, money would not drive her, so much as latitude for research. Sarah assured her she would have no worries.

Her interview with Sarah Grayson of York Targeted Technologies had been one of the strangest interviews she had ever experienced. It left her unsettled.

It started well; they met over an exquisite dinner.

Then, a Mr. G. Augustine joined them. He spoke of 'bucking the system', goals, and aspirations to fame. Laurel asked pointed, detailed questions about what his company developed and manufactured to which he provided both specific and vague answers. She also inquired about where they were going with Research and Development. York Targeted Technologies currently produced nothing which needed her level of expertise in her assessment. In their in-depth R&D discussion, Mr. Augustine referred often to 'accuracy targeted biologics', yet he would not answer direct questions about what investigative genetic lines York Targeted Technologies specialized in. Mr. Augustine's evasiveness when all other pharmaceutical firms were specific made her uncomfortable.

YTT offered her an obscene salary and fifty percent lab time for her own research, causing her further unease while considering the position.

Mr. Augustine reminded her of the mob boss from "The Godfather". Her sixth sense screamed at her to get the hell away from him and all he touched.

Laurel closed the interview with Mr. Augustine with a handshake, which sent an immediate bolt of nausea to her insides. She could not wait to wash her hands. She did promise to 'think about it', so that he would let her go. She had already decided she would not accept the position with YTT but did not let on.

The next day, chest deep in the weeds of protein expression for the lung cancer genetic marker she had pinned down, she did not hear Mr. Jacobs come into her lab.

In silence, unnoticed, Malachi watched Doctor Heatherton work for over an hour. He found Laurel's ability to be lost in her work fascinating and enjoyed watching the way her mind worked on multiple levels at once.

Malachi shifted on his stool. It creaked.

Laurel jumped and exclaimed, "Oh!" She turned toward him, not being able to look at him from the side of her eye with the integrated visor of the bunny suit.

"My apologies, Doctor Heatherton, I did not intend to startle you." He gave her a bemused smile and a salute with the stylus with which he had been making notes on his tablet. "Please, carry on."

"Oh, I am sorry, Mr. Jacobs. Please excuse my rude behavior. I have just been working away while you are sitting here."

"Not at all, Doctor Heatherton. This has given me a chance to observe your work unfettered. You may have done things in a different manner if you were aware, self-conscious."

"Hmm, that makes sense. You don't think I'm rude?"

Malachi laughed, "Rude? No, Doctor Heatherton, not rude at all. I found watching you work to be symmetry in motion. Beautiful."

Laurel looked at him as though he had grown another head. "Surely, you're joking!"

In silence, her eyes searched his. The moment stretched for eons. She had known him forever.

"Do I look like I am joking?"

The churning storms in his eyes took her breath away. Never had she had someone's gaze on her own as intense, appreciative. The sensation she was falling off a cliff into his eyes filled her.

Unbidden tears burned. She turned back to her monitor, blinking them back.

"Well, then…" Uncertainty hung in the air between them. "I shall continue," she said.

Relief she could return to her work removed tension from her shoulders and the room.

Malachi dove into his observations of her use of tied-together systems and communication with other researchers both in and outside of Pacific Pharmaceuticals.

The day passed for both of them before either knew it.

Malachi Jacobs spent the next few days elsewhere in Pacific Pharmaceuticals. Laurel berated herself for looking for him.

The following Monday opened with her and her lab assistant, Hanson, delving into replicating their protein expression results, only to find Jacobs observing in silence, once again. Laurel advised Hanson to go about business as usual and soon she fell back into the rhythm of her work alongside him.

The long day ended on a good note and the sun shone outside, tempting Laurel to enjoy the outdoors.

"God, I cannot wait to go for a good hike. With the days longer, there is time after work," remarked Laurel, as she rubbed her temples.

Malachi, walking past her toward his temporary office, stopped short and backed up. "A hike? That sounds very tempting." His Old-World accent added charm to what she knew would be his request to join her.

"Would you mind some company if I promise to be a silent partner? Unless I fall off a cliff or something else catastrophic."

Laurel enjoyed the way he pronounced 'catastrophic' and could not help but laugh with his humor. "Yes, but only with major catastrophes. Minor disasters still require your vow of silence. Do you know the West Duwamish Greenbelt Trails? Your biggest risk there is a run in with a fox or a tree, so the 'Vow of Silence' shall be yours."

"The WDGT? That is a beautiful place, so wild, in the middle of the city. You make me ashamed I do not take advantage of it nearly enough. You do drive a hard bargain, Heatherton. Deal. I shall be as quiet as a country mouse."

"A country mouse?"

Malachi nodded.

"I did not know we had country mice. And, I assume, also urban mice, Mr. Jacobs. The country mouse is less noisy than the urban mouse, I presume?" Laurel laughed. "See you in the lobby in thirty, Jacobs. You can follow me to the trailhead at the tennis courts at South Seattle College."

Deep into the forest in the city, the pact of silence slipped into a mutual vow. The sounds and smells of the forest all the more vibrant and alive for Laurel, as Malachi trod the path behind her. She wondered what he perceived of the forest. She heard rustling in the dense stand of trees off to her left. Pulling out her binoculars, she spotted a doe and two fawns. Then caught a flash of a fox bounding behind them.

"Oh, wow, how sweet," she whispered, watching the spotted fawns as part of the magic of the forest.

"'Til they eat your hydrangeas," whispered Malachi, in the barest wraith of a comment.

"What happened to your vow of silence?"

"There's a fawn exception."

"Jacobs, you are full of shit."

Laurel turned to keep walking. The doe's ears perked up, whether from her turning or Malachi's soft snort of amusement, she would not know.

Light suffused them as the path exited the trees and wound along the water. Malachi touched Laurel's shoulder and pointed up to the sky. A majestic osprey dove toward the water, swooping back up into the air with a wiggling fish in its talons.

"Wow. One does not get to see that in person often," breathed Laurel in awe. She glanced at her watch, then looked back out over the water. "It will be dusk soon. Are you in any hurry? I don't like to hike in the dark since I am usually by myself. It is such a beautiful evening. We could always use the flashlights on our phones." She turned from the water to him. "Are you game, Jacobs?"

Malachi smiled, waiting for her to remember he had a 'vow of silence'.

"Are you?" she asked, again.

Malachi gave a thumbs up.

"Oh, yeah, right. 'Vow of silence'," she laughed, "I have to give you credit for sticking with it."

Malachi gave her another thumbs up. *This 'vow of silence' joke of hers turned out to be serendipitous.* He did not need to worry about trying to make small talk with the woman he had loved for centuries and she had no idea of it.

Laurel found a large, wide boulder and sat on it as the sun began to set.

Malachi settled next to her.

They relaxed, a light brown and a raven black ponytail hanging down their backs, side by side. Both took joy in watching the brilliant orange and pink shifting colors of the sky, in companionable quiet.

Whispers of contentment ribboned through Malachi's soul. He dared not grasp at them, for fear they would slip away, again. He enjoyed the beauty of the moment and solace in his heart.

Darkness fell. Malachi found he had an immediate need rise up through him to get Laurel away from the water's edge. Memories from the worst night of his life corrupted the enchanted moment.

He stood and did his best not to be obvious in his need to drag her away from the water, but to get them both onto the path and back to their cars.

Confused by the sudden tension pouring from Malachi, she wondered what the heck she had said or done, as he hurried them down the path.

"Jacobs," she called.

He did not stop.

"Jacobs!"

Malachi turned around.

"Okay, the fucking 'vow of silence' thing is over now. What the fuck? Here we are having a great hike, a beautiful sunset, and suddenly, 'boom!'," she flicked out her hands above her head, lowered them. "I do something to piss you off, which I don't even know about! And we need to head away like the hounds of hell are after us. What the fuck?"

"Cursing does not become you, Laurel. My apologies, for the disruption in our evening, Doctor Heatherton."

"'Cursing does not become me?' Fuck you, Jacobs," Laurel ground out, then guilt seeped in when she saw him flinch. "Look. I am sorry." She really did not want their beautiful night to go south, but the man did need to come to the twenty-first century. "And please don't admonish me like I am a child over my use of language." She twisted her ponytail in her hand, nervous and having a desire to rescue their pleasant evening. She asked him, "Tell me, what did I say to upset you?"

Malachi's eyes teared up.

Laurel looked at him, shocked. "Oh, Malachi. Tell me. I did not do or say anything, did I?" She took his hand. Her eyes became round. "Our night brought something back. Something awful," she said, while she held his hand.

Malachi yanked his hand back from her. His pupils dilated, his eyes even darker in his pale face.

Laurel grasped his hand again, and held on, closing her eyes.

Her eyes popped open, terror making her pupils dilate and her eyes tear. She dragged in a breath, shaking, "Oh, my God, Malachi. She drowned. And you could not stop it. I am so sorry." She squeezed his hand.

Malachi returned the clasp and said, hoarse with emotion, "It's okay. It was a long time ago, Laurel. But, thank you." Malachi gave a wan smile. "We both have a long day at work tomorrow. Let's get ourselves home."

Laurel looked at Malachi with a question in her eyes. "Jacobs, are you sure you'll be okay?"

"I am sure, Heatherton."

A headache made itself at home in Laurel's head the next morning. Her dreams had been full of bizarre nightmares of giant snakes, large birds, an ancient Bain Marie, and nuns constantly interrupting her sleep.

She walked into the lab, looking forward to falling into her familiar routine with Hanson, only to find they needed to put together an unexpected report on the safety procedures and incident statistics for the past year for their lab. An incident had occurred at another Pacific Pharmaceuticals Lab, last week.

The report finished, they worked hard to play catch up for the remainder of the day. Laurel made an effort not to be cranky with Hanson, the nicest man (and best lab assistant) on the face of the Earth, in her opinion. She did not want him upset with her.

Wrapping up, tired, Laurel stared off into nothing from her countertop workspace, curious as to how Malachi seemed so familiar when she had never met him. She headed to the firm's gym for a much-needed workout at the end of the long and arduous day. She had a driving need to push the disturbing questions from her mind for which she had no answers.

Via instant message, Malachi clarified IT processes with Laurel over the following week as he compiled his data. His sardonic humor added an edge now and then in the messages they traded.

Laurel's comfort with Malachi increased with each conversation. She admonished herself, finding that her heart would jump like a schoolgirl's when she would see an IM from Jacobs pop up.

Laurel heard through Pacific's grapevine Jacobs had shadowed several other researchers and all the executive, administrative and IT personnel. She chuckled over her avocado and cheese sandwich as she pictured him lurking in the corners of the various C-suite offices. Victoria's unstoppable charm was not the norm. Both the CFO and the CIO had dour and cranky dispositions. Word filtered through that the CIO threw a tantrum over Mr. Jacob's unflappable line of questioning. Laurel postulated a fly on that wall would have had a grand time with that one.

After finishing her lunch, Laurel decided a cup of coffee would hit the spot. She made her way to the well-appointed employee lounge. The aroma of fresh coffee made her mouth water when she filled her cup from the carafe. *Damn!* She thought as the heat soaked into her fingers. She had forgotten to grab a cardboard sleeve, again.

"Are you looking for one of these?"

Laurel almost dropped her coffee hearing Malachi's voice coming from behind her and seeing a cardboard sleeve appear at her left. Irritation sifted through her. She wanted to say no, but that that would be cutting off her nose to spite her face. *The bastard knows my fingers are burning, I can just tell by the smug tone in his voice.* She snatched the cardboard sleeve out of his hand without a word. Placed her cup in it, then took a sip. She then said, "You know, if I had not heard that you took no prisoners in the C-Suite, I might have told you what to do with your cardboard sleeve." She paused and looked at him instead of the coffee carafe. "That is much better, thank you." She knew common courtesy dictated she offer him a cup. She really did not want to spend any more time in Jacob's presence than necessary. The words tumbled out before she could stop them, "Could I get you anything?"

"I would love a hot tea, Dr. Heatherton."

"Of course, you would, Jacobs," she replied while she turned back to find the hot water carafe. She tried to keep from grinning when she heard a soft snort of amusement from behind her. The corners of her lips twitched. "One lump or two, Jacobs?"

They both know she referred to lumps on the head and not sugar cubes.

"I'll take it black, Laurel. Thank you."

Handing him his cup without a sleeve, Laurel moved to pull a chair out from under a table. She surreptitiously watched Malachi walk over to the sleeves in the organically intrepid way he had. It bothered her because it intrigued her. She did not want to be intrigued; she found her comfort in her work. *Damn.* Then his eyes landed on her. *Oh no, please don't come over here.*

Malachi stopped at a chair at her table. "May I?"

Laurel made a show of taking a long sip of her coffee.

He stood there a moment, then lifted his hand from the chair and turned to go.

Guilt sifted through her. "Mr. Jacobs, I would enjoy the company." *Well, white lies can be better than bad manners.*

"It seems I owe you thanks yet again, Laurel," Malachi said as he pulled out the chair and sat.

"You're welcome," Laurel said as she pulled out her phone

and scrolled through the latest science news. She came across an article about the alchemist and physician, Paracelsus. "This is fascinating! This alchemist, from the 16th century, developed scientific methodology as we know it today and is known 'as the father of toxicology'! He figured out how to determine how dosing regimens work!" Laurel went on to quote much of the article. She was pleased to see that Malachi appeared to be genuinely fascinated.

Malachi replied, "We are most fortunate he researched as he did! I too find his story to be fascinating!"

Laurel replied, "I find it interesting that he was both an alchemist and a physician. I would have thought the two were mutually exclusive."

"There was a time when alchemists were respected. They laid much of the groundwork for today's chemistry."

Laurel looked at Malachi with renewed interest. "Tell me more."

Thursday morning, a week later, Laurel walked into her lab to see Malachi chatting with her assistant. Her stomach did a little flip and a silly grin popped up the corners of her mouth, unbidden. *What the hell?* she admonished herself.

"Good morning, Doctor Heatherton."

"Good morning, Mr. Jacobs." She looked to Hanson, her assistant, and asked, "Are you up for the challenge of our day, Hanson? We have a ton of new specimens to go through."

"On it, Boss," he said as he saluted her and nodded to Mr. Jacobs. Hanson continued to set up for the day.

Immersed in their work, Laurel never noticed that Malachi had left. Appreciation he did not interrupt them with a "goodbye" filled her. As usual, synergy flowed between her and Hanson, and they wrapped up a satisfying day, having only broken for a quick lunch. Walking out of the lab with Hanson, she spotted Malachi sitting at one of the flexible work pods dotted around the firm, for use when inspiration hit when not in one's workspace.

"See you in the morning, Doctor Heatherton," Hanson called out while he continued on his way.

Laurel watched him walk down the hall, admiration in her eyes for her astute lab assistant. Not everyone had as good of a working relationship as she and Hanson.

"He seems to be a stellar assistant and work-mate," Malachi's voice interrupted her reverie.

"Yes, yes, he is. Quite so. I am fortunate," she said, turning to Malachi, smiling. "I heard you got the CIO in a lather." She grinned and continued, "He is an arrogant SOB. I so wish I could have seen that."

"Yes, well, his arrogance may be taken down a few notches after Victoria and the board get my report… and that is not to be repeated."

"No, no. of course not." She walked over to him, pulled out a nearby chair. "How is it going otherwise?"

"I believe I will be wrapped up here in two days. A few days to finish my report. It is going well," Malachi answered.

An unexpected sadness that he planned on leaving soon moved over her.

"I feel the same," Malachi said, in such a low voice, she almost did not hear him.

Her eyes flew to his. "W— what do you mean?" she asked, surprised he seemed to have caught her thoughts. Breathless, her pulse ricocheted in her ears.

"Laurel, you fascinate me."

Laurel could not help it; a bitter laugh exploded from her mouth.

Consternation crossed Malachi's face. "What? Tell me."

Heat and embarrassment moved up her neck. She shared, "I fascinate no one, Malachi."

"Laurel, I dream of spending time with you. I love watching you work."

"Jacobs, either you are full of shit or you are crazy." Indignation filled Laurel. Her eyes flashed doubtful hurt at him. "What's your endgame," she asked.

"Laurel, understand. I never converse with people in my professional life as you and I are right now. Ever.

"You… this is different. You are a beautiful woman in so many ways, so many layers. I am captivated," he explained.

Dumbfounded, she could not think of a response. Never before had she a lack of words. She knew as sure as she knew DNA, sincerity and truth rang through every word which had just spilled from his mouth and poured over her as precious honey made of mountain wildflowers.

A single tear rolled down her cheek, marking her heart as his.

"Laurel, you and I both put in long hours. Let's leave now and go for dinner, coffee, ice cream, anything. Let's just go," Malachi said, as he stood up and held out his hand.

"A date?" she asked.

"Yes, a date."

"A real date. Even though I like work better than sex?"

Mirth lit his eyes. "I was not expecting that." He smiled. "You are beautifully unpredictable," he said, while he brushed his thumb over her cheek. He dropped his hand from her face. "We are in your place of work, Laurel. I am not even going to begin to touch that one… for now."

His sensual hint of a promise hung in the air. Heat wound through her belly.

A grin crossed Malachi's face. He knew he was taking a chance, but it appeared the pieces were falling into place. Fate, fickle as she could be, worked in such a way. He was not about to ignore her—one could pay a heavy price if one did not pay attention when Fate smiled upon them.

Malachi escorted Laurel into the small Italian restaurant. He knew the owners well, they greeted both him and Laurel with warm enthusiasm. Mrs. Venturino pinched his savage cheek, much to the amusement of Laurel.

Malachi chatted with her over cheese and wine while they waited for their dinner. Laurel found herself bemused with how fierce Malachi came across in appearance and demeanor, yet intimidation or fear did not count among the emotions she experienced with him. Rather, she sensed from him a deep appreciation for her and how her mind worked. She found herself tumbling hard and fast, with a burning desire to grasp everything about them together, and him, and not let go.

"Laurel."

Goosebumps rose over her with the way he rolled her name off his tongue with his beautiful, and unique accent.

"'Laurel' is to what Zeus transformed Daphne, so she could hide from the relentless pursuit of Apollo," he said as he peered at her, emotions churning in his dark eyes as he spoke.

"Yes, my parents shared that story with me."

"I find your name a most beautiful and interesting name, Laurel."

Malachi—undeniable and hot as sin, yet comfortable, those juxtaposed words came to mind in her thoughts of him.

He curled his fingers about her hand and pressed his sensual, firm lips to her knuckles.

An orgasm almost overtook her, in her seat, in public, shocking her in her immediate and strong reaction to him. "Don't," she hissed at him, from across the table. Yet her hand remained held in his. She picked up a menu with her other hand

and fanned herself, shooting him a look full of hunger and indignation, then glanced at the unlit candle only to have the wick flare and flame.

Laurel's eyes shot to his, horrified she had done such in front of another. Her cheeks burned in embarrassment.

"Impressive," Malachi said, with a nonchalant chuckle. His gaze shifted from hers to the candle flame.

The mortified pounding of her heart settled. Laurel thought she would give her eye teeth to hear and feel that low and sexy chuckle of Malachi's fan past her ear. *Christ, I am a ball of orgasmic energy, here! What gives?*

The sensual, wicked gleam in Malachi's eye moved from the candle flame back to her, his obsidian gaze hot and enthralling.

"Tell me, Laurel, do you still think you will find work more interesting than sex," he asked, his deep voice with its Old-World accent rained over her.

Carnal, edgy thoughts of how his voice would sound whispering past her ear as he thrust into her with his fierce body flowed through her mind. She desired to feel his raven's hair with the mysterious, captivating white streak at either temple, cascading over her.

His question hovered between them, at their table, then wound its way into her belly and between her legs. She squirmed in her chair, pressing her womanhood against it. Sudden awareness peaked, realizing what she was doing, heat rose into her cheeks. Laurel gasped, her mouth a round "O" as she lifted her free hand to it in embarrassment.

Malachi held her gaze in his, set his lips to her knuckles again. He soothed his tongue over her middle knuckle. He watched every subtle, yet Earth-moving reaction in her eyes and face.

Falling fast and hard, Laurel could not wait to be alone with this enigmatic man who made her feel like she had known him for a hundred years and made it obvious he worshipped every molecule of her body.

"Do you think we could get our dinner to go, Malachi?" she asked, plumbing the depths of his soul. She gathered his angst, strength, and deep love into her heart.

His eyes flared, rooted to her gaze. After what seemed an eternity, he answered, "How can I deny you, or me, Laurel?"

"I don't know, Malachi. How can you?" she asked. Then laughed, knowing she asked an impossible question to answer.

Promises of love and lust danced in her eyes, sprinkled with her warm laughter. His heart was still.

He helped her with her coat.

The drive to his house seemed to take forever. Malachi parked. He walked in his intrepid way, which she found to be so sexy, around his car to her door. Next thing she knew, his hand was there to help her out of her seat.

Once in the foyer, Laurel turned toward Malachi.

He held her face between his hands, ran his rough thumb over her lips.

Sensuality, love galvanized them both. Their mouths came together. A sunburst, their kiss deepened, and their tongues entwined.

Laurel turned her mouth a bit to haul in a breath, she could pull enough air through her nose, while he evoked molten ribbons through her sex, belly, breasts, with his soul-burning kiss. His passion enveloped her psyche, her heart, all of her.

Hungry, she shoved his suit jacket off his shoulders. He tugged her sweater up over her head. She unbuttoned his shirt. It landed on his suit jacket, forming a sensual pile with unplanned folds and planes in the discarded clothes.

Embers of his gaze on hers, Malachi pushed her pants down her legs. She stepped out of the fine wool pants, now pooled at her feet. His black raven's wing hair brushed against her thigh as he moved to stand back up. Heat, nectar flowed in her nether lips and curled about deep inside. She sighed with longing.

Once Malachi stood straight, Laurel gathered her thoughts enough to undo his fly. Passion burgeoning, she ground against his muscular thigh as her knuckles brushed over his erection while she lowered his zipper. She yanked his trousers over his hips and down over his powerful legs. Her hands traced the planes of his muscles as she pushed the fine material down his legs, over his wide, hard calves. Malachi stepped out of his trousers.

He grasped her forearms, brought her to stand with him, and embraced her, "You are an incredible woman, Laurel," he feathered past her ear, his hot breath a beautiful caress. He reached behind her and undid her bra.

Cool air moved over her back as his nimble fingers undid the clasps. Erect, her nipples strained toward him, aching to be bare, attention laved upon them.

Solemn, his raven gaze on her gray one, he slid the bra straps down over her arms, slow, inexorable. Time suspended, breathed, wavered, his eyes never leaving hers. Memories of the fires of hell disappeared, they had only here and now.

Reverent, he lowered his lips to hers and dropped her scrap of silk on top of her pile of clothes.

His velvety, rock hard erection brushed against her hip while Malachi suckled at her breast. Heat, sweet nectar flowed as her nether lips pulsed and blossomed.

Malachi inhaled the fragrance of her blooming womanhood as he laved her burgeoning nipple. Laurel mewled, the sound heaven to his ears. He slid his hard, rough, splayed hand down her belly, then slid two fingers between her lips, and growled as he swiped his fingers through her silk.

"Dear Isis, Laurel," He moved his hot mouth against the side of her breast while he spoke.

Malachi led her to his davenport, set her on the edge and

kneeled before her. He planted a reverent kiss upon her forehead.

With his worshipful kiss, trust poured through her.

Leaning her back, Malachi lifted her feet one at a time, to rest her heels on his broad shoulders. Into her silk, he slid his knowing fingers. He bent to kiss her nether lips, his love imbuing every touch.

A nova built as Malachi stoked her tension. She crested, he pushed her over, and she rode the zenith, tears running down her cheeks.

"Yes, Love, yes." His gaze burned with the fires of hell he crossed to be with her. "You are exquisite," he said, his voice a reverent whisper. "Everything about you is amazing."

Laurel opened her eyes to see a tear tracking down his cheek.

Malachi helped her to stand, he bent her over the arm of his couch, her derriere enticing and raised. The wolf and the raven within him leapt in joy of the ancients.

Primal drive flowed through Laurel; power hummed through her. She keened and lifted her rear higher for him. Teeth bared, she huffed then snarled.

"Ready?" He whispered the question against her ear, blending with the thrum of sensual, sexual energy.

Laurel nodded and threw her head back and again keened as he sunk into her.

Back against Malachi, Laurel ground. Filled with an undeniable need to take him deeper into her. Her muscles clenched about his hot, wide length.

Malachi pulled back, he grasped her hips, then surged over and over.

To the back of his flexing thigh she wound her hand, pulled him tight against her and lifted her derriere to take him as deep as possible into her silken channel with each thrust. She clenched hold of him firmly with each stroke. Perspiration pooled in the small of her back and her light brown hair spilled across her shoulder blades, increasing her sense of power and primal desire.

Teeth gritted, a sheen of sweat covering him, Malachi threw his head back, grasped her hips more firmly and plunged one last time. He growled low and carnal, then orgasmed. "I love you, Laurel. Like nothing else, I love you," he ground out, his breath heaving, laying his forehead onto the middle of her back.

Malachi pulled Laurel to standing, turned and kissed her. They curled up together on the couch. Malachi pulled a throw over them both. Their hearts both still pounding, they descended as one from their spiritual and sensual heights.

Laurel lifted locks of his long hair, watching as the strong, silky strands fell through her fingers. "I love you, Malachi."

They fell into a sweet, light sleep of peace, a spell together.

Laurel nudged Malachi awake, needing to move. Stiffness had started to invade her joints. "Malachi?"

"Yes, Love."

"To answer your question. Sex with you is better than work."

A laugh, low and warm, erupted from Malachi. His black eyes shone in his sincere pleasure. He made love to her again, long and sweet, on the davenport.

CHAPTER THIRTY

REGRET LEFT a bitter taste in her mouth. Laurel followed Mr. Gideon Augustine through his plant he had insisted on showing her with his last bid to win her over to working for YTT.

His perfect delivery and cultured British dialect had begun to grate on her nerves. At this point, Laurel just wanted to get home and back to Malachi, wishing she could recover the precious hour of time she had wasted with Mr. Augustine.

Awareness rose in Laurel, his words regarding biological warfare filtering through her drifting mind. Laurel reeled in disbelief as nausea roiled in her stomach. Incredulous, shaking inside, her eyes widened, she asked, "Mr. Augustine, you are explaining to me that you have discovered a way to target an individual or group of individuals with a rapid leukemia? A leukemia which will cause their death in about one hour but will not affect anyone else you have not targeted?"

"Yes, Doctor Heatherton. That is correct," he answered, as he pinned her under his now zealous gaze of silvery fire. "Is it not beautiful? Innocent people will no longer be collateral damage, and blanket mass destruction will not be the norm.

"We need you, your expertise to further develop our targeted technology. This is so much better than what has been or what could be, Doctor Heatherton. Much more merciful, do you not agree?"

Laurel took a deep breath, trying to keep the fearful quaver out of her voice, and said "I cannot work for you, Mr. Augustine. I cannot put my conscious effort into something which causes death. Even if you consider it humane." She glanced past his shoulder to gauge her best route of escape, then looked back to him. "Who decides who dies and who lives?"

A barked laugh burst from him, then he answered, "Your humor is precious, Laurel." Cold-blooded purpose eddied in his eyes. "Me. Who else?"

She did not laugh with him. Uncomfortable silence hung in the air.

Gideon's silver gaze glinted with hard, cold evil, his eyes windows into his black soul.

"I see, Doctor Heatherton. This is unfortunate. I am afraid I will have to dispatch you. I cannot let the world in on my secret. At least, not yet."

His cool pronouncement sent gnarled, icy fingers down her back and around her stomach.

He pulled a remote from his pocket, hit a button and a metal garage door whooshed to the right. Through the opening appeared a breathtaking cliff top view over the ocean.

"I regret, Doctor Heatherton, you will meet with a tragic accident while visiting our facility," he said, as his hand encircled her elbow and he made as though to escort her outdoors, walking next to her.

Laurel yanked her arm from his grasp and made to turn and run from him. With his cold, strong grip, he pulled both of her arms behind her, then held fast both of her wrists with one hand, and resumed forcing Laurel outside to the bluff as she dipped and turned in attempts to break free of his hold.

The salt-laden ocean breeze ruffled her hair, it seemed his dirty fingers were running through it, with sticky pieces of gore on them from those who would later perish because of him.

Panic filled Laurel as the bluff's edge loomed closer, she screamed in her mind for Malachi, for dear life.

Seagulls cried above her, as the ocean breeze whipped her hair about. She twisted her torso and face up toward him, that her words would not be lost to him in the wind, and pleaded, "Please let me go, Mr. Augustine, I can do nothing to hurt you." He said nothing and continued on his path with her to the cliff top.

He stopped. His silver eyes captured hers. They were without remorse. "It really is a pity you did not take the job offer, Doctor Heatherton."

He again pushed her before him as she tried to dig her feet into the sandy grass to halt their progress to the edge. Her inner spirit cried out for her to listen to her Elemental self.

The edge. Laurel glanced down at the water, waves crashed against the rocks below, bile and terror rose within her. She dipped then swung her body away from the bluff's edge, desperation warring with her inner self screaming at her to listen.

Augustine growled and hauled her back, lifting her body, her feet pedaling the air.

Laurel closed her eyes. She listened. It was all she had left. Her intervention now revealed by the Elemental voices within her. Strength grew within her. Laurel reached deep inside and pulled on the powers she had experimented with but never really developed, praying they would cooperate with her for now. She pushed fear aside and thought of power, the beauty of Elements and the charge they held.

Augustine shoved her off the bluff.

The change! The change occurred. Laurel knew the moment she became living current.

She hovered a moment then flew back onto the bluff's edge. Augustine's eyes bugged with disbelief.

He grabbed her arm and made to fling her off the cliff.

With a cry worthy of a Valkyrie, Laurel broke her arm free of Augustine's grasp, and stepped further onto the solid land. She held her hands before her, Elemental forces moving though her and a high-pitched whine from her own body sounded in her ears. She sent a bolt of lightning into him.

She just about shit herself to see it happen, but recovered in a split second.

Augustine's jaw dropped open, caught off guard, as he stood there, his arms limp at his sides, smoke, and steam escaping from his sleeves.

Laurel took advantage of the moment and pummeled him with more bolts. She learned how her power worked as she attacked him. Laurel advanced toward Augustine, relentless in the offensive, bolt after bolt flew into him. He backed away from her and the bluff top.

Singed, more smoke rose from him, an acrid odor hung in the air. Augustine regained his wits. His eyes cleared. He made a long, quick movement with his hands, forming a humming gray and black sword.

Laurel noticed the eerie silence in the absence of the cries of the gulls, hearing only the wind and the continuous crash of the waves below. She realized the gulls knew to hide.

Terror filled her, she wished to the heavens for a shield.

Augustine brought the massive gray blade down toward

her. It would cleave her in half. She dove and rolled, knowing it was fruitless, and braced for the death blow. The blade stopped within millimeters of her face and the blow concussed her, but it did not strike. Cognizance dawned in the heated moment that somehow, she had conjured a shield. *Holy shit, okay then.* Hope flared that she might survive.

Augustine howled in rage, yanking her attention back to him. His face suffused in crimson his silver eyes burned bright from his livid countenance. Saliva flew from his mouth as he advanced on her with a battle cry and another mighty arc of his sword.

Laurel imagined her shield weaponized with energy. His sword struck, clanging, coming to a dead stop. The momentum instead jarred Augustine's body. Confusion sifted across his face.

Holy fucking shit, it worked! flashed through her mind while she kept up her concentration on staying alive. Gilded lightning entwined the tip of Augustine's blade and snaked up his sword. He watched in horror, heaving in great deep breaths. The vine of golden light sprouted leaves and swallowed his blade, ashes falling to the ground beneath. Leaves and vine progressed to his hand.

At the same time, Malachi materialized beside Laurel. He watched with great pride the skill with which she threw vines of lightning from her shield up Gideon's arm.

Shrieks of combined agony, indignation and anger issued from Gideon's gaping mouth. He jerked his arm free of the climbing, hungry golden electrified vine and pulled his arm close to his chest. The stink of burnt flesh hung pungent in the sea air.

Both Malachi and Laurel looked with disgust at the smoking, cauterized stump where his hand had been. The vine dissipated into gilt motes and evaporated.

Malachi's gaze moved between Laurel and Gideon. He remained silent.

Gideon turned his blazing silver gaze on Laurel. "Heatherton, I vow I shall return, and I will slaughter you and Malachi. You will regret not staying dead, Daphne," he growled, then disappeared.

Laurel, now on her knees, bent her head to the ground, and gulped in large breaths. She wrapped her arms about herself, her trembling unstoppable. *Daphne? Who the fuck is Daphne?* The world about Laurel narrowed into a tunnel, the walls whooshing by as she slid through it. Lights flashed around her like she was on a train, passing another train. Images sped past from the other train's windows. She lifted her right hand, turned it over and stared. The realization sinking in that the woman in the flashes from the past, the alchemist, and her were the same. Malachi's presence and warmth next to her kept her from going mad.

Malachi knelt beside her, catching glimpses of what she saw, not touching her. He thought it better to let her assimilate the information without additional sensations.

Vertigo remained her world. She kept her head down, as she knelt, breathing heavily. She listened to her breath move in and out of her body and took comfort from it.

"Laurel," Malachi whispered, sensing she had calmed.

Her deliberate breaths in and out remained the only sound she made.

"Laurel, what might I do for you?"

She swallowed and thought about his question. Then asked, "Am I in a dream, Malachi?"

He was not sure if this was her humor talking or if she were serious. He decided to take the path of serious. "You are not in a dream, Laurel."

"Is he really gone from here?"

"Yes, he is gone."

She nodded. "Okay. So, I really did just shoot fucking lightning bolts. I am not delusional."

"You are not delusional, Laurel," answered Malachi, his voice low and steady.

"Okay. Okay. I have to figure this out," she said, her head still to the ground as she knelt, eyes shut tight. "Please don't leave me, Malachi. Help me figure this out. Please," she implored him, ending on sobs which wracked through her.

Malachi gathered her to him, moving with care. "Laurel, my love. I believe I do have many of the answers. We can talk this through at your pace, over days, weeks. You need to let your body and mind work through this initial shock." He hugged her tight and kissed her head as he said, "You have always had this Elemental force in you, even long ago. It needed to explode out of you today, so that you might live. For that, I am thankful. But it does not make it any less difficult for you to comprehend."

"Well, yeah." She gave a sardonic laugh, and retorted, "It sure did come out today. In spades, Malachi."

"Umm, hmm," Malachi murmured against her head in agreement. "Remind me not to piss you off or take the last piece of pizza again, Laurel," he said, his chin moving near her ear.

She began to laugh, then pulled away and sat up and doubled over laughing. "I fucking melt some dickhead's hand off, who disappears into thin air, and you worry about me smiting you over pizza?" She calmed, laughter truly the best medicine.

"Laurel, you fought a battle of battles. I am in awe." He paused, then continued, "You managed to rout out Gideon Augustine. The CIA and my company have been hunting him for months. YTT is being raided now, as we speak."

He wrapped his arms about her and rested his cheek on the crown of her head.

"Daphne?" she whispered the question, knowing part of the answer.

He kissed her palm. "There is so much for me to share with you, Laurel. My formidable, brilliant Laurel." He kissed her hair again. "We will have several lifetimes. If you will have me."

"Malachi," she said and moved their joined hands toward her face. She laid the back of his hand against her cheek, and looked up at him. "I cannot imagine being without you."

They sat together for some time on the bluff. The sea breeze lifted Malachi's hair like the wings of the sly raven.

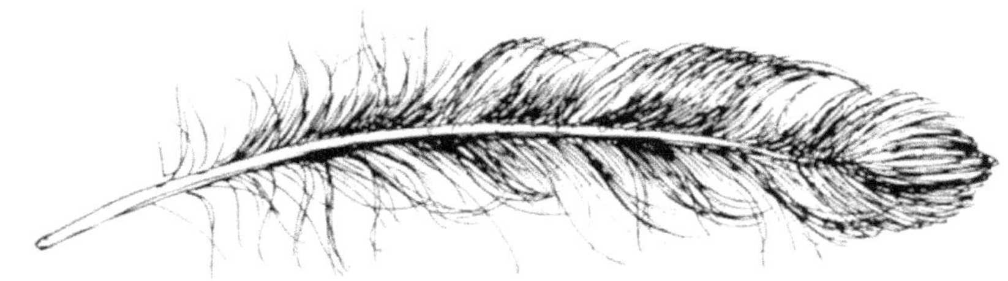

To be continued with Katherine's story in

DANTE'S

FIRE

OF ALCHEMY & ANGELS
BOOK TWO

Coming February 2, 2022

Danielle Ancona is a mixer of things. To prevent having a lonely fact, lore, or myth, she combines them together. They, however, may or may not like it, and she won't know until she sees the resulting chemical reaction. But it is never boring and provides for very interesting conversations—sometimes arguments—with her characters as she is writing.

Danielle and her husband enjoy overnight bicycling excursions and long day rides.

The alchemy, mythological & historical research for the *Of Alchemy & Angels* series has been of great interest to her and she is passionate about her work in Oncology. She adores the hard and soft sciences, yet has a healthy respect for the Ethereal.

REFERENCES

Several sources served as references throughout the writing of this book, and I'd like to give both credit and thanks to them for an amazing journey of discovery.

— Danielle Ancona

Benedictow, Ole. *The Black Death: The Greatest Catastrophe Ever.* History Today, Volume 55, Issue 3. March, 2005 https://www.historytoday.com/archive/black-death-greatest-catastrophe-ever

Borzelleca, Joseph F. *Paracelsus: Herald of Modern Toxicology.* Toxicological Sciences, Volume 53, Issue 1. January, 2000. https://doi.org/10.1093/toxsci/53.1.2

Bosveld, Jane. *Isaac Newton, World's Most Famous Alchemist.* Discover Magazine. December, 2010. https://www.discovermagazine.com/the-sciences/isaac-newton-worlds-most-famous-alchemist

Campbell, Dylan. *Aristotle's "On the Heavens"*. Ancient History Encyclopedia. 16 October, 2016. https://member.ancient.eu/article/959/aristotles-on-the-heavens/#citation_info

Cartwright, Mark. *Food & Drink in the Elizabethan Era*. Ancient History Encyclopedia. 8 July, 2020. https://member.ancient.eu/article/1578/food--drink-in-the-elizabethan-era/

Cartwright, Mark. *Hoplite*. Ancient History Encyclopedia, Ancient History Encyclopedia. February, 2013. https://ancient.eu/hoplite/

Conniff, Richard. *Alchemy May Not Have Been the Pseudoscience We Thought it Was*. Smithsonian Magazine. February, 2014. https://www.smithsonianmag.com/history/alchemy-may-not-been-pseudoscience-we-thought-it-was-180949430/

Debaskcsy, Dale. *The Life Of Laura Bassi (1711-1778), The World's First Female Full Professor Of Science*. Women You Should Know. June, 2018. https://womenyoushouldknow.net/laura-bassi-worlds-first-female-professor-science/

Erikson, Amy. *Mistress, Mrs, Ms or Miss: Untangling the Shifting History of Women's Titles*. New Statesman. 12 September, 2014. https://www.newstatesman.com/cultural-capital/2014/09/mistress-miss-mrs-or-ms-untangling-shifting-history-women-s-titles

Eschner, Kat. *England's Witch Trials Were Lawful*. Smithsonian Magazine. 18 August, 2017. https://www.smithsonianmag.com/smart-news/englands-witch-trials-were-lawful-180964514/

Gilbert, Robert Andrew & Multhauf, Robert P. *Alchemy*. Encyclopedia Britannica. March 2019. https://www.britannica.com/topic/alchemy

Harris, Karen. *Trees of the Gods: Worshiping the Mighty Oak Tree.* British History. *History Daily.* 11 August, 2019. https://historydaily.org/tree-gods-worshiping-mighty-oak-trees.

Helmenstine, Anne Marie, Ph.D. *Aether Definition in Alchemy and Science.* ThoughtCo. Feb. 11, 2020. https://www.thoughtco.com/aether-in-alchemy-and-science-604750#

Hill, Jenny. *Sekhmet.* Ancient Egypt Online. 2008 https://ancientegyptonline.co.uk/sekhmet/

Huntley, D. *English Cheddar Cheese.* British Heritage. May, 2020 https://britishheritage.com/food-drink/english-cheddar-cheese

Kraut, Richard. *Socrates.* Encyclopedia Britannica. 6 May, 2020. https://www.britannica.com/biography/Socrates

Lee, Jookyung Lee & Borukhov, Sergei. *Bacterial RNA Polymerase-DNA Interaction — The Driving Force of Gene Expression and the Target for Drug Action.* Frontiers in Molecular Sciences. November, 2016. https://www.frontiersin.org/articles/10.3389/fmolb.2016.00073/fullPolymerase-DNA Interaction—The Driving Force of Gene Expression and the Target for Drug Action

Mansoor, Pete. *Armour (History of).* Encyclopedia Britannica. May, 2019 https://www.britannica.com/topic/armour-protective-clothing

Mark, Joshua J. *Alexander the Great*. Ancient History Encyclopedia. 14 November, 2013. https://www.ancient.eu/Alexander_the_Great/

Mark, Joshua J. *Aristotle*. Ancient History Encyclopedia. 22 May, 2019 https://ancient.eu/aristotle/

Mark, Joshua J. *Sekemet*. Egyptian Gods - The Complete List. *Ancient History Encyclopedia*. 14 April, 2016. https://member.ancient.eu/article/885/egyptian-gods---the-complete-list/

Mark, Joshua J. *Thoth*. Ancient History Encyclopedia. 26 July, 2016 https://www.ancient.eu/Thoth/

Mather, Lee. *Laser Microscope Demonstrates Gene Splicing in Real Time*. Bio-Optics World. 22 March, 2011. Laser microscope demonstrates gene splicing process in real time

McFarling, Usha Lee. *Making Ink from Oak Galls*. Verso - The Blog of the Huntington Library, Art Museum, and Botanical Gardens. 1 May, 2019. https://www.huntington.org/verso/2019/05/making-ink-oak-galls

Meinwald, Constance C. *Plato*. Encyclopedia Britannica. March, 2020 https://www.britannica.com/biography/Plato

Peyton, Jane. *The Origins and History of Cider*. Great British Chefs. February 13, 2019. https://www.greatbritishchefs.com/features/cider-history-origins

Sack, Harold. *Mary the Jewess and the Origins of Chemistry*. Science History Blog. May, 2020. http://scihi.org/mary-the-jewess-origins-chemistry/

Schulz, Nicole. *Cancer Cell Mechanics: Adhesion G Protein-coupled Receptors in Action?*. Frontiers in Oncology. March, 2018. Cancer Cell Mechanics: Adhesion G Protein-coupled Receptors in Action?

Syme, Ruth Lewin. *Lise Mietner's Escape From Germany*. American Journal of Physics, Vol 8, no. 53. March, 1990. https://www.researchgate.net/publication/252687986_Lise_Meitner's_escape_from_Germany

Editors of Encyclopedia Britannica. *Artemis*. Encyclopedia Britannica. May, 2020. https://www.britannica.com/topic/Artemis-Greek-goddess

Editors, Encyclopedia Britannica. *Cuirass*. Encyclopedia Britannica. March, 2016. https://www.britannica.com/technology/cuirass

Bia. Greek Gods & Goddesses. June 10, 2018. https://greekgodsandgoddesses.net/goddesses/bia/

Cheddar: Ancient Cheese of Monarchs. The Nibble https://www.thenibble.com/reviews/main/cheese/cheese2/whey/2006-04-2.asp#index

Hoplite Arms and Armor. Hoplite Warfare. *Penn State University*. https://sites.psu.edu/hoplitewarfare/hoplite-arms-and-armor/

Kratos. Greek Gods & Goddesses. February 9, 2017. https://greekgodsandgoddesses.net/gods/kratos/

Laser Scanning Microscopy Tutorial. Thor Labs. https://www.thorlabs.com/newgrouppage9.cfm?objectgroup_id=10765

Laura Bassi. Famous People, Guests, and Illustrious Students. *University of Bologna.* https://www.unibo.it/en/university/who-we-are/our-history/famous-people-guests-illustrious-students/laura-bassi/

Transport yourself to another fantasy world.

The Frost Eater
by Carol Beth Anderson

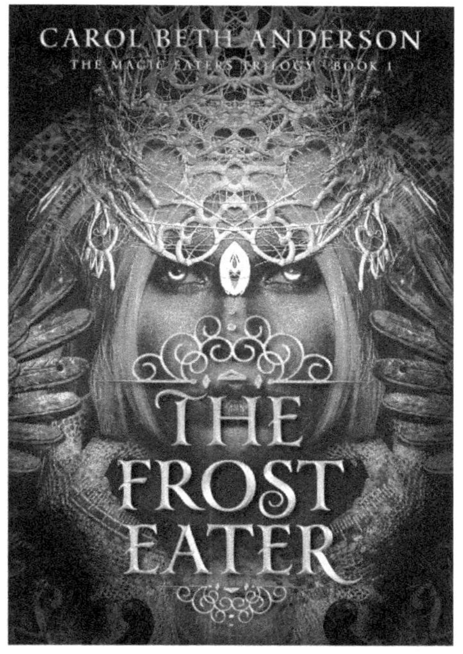

A spoiled royal hungry for excitement.

A young man who hates nobles.

Can they foil a kidnapping before they fall prey to an enemy's deadly magic?

9 781952 152276